TOE TO TOE
WITH THE ENEMY!

"Detail . . . *stop!*" the little brown girl called out. She seemed about seven years old. The robot halted. "Detail . . . Oh, I don't know what I'm supposed to say. Stand with your feet apart and put your gun down." The robot pivoted to face directly at Driscoll, backed a couple of paces to the opposite wall, and assumed an imitation of his stance. The top half of its head was a transparent dome inside which a row of colored lights blinked on and off, while the lower half contained a metal grille for a mouth, a TV lens-housing for a nose. It appeared to be grinning.

"Stay . . . there!" The girl instructed. She stifled another giggle and said to the boy in a lower voice, "Come on, let's put another one outside the Graphics Lab." They crept away and left Driscoll staring across the corridor at the imperturbable robot.

VOYAGE
FROM
YESTERYEAR

James P. Hogan

A Del Rey Book

BALLANTINE BOOKS • NEW YORK

Library of Congress Catalog Card Number: 81–22890

ISBN 0–345–29472–6

Manufactured in the United States of America

First Edition: July 1982

Cover art by Darrell K. Sweet

To ALEXANDER JAMES—
who was conceived at about the same time
as the book. Nature delivered faster.

PROLOGUE

". . . LADIES AND GENTLEMEN, our guest of honor tonight—
Henry B. Congreve." The toastmaster completed his intro-
duction and stepped aside to allow the stocky, white-haired
figure in black tie and dinner jacket to move to the podium.
Enthusiastic applause arose from the three hundred guests
gathered in the Hilton complex on the western outskirts of
Washington, D.C. The lights around the room dimmed,
fading the audience into white shirtfronts, glittering throats
and fingers, and masklike faces. A pair of spotlights picked
out the speaker as he waited for the applause to subside.
In the shadows next to him, the toastmaster returned to
his chair.

After sixty-eight years of tussling with life, Congreve's
bulldog frame still stood upright, his shoulders jutting
squarely below his close-cropped head. The lines of his
roughly chiseled face were still firm and solid, and his eyes
twinkled good-humoredly as he surveyed the room. It
seemed strange to many of those present that a man so
vital, one with so much still within him, should be about
to deliver his retirement address.

Few of the younger astronauts, scientists, engineers, and
North American Space Development Organization execu-
tives could remember NASDO without Congreve as its
president. For all of them, things would never be quite the
same again.

"Thank you, Matt." Congreve's voice rumbled in a
gravelly baritone from the speakers all around. He glanced
from side to side to take in the whole of his audience. "I,
ah—I almost didn't make it here at all." He paused, and
the last whispers of conversation died away. "A sign in the

1

hall outside says that the fossil display is in twelve-oh-three upstairs." The American Archeological Society was holding its annual convention in the Hilton complex that week. Congreve shrugged. "I figured that had to be where I was supposed to go. Luckily I bumped into Matt on the way, and he got me back on the right track." A ripple of laughter wavered in the darkness, punctuated by a few shouts of protest from some of the tables. He waited for silence, then continued in a less flippant voice. "The first thing I have to do is thank everybody here, and all the NASDO people who couldn't be with us tonight, for inviting me. Also, of course, I have to express my sincere appreciation for this, and even more my appreciation for the sentiments that it signifies. Thank you—all of you." As he spoke, he gestured toward the eighteen-inch-long, silver and bronze replica of the as yet unnamed, untried SP3 starprobe that stood on its teak base before Congreve's place at the main table.

His voice became more serious as he continued. "I don't want to go off into a lot of personal anecdotes and reminiscences. That kind of thing is customary on an occasion such as this, but it would be trivial, and I wouldn't want my last speech as president of NASDO to be marked by trivia. The times do not permit such luxury. Instead, I want to talk about matters that are of global significance and which affect every individual alive on this planet, and indeed the generations yet to be born—assuming there will be future generations." He paused. "I want to talk about survival—the survival of the human species."

Although the room was already quiet, the silence seemed to intensify with these words. Here and there in the audience, faces turned to glance curiously at one another. Clearly, this was not to be just another retirement speech. Congreve went on. "We have already come once to the brink of a third world war and hung precariously over the edge. Today, in 2015, twenty-three years have passed since U.S. and Soviet forces clashed in Baluchistan with tactical nuclear weapons, and although the rapid spread of a fusion-based economy at last promises to solve the energy problems that brought about that confrontation, the jealousies, mistrusts, and suspicions which brought us to the point of war thcn and which have persistently plagued our race throughout its history are as much in evidence as ever.

"Today the sustenance that our industries crave is not oil, but minerals. Fifty years from now our understanding of controlled-fusion processes will probably have eliminated that source of shortages too, but in the meantime shorter-sighted political considerations are recreating the climate of tension and rivalry that hinged around the oil issue at the close of the last century. Obviously, South Africa's importance in this context is shaping the current pattern of power maneuvering, and the probable flashpoint for another East-West collision will again be the Iran-Pakistan border region, which our strategists expect the Soviets to contest to gain access to the Indian Ocean in preparation for the support of a war of so-called black African liberation against the South."

Congreve paused, swept his eyes from one side of the room to the other, and raised his hands in resignation. "It seems that as individuals we can only stand by as helpless observers and watch the events that are sweeping us onward collectively. The situation is complicated further by the emergence and rapid economic and military growth of the Chinese-Japanese Co-Prosperity Sphere, which threatens to confront Moscow with an unassailable power bloc should it come to align with ourselves and the Europeans. More than a few Kremlin analysts must see their least risky gamble as a final resolution with the West now, before such an alliance has time to consolidate. In other words, it would not be untrue to say that the future of the human race has never been at greater risk than it is at this moment."

Congreve pushed himself back from the podium with his arms and straightened. When he resumed speaking, his tone had lightened slightly. "In the area that concerns all of us here in our day-to-day lives, the accelerating pace of the space program has brought a lot of excitement in the last two decades. Some inspiring achievements have helped offset the less encouraging news from other quarters: We have established permanent bases on the Moon and Mars; colonies are being built in space; a manned mission has reached the moons of Jupiter; and robots are out exploring the farthest reaches of the Solar System and beyond. But" —he extended his arms in an animated sigh—"these operations have been national, not international. Despite the hopes and the words of years gone by, militarization has followed everywhere close on the heels of exploration, and we are led to the inescapable conclusion that a war, if it comes, would soon spread beyond the confines of the surface and jeopardize our species everywhere. We must face up to the fact that the danger now threatening us in the years ahead is nothing less than that."

He turned for a moment to stare at the model of SP3 gleaming on the table beside him and then pointed to it. "Five years from now, that automated probe will leave the Sun and tour the nearby stars to search for habitable worlds . . . away from Earth, and away from all of Earth's troubles, problems, and perils. Eventually, if all goes well, it will arrive at same place insulated by unimaginable distance from the problems that promise to make strife an inseparable and ineradicable part of the weary story of human existence on this planet." Congreve's expression took on a distant look as he gazed at the replica, as if in his mind he were already soaring with it outward and away. "It will be a new place," he said in a faraway voice. "A new, fresh, vibrant world, unscarred by Man's struggle to elevate himself from the beasts, a place that presents what might be the only opportunity for our race to preserve an extension of itself where it would survive, and if necessary begin again, but this time with the lessons of the past to guide it."

An undercurrent of murmuring rippled quickly around the hall. Congreve nodded, indicating his anticipation of the objections he knew would come. He raised a hand for attention and gradually the noise abated.

"No, I am not saying that SP3 could be modified from a robot craft to carry a human crew. The design could not feasibly be modified at this late stage. Too many things would have to be thought out again from the beginning, and such a task would require decades. And yet, nothing comparable to SP3 is anywhere near as advanced a stage of design at the present time, let alone near being constructed. The opportunity is unique and cannot, surely, be allowed to pass by. But at the same time we cannot afford the delay that would be needed to take advantage of that opportunity. Is there a solution to this dilemma?" He looked around as if inviting responses. None came.

"We have been studying this problem for some time now, and we believe there is a solution. It would not be feasible to send a contingent of adult humans, either as a functioning community or in some suspended state, with the ship; it is in too advanced a stage of construction to change its primary design parameters. But then, why send *adult* humans at all?" He spread his arms appealingly. "After all, the objective is simply to establish an extension of our race where it would be safe from any calamity that might befall us here, and such a location would be found only at the end of the voyage. The people would not be required either during the voyage or in the survey phase, since machines are perfectly capable of handling everything connected with those operations. People become relevant only when those phases have been successfully completed. Therefore we can avoid all the difficulties inherent in the idea of sending people along by dispensing with the conventional notions of interstellar travel and adopting a totally new approach: by having the ship *create* the people after it gets there!"

Congreve paused again, but this time not so much as a whisper disturbed the silence.

Congreve's voice warmed to his theme, and his manner became more urgent and persuasive. "Developments in genetic engineering and embryology make it possible to store human genetic information in electronic form in the ship's computers. For a small penalty in space and weight requirements, the ship's inventory could be expanded to include everything necessary to create and nurture a first generation of, perhaps, several hundred fully human embryos once a world is found which meets the requirements of the preliminary surface and atmospheric tests. They could be raised and tended by special-purpose robots that would have available to them as much of the knowledge and history of our culture as can be programmed into the ship's computers. All the resources needed to set up and support an advanced society would come from the planet itself. Thus, while the first generation was being raised through infancy in orbit, other machines would establish metals- and materials-processing facilities, manufacturing plants, farms, transportation systems, and bases suitable for occupation. Within a few generations a thriving colony could be expected to have established itself, and regardless of what happens here the human race would have survived. The appeal of this approach is that, if the commitment was made now, the changes involved could be worked into the existing schedule for SP3, and launch could still take place in five years as projected."

By this time life was flowing slowly back into his listeners. Although many of them were still too astonished by his proposal to react visibly, heads were nodding, and the murmurs running around the room seemed positive. Congreve nodded and smiled faintly as if savoring the thought of having kept the best part until last.

"The second thing I have to announce tonight is that such a commitment has now been made. As I mentioned a moment ago, this subject has been under study for a considerable period of time. I can now inform you that, three days ago, the President of the United States and the Chairman of the Eastern Co-Prosperity Sphere signed an agreement for the project which I have briefly outlined to be pursued on a joint basis, effective immediately. The activities of the various national and private research institutions and other organizations that will be involved in the venture will be coordinated with those of the North American Space Development Organization and with those of our Chinese and Japanese partners under a project designation of Starhaven."

Congreve's face split into a broad smile. "My third announcement is that tonight does not mark my retirement from professional life after all. I have accepted an invitation from the President to take charge of the Starhaven project on behalf of the United States as the senior member nation, and I am relinquishing my position with

NASDO purely in order to give undivided attention to my new responsibilities. For those who might believe that I've given them some hard times in the past, I have to say with insincere apologies that I'm going to be around for some time longer yet, and that before this project is through the times are going to get a lot harder."

Several people at the back stood up and started clapping. The applause spread and turned into a standing ovation. Congreve grinned unabashedly to acknowledge the enthusiasm, stood for a while as the applause continued, and then grasped the sides of the podium again.

"We had our first formal meeting with the Chinese yesterday, and we've already made our first official decision." He glanced at the replica of the star-robot probe again. "SP3 now has a name. It has been named after a goddess of Chinese mythology whom we have adopted as a fitting patroness: *Kuan-yin*—the goddess who brings children. Let us hope that she watches over her children well in the years to come."

PART ONE

THE
VOYAGE
OF
THE MAYFLOWER II

CHAPTER ONE

ABOUT TWO HUNDRED feet below the ridgeline, the Third Platoon of D Company had set up its Tactical Battle Station in a depression surrounded by interconnecting patches of sagebrush and scrub. A corner in a low rock wall sheltered it on two sides, a large boulder closed in the third, and a parapet of smaller, flat rocks protected it from the front; a thermal shield stretched across the top hid the body heat of its occupants from the ever-vigilant sensors of hostile surveillance satellites.

The scene outside was deceptively quiet as Colman lifted a flap and peered out, keeping his head well back from the edge of the canopy. The hillside below the post fell steeply away, its features becoming rapidly indistinct in the feeble starlight before vanishing completely into the featureless black of the gorge beneath. There was no moon, and the sky was clear as crystal. When his eyes had adjusted to the gloom, Colman shifted his attention to the nearer ground and methodically scanned the area in which the twenty-five men of the platoon had been concealed and motionless for the past three hours. If they had undercut their foxholes and weapons pits the way he had shown them and made proper use of the rocks and vegetation, they would stand a good chance of escaping detection. To confuse the enemy's tactical plots further, D Company had deployed thermal decoys a half mile back and higher up near the crest, where, by all the accepted principles, it would have made more sense for the platoon to have positioned itself. Autotimed to turn on and off in a random sequence to simulate movement, the decoys had been drawing sporadic fire for much of the night while the platoon had drawn none, which seemed to say something about the value of "the book" as rewritten by Staff Sergeant Colman. "There are two ways to do anything," he told the recruits. "The Army way and the wrong way. There isn't any other way. So when I tell you to do something the Army way, what does it mean?"

"It means do it your way, Sergeant."

"Very good."

A tiny pinpoint of orange glowed bright for a second, about fifty feet away, where Stanislau and Carson were covering the trail from the gorge with the submegajoule laser. Colman scowled to himself. He turned his head a fraction to whisper to Driscoll. "The LCP's showing a cigarette. Tell them to get rid of it."

Driscoll tapped into the fingerpanel of the compack, and from a spike pushed into the ground, ultrasonic vibrations spread outward through the soil, carrying the call sign of the Laser Cannon Post. "LCP reading," a muted voice acknowledged from the compack.

Driscoll spoke into the microphone boom projecting from his helmet. "Red Three, routine check." This would leave an innocuous record in the automatic signal logging system. In the darkness Driscoll pressed a key to deactivate the recording channel momentarily. "You're showing a light, shitheads. Douse it or cover it." His finger released the key. "Report status, LCP."

"Ready and standing by," the voice replied neutrally. "Nothing to report." Outside, the pinpoint of light vanished abruptly.

"Remain at ready. Out."

Colman grunted to himself, made one final sweep of the surroundings, then dropped the flap back into place and turned to face inside. Behind Driscoll, Maddock was examining the bottom of the gorge through the image intensifier, while in the shadows next to him the expression of concentration on Corporal Swyley's face was etched sharply by the subdued glow of the forward terrain display screen propped in front of him.

The image that so held his attention was transmitted from an eighteen-inch-long, infantry reconnaissance drone that they had managed to slip in a thousand feet above the floor of the gorge and almost over the enemy's forward positions and was supplemented by additional data collected from satellite and other ELINT network sources. The display showed the target command bunker at the bottom of the gorge, known enemy weapons emplacements as computed from backplots of radar-tracked shell trajectories, and the locations of observation and fire-command posts from source analysis triangulations of stray reflections from control lasers. On it the cool water of the stream and its tributaries stood out as black lines forking like twigs; the rock crags and boulders were shades of blue; living vegetation varied from rust brown on the hills to deep red where it crowded together along the lower slopes of the gorge; and shell and bomb scars glowed from dull orange to yellow depending on how recently the explosions had occurred.

But what Corporal Swyley was concentrating on so intently were the minute specks of brighter reds that might or might not have been imperfectly obscured defensive positions, and the barely discernible hairline fragments that could have been the thermal footprints of recent vehicle movements.

How Swyley did what only he did so well was something nobody was quite sure of, least of all Swyley himself. Whatever the reason, Swyley's ability to pick out significant details from a hopeless mess of background garbage and to distinguish consistently between valid information and decoys was justly famed—and uncanny. But since Swyley himself didn't understand how he did it, he was unable to explain it to the systems programmers, who had hoped to duplicate his feats with their image-analysis programs. That had been when the "-ists" and the "-ologists" began their endless batteries of fruitless tests. Eventually Swyley made up plausible-sounding explanations for the benefit of the specialists, but these were exposed when the programs written to their specifications failed to work. Then Swyley began claiming that his mysterious gift had suddenly deserted him completely.

Major Thorpe, Electronics Intelligence Officer at Brigade H.Q., had read somewhere that spinach and fish were sure remedies for failing eyesight, so he placed Corporal Swyley on an intensive diet. But Swyley hated spinach and fish even more than he hated being tested, and within a week he was afflicted by acute color-blindness, which he demonstrated by refusing to see anything at all in even the simplest of training displays.

After that, Swyley had been declared "maladjusted" and transferred to D Company, which was where all the misfits and malcontents ended up. Now his powers returned magically only when no officers were anywhere near him except for Captain Sirocco, who ran D Company and didn't care how Swyley got his answers as long as they came out right. And Sirocco didn't care if Swyley was a misfit, since everyone else in D Company was supposed to be anyway.

It probably meant that there was no easy way of getting out of D Company again let alone out of the regular service, Colman reflected as he watched in the darkness and waited for Swyley to deliver his verdict. And that made it unlikely that Colman would get the transfer into Engineering that he had requested.

It seemed self-evident to him that nobody in his right mind would want to get killed, or to be sent to places he'd never heard of by people he'd never met in order to kill other people he didn't know. Therefore nobody in his right mind would be in the Army. But since the Army was full of people whom it had judged to be acceptably sane and normal, it seemed to follow that the Army's ideas of what was normal had to be very strange. Now, to transfer into something like Engineering seemed on the face of it to be a perfectly natural, reasonable, constructive, and desirable thing to want to do. And that seemed enough to guarantee that the Army would find the request unreasonable and him unsuitable.

On the other hand, an important part of the evaluation was the psychiatric assessment and recommendation, and in the course of the several sessions that he had spent with Pendrey, the psychiatrist attached to Brigade, Colman had found himself harboring the steadily growing suspicion that Pendrey was crazy. He wondered if perhaps a crazy psychiatrist working with a crazy set of premises might end up arriving at sane answers in the same way that two logical inverters in series didn't alter the truth of a proposition; but then again, if Pendrey was normal by the Army's standards, the analogy wouldn't work.

Sirocco had endorsed the request, it was true, but Colman wasn't sure it would count for very much since Sirocco ran D Company, and anything he said was probably inverted somewhere along the chain as a matter of course. Perhaps he should have persuaded Sirocco not to endorse the request. On the other hand, if anything recommended by Sirocco was inverted to start with, and if Pendrey was crazy but normal by the Army's standards, and if the premises that Pendrey was working with were also crazy, then the decision might come out in Colman's favor after all. Or would it? His attempt to think the tortuous logic of the situation once again was interrupted by Swyley at last leaning back and turning his face away from the screen.

"They've got practically all their strength out on the flanks both ways along the gorge," Swyley announced. "There are some units moving down the opposite slope, but they won't be in position for about another thirty minutes." The glow from the screen highlighted the mystified look that flashed across his face. He shrugged. "Right now they're wide open, right down below us."

"They don't have anything here?" Colman checked, touching the screen with a finger to indicate the place where the bottom of the trail emerged from a small wood on the edge of a grassy flat and just a few hundred feet from the enemy bunker. The display showed a faint pattern of smudges on either side of the trail in just the positions where defensive formations would be expected.

Swyley shook his head. "Those are decoys. Like I said, they've moved practically all the guys out to the flanks"—he jabbed at the screen with a finger—"here, here, and here."

"Getting round behind B Company, and up over spur Four-nine-three," Colman suggested as he studied the image.

"Could be," Swyley agreed noncommittally.

"Looks dead as hell down there to me," Maddock threw in without taking his eyes from the viewpiece of the intensifier.

"What do the seismics and sniffers say about Swyley's decoys?" Colman asked, turning his head toward Driscoll.

Driscoll translated the question into a computer command and peered at the data summary on one of the compack screens. "Insignificant seismic above threshold at eight hundred yards. Downwind ratio less than five points up at four hundred. Negative corroboration from acoustics—background swamping." The computers were unable to identify vibrational patterns correlating with human activity in the data coming in from the sensing devices quietly scattered around the gorge by low-flying, remote-piloted "bees" on and off throughout the night; the chemical sensors located to the leeward of the suspected decoys were detecting little of the odor molecules characteristic of human bodies; the microphones had yielded nothing in the way of coherent sound patterns, but this was doubtless because of the white-noise background being generated in the vicinity of the stream. Although the evidence was only partial and negative at that, it supported Swyley's assertion that the main road down to the objective was, incredibly, virtually undefended for the time being.

Colman frowned to himself as his mind raced over the data's significance. No sane attacking force would contemplate taking an objective like that by a direct frontal assault in the center—the lowermost stretch of the trail was too well covered by overlooking slopes, and there would be no way back if the attack bogged down. That was what the enemy commander would have thought anyone would have thought. So what would be the point of tying up lots of men to defend a point that would never be attacked? According to the book, the correct way to attack the bunker would be along the stream from above or by crossing the stream below and coming down from the spur on the far side. So the other side was concentrating at points above both of the obvious assault routes and setting themselves up to ambush whichever attack should materialize. But in the meantime they were wide open in the middle.

"Alert all section leaders on the grid," Colman said to Driscoll. "And open a channel to Blue One."

Sirocco came through on the compack a few moments later, and Colman summarized the situation. The audacity of the idea appealed to Sirocco immediately. "We'd have to handle it ourselves. There isn't enough time to involve Brigade, but we could pin down those guys on the other side while you went in, and roll a barrage in front of you to clear obstacles." He was referring to the Company-controlled robot batteries set up to the rear, below the crestline of the ridge. "It would mean going in without any counterbattery suppression when you break though. What do you think?"

"If we went fast, we could make it without." Colman answered.

"Without CB suppression there wouldn't be time to move any of the other platoons round to back you up. You'd be on your own," Sirocco said.

"We can use the robot batteries to lay down a close-cover screen from the flanks. If you give us an optical and IR blanket at twelve hundred feet, we can make it."

Sirocco hesitated for a split second. "Okay" he finally said. "Let's do it."

Ten minutes later, Sirocco had worked out a hastily contrived fire-plan with his executive officer and relayed details to First, Second, and Fourth platoons, and Colman had briefed Third Platoon via his section leaders. Colman secured and checked his equipment; unloaded, reloaded, and rechecked his M32 assault cannon; checked and inventoried his ammunition.

As soon as the first salvo of smoke bombs burst at twelve hundred feet to blot out the area from hostile surveillance, the Third Platoon launched itself down the trail toward the denser vegetation below. Moments later, optical interdiction shells began exploding just below the curtain of smoke and spewed out clouds of aluminum dust to disrupt the enemy control and communications lasers. Ahead of the attacking troops, a concentrated point-barrage of shells and high-intensity pulsed beams fired from the flanking platoons rolled forward along the trail to clear the way of mines and other antipersonnel ordnance. Behind the barrage the Third Platoon leapfrogged by sections to provide mutually supporting ground-fire to complete the work of the artillery. There was no opposition. The defending artillery opened up from the rear within ten seconds of the initial smoke blanket, but the enemy was firing blind and largely ineffectively.

In thirteen minutes the firefight was all over. Colman stood on the gravel bank of the stream and watched as a bewildered major was led from the enemy bunker, followed by his numb staff, who joined the gaggle of disarmed defenders being herded together under the watchful eyes of smirking Third Platoon guards. The primary objective had been to take prisoners and obtain intelligence, and the crop had yielded two captains in addition to the major, a first and a second lieutenant, a chief warrant officer, a sergeant major, two sergeants, and over a dozen enlisted men. Moreover, the call-sign lists and maps had been seized intact, along with invaluable communications and weapons-control equipment. Not a bad haul at all, Colman reflected with satisfaction.

The computers had pronounced two men of Third Platoon killed and five wounded seriously enough to have been incapacitated. Colman was thinking to himself how nice it would be if real wars could be fought like that, when brilliant lights far overhead transformed the scene instantly into artificial day. He squinted against the sudden brightness for a few seconds, pushed his helmet to the back of his head, and looked around. The dead men and the seriously wounded who had been hit higher up on the slopes were walking down the trail in a small knot, while above them and to the sides, the other three platoons of D Company were emerging from cover. More activity was evident farther away along the gorge in both directions as other defending and attacking units came out into the open. Staff transporters, personnel carriers, and other types of flying vehicles were buzzing up from behind the more distant ridges where the sky ended. Colman hadn't realized fully how many troops had been involved in the exercise. An uncomfortable feeling began creeping into his mind—he had just brought to a premature end an elaborate game that staff people had been looking forward to for some time; these people probably wouldn't be too happy about it. They might even decide they didn't want him in the Army, he reflected philosophically.

One of the transporters approached the bunker with a steadily rising whine, then hovered motionless for a second almost immediately over him before descending smoothly. Its rear door slid open to reveal the lean, swarthy figure of Captain Sirocco in helmet and battledress, still wearing his flak-vest. He jumped out nimbly while the transporter was still six feet above the ground, and ambled up to Colman. Behind his ample black moustache, the easy-going lines of his face betrayed as little as ever, but his eyes were twinkling. "Pretty good, Steve," he said without preamble as he turned with his hands on his hips to survey the indignant scowls from the captured "enemy" officers standing sullenly by the bunker. "I don't think we'll get any Brownie points for it though. We broke just about every rule in the book." Colman grunted. He hadn't expected much else. Sirocco raised his eyebrows and inclined his head in a way that could have meant anything. "Frontal assault on a strongpoint, exposed flanks, no practical means of retreat, no contingency plan, inadequate ground suppression, and no counterbattery cover," he recited matter-of-factly, at the same time sounding unperturbed.

"What about leaving your chin wide open?" Colman asked. "Isn't there anything in the rules about that?"

"Depends who you are. For D Company all things are relative."

"Ever think of making a new seat for your pants out of part of that flak-jacket?" Colman asked after a pause. "You're probably gonna need it."

"Ah, who gives a shit?" Sirocco looked up. "Anyhow, won't be much longer before we find out."

Colman followed his gaze. An armored VIP carrier bearing a general's insignia on its nose was angling toward them. Colman shifted his M32 to the other shoulder and straightened up to watch. "Smarten it up," he called to the rest of Third Platoon, who were smoking, talking, and lounging in groups by the stream and around the bunker. The cigarettes were ground out under the heavy soles of combat boots, the chattering died away, and the groups shuffled themselves into tidier ranks.

"On what did you base your analysis of the situational display, Sergeant?" Sirocco asked, speaking in a clipped, high-pitched voice mimicking the formal tones of Colonel Wesserman, who was General Portney's aide. He injected a note of suspicion and accusation into the voice. "Was Corporal Swyley instrumental in the formulation of your tactical evaluation?" The question was bound to arise; the image analysis routines run at Brigade would have yielded nothing to justify the attack.

"No, sir," Colman replied stiffly, keeping his eyes fixed straight ahead. "Corporal Swyley was manning the compack. He would not have been assigned to ELINT analysis. He's color-blind."

"Then how do you explain your extraordinary conclusions?"

"I suppose we just guessed lucky, sir."

Sirocco sighed. "I suppose I'll have to put it in writing that I authorized the assault on my own initiative and without any substantiating data." He cocked his head at Colman. "Happen to know anyone around here who makes a good pair of pants?"

Ahead of them the door of the VIP carrier opened to expose the rotund form of Colonel Wesserman. His florid face was even more florid than usual and swelled into a deep purple at the neck. He seemed to be choking with suppressed fury.

"I guess he doesn't have a nose for the sweet smell of success," Colman murmured as they watched.

Sirocco twirled one side of his moustache pensively for a second or two. "Success is like a fart," he said. "Only your own smells nice."

CHAPTER TWO

A SUDDEN CHANGE in the colors and format of one of the displays being presented around him in the monitor room of the Drive Control Subcenter caught Bernard Fallows's eye and dismissed other thoughts from his mind. The display was one of several associated with Number 5 Group of the Primary Fuel Delivery System and related to one of the batteries of enormous hydrogen-feed boost pumps located in the tail section of the vessel, five miles from where Fallows was sitting.

"What's happening on Five-E, Horace?" he asked the empty room around him.

"Low-level trend projection," the subcenter executive computer replied through a small grille set to one side of Fallow's console. "Booster five-sub-three's looking as if it's going to start running hot again. Correlation integral sixty-seven, check function positive, expansion index eight-zero."

"Reading at index six?"

"Insignificant."

Fallows took in the rest of the information from the screen. The changes that the computers had detected were tiny—the merest beginnings of a trend which, if it continued at the present rate, wouldn't approach anything serious for a month or more. With only another three months to go before the ship reached Chiron there was no cause for alarm since the rest of the pump-group had enough design margin to make up the difference even without the backup. But even so, there was little doubt that Merrick would insist on the primary's being stripped down to have its bearings reground, alignment rechecked, and rotor rebalanced again. They had been through that routine twice already in the three months that the main drive had been firing. That meant another week of working in near-zero g and klutzing around in heavy-duty protective suits on the wrong side of the stern radiation shield. "Bloody pump," Fallows muttered sourly.

"Since a pump is not an organic system, I presume the expression is an expletive," Horace observed chattily.

"Aw, shuddup." The computer returned obediently to its meditations.

Fallows sat back in his chair and cast a routine eye around the monitor room. Everything seemed to be running smoothly at the crew stations beyond the glass partition behind his console, and the other displays confirmed that all else was as it should be. The reserve tank to Number 2 vernier motor had been recharged after a slight course-correction earlier and was checking out at "Ready" again. All the fuel, coolant, primary and standby power, hydraulic, pneumatic, gas, oil, life-support, and instrumentation subsystems servicing the Drive Section were performing well within limits. Way back near the tail, the banks of gigantic fusion reactors were gobbling up the 35 million tons of hydrogen that had been magnetically ramscooped out of space throughout the twenty-year voyage and converting over two tons of its mass into energy every second to produce the awesome, 1.5-mile-diameter blast of radiation and reaction products that would have to burn for six months to slow the 140-million-ton mass of the *Mayflower II* down from its free-cruise velocity.

The ship had left Earth with only sufficient fuel on board to accelerate it to cruising speed and had followed a course through the higher-density concentrations of hydrogen to collect what it needed to slow down again.

Fallows glanced at the clock in the center of the console. Less than an hour before Walters was due to take over the watch. Then he would have two days to himself before coming back on duty. He closed his eyes for a moment and savored the thought.

Only three months to go! His children had often asked him why a young man in his prime would turn his back on everything familiar and exchange twenty years of his life for a one-way journey to Alpha Centauri. They had good reason, since their futures had been decided more than a little by his decision. Most of the *Mayflower II*'s thirty thousand occupants were used to being asked that question. Fallows usually replied that he had grown disillusioned by the spectacle of the world steadily rearming itself toward the same level of insanity that had preceded the devastation of much of North America and Europe and the end of the Soviet empire in the brief holocaust of 2021, and that he had left it all behind to seek a new start somewhere else. It was one of the standard answers, given as much for self-reassurance as anything else. But in his private moments Fallows knew that he really didn't believe it. He tried to pretend that he didn't remember the real reason.

He had been born almost at the end of the Lean Years following the war, so he didn't remember about that period, but his father had told him about the times when fifty million people lived amid shantytown squalor around the blackened and twisted skeletons of their cities and huddled in lines in the snow for their ration of soup and bread at government field-kitchens; about his mother laboring fifteen hours a day cutting boards for prefabricated houses to put two skimpy meals of beef broth and rice from the Chinese food ships on the table each day and to buy one pair of utility-brand pressed-paper shoes per person every six months; about his older brother killed in the fighting with the hordes that had come plundering from the Caribbean and from the south.

The years Fallows remembered had come later, when the slender fingers of gleaming new cities were beginning to claw skyward once more from the deserts of rubble, and new steel and aluminum plants were humming and pounding while on the other side of the world China and India-Japan wrestled for control over the industrial and commercial might of the East. Those had been stirring years, vibrant years, inspiring years. Fallows remembered the floodlit parades in Washington on the Fourth of July— the color and the splendor of the massed bands, the columns of marching soldiers with uniforms glittering and flags flying, the anthems and hymns rising on the voices of tens of thousands packed into Capitol Square, where the famous building had once stood. He remembered strutting into a high-school ball in his just acquired uniform of the American New Order Youth Corps and pretending haughtily not to notice the admiring looks following him wherever he went. How he had bragged to his envious friends after the first weekend of wargaming with the Army in the New Mexico desert . . . the exhilaration when America reestablished a permanently manned base on the Moon.

Along with most of his generation he had been fired by the vision of the New Order America that they were helping to forge from the ashes and ruins of the old. Even stronger than what had gone before, morally and spiritually purer, and confident in the knowledge of its God-ordained mission, it would rise again as an impregnable sanctuary to preserve the legacy of Western culture from the corrosive flood of heathen decadence and affluent brashness sweeping across the far side of the globe. So the credo had run. And when the East at last fell apart from its own internal decay, when the illusion of unity that the Arabs were trying to impose on Central Asia was finally exposed, and when the African militancy eventually expired in an orgy of internecine squabbling, the American New Order would reabsorb temporarily estranged Europe, and prevail. That had been the quest.

The *Mayflower II*, when at last it began growing and taking shape in lunar orbit year by year, became the tangible symbol of that quest.

Although he had been only eight years old in 2040, he could remember clearly the excitement caused by the news that a signal had come in from a spacecraft called the *Kuan-yin*, which had been launched in 2020, just before the war broke out. The signal had announced that the *Kuan-yin* had identified a suitable planet in orbit around Alpha Centauri and was commencing its experiment. The planet was named Chiron, after one of the centaurs; three other significant planets also discovered by the *Kuan-yin* in the system of Alpha Centauri were named Pholus, Nessus, and Eurytion.

Ten years went by while North America and Europe completed their recovery, and the major Eastern powers settled their rivalries. At the end of that period New America extended from Alaska to Panama, Greater Europe had incorporated Russia, Estonia, Latvia, and the Ukraine as separate nations, and China had come to dominate an Eastern Asiatic Federation stretching from Pakistan to the Bering Strait. All three of the major powers had commenced programs to reexpand into space at more or less the same time, and since each claimed a legitimate interest in the colony on Chiron and mistrusted the other two, each embarked on the construction of a starship with the aim of getting there first to protect its own against interference from the others.

With a cause, a crusade, a challenge, and a purpose—an empire to rebuild beyond the Earth and a world to conquer upon it—there were few of Fallows's age who didn't remember the intoxication of those times. And with the *Mayflower II* growing in the lunar sky as a symbol of it all, the dream of flying with the ship and of being a part of the crusade to secure Chiron against the Infidel became for many the ultimate ambition. The lessons of discipline and self-sacrifice that had been learned during the Lean Years served to bring the *Mayflower II* to completion two years ahead of its nearest rival, and so it came about that Bernard Fallows at the age of twenty-eight had manfully shaken his father's hand and kissed his tearful mother farewell before being blasted upward from a shuttle base in Arizona to join the lunar transporter that would bear him on the first stage of his crusade to carry the American New Order to the stars.

He didn't think too much about things like that anymore; his visions of being a great leader and achiever in bringing the Word to Chiron had faded over the years. And instead . . . what? Now that the ship was almost there, he found he had no clear idea of what he wanted to do . . . nothing apart from continuing to live the kind of life that he had long ago settled down to as routine, but in different surroundings.

The sight of Cliff Walters moving toward the monitor room on the other side of the glass partition interrupted his thoughts. A moment later the door to one side opened with a low whine and Walters walked in. Fallows swung his chair round to face him and looked up in surprise. "Hi. You're early. Still forty minutes to go."

Walters slipped off his jacket and hung it in the closet by the door after taking a book from the inside pocket. Fallows frowned but made no comment.

"Logging on early," Walters replied. "Merrick wants to talk to you for a minute before you go off duty. He told me to tell you to stop by the ECD. You can take off now and see him on the company's time." He moved over to the console and nodded at the array of screens. "How are we doing? Lots of wild and exciting things happening?"

"Five-sub-three primary's starting to play up again, you'll be happy to hear. Low-level profile, but it's positive. We had a one-fifteen second burn on vernier two at seventeen hundred hours, which went okay. The main burn is behaving itself fine and correcting for trim as programmed. . . ." He shrugged. "That's about it."

Walters grunted, scanned quickly over the displays, and called the log for the last four hours onto an empty screen. "Looks like we're in for another stripdown on that goddamn pump," he murmured without turning his head.

"Looks like it," Fallows agreed with a sigh.

"Not worth screwing around with," Walters declared. "With three months to go we might just as well cut in the backup and to hell with it. Fix the thing after we get there, when the main drive's not running. Why lose pounds sweating in trog-suits?"

"Tell it to Merrick," Fallows said, making an effort not to show the disapproval that he felt. Talking that way betrayed a sloppy attitude toward engineering. Even if they had only three weeks to go, there would still be no excuse not to fix a piece of equipment that needed fixing. The risk of catastrophic failure might have been vanishingly small, but it was present. Good practice lay with reducing possibilities like that to zero. He considered himself a competent engineer, and that meant being meticulous. Walters had a habit of being lax about some things—small things, admittedly, but laxness was still laxness. To be ranked equally irked Fallows. "Log change of watch duty, Horace," he said to the grille on the console. "Officer Fallows standing down. Officer Walters taking over."

"Acknowledged," Horace replied.

Fallows stood up and stepped aside, and Walters eased himself into the subcenter supervisor's chair. "You're off on a forty-eight, that right?" Walters asked.

"Uh-huh."

"Any plans?"

"Not really. Jay's playing on one of the teams in the Bowl tomorrow. I'll probably go and watch that. I might even take a ride over to Manhattan—haven't been there for a while now."

"Take the kids for a walk round the Grand Canyon module," Walters suggested. "It's being resculpted again—lots of trees and rocks, with plenty of water. Should be pretty."

Fallows appeared surprised. "I thought it was closed off for another two days. Isn't the Army having an exercise in there or something?"

"They wound it up early. Anyhow, Bud told me it'll be open again tomorrow. Check it out and give it a try."

"I might just do that," Fallows said, nodding slowly. "Yeah . . . I could use being out and about for a few hours. Thanks for the tip."

"Anytime. Take care."

Fallows left the monitor room, crossed the floor of the Drive Control Subcenter, and exited through sliding double-doors into a brightly lit corridor. An elevator took him up two levels to another corridor, and minutes later he was being shown into an office that opened onto one side of the Engineering Command Deck. Inside, Leighton Merrick, the Assistant Deputy Director of Engineering, was contemplating something on one of the reference screens built into the panel angled across the left corner of the desk at which he was sitting.

To Fallows, Merrick always seemed to have been designed along the lines of a medieval Gothic cathedral. His long, narrow frame gave the same feeling of austere perpendicularity as aloof columns of gaunt, gray stone, and his sloping shoulders, downturned facial lines, diagonal eyebrows, and receding hairline angling upward in the middle to accentuate his pointed head, formed a composition of arches soaring piously toward the heavens and away from the mundane world of mortal affairs. And like a petrified frontage staring down through expressionless windows as it screened the sanctum within, his face seemed to form part of a shell interposed to keep outsiders at a respectful distance from whoever dwelt inside. Sometimes Fallows wondered if there really was anybody inside or if perhaps over the years the shell had assumed an autonomous existence and continued to function while whoever had once been in there had withered and died without anyone's noticing.

Despite having worked under him for several years, Fallows had never been able to master the art of feeling at ease in Merrick's presence. Displays of undue familiarity were hardly to be expected between echelon-six and echelon-four personnel, naturally, but even allowing for that, Fallows always found himself in acute discomfort within seconds of entering a room with Merrick in it, especially when nobody else was present. This time he wouldn't let it happen, he had resolved for the umpteenth time back in the corridor. This time he would be rational about how irrational the whole thing was and refuse to be intimidated by his own imagination. Merrick had not singled him out as any special object of his disdain. He behaved that way with everybody. It didn't mean anything.

Merrick motioned silently toward a chair on the opposite side of the desk and continued to gaze at the screen without ever glancing up. Fallows sat. After some ten seconds he began feeling uncomfortable. What had he done wrong in the last few days? Had there been something he'd forgotten? . . . or failed to report, maybe? . . . or left with loose ends dangling? He racked his brains but couldn't think of anything. Finally, unnerved, Fallow managed to stammer, "Er . . . you wanted to see me, sir."

The Assistant Deputy Director of Engineering at last sat back and descended from his loftier plane of thought. "Ah, yes, Fallows." He gestured toward the screen he had been studying. "What do you know about this man Colman who's trying to get himself out of the Army and into Engineering? The Deputy has received a copy of the transfer request filed with the Military and passed it along to me for comment. It seems that this Colman has given your name as a reference. What do you know about him?" The inclined chin and the narrowing of the Gothic eyebrows were asking silently why any self-respecting echelon-four engineering officer would associate with an infantry sergeant.

It took Fallows a moment or two to realize what had happened. Then he groaned inwardly as the circumstances came back to him.

"I, er . . . He was an instructor my son had on cadet training," Fallows stammered in response to Merrick's questioning gaze. "I met him at the end-of-course parade . . . talked to him a bit. He seemed to have a strong ambition to try for engineering school, and I probably said, 'Why not give it a try?,' or something like that. I guess maybe he remembered my name."

"Mmmm. So you don't really know anything about his experience or aptitude. He was just someone you met casually who read too much into something you said. Right?"

Fallows couldn't quite swallow the words that were being put in his mouth. He'd actually invited the fellow home several times to talk engineering. Colman had some fascinating ideas. He frowned and shook his head before he could stop himself. "Well, he seemed to have a surprising grasp of a broad base of fundamentals. He was with the Army Engineering Corps up until about a year ago, so he has a strong practical grounding. And he's studied extensively since we left Earth. I do—I did get the im-

pression that perhaps he might be worth some considera-
tion. But of course that's just an opinion."

"Worth considering for what? You're not saying he'd
make an engineering officer, surely."

"Of course not! But one of the Tech grades maybe . . .
Two or Three perhaps. Or maybe the graduate entry
stream."

"Hmph." Merrick waved a hand at the screen. "Doesn't
have the academics. He'd need to do at least a year with
kids half his age. We're not a social rehabilitation unit, you
know."

"He has successfully self-taught Eng Dip One through
Five," Fallows pointed out. Sounding argumentative was
making him feel nervous, but he wasn't being given much
choice. "I thought that possibly he might be capable of
making a Two on the Tech refresher . . ."

Merrick glared across the desk suspiciously. Evidently
he wasn't getting the answers he wanted. "His Army record isn't exactly the best one could wish for, you know.
Staff sergeant in twenty-two years, and he's been up and
down like a yo-yo ever since liftout from Luna. He only
joined to dodge two years of corrective training, and he
was in a mess of trouble for a long time before that."

"Well, I—I can't pretend to know anything about that
side of things, sir."

"You do now." Merrick arched his fingers in front of
his face. "Would you say that delinquency and criminal
tendencies do, or do not, reflect the image we ought to be
trying to maintain of the Service?"

Faced with a question slanted like that, Fallows could
only reply, "Well . . . no, I suppose not."

"Aha!" Merrick seemed more satisfied. "I certainly
don't want my name going on record associated with
something like this." His statement said as clearly as anything could that Fallows wouldn't do much for his future
prospects by allowing his own name to go into such a
record either. Merrick screwed his face up as if he were
experiencing a sour taste. "Low-echelon rabble trying to
rise above themselves. We've got to keep them in their
places, you know, Fallows. That was what went wrong

with the Old Order. It let them climb too high, and they took over. And what happened? They dragged it down— civilization. Do you want to see that happen again?"

"No, of course not," Fallows said, not very happily.

"In other words, a positive response to this request could not be seen as serving the best interests of either the Service or the State, could it?" Merrick concluded.

Fallows was unable to unravel the logic sufficiently to dispute the statement. Instead, he shook his head. "It doesn't sound like it, I suppose."

Merrick nodded gravely. "An officer who abets an act contrary to the best interests of the Service is being disloyal, and a citizen who acts against the interests of the State could be considered subversive, wouldn't you agree?"

"Well, that's true, but—"

"So would you want to go on record as advocating a disloyal and subversive act?" Merrick challenged.

"Definitely not. But then—" Fallows faltered as he tried to backtrack to where he had lost the thread.

"Thank you," Merrick said, pouncing on the opportunity to conclude. "I agree with and endorse your assessment. Very good, Fallows. Enjoy your leave." Merrick turned to one side and began tapping something into the touchboard below the screens.

Fallows stood awkwardly and began moving toward the door. When he was halfway there he stopped, hesitated, then turned round again. "Sir, there's just one thing I'd like—"

"That's all, Fallows," Merrick murmured without looking up. "You are dismissed."

Fallows was still brooding fifteen minutes later in the transit capsule as it sped him homeward around the *Mayflower II*'s six-mile-diameter Ring. Merrick was right, he had decided. He had been a fool. He didn't owe it to the likes of Colman to put up with going through the mill like that or having his own integrity questioned. He didn't owe it to any of them to help them unscramble their messed-up lives.

Cliff Walters would never have gotten himself into a

stupid situation like that. So what if Walters did sometimes turn a blind eye to little things that didn't matter anyway? Walters was a lot smarter when it came to the things that did matter. So much for Fallows, the smartass kid shuttling up from Arizona to save the universe, who still hadn't learned how to keep his nose clean. Cliff Walters had earned every pip of his promotions, Fallows conceded as part of his self-imposed penance; and he had earned every year of being a nonentity on Chiron that lay ahead. Someday, maybe, he'd learn to listen to Jean.

CHAPTER THREE

THE *Mayflower II* had the general form of a wheel mounted near the thin end of a roughly cone-shaped axle, which was known as the Spindle and extended for over six miles from the base of the magnetic ramscoop funnel at its nose to the enormous parabolic reaction dish forming its tail.

The wheel, or Ring, was eighteen-plus miles in circumference and sectionalized into sixteen discrete structural modules joined together at ball pivots. Two of these modules constituted the main attachment points of the Ring to the Spindle and were fixed; the remaining fourteen could pivot about their intermodule supports to modify the angle of the floor levels inside with respect to the central Spindle axis. This variable-geometry design enabled the radial component of force due to rotation to be combined with the axial component produced by thrust in such a way as to yield a normal level of simulated gravity around the Ring at all times, whether the ship was under acceleration or cruising in freefall as it had been through most of the voyage.

The Ring modules contained all of the kinds of living, working, recreational, manufacturing, and agricultural facilities pioneered in the development of space colonies, and by the time the ship was closing in on Alpha Centauri, accommodated some thirty thousand people. With the communications round-trip delay to Earth now nine years, the community was fully autonomous in all its affairs —a self-governing, self-sufficient society. It included its own Military, and since the mission planners had been obliged to take every conceivable circumstance and sce-

33

nario into account, the Military had come prepared for anything; there could be no sending for reinforcements if they got into trouble.

The part of the *Mayflower II* dedicated to weaponry was the mile-long Battle Module, attached to the nose of the Spindle but capable of detaching to operate independently as a warship if the need arose, and equipped with enough firepower to have annihilated easily either side of World War II. It could launch long-range homing missiles capable of sniffing out a target at fifty thousand miles; deploy orbiters for surface bombardment with independently targeted bombs or beam weapons; send high-flying probes and submarine sensors, ground-attack aircraft, and terrain-hugging cruise missiles down into planetary atmospheres; and land its own ground forces. Among other things, it carried a lot of nuclear explosives.

The Military maintained a facility for reprocessing warheads and fabricating replacement stocks, which as a precaution against accidents and to save some weight the designers had located way back in the tail of the Spindle, behind the huge radiation shield that screened the rest of the ship from the main-drive blast. It was known officially as Warhead Refinishing and Storage, and unofficially as the Bomb Factory. Nobody worked there. Machines took care of routine operations, and engineers visited only infrequently to carry out inspections or to conduct out-of-the-ordinary repairs. Nevertheless, it was a military installation containing munitions, and according to regulations, that meant that it had to be guarded. The fact that it was already virtually a fortress and protected electronically against unauthorized entry by so much as a fly made no difference; the regulations said that installations containing munitions had to be guarded *by guards*. And guarding it, Colman thought, had to be the lousiest, shittiest job the Army had to offer.

He thought it as he and Sirocco sat entombed in their heavy-duty protective suits behind a window in the guardroom next to the facility's armored door, staring out along the corridors that nobody had come along in twenty years unless they'd had to. Behind them PFC Driscoll was

wedged into a chair, watching a movie on one of the companel screens with the audio switched through to his suit
radio. Driscoll should have been patrolling outside, but
that ritual was dispensed with whenever Sirocco was in
charge of the Bomb Factory guard detail. A year or so
previously, somebody in D Company had taken advantage
of the fact that everyone looked the same in heavy-duty
suits by feeding a video recording of some dutiful, long-
forgotten sentry into the closed-circuit TV system that
senior officers were in the habit of spying through from
time to time, and nobody from the unit had done any
patrolling since. The cameras were used instead to afford
early warning of unannounced spot checks.

"You never know. The chances might be better after we
reach Chiron," Sirocco said. Colman's transfer application
had been turned down by Engineering. "With the population exploding like crazy, there might be all kinds of
prospects. That's what you get."

"What's what I get?"

"For being a good soldier and a lousy citizen."

"Not liking killing people makes a good soldier?"

"Sure." Sirocco tossed up a gauntleted hand as if the
answer were obvious. "Guys who don't like it but have to
do it get mad. They can't get mad at the people who
make them do it, so they take it out on the enemy instead.
That's what makes them good. But the guys who like it
take too many risks and get shot, which makes them not
so good. It's logical."

"Army logic," Colman murmured.

"I never said it had to make sense." Sirocco brought
his elbows up level with his shoulders, stretched for a few
seconds, and sighed. After a short silence he cocked a
curious eye in Colman's direction. "So . . . what's the latest
with that cutie from Brigade?"

"Forget it."

"Not interested?"

"Dumb."

"Too bad. How come?"

"Astrology and cosmic forces. She wanted to know what
sign I was born under. I told her MATERNITY WARD." Col-

man made a sour face. "Hell, why should I have to humor people all the time?"

Sirocco wrinkled his lip, showing a glimpse of his moustache. "You can't fool me, Steve. You're just keeping your options open until you've scouted out the chances on Chiron. Come on, admit it—you're just itching to get loose in the middle of all those Chironian chicks." The first, machine-generated Chironians were the ten thousand individuals created through the ten years following the *Kuan-yin*'s arrival, the oldest of whom would be in their late forties. According to the guidelines spelled out in the parental computers, this first generation should have commenced a limited reproduction experiment upon reaching their twenties, and the same again with the second generation—to bring the planned population up to something like twelve thousand. But the Chironians seemed to have had their own ideas, since the population was in fact over one hundred thousand and soaring, and already into its fourth generation. The possible implications were intriguing.

"I'm not that hung up about it," Colman insisted, not for the first time. "Maybe it is like some of the guys think, and maybe it's not. Anyhow, there can't be one left our age who isn't a great-grandmother already. Look at the statistics."

"Who said anything about them? Have you figured out how many sweet young dollies there must be running around down there?" Sirocco chuckled lasciviously over the intercom. "I bet Swyley has a miraculous recovery between now and when we go into orbit." Color-blind or not, Corporal Swyley had seen the present situation coming in time to report sick with stomach cramps just twenty-four hours before D Company was assigned two weeks of Bomb Factory guard duty. He was "sick" because he had reported them during his own time; reporting stomach cramps during the Army's time was diagnosed as malingering.

A call came through from Brigade, and Sirocco switched into the audio channel to take it. Colman sat back and looked around. The indicators and alarms on the console in front of him had nothing to report. Nobody was creeping about under the floor, worming their way between the structure's inner and outer skins, tampering with any doors or hatches, cutting a hole through from the booster compartments, crawling down from the accelerator level above, or climbing furtively across the outside. Nobody, it seemed, wanted any thermonuclear warheads today. He rose and moved round behind the chair. "Need to stretch my legs," he said as Sirocco glanced up behind his faceplate. "It's time to do a round anyhow." Sirocco nodded and carried on talking inside his helmet. Colman shouldered his M32 and left the guardroom.

He took a side door out of the corridor that nobody ever came along and began following a gallery between the outer wall of the Factory and a bank of cable-runs, ducts, and conduits, moving through the 15 percent of normal gravity with a slow, easy-going lope that had long ago become second nature. Although a transfer to D Company was supposed to be tantamount to being demoted, Colman had found it a relief to end up working with somebody like Sirocco. Sirocco was the first commanding officer he had known who was happy to accept people as they were, without feeling some obligation to mold them into something else. He wasn't meddling and interfering all the time. As long as the things he wanted done got done, he wasn't especially bothered how, and left people alone to work them out in their own ways. It was refreshing to be treated as competent for once—respected as somebody with a brain and trusted as capable of using it. Most of the other men in the unit felt the same way. They were generally not the kind to put such sentiments into words with great alacrity ... but it showed.

Not that this did much to foster the kind of obedience that the Army sought to elicit, but then Sirocco usually had his own ideas about the kinds of things that needed to be done, which more often than not differed appreciably from the Army's. Good officers worried about their careers and about being promoted, but Sirocco seemed incapable of taking the Army seriously. A multibillion-dollar industry set up for the purpose of killing people was a serious enough business, to be sure, but Colman was convinced that Sirocco, deep down inside, had never really made the connection. It was a game that he enjoyed playing. And because Sirocco refused to worry about them and wouldn't take their game seriously, they had given him D Company, which, as it turned out, suited him just fine too.

Colman had reached the place where a raised catwalk joined the gallery from a door leading through a bulkhead into one of the booster-pump compartments, where tritium bred in the stern bypass reactors was concentrated to enrich the main-drive fusion plasma before it was hurled away into space. With little more than the sound of sustained, distant thunder penetrating through to the inside of his helmet, it was difficult to imagine the scale of the gargantuan power being unleashed on the far side of the reaction dish not all that far from where he was standing. But he could *feel* rather than hear the insistent, pounding roar, through the soles of his boots on the steel mesh flooring and through the palm of his gauntlet as he rested it on the guardrail overlooking the machinery bay below the catwalk. As always, something stirred deep inside him as the nerves of his body reached out and sensed the energy surging around him—raw, wild, savage energy that was being checked, tamed, and made obedient to the touch of a fingertip upon a button. He gazed along the lines of superconducting busbars with core maintained within mere tens of degrees from absolute zero just feet from hundred-million-degree plasmas, at the accelerator casing above his head, where pieces of atoms flashed at almost the speed of light along paths controlled to within millionths of an inch, at the bundles of data cables marching away to carry details of everything that happened from microsecond to microsecond to the ever-alert control computers, and had to remind himself that it had all been constructed by men. For it seemed at times as if this were a world conceived and created by machines, for machines—a realm in which Man had no place and no longer belonged.

But Colman felt that he did belong here—among the machines. He understood them and talked their language, and they talked his. They were talking to him now in the vibrations coming through his suit. The language of the machines was plain and direct. It had no inverted logic or double meanings. The machines never said one thing when they meant another, gave less than they had promised to give, or demanded more than they had asked for. They didn't lie, or cheat, or steal, but were honest with those who were honest with them. Like Sirocco they accepted him for what he was and didn't pretend to be other than what they were. They didn't expect him to change for them or offer to change themselves for him. Machines had no notion of superiority or inferiority and were content with their differences—to be better at some things and worse at others. They could understand that and accept it. Why, Colman wondered, couldn't people?

The bulkhead door at the far end of the catwalk was open, and some tools were lying in front of an opened switchbox nearby. Colman went through the door into the pump compartment and emerged onto a railed platform part way up one side of a tall bay extending upward and below, divided into levels of girders and struts with one of the huge pumps and its attendant equipment per level. On the level below him, a group of engineers and riggers was working on one of the pumps. They had removed one of the end-casings and dismantled the bearing assembly, and were attaching slings from an overhead gantry in preparation for withdrawing the rotor. Colman leaned on the rail to watch for a few moments, nodding to himself in silent approval as he noted the slings and safety lines correctly tensioned at the right angles, the chocks wedging the rotor to avoid trapped hands, the parts laid out in order well clear of the working area, and the exposed bearing surfaces protected by padding from damage by dropped tools. He liked watching professionals.

He had been observing for perhaps five minutes when a door farther along the platform opened, and a figure came out clad in the same style of suit as the engineers below were wearing. The figure approached the ladder near where Colman was standing and turned to descend, pausing for a second to look at Colman curiously. The nametag on the breast pocket read B. FALLOWS. Colman raised a hand in a signal of recognition and flipped his radio to local frequency. "Hey, Bernard, it's me—Steve Colman. I don't know if you're heard yet, but that transfer didn't go through. Thanks for trying anyway."

The features behind the other's visor remained unsmiling. "*Mister* Fallows to you, Sergeant." The voice was icy. "I'm sorry, but I have work to do. I presume you have as well. Might I suggest that we both get on with it." With that he clasped the handrails of the ladder, stepped backward off the platform to slide gently down to the level below, and turned away to rejoin the others.

Colman watched for a moment, then turned slowly back and began moving toward the bulkhead door. He didn't feel resentful, nor particularly surprised. He'd seen it all too many times before. Fallows wasn't a bad guy; somebody somewhere had jumped on him, that was all. "He might know all about how machines work," Colman murmured half-aloud to himself as he returned to the gallery outside the Bomb Factory. "But he doesn't understand how they think."

CHAPTER FOUR

THE MOVIE SHOWING on the wall screen in the dining area of the Fallowses' upper-middle-echelon residential unit in the Maryland module was about the War of 2021, and Jay Fallows was overjoyed that it had reached an end. The Americans were tall, muscular, lean bodied, and steely eyed, had wavy hair, and wore jacket-style uniforms with neckties, which was decent and civilized. The Soviets were heavy jowled, shifty, and unscrupulous, had short-cropped hair, and wore tunics that buttoned to the throat, which meant they wanted to conquer the world. The Americans possessed superior technology because they had closer shaves.

"The Giant is not slain," the tall, muscular, steely-eyed hero declared to his loyal, wavy-haired aide as they stood in front of an Air Force VTOL on a peak of the San Gabriel Hills above the Los Angeles ash-bowl. "It must sleep a while to mend its wounds now its task is done. But it will rise again, hardened and tempered from the furnace. This will not have been for naught." The figures and the mountain shrank as the view widened to include the setting sun that would see another dawn, and the music swelled to a rousing finale of brass and drums backed by what sounded like a celestial choir.

Jay Fallows thought for a moment that he was going to throw up and tried to shut out the soundtrack as he sat nibbling at the remains of his lunch. An astronomy book lay propped open on the table in front of him. Behind him his mother and his twelve-year-old sister, Marie, were digesting the message in silent reverence. The page he was looking at showed the northern constellations of stars as

41

they appeared from Earth. They looked much as they did from the *Mayflower II*, except in the book Cassiopeia was missing a star—the Sun. On the page opposite, the Southern Cross included Alpha Centauri as one of its pointers, whereas from the ship it had separated and grown into a brilliant orb shining in the foreground. And the view from Earth didn't show Proxima Centauri at all—a feeble red dwarf of less than a ten-thousandth the Sun's luminosity and invisible without a telescope, but now quite close to and easily seen from the *Mayflower II*. Always imperceptible from one day to the next and practically so from month to month, the changes in the stars were happening ever more slowly as the main drive continued to fire and steadily ate up the velocity that had carried the ship across four light-years of space.

Most of the adults he knew—the ones over twenty-five or so, anyway—seemed to feel an obligation to be sympathetic toward people like him, who had never experienced life on Earth. From what he had seen he wasn't sure that he'd missed all that much. Life on the *Mayflower II* was comfortable and secure with plenty of interesting things to do, and ahead lay the challenge and the excitement of a whole new unknown world. Certainly that was something no one back on Earth could look forward to.

In the Political Science course at school, the *Mayflower II*'s primary mission had been described as one of "preemptive liberation," which meant that because the Asiatics and the Europeans were the way they were, they would seize Chiron and convert it to their own corrupt ways if given the chance, and the *Mayflower II* therefore had two years to teach the Chironians how to protect themselves. There were other, more abstract reasons why it was so important for the Chironians to be educated and enlightened, which Jay didn't fully understand, but which he accepted as being among the many mysteries that would doubtless reveal themselves in their own good time as part of the complicated business of growing up.

Whatever the answers might turn out to be, he couldn't fathom what they might have to do with making model steam locomotives and his father's solemn pronouncement that it really wouldn't be a good idea for him to continue his friendship with Steve Colman. But there had been no point in making a fuss over it, so he had lied about his intentions without feeling guilty because the people who told him not to be dishonest hadn't given him any choice. Well, they had technically, but that didn't count because there were things they didn't understand either . . . or had forgotten, maybe. But Steve would understand.

"I'm glad I wasn't alive *then*," Marie said from behind him. "I can't imagine whole cities burning. It must have been *horrible*."

"It was," Jean agreed. "It's a lesson that we all have to remember. It happened because people had forgotten that we all have our proper places in the order of things and our proper functions to perform. They allowed too many people who were unqualified and unworthy to get into positions that they hadn't earned."

"Pay our debt, collect our due/Each one proud for what we do," Marie recited.

"Very good," her mother said.

Little snot, Jay thought to himself and turned the page. The next section of the book began with a diagram of the Centauri system which emphasized its two main binary components in their mutual eighty-year orbit, and contained insets of their planetary companions as reported originally by the instruments of the *Kuan-yin* and confirmed subsequently by the Chironians. Beneath the main diagram were pictures of the spectra of the Sunlike Alpha G2v primary with numerous metallic lines; the cooler, K1-type-orange Beta Centauri secondary with the blue end of its continuum weakened and absorption bands of molecular radicals beginning to appear; and M5e, orange-red Proxima Centauri with heavy absorption in the violet and prominent CO, CH, and TiO bands.

"There won't be a war on Chiron, will there?" Marie asked.

"Of course not, dear. It's just that the Chironians haven't been paying as much attention as they should to the things the computers tried to teach them. They've always had machines to give them everything they want, and they think life is all one long playtime. But it's not really their fault because they're not really people like us." The conviction was widespread even though the *Mayflower II*'s presiding bishop was carrying a special ordinance from Earth decreeing that Chironians had souls. Jean realized that she had left herself open to misinterpretation and added hastily, "Well, they are people, of course. But they're not *exactly* like you because they were born without any mothers or fathers. You mustn't hate them or anything. Just remember that you're a little better than they are because you've been luckier, and you know about things they've never had a chance to learn. Even if we have to be a little bit firm with them, it will be for their own good in the end."

"You mean when the Chinese and the Europeans get here?"

"Quite. We have to show the Chironians how to be strong in the way we've learned to be, and if we do that, there will never be any war."

Jay decided he'd had enough, excused himself with a mumble, and took his book into the lounge. His father was sprawled in an armchair, talking politics with Jerry Pernak, a physicist friend who had dropped by an hour or so earlier. Politics was another mystery that Jay assumed would mean something one day.

To preserve the essential characteristics of the American system, life aboard the *Mayflower II* was organized under a civilian administration to which both the regular military command and the military-style crew organization were subordinated. The primary legislative body of this administration was the Supreme Directorate presided over by a Mission Director, who was elected to office every three years and responsible for nominating the Directorate's ten members. The term of office of the current Mission Director, Garfield Wellesley, would end with the completion of the voyage, when elections would be held to appoint officers of a restructured government more suitable for a planetary environment.

"Howard Kalens, no doubt about it," Bernard Fallows was saying. "If we've only got two years to knock the place into shape, he's just the kind of man we need. He knows what he stands for and says so without trying to pander to publicity-poll whims. And he's got the breeding for the position. You can't make a planetary governor out of any rabble, you know."

Pernak didn't seem overeager to accept the implied invitation to agree. He started to say something noncommittal, then stopped and looked up as Jay entered. "Hi, Jay. How was the movie?"

"Aw, I wasn't watching it." Jay waved vaguely with the book and returned it to its shelf. "Usual stuff."

"What are the girls still talking about in there?" Bernard asked.

"I'm not sure. I guess I couldn't have been listening that much."

"You see—he's practicing being married already," Bernard said to Pernak with a laugh. Pernak grinned momentarily. Bernard looked at his son. "Well, it's early yet. Figured out what you're doing this afternoon?"

"I thought maybe I'd go over to Jersey and put in a few hours on the loco."

"Fine." Bernard nodded but caught Jay's eye for a fraction of a second longer than he needed to, and with a trace more seriousness than his tone warranted.

"How's it coming along?" Pernak asked.

"Pretty good. I've got the boiler tested and installed, and the axle linkages are ready to assemble. Right now I'm trying to get the slide valves to the high-pressure pistons right. They're tricky."

"Got far with them?" Pernak asked.

"I had to scrap one set." Jay sighed. "I guess it's back to square one on another. That's what I reckon I'll start today."

"So when are you going to show it to me?"

Jay shrugged. "Any time you like."

"You going to Jersey right now?"

"I was going to. I don't have to make it right now."

Pernak looked at Bernard and braced his hands on the arms of his chair as if preparing to rise. "Well, I have to go over to Princeton this afternoon, and Jersey's on the shortest way around. Jay and I could share a cab."

Bernard stood up. "Sure . . . don't let me keep you if you have things to do. Thanks for letting me have the cutter back." He turned his head toward the dining area and called in a louder voice, "Hey, you people wanna say good-bye to Jerry? He's leaving." Pernak and Jay waited by the door for Jean and Marie to appear.

"On your way?" Jean asked Pernak.

"Things won't do themselves. I'm stopping off at Jersey with Jay to see how his loco's coming along."

"Oh, that locomotive!" Jean looked at Jay. "Are you working on it again?"

"For a few hours maybe."

"Well, try not to make it half the night this time, won't you." And to Pernak: "Take care, Jerry. Thanks for dropping by. Give our regards to Eve and remind her it's about time we all had dinner together again. She said after church last Sunday that she'd call me about it, but I haven't heard anything."

"I'll remind her," Pernak promised. "Ready, Jay? Let's go."

Pernak had short, jet-black hair, a broad, solid frame, and rubbery features that always fascinated Jay with their seemingly endless variety of expressions. He had lectured on physics topics several times at Jay's school and had proved popular as much for his entertainment value as for his grasp of the subject matter, which he always managed to make exciting with tantalizing glimpses inside black holes, mind-bending accounts of the first few minutes of the universe, and fantastic speculation about living in twisted spacetimes with unusual geometries. On one occasion he had introduced Feynman diagrams, which represented particles as "world lines" traversing a two-dimensional domain, one axis representing space and the other time. Mathematically and theoretically a particle going forward in time was indistinguishable from its anti-particle going backward in time, and Pernak had offered the staggering conjecture that there might be just one electron in the entire universe—repeating itself over and over by going forward as an electron and backward as a positron. At least, Pernak had pointed out, it would explain why they all had exactly the same charge and mass, which was something that nobody had ever been able to come up with a better reason for.

Pernak had a surprisingly long stride for his height, and Jay had to hurry to keep up as they walked a couple of blocks through densely packed but ingeniously secluded interlocking terraces of Maryland residential units. It wasn't long before Pernak was talking about phase-changes in the laws of physics and their manifestation through the process of evolution. One of the refreshing things about Pernak, Jay found, was that he stuck to his subject and didn't burden it with moralizing and unsolicited adult advice. He had never been able to make up his mind whether Pernak was secretly a skeptic about things like that or just believed in minding his own business, but he had never found a way of leading up to the question.

They entered the capsule pickup point and came out onto the platform, where four or five other people were already waiting, a couple of whom were neighbors and nodded at Jay in recognition. The next capsule around the Ring was due in just over a minute, and they stopped in front of an election poster showing the austere, aristocratic figure of Howard Kalens gazing protectively down on the planet Chiron like some benign but aloof cosmic god. The caption read simply: PEACE AND UNITY.

"Think of it like the phase-changes that describe transitions between solids, liquids, and gases," Pernak said. "The gas laws are only valid over a certain limited range. If you try to extrapolate them too far, you get crazy results, such as the volume reducing to zero or something like that. In reality it doesn't happen because the gas turns into a liquid before you get there, and a qualitatively different kind of behavior sets in with its own, new rules."

"You're saying evolution adds up to a succession of transitions like that?"

"Yes, Jay. Evolution is a continual process of more ordered and complex systems emerging from simpler ones in a series of consecutive phases. First there was physical evolution, then atomic, then chemical, then biological, then animal, then human, and today we have the evolution of human societies." Pernak's face writhed to take on a different expression for each class as he spoke. "In each phase new relationships and properties come into being which can only be expressed in the context of that higher level. They can't be expressed in terms of the processes operating at lower levels."

Jay thought about it for a few seconds and nodded slowly. "I think I get it. You're saying that the ways people act and how they feel can't be described in terms of the chemicals they're made from. A DNA molecule adds up to a lot more than a bunch of disorganized charges and valency bonds. The way you organize it makes its own laws."

"Exactly, Jay. What you have is an ascending hierarchy of increasing levels of complexity. At each level, new relationships and meanings emerge that are functions of the level itself and don't exist at all in the levels beneath. For instance, there are twenty-six letters in the alphabet. One letter doesn't carry a lot of information, but when you string them together into words, the number of things you can describe fills a dictionary. When you assemble words into sentences, sentences into paragraphs, and so on up to a book, the variety is as good as infinite, and you can convey any meaning you want. Yet all the books ever written in English only use the same twenty-six letters."

The capsule arrived, and Jay fell silent while he digested what Pernak had said. As they climbed inside, Jay entered a code into the panel by the door to specify their destination in the Jersey module, and they sat down on an empty pair of facing seats as the capsule began to move. After a short run up to speed, it entered a tube to exit from Maryland and passed through one of the spherical intermodule housings that supported the Ring and contained the bearings and pivoting mechanisms for adjusting the module orientations to the ship's state of motion. For a brief period they were looking out through a transparent outer shell at the immensity of the Spindle, seemingly supported by a web of structural booms and tie-bars three miles above their heads, with the vastness of space extending away on either side, and then they entered the Kansas module where the scene outside changed to animal grazing enclosures, level upon level of agricultural units, fish farms, and hydroponic tanks.

"Okay, so you track it all back to the Big Bang," Jay said at last. "Then where do you go?"

"Classically, you can't go anywhere. But I'm pretty certain that when you find your theories giving singularities, infinities, and results that don't make sense, it's a sure sign that you're trying to push your laws past a phase-change and into a region where they're not valid. I think that's what we're up against."

"So where do you go?" Jay asked again.

"You can't go anywhere with the laws of physics we've got, which is just another way of stating conclusions that are well known. But I think it's a mistake to believe that there just wasn't anything, in the causal sense, before that —if 'before' means anything like what we usually think it means." Pernak sat forward and moistened his lips. "I'll give you a loose analogy. Imagine a flame. Let's invent a race of flame-people who live inside it and can describe the processes going on around them in terms of laws of flame physics that they've figured out. Okay?" Jay frowned but nodded. "Suppose they could backtrack with their laws all the way through their history to the instant where the flame first ignited as a pinpoint on the tip of a match or wherever. To them that would be the origin of their universe, wouldn't it."

"Oh, okay," Jay said. "*Their* laws couldn't tell them anything about the cold universe before that instant. Flame physics only came into existence when the flame did."

"A phase-change, evolving its own new laws," Pernak confirmed, nodding.

"And you're saying the Big Bang was something like that?"

"I'm saying it's very likely. What triggers a phase-change is a concentration of energy—energy *density*—like at the tip of a match. Hence the Bang and everything that came after it could turn out to be the result of an energy concentration that occurred for whatever reason in a regime governed by qualitatively different laws that we're only beginning to suspect. And that's what my line of research is concerned with."

Another flash of stars and they were in Idaho, one of the two fixed modules that carried the main support arms to the Spindle. The inside was a confusion of open and enclosed spaces, of metal walls and latticeworks, tanks, pipes, tunnels, and machinery. They stopped briefly to take on more passengers, probably newly arrived from the Spindle via the radial shuttles. Then the capsule moved away again.

"It could open up possibilities that'll blow your mind," Pernak resumed. "Suppose, for instance, that we could get to understand those laws and create our own concentrations on a miniature scale to inject energy from . . . let's call it a hyperrealm, into our own universe—in other words make 'small bangs'—mini white holes. Think what an energy source that would be. It'd made fusion look like a firecracker." Pernak waved his hands about. "And how about this, Jay. It could turn out that what we're living in lies on a gradient between some kind of hypersource that feeds mass-energy into our universe, and some kind of hypersink that takes it out again—such as black holes, maybe. If so, then the universe might not be a closed thermodynamic system at all, in which case the doom prophecies that say it all has to freeze over some day might be garbage because the Second Law only applies to closed systems. In other words we might find we're flame people living in a match factory."

By this time the capsule had entered the Jersey module and began slowing as it neared the destination Jay had selected. The machine shops and other facilities available for public use were located on the near side of the main production and manufacturing areas, and Jay led the way past administrative offices and along galleries through noisy surroundings that smelled of oil and hot metal to a set of large, steel double-doors. A smaller side door brought them to a check-in counter topped by a glass partition behind which the attendant and a watchman were playing cribbage across a scratched and battered metal desk. The attendant stood and shuffled over when Jay and Pernak appeared, and Jay presented a school pass which entitled him to free use of the facilities. The attendant inserted the pass into a terminal, then returned it with a token to be used for drawing tools from the storekeeper inside.

"There's something for you here," the attendant noted as Jay was turning away. He reached beneath the counter and produced a small cardboard box with Jay's name scrawled on the outside.

Puzzled, Jay broke the sealing tape and opened the box to reveal a layer of foam padding and a piece of folded notepaper. Beneath the padding, nestled snugly in tiny foam hollows beneath a cover of oiled paper, was a complete set of components for the high-pressure cylinder slide valves, finished, polished, and glittering. The note read:

> Jay,
>   I thought you might need a hand with these so I did them last night. If my hunch is right, things have probably gotten a bit difficult for you. There's no sense in upsetting people who don't mean any harm. Take it from me, he's not such a bad guy.
>   STEVE

Jay blinked and looked up to find Pernak watching him curiously. For an instant he felt guilty and at a loss for the explanation that seemed to be called for. "Bernard told me about it," Pernak said before Jay could offer anything. "I guess he's under a lot of pressure right now, so don't read too much into it." He stared at the box in Jay's hand. "I don't see anything—not a darn thing. Come on, Jay. Let's take a look at that loco of yours."

CHAPTER FIVE

CHIRON WAS ALMOST nine thousand miles in diameter, but its nickel-iron core was somewhat smaller than Earth's, which gave it a comparable gravitational force at the surface. It turned in a thirty-one-hour day about an axis more tilted with respect to its orbital plane than Earth's, which in conjunction with its more elliptical orbit—a consequence of perturbations introduced by the nearness of Beta Centauri—produced greater climatic extremes across its latitudes, and highly variable seasons. Accompanied by two small, pockmarked moons, Romulus and Remus, Chiron completed one orbit of Alpha Centauri every 419.66 days.

Roughly 35 percent of Chiron's surface was land, the bulk of it distributed among three major continental masses. The largest of these was Terranova, a vast, east-west sprawling conglomeration of every conceivable type of geographic region, dominating the southern hemisphere and extending from beyond the pole to cross the equator at its most northerly extremity. Selene, with its jagged coastlines and numerous islands, was connected to the western part of Terranova via an isthmus that narrowed to a neck below the equator; Artemia lay farther to the east, separated by oceans.

Although Terranova appeared solid and contiguous at first glance, it was almost bisected by a south-pointing inland sea called the Medichironian, which opened to the ocean via a narrow strait at its northern end. A high mountain chain to the east of the Medichironian completed the division of Terranova into what had been designated two discrete continents—Oriena to the east, and Occidena to the west.

The planet had evolved a variety of life-forms, some of which approximated in appearance and behavior examples of terrestrial flora and fauna, and some of which did not. Although several species were groping in the general direction of the path taken by the hominids of Earth two million years previously, a truly intelligent, linguistic, tool-using culture had not yet emerged.

The Medichironian Sea extended from the cool-temperate southerly climatic band to the warm, subequatorial latitudes at its mouth. Its eastern shore lay along narrow coastal plains, open in some parts and thickly forested in others, that rapidly rose into the foothills of the Great Barrier Chain, beyond which stretched the vast plains and deserts of central Oriena. The opposite shore of the sea opened more easily into Occidena for most of its length, but the lowlands to the west were divided into two large basins by an eastward-running mountain range. An extension of this range projected into the sea as a rocky spine of fold valleys fringed by picturesque green plains, sandy bays, and rugged headlands, and was known as the Mandel Peninsula, after a well-known statesman of the 2010s. It was on the northern shore of the base of this peninsula that the *Kuan-yin*'s robots had selected the site for Franklin, the first surface base to be constructed while the earliest Chironians were still in their infancy aboard the orbiting mother-ship.

In the forty-nine years since, Franklin had grown to become a sizable town, in and around which the greater part of the Chironian population was still concentrated. Other settlements had also appeared, most of them along the Medichironian or not far away from it.

Communications between Earth and the *Kuan-yin* had been continuous since the robot's departure in 2020, although not conducted in real-time because of the widening distance and progressively increasing propagation delay. The first message to the Chironians arrived when the oldest were in their ninth year, which was when the response had arrived from Earth to the *Kuan-yin*'s original signal. Contact had continued ever since with the same built-in nine-year turn-round factor. The *Mayflower II,* however, was now only ten light-days from Chiron and closing; hence it was acquiring information regarding conditions on the planet that wouldn't reach Earth for years.

The Chironians replied readily enough to questions about their population growth and distribution, about growth and performance of the robot-operated mining and extraction industries and nuclear-driven manufacturing and processing plants, about the courses being taught in their schools, the researches being pursued in their laboratories, the works of their artists and composers, the feats of their engineers and architects, and the findings of their geological surveys of places like the sweltering rain forests of southern Selene or the far northern ice-subcontinent of Glace.

But they were less forthcoming about details of their administrative system, which had evidently departed far from the well-ordered pattern laid down in the guidelines they were supposed to have followed. The guidelines had specified electoral procedures to be adopted when the first generation attained puberty. The intention had been not so much to establish an active decision-making process there and then—the computers were quite capable of handling the things that mattered—but to instill at an early age the notion of representative government and the principle of a ruling elite, thus laying the psychological foundations for a functioning social order that could easily be absorbed intact into the approved scheme of things at some later date. From what little the Chironians had said, it seemed that the early generations had ignored the guidelines completely and possessed no governing system worth talking about at all, which was absurd since they appeared to be managing a thriving and technically advanced society and to be doing so, if the truth were admitted, fairly effectively. In other words, they had to be covering a lot of things up.

Although they came across as polite but frank in their laser transmissions, they projected a coolness that was enough to arouse suspicions. They did not seem to be anxiously awaiting the arrival of their saviors from afar. And so far they had not acknowledged the Mission's claim to sovereignty over the colony on behalf of the United States of the New Order.

"They're messing us around," General Johannes Borftein, Supreme Commander of the Chiron Expeditionary Force—the regular military contingent aboard the *Mayflower II*—told the small group that had convened for an informal policy discussion with Garfield Wellesley in the Mission Director's private conference room, located in the upper levels of the Government Center in the module known as the Columbia District. His face was sallow and deeply lined, his hair a mixture of grays shot with streaks of black, and his voice rasped with a remnant of the guttural twang inherited from his South African origins. "We've got two years to get this show organized, and they're playing games. We don't have the time. We haven't seen any evidence of a defense program down there. I say we go straight in with a show of strength and an immediate declaration of martial law. It's the best way."

Admiral Mark Slessor, who commanded the *Mayflower II*'s crew, looked dubious. "I'm not so sure it's that simple." He rubbed his powerful, blue-shadowed chin. "We could be walking into anything. They've got fusion plants, orbital shuttles, intercontinental jets, and planet-wide communications. How do we know they haven't been working on defense? They've got the know-how and the means. I can see John's point, but his approach is too risky."

"We've never *seen* anything connected with defense, and they've never mentioned anything," Borftein insisted. "Let's stick to reality and the facts we know. Why complicate the issue with speculation?"

"What do you say, Howard?" Garfield Wellesley inquired, looking at Howard Kalens, who was sitting next to Matthew Sterm, the grim-faced and so-far silent Deputy Mission Director.

As Director of Liaison, Kalens headed the diplomatic team charged with initiating relationships with the Chironian leaders and was primarily responsible for planning the policies that would progressively bring the colony into a

Terran-dominated, nominally joint government in the months following planetfall. Hence the question probably concerned him more than anybody else. Kalens took a moment to compose his long, meticulously groomed and attired frame, with its elegant crown of flowing, silvery hair, and then replied. "I agree with John that a rigid rule needs to be asserted early on . . . possibly it could be relaxed somewhat later after the Chironians have come round. However, Mark has a point too. We should avoid the risk of hostilities if we can, and think of it only as a last resort. We're going to need those resources working *for* us, not against. And they're still very thin. We can't permit them to be frittered away or destroyed. Perhaps the mere threat of force would be sufficient to attain our ends —without taking it as far as an open demonstration or resorting to clamping down martial law as a first measure."

Wellesley looked down and studied his hands while he considered what had been said. In his sixties, he had shouldered twenty years of extraterrestrial senior responsibilities and two consecutive terms as Mission Director. Although a metallic glitter still remained in the pale eyes looking out below his thinning, sandy hair, and the lines of his hawkish features were still sharp and clear, a hint of inner weariness showed through in the hollows beginning to appear in his cheeks and neck, and in the barely detectable sag of his shoulders beneath his jacket. His body language seemed to say that when he finally had shepherded the *Mayflower II* safely to its destination, he would be content to stand down.

"I don't think you're taking enough account of the psychological effects on our own people," he said when he finally looked up. "Morale is high now that we're nearly there, and I don't want to spoil it. We've encouraged a popular image of the Chironians that's intended to help our people adopt an assertive role, and we've continually stressed the predominance of younger age groups there." He shook his head. "Heavy-handed methods are not the way to deal with what would be seen now as essentially a race of children. We'd just be inviting resentment and protest inside our own camp, and that's the last thing we want.

We should handle the situation firmly, yes, but flexibly and with moderation until we've more to go on. Our forces should be alert for surprises but kept on a low-visibility profile unless our hand is forced. That's my formula, gentlemen—firm, low-key, but flexible."

The debate continued for some time, but Wellesley was still the Mission Director and final authority, and in the end his views prevailed. "I'll go along with you, but I have to say I'm not happy about it," Borftein said. "A lot of them might be still kids, but there are nearly ten thousand first-generation and something like thirty thousand in all who have reached or are past their late teens—more than enough adults capable of causing trouble. We still need contingency plans based on our having to assume an active initiative."

"Is that a proposal?" Wellesley asked. "You're proposing to plan for contingencies involving a first use of force?"

"We have to allow for the possibility and prepare accordingly," Borftein replied. "Yes, it is."

"I agree," Howard Kalens murmured.

Wellesley looked at Slessor, who, while still showing signs of apprehension, appeared curiously to feel relieved at the same time. Wellesley nodded heavily. "Very well. Proceed on that basis, John. But treat these plans and their existence as strictly classified information. Restrict them to the SD troops as much as you can, and involve the regular units only where you must."

"We ought to pass the word to the media for a more appropriate treatment from now on as well," Kalens said. "Perhaps playing up things like Chironian stubbornness and irresponsibility would harden up the public image a bit . . . just in case. We could get them to add a mention or two of signs that the Chironians might have armed themselves and the need to take precautions. It could always be dismissed later as overzealous reporting. Should I whisper in Lewis's ear about it?"

Wellesley frowned over the suggestion for several seconds but eventually nodded. "I suppose you should, yes."

Sterm watched, listened, and said nothing.

CHAPTER SIX

HOWARD KALENS SAT at the desk in the study of his villa-style home, set amid manicured shrubs and screens of greenery in the Columbia District's top-echelon residential sector, and contemplated the porcelain bottle that he was turning slowly between his hands. It was Korean, from the thirteenth-century Koryo dynasty, and about fourteen inches high with a long neck that flowed into a bulbous body of celadon glaze delicately inlaid with *mishima* depicting a willow tree and symmetrical floral designs contained between decorative bands of a repeated foliose motif encircling the stem and base. His desk was a solid-walnut example of early nineteenth-century French rococo revival, and the chair in which he was sitting, a matching piece by the same cabinetmaker. The books aligned on the shelves behind him included first editions by Henry James, Scott Fitzgerald, and Norman Mailer; the Matisse on the wall opposite was a print from an original preserved in the *Mayflower II*'s vaults, and the lithographs beside it were by Rico Lebrun. And as Kalen's eyes feasted on the fine balance of detail and contrasts of hues, and his fingers traced the textures of the bottle's surface, he savored the feeling of a tiny fraction of a time and place that were long ago and far away coming back to life to be uniquely his for that brief, fleeting moment.

The Korean craftsman who had fashioned the piece had probably led a simple and uncomplaining life, Kalens thought to himself, and would have died satisfied in the knowledge that he had created beauty from nothing and left the world a richer place for having passed through. Would his descendants in the Asia of eight hundred years

58

later be able to say the same or to feel the same fulfillment as they scrambled for their share of mass-produced consumer affluence, paraded their newfound wealth and arrogance through the fashion houses and auction rooms of London, Paris, and New York, or basked on the decks of their gaudy yachts off Australian beaches? Kalens very much doubted it. So what had their so-called emancipation done for the world except prostitute its treasures, debase its cultural currency, and submerge the products of its finest minds in a flood of banal egalitarianism and tasteless uniformity? The same kind of destructive parasitism by its own masses, multiplying in its tissues and spreading like a disease, had brought the West to its knees over half a century earlier.

In its natural condition a society was like an iceberg, eight-ninths submerged in crude ignorance and serving no useful purpose other than to elevate and support the worthy minority whose distillation and embodiment of all that was excellent of the race conferred privilege as a right and authority as a duty. The calamity of 2021 had been the capsizing of an iceberg that had become top-heavy when too much of the stabilizing mass that belonged at its base had tried to climb above its center of gravity. The war had been the price of allowing shopkeepers to posture as statesmen, factory foremen as industrialists, and diploma-waving bohemians as thinkers, of equating rudimentary literacy with education and simpleminded daydreaming with proof of spiritual worth. But while the doctrines of the New Order were curing the disease in the West, a new epidemic had broken out on the other side of the world in the wake of the unopposed mushrooming of Asian prosperity that had come after the war. Mankind as a whole, it seemed, would never learn.

"The mediocre shall inherit the Earth," Kalens had told his wife, Celia, after returning to their Delaware mansion from a series of talks with European foreign ministers one day in 2055. "Or else, eventually, there will be another war." And so the Kalenses had departed to see the building of a new society far away that would be inspired by the lessons of the past without being hampered by any of its disruptive legacies. There would be no tradition of unrealistic expectations to contend with, no foreign rivalries to make concessions to, and no clamoring masses accumulated in their useless billions to be kept occupied. Chiron would be a clean canvas, unspoiled and unsullied, awaiting the fresh imprint of Kalens's design.

Three obstacles now remained between Kalens and the vision that he had nurtured through the years of presiding over the kind of neofeudal order that would epitomize his ideal social model. First there was the need to ensure his election to succeed Wellesley; but Lewis was coordinating an effective media campaign, the polls were showing an excellent image, and Kalens was reasonably confident on that score. Second was the question of the Chironians. Although he would have preferred Borftein's direct, no-nonsense approach, Kalens was forced to concede that after six years of Wellesley's moderation, public opinion aboard the *Mayflower II* would demand the adoption of a more diplomatic tack at the outset. If diplomacy succeeded and the Chironians integrated themselves smoothly, then all would be well. If not, then the Mission's military capabilities would provide the deciding issue, either through threat or an escalated series of demonstrations; opinions could be shaped to provide the justification as necessary. Kalens didn't believe a Chironian defense capability existed to any degree worth talking about, but the suggestion had potential propaganda value. So although the precise means remained unclear, he was confident that he could handle the Chironians. Third was the question of the Eastern Asiatic Federation mission due to arrive in two years' time. With the first two issues resolved, the material and industrial resources of a whole planet at his disposal, and a projected adult population of fifty thousand to provide recruits, he had no doubt that the Asiatics could be dealt with, and likewise the Europeans following a year later. And then he would be free to sever Chiron's ties to Earth completely. He hadn't confided that part of the dream to anyone, not even Celia.

But first things had to come first. It was time to begin mobilizing the potential allies he had been quietly sounding out and cultivating for the three years since the last elections. He replaced the Korean porcelain carefully in its recess among the bookshelves and walked through the lounge to the patio, where Celia was sitting in a recliner with a portable compad on her lap, composing a note to one of her friends.

The young, sophisticated wife that Howard Kalens had taken with him to Luna to join the *Mayflower II* was now in her early forties, but her face had acquired character and maturity along with the womanly look that had evolved from girlish prettiness, and her body had filled out to a voluptuousness that had lost none of its femininity. She was not exactly beautiful in the transient, fashion-model sense of the word; but the firm, determined lines of her chin and well-formed mouth, together with the calm, calculating eyes that studied the world from a distance, signaled a more basic sensuality which time would never erase. Her shoulder-length auburn hair was tied back in a ponytail, and she was wearing tan slacks with an orange silk blouse covering firm, full breasts.

She looked up as Howard came out of the house. Her expression did not change. Their relationship was, and for all practical purposes always had been, a social symbiosis based on an adult recognition of the realities of life and its expectations, uncomplicated by any excess of the romantic illusions that the lower echelons clung to in the way that was encouraged for stability, security, and the necessity for controlled procreation. Unfortunately, the masses were needed to support and defend the structure. Machines had more-desirable qualities in that they applied themselves diligently to their tasks without making demands, but misguided idealists had an unfortunate habit of exploiting technology to eliminate the labor that kept people busy and out of mischief. Too, the idealists would teach them how to think. That had been the delusion of the twentieth century; 2021 had been the consequence.

"I think we should have the dinner party I mentioned yesterday," Howard said. "Can you put together an invitation list and send it out? The end of next week might be suitable—say Friday or Saturday."

"If we're going to want a suite at the Françoise again, I'd better reserve it now," Celia answered. "Any idea how many people we're talking about?"

"Oh, not a lot, I want it to be cosy and private. Here should be fine. Probably about a dozen. There's Lewis, of course, and Gerrard. And it's about time we started bringing Borftein closer into the family."

"That man!"

"Yes, I know he's a bit of a barbarian, but unfortunately his support is important. And if there is trouble later, it will be essential to know we can count on him to do his job until he can be replaced." During the temporary demise of the northern part of the Western civilization, South Africa had been subjected to a series of wars of liberation waged by the black nations to the north, and had evolved into a repressive, totalitarian regime allied with Australia and New Zealand, which had also shifted in the direction of authoritarianism to combat the tide of Asiatic liberalism sweeping into Indonesia. Their methods had merit, but produced Borfteins as a by-product.

"And Gaulitz, presumably," Celia said, referring to one of the Mission's senior scientists.

"Oh, yes, Gaulitz definitely. I've plans for Herr Gaulitz."

"A government job?"

"A witch doctor." Kalens smiled at the frown on Celia's face. "One of the reasons America declined was that it allowed science to become too popular and too familiar, and therefore an object of contempt. Science is too potent to be entrusted to the masses. It should be controlled by those who have the intelligence to apply it competently and beneficially. Gaulitz would be a suitable figure to groom as a . . . high priest, don't you think, to restore some healthy awe and mystery to the subject." He nodded knowingly. "The Ancient Egyptians had the right idea." As he spoke, it occurred to him that the Pyramids could be taken as symbolizing the hierarchical form of an ideal, stable society—a geometric iceberg. The analogy was an interesting one. It would make a good point to bring up at the dinner party. Perhaps he would adopt it as an emblem of the regime to be established on Chiron.

"Have you made your mind up about Sterm?" Celia asked.

Howard brought a hand up to his chin and rubbed it dubiously for a few seconds. "Mmm . . . Sterm. I can't make him out. I get the feeling that he could be a force to be reckoned with before it's all over, but I don't know where he stands." He thought for a moment longer and at last shook his head. "There are some confidential matters that I'll want to bring up. Sterm could turn out to be an adversary. It wouldn't be wise to show too much of our hand this early on. You'd better leave him out of it. Later on it might change . . . but let's keep him at a distance for the time being."

CHAPTER SEVEN

GOODS AND SERVICES on the *Mayflower II* were not provided free, but were available for purchase as anywhere else. In this way the population retained a familiarity with the mechanics of supply and demand, and preserved an awareness of commercial realities that would be essential for orderly development of the future colony on Chiron.

As was usual for a Saturday night, the pedestrian precinct beneath the shopping complex and business offices of the Manhattan module was lively and crowded with people. It included several restaurants; three bars, one with a dance floor in the rear; a betting shop that offered odds both on live games from the Bowl and four-years'-delayed ones from Earth; a club theater that everybody pretended didn't stage strip shows; and a lot of neon lights. The Bowery bar, a popular haunt of off-duty regular troops, was squeezed into one corner of the precinct next to a coffee shop, behind a studded door of imitation oak and a high window of small, tinted glass panes that turned the inside lights red.

The scene inside the Bowery was busy and smoky, with a lot of uniforms and women visible among the crowd lining the long bar on the left side of the large room inside the door, and a four-piece combo playing around the corner in the smaller room at the back. Colman and some of D Company were sitting at one of the tables standing in a double row along the wall opposite the bar. Sirocco had joined them despite the regulation against officers' fraternizing with enlisted men, and Corporal Swyley was up and about again after the dietitian at the Brigade sick bay had enforced a standing order to put Swyley on spinach and fish whenever he was admitted. Bret Hanlon, the sergeant in charge of Second Platoon and a long-standing buddy of Colman, was sitting on the other side of Sirocco with Stanislau, Third Platoon's laser gunner, and a couple of civilian girls; a signals specialist called Anita, attached to Brigade H.Q. was snuggling close to Colman with her arm draped loosely through his.

Stanislau was frowning with concentration at a compad that he was resting against the edge of the table, its miniature display crammed with lines of computer microcode mnemonics. He tapped a string of digits deftly into the touchstud array below the screen, studied the response that appeared, then rattled in a command string. A number appeared low down in a corner. Stanislau looked up triumphantly at Sirocco. "3.141592653," he announced. "It's *pi* to ten places." Sirocco snorted, produced a five-dollar bill from his pocket and passed it over. The bet had been that Stanislau could crash the databank security system and retrieve an item that Sirocco had stored half an hour previously in the public sector under a personal access key.

"How about that?" Hanlon shouted delightedly. "The guy did it!"

"Don't forget—a round of beers too," Colman reminded Sirocco. The girls whooped their approval.

"Where did you learn that, Stan?" Paula, one of the civilian girls, asked. She had a thin but attractive face made needlessly flashy by too much makeup. Her clothes were tight and provocative.

Stanislau slipped the compad into his pocket. "You don't wanna know about that," he said. "It's not very respectable."

"Come on, Stan. Give," Terry, Paula's companion, insisted. Colman gave Stanislau a challenging look that left him no way out.

Stanislau took a long draught from his glass and made a what-the-hell? gesture. "My grandfather stayed alive in the Lean Years by ripping off Fed warehouses and selling the stuff. He could bomb any security routine ever dreamed up. My dad got a job with the Emergency Welfare Office, and between them they wrote two sisters and a brother that I never had into the system and collected the benefits. So life wasn't too bad." He shrugged, almost apologetically. "I guess it got to be kind of a tradition . . . sort of handed down in the family."

"A real pro burglar!" Terry exclaimed.

"You son-of-a-gun." Hanlon said admiringly.

"Son-of-a-something, anyway," Anita added. They all laughed.

Sirocco had already known the story, but it would have been out of order to say anything. Stanislau's transfer to D Company had followed an investigation of the mysterious disappearance from Brigade stores of tools and electrical spares that had subsequently appeared on sale in the Home Entertainment department of one of the shopping marts.

Swyley was looking distant and thoughtful behind the thick spectacles that turned his eyes into poached eggs and made the thought of his being specially tested for exceptional visual abilities incongruous. He was wondering how useful Stanislau's nefarious skills might be for inserting a few plus-points into his own record in the Military's administrative computer, but couldn't really say anything about the idea in Sirocco's presence. There was such a thing as being too presumptuous. He would talk to Stanislau privately, he decided.

"Where's Tony Driscoll tonight?" Paula asked, straightening up in her chair to scan the bar. "I don't see him around anywhere."

"Don't bother looking," Colman said. "He's got the late duty."

"Don't you ever give these guys a break?" Terry asked Sirocco.

"Somebody has to run the Army. It's just his turn. He's as qualified to do it as anyone else."

"Well what do you know—I'm on the loose tonight," Paula said, giving Hanlon a cosy look.

Bret Hanlon held up a hand protectively. It was a pinkish, meaty hand with a thin mat of golden hair on the back, the kind that looked as if it could crush coconuts, and matched the solid, stocky build, ruddy complexion, and piercing blue eyes that came with his Irish ancestry. "Don't look at me," he said. "I'm contracted now, all nice and respectable. *That's* the fella you should be making eyes at." He nodded toward Colman and grinned mischievously.

"Do him good too," Sirocco declared. "Then they might make him an engineer. But you'll have a hard time. He's holding out till he's found out what the talent's like on Chiron."

"I didn't know you had a thing about little girls, Steve," Anita teased. "You don't look the type." Hanlon roared and slapped his thigh.

"I've got two sisters you can't get in trouble with," Stanislau offered.

"You got it wrong," Colman told them. "It's not the little ones at all." He widened his eyes in a parody of lewd anticipation and grinned. "Think of all those *grandmothers*." Terry and Paula laughed.

Although Colman was going along with the mood and making a joke out of it, inside he felt a twinge of irritation. He wasn't sure why. Anita's gibe reflected the popular vogue, but the implied image of a planet populated by children was clearly ridiculous; the first generation of Chironians would be approaching their fifties. He didn't like foolish words going into people's heads and coming out again without any thought about their meaning having transpired in between. Anita was an attractive girl, and not stupid. She didn't have to do things like that. Then it occurred to him that perhaps he was being too solemn. Hadn't he just done the same thing?

"Some grandmothers!" Terry exclaimed. "Did anybody see the news today? Some scientist or other thinks the Chironians could be building bombs. There was an interview with Kalens too. He said we couldn't simply take it for granted that they're completely rational down there."

"You're not suggesting there'll be a fight, are you?" Paula said.

"I didn't say that. But they're funny people . . . cagey. They're not exactly giving straight answers about everything."

"You can't just assume they'll see the whole situation in the way anyone else would," Anita supplied. "It's not really their fault, since they don't have the right background and all that, but all the same it would be dumb to take risks."

"It makes sense, I guess," Paula agreed absently.

"Do you figure they might start trouble, chief?" Stanislau asked, turning his head toward Sirocco.

Sirocco shrugged noncommittally. "Can't say. I wouldn't worry too much about it. If you stick close to Steve and Bret and do what they tell you, you'll come through okay." Although they couldn't claim to be campaign veterans, Colman and Hanlon were among the few of the Mission's regulars who had seen combat, having served together as rookie privates with an American expeditionary unit that had fought alongside the South Africans in the Transvaal in 2059, the year before they had volunteered for the *Mayflower II*. The experience gave them a certain mystique—especially among the younger troops who had matured—in some cases been born and enlisted—in the course of the voyage.

"I think it will be all right if Kalens gets elected," Terry told them. "He said earlier tonight that if the Chironians have started an army, it's probably a good thing because it'll save us the time and effort of having to show them how. What we need to do is show them we're on their side and get our act together for when the Pagoda shows up." The EAF starship was designed differently from the *Mayflower II*. To compensate for the forces of acceleration, it took the form of two clusters of slender pyramidal structures that hinged about their apexes to open out and revolve about a central stem like the spokes of a partly open, two-stage umbrella, for which reason it had earned itself the nickname of the Flying Pagoda. Terry sipped her drink and looked around the table. "The guy's got it figured realistically. You see, there's no need for a fight. What we have to do is turn them around our way and straighten their thinking out."

"But that doesn't mean we have to take chances," Anita pointed out.

"Oh, sure . . . I'm just saying there doesn't have to be anything to get scared about."

Colman was becoming irritated again. No one on the

ship had met a Chironian yet, but everyone was already an expert. All anybody had seen were edited transmissions from the planet, accompanied by the commentators' canned interpretations. Why couldn't people realize when they were being told what to think? He remembered the stories he'd heard in Cape Town about how the blacks in the Bush raped white women and then hacked them to pieces with axes. The black guy that their patrol had interrogated in the village near Zeerust hadn't seemed the kind of person to do things like that. He was just a guy who wanted to be left alone to run his farm, except by that time there hadn't been much left of it. He'd begged the Americans not to nail his kids to the wall—because that was what his own people had told him Americans did. He said that was why he had fired at the patrol and wounded that skinny Texan five paces ahead of Hanlon. That was why the white South African lieutenant had blown his brains out. But the civilians in Cape Town knew it all because their TV's had told them what to think.

Corporal Swyley wasn't saying anything, which was significant because Swyley was usually a pretty good judge of what was what. His silence meant that he didn't agree with what was being said. When Swyley agreed with something, he said he didn't agree. When he really didn't agree, he said nothing. He never said he agreed with anything. When he had decided that he felt fine after the dietitian discovered the standing order for spinach and fish, the Medical Officer hadn't been able to accuse him of faking anything because Swyley had never agreed with anybody that he was sick; all he'd said was that he had stomach cramps. The M.O. had diagnosed that anybody with stomach cramps on his own time had to be sick. Swyley hadn't. In fact, Swyley had disagreed, which should have been obvious because he hadn't said anything.

"Well, I think there's something to be scared about," Paula said. "Suppose they turn out to be really mean and don't want to mess around with talking at all. Suppose they send a missile up at us without any warning or anything . . . I mean, we'd be stuck out in space like a sitting duck, wouldn't we. Then where would we be?"

Sirocco gave a short laugh. "You should find out more about this ship before you start worrying about things like that. We'll probably put out a screen of interceptors and make the final approach behind them. They'll stop anything before it gets within ten thousand miles. You have to give the company some credit."

Hanlon made a throwing-away motion in the air. "Ah, this is all getting to be too serious for a Saturday night. Why are we talking like this at all? Are we letting silly rumors get to us?" He looked at Sirocco. "Our glasses are nearly empty, Your Honor. A round was part of the bet."

Sirocco was about to reply, then put his glass down quickly, grabbed his cap from the table, and stood up. "Time I wasn't here," he muttered. "I'll be up in Rockefeller's if anyone wants to join me there." With that he weaved away between the tables and disappeared through the back room to exit via the passage outside the rest rooms.

"What in hell's come over him?" Hanlon asked, nonplussed. "Aren't they paying captains well these days?"

"SD's," Swyley murmured, without moving his mouth. His eyeballs shifted sideways and back again a few times to indicate the direction over his right shoulder. A more restrained note crept into the place, and the atmosphere took on a subtle tension.

Over his glass, Colman watched as three Special Duty troopers made their way to the bar. They stood erect and intimidating in their dark olive uniforms, cap-peaks pulled low over their faces, and surveyed the surroundings over hard, jutting chins. Nobody met their stares for long before looking away. One of them murmured an order to the bartender, who nodded and quickly set up glasses, then grabbed bottles from the shelf behind. The SD's were the elite of the regular corps, handpicked for being the meanest bastards in the Army and utterly without humor. They reminded Colman of the commando units he had seen in the Transvaal. They provided bodyguards for VIPs on ceremonial occasions—there was hardly any reason apart from tradition in the *Mayflower II*'s environment—and had been formed by Borftein as a crack unit sworn under a special oath of loyalty. Their commanding officer was a general named Stormbel. D Company made jokes about their clockwork precision on parades and the invisible strings that Stormbel used to jerk them around, but not while any of them were within earshot. They called the SD's the Stromboli Division.

"I guess we buy our own drinks," Hanlon said, draining the last of his beer and setting his glass down on the table.

"Looks like it," Stanislau agreed.

"I got the last one," Colman reminded them. Somehow the enthusiasm had gone out of the party.

"Ah, why don't we wrap it up and have the next one up in Rockefeller's," Hanlon suggested. "That was where Sirocco said he was going."

"Great idea," Colman said and stood up. Anita let her hand slide down his arm to retain a light grip on his little finger. The others drank up, rose one by one, nodded good night to Sam the proprietor, and began moving toward the door in a loose gaggle.

Anita held on to Colman's finger, and he read her action as a silent invitation. He had slept with her a few times, many months ago now, and enjoyed it. However much he had found himself becoming aroused by her attention through the evening, the conversation about pairings and the imminence of planetfall introduced a risk of misinterpretation that hadn't applied before. Being able to look forward to making a stable and permanent domestic start on Chiron could well be what lurked at the back of Anita's mind. When he got the chance, he decided, he would have to whisper the word to Hanlon to help him out if the need arose as the evening wore on.

The precinct outside was full of people wasting the evening while trying to figure out what to do with it, when Colman and Anita emerged from the Bowery and turned to follow the others, who were already some distance ahead. Anita stopped to fish for something in her pocketbook, and Colman slowed to a halt to wait. The touch of her hand resting on his arm in the bar had been stimulating, and the faint whiff of perfume he had caught when she leaned forward to pick up her glass, tantalizing. What the hell? he thought. She's not a kid. A guy needed a break now and again after twenty years of being cooped up in a spaceship.

He turned back to find her holding a phial of capsules. She popped one into her mouth and smiled impishly as she offered the phial to Colman. "It's Saturday, why not live it up a little?" He scowled and shook his head. Anita pouted. "They're good. Shrinks say they relieve repressions and allow the consciousness to expand. We should get to know ourselves."

"I've talked to shrinks. They're all crazy. How do they know whether I know me or not? Do you know how your head works inside?" Anita shook it in a way that said she didn't care all that much either. Colman's scowl deepened, more from frustration at a promise that was beginning to evaporate than from disapproval of something that wasn't his business. "Then how do you expect a pill to figure it out?"

"You should try to find yourself, Steve. It's healthy."

"I never lost myself."

"Zangreni needs stimulants to catalyze her psychic currents. That's how she make predictions."

"For Christ's sake, that's TV fiction. She doesn't exist. It's not real life. There isn't anything like that in real life."

"Who cares? It's more fun. Why be a drag?"

Colman looked away in exasperation. She could have been a unique, thinking person. Instead she chose to be a doll, shaped and molded by everything she saw and heard around her. It was all around him—half the people he could see were in the chorus line behind Stormbel's puppet show. They could be told what to think because they didn't want to think. Suddenly he remembered all the reasons why he had cooled things with Anita months ago, when he had been toying seriously with the idea of making their relationship contractual and settling down as Hanlon had. He had tried to tune into her wavelength and found nothing but static. But what had infuriated him more was that her attitude had been unnecessary—she had a head but wouldn't use it.

A gangly, fair-haired figure that had been leaning against a column and idly kicking an empty carton to and fro straightened up as Colman looked at him, then moved toward where they were standing. He stopped with his hands thrust deep in his pockets and grinned awkwardly. Colman stared at the boy in surprise. It was Jay Fallows. "What the hell are you doing here?"

"Oh, I figured you'd be around here somewhere."

"Is this the guy who makes trains?" Anita asked.

"Yeah. This is Jay. He's okay . . . and smart."

"Smart . . . brains." A faraway look was coming into Anita's eyes. "Brains and trains. I like it. It's lyrical. Don't you think it's lyrical?" She smiled at Jay and winked saucily. "Hi, Jay." The pill was mixing with the drinks and getting to her already. Jay grinned but looked uncomfortable.

"Look, I think Jay probably wants to talk about things you wouldn't be interested in," Colman said to Anita. "Why don't you go on after the others. I'll catch up later."

"You don't want me around?"

Colman sighed. "It's not anything like that. It's just—"

Anita waved a hand in front of her face. "It's okay. You don't want me around . . . you don't want me around. It's okay." Her voice was starting to rise and fall singsong fashion. "Who says I need anybody to have a good time, anyhow? I'm fine, see. It's okay. . . . You and Jay can go talk about brains and trains." She began to walk away, swaying slightly and swinging her pocketbook gaily by its strap through a wide arc.

"Look, I-I didn't mean to bust into anything," Jay stammered. "I mean, if you and her are . . ."

Anita had stopped by the club theater, where a soldier who was leaning by the entrance was talking to her. She slipped an arm through his and laughed something in reply. "About as much as that." Colman said, nodding his head. "Forget it. Maybe you did me a favor." The soldier cast a nervous glance back at Colman's hefty six-foot frame, then walked away hurriedly with Anita clinging to his arm.

Colman watched them go, then dismissed them from his

mind and turned to look at Jay for a few seconds. "Can't figure life out, huh?" he said gruffly. It saved a lot of pointless questions.

Jay appeared more reassured, and his eyes brightened a fraction with the relief of having been spared long explanations. "It's all screwed up," he replied simply.

"Would you feel better if I said I haven't figured it out yet either?"

Jay shook his head. "It'd just mean we've got the same problem. It wouldn't solve anything."

"I didn't think it would, so I won't say it."

"So does that mean you've got it figured?" Jay asked.

"Would it make any difference to your problem if I had?"

"No. It'd be your solution, not mine."

"Then that's the answer."

Jay nodded, straightened his arms into his pockets with his shoulders bunched high near his ears, held the posture for a few seconds, and then relaxed abruptly with a sigh. "Can I ask you something?" he said, looking up.

"Do I have to answer it?"

"Not if you don't want to, I guess."

"Go ahead."

"Why is it the way it is? How does what you and I do in Jersey have anything to do with my dad's job? It doesn't make any sense."

"Did you ask him about it?"

"Uh-huh."

"And?"

Jay squinted into the distance and scratched his head. "Pretty much what I expected. Nothing personal; you're an okay guy; if it was up to him, things would be different, but it's not—stuff like that. But he was only saying that so as not to sound mean—I could tell. It goes deeper than that. It's not a case of it being up to him or not. He really believes in it. How do people get like that?"

Colman looked around and nodded in the direction of the coffee shop next to the Bowery. "Let's not stand around here all night," he said. "Come on inside. Could you use a coffee?"

"Sure . . . thanks." They began walking toward the door. "And thanks for the valves," Jay said. "They fit perfectly."

"How's it coming along?"

"Pretty good. The axle assembly's finished. You'll have to come and take a look."

"I sure will."

Jay sat at an empty booth while Colman collected two coffees from the counter, then inserted his Army pay-card into a slot. In a lot of ways Jay reminded Colman of himself when he was a lot younger. Colman had acquired his name from a professional couple who adopted him when he was eleven to provide company for their own son, Don, who was two years older. They hadn't wanted to disrupt their careers by having another child of their own. Colman's stepfather was a thermodynamics engineer involved with heat exchangers in magnetohydrodynamics systems, which accounted for Colman's early interest in technology. Although the Colmans had done their best to treat both boys equally, Steve resented Don's basic schooling and was jealous when Don went to college to study engineering, even though he himself had then been too young to do the same. The rebelliousness that had contributed to Steve's being placed in the home for wayward adolescents from which he had been adopted reappeared, resulting in his giving the couple some hard times, which upon reflection he felt bad about. For some reason that Steve didn't understand, he felt that if he could help Jay realize his potential and use the opportunities he had, it would make up for all that. Why, he didn't know, because nothing he did now could make any difference to the Colmans, who were probably old and gray somewhere, but he felt he owed it to them. People's minds worked like that. Minds could be very strange.

He set the coffees down and slid into the seat opposite Jay. "Ever been thirsty?" he asked as he stirred sugar into his cup.

Jay looked surprised. "Why . . . sure. I guess so. Hasn't everybody?"

"Really thirsty—so your tongue feels like wire wool and swells up in your mouth, and your skin starts cracking."

"Well . . . no. Why?"

"I have. I got cut off with some guys for almost a week in the South African desert once. All you think about is water. You can't describe the craving. You'd cut off your arm for a cup." He paused, and Jay waited with a puzzled expression on his face. "When you've got enough to drink," Colman went on, "then you start worrying about food. That takes longer to build up, but it gets as bad. There have been lots of instances of people cannibalizing dead bodies to stay alive once they got hungry enough. They've killed each other over potato peels."

"So-o-o-o?"

"When you've got enough to eat and drink, then you worry about keeping warm. And when you're warm enough, you start thinking about staying safe." Colman opened his hands briefly. "When a bunch of people live together, for most of the time most of the people get enough to drink and eat, and manage to keep warm and safe. What do you think they start worrying about then?"

Jay frowned and looked mildly uncomfortable. "Sex?" he hazarded.

Colman grinned. "You're right, but you're supposed to pretend you don't know about that. I was thinking of something else—recognition. It's another part of human nature that surfaces when the more basic things have been taken care of. And when it does, it gets to be just as powerful as the rest. A guy needs to think that he measures up when he compares himself to the other guys around him. He needs to be recognized for what's good about him and to stand out. Like you said, it's probably sex, because he thinks the girls are taking notice, but whatever the reason, it's real."

Jay was beginning to see the connection. "Measures up with respect to what?" he asked. "What's the standard?"

"It doesn't matter," Colman told him. "It's different in different places. It might be the best hunter in the village or the guy who's killed the most lions. It might be the way you paint your face. Through most of history it's been money. What you buy with it isn't important. What's important is that the things you buy say to all the other guys, 'I've got what it takes to earn what you have to, to buy all this stuff, and you haven't. Therefore I'm better than you.' That's what it's all about."

"Why's it so important to be better than somebody?"

"I told you, it's an instinct. You can't fight it. It's like being thirsty."

"Am I supposed to feel that way?"

"You do. Don't you like it when your team wins in the Bowl? Why do you work hard at school? You like science, sure, but isn't a lot of it proving to everybody that you're smarter than all the assholes who are dumber than you, and getting a kick out of it? Be honest. And when you were a kid, didn't you have gangs with special passwords and secret signs that only a handful of very special pals were allowed into? I bet you did."

Jay nodded and smiled. "You're right. We did."

"We all did. And it doesn't change when you get older. It gets worse. Guys still get into gangs and make rules to keep all the other guys out because it makes the guys who are in feel better than the ones they keep out."

"But the rules are so dumb," Jay protested. "They don't make sense. Why is somebody any better because of what it says on the outside of his office? It's what he does inside that matters."

"They don't have to make sense. All they have to do is say you're different. Now do you get it? Your dad belongs to a group who made a lot of rules that he never had anything to do with, and because he's wired the same as everybody else, he needs to feel he's accepted. To be accepted, he has to be seen to go by the rules. If he didn't he'd become a threat to the group, and they'd reject him. And nobody can take that. Look around and watch all the crazy things people get into just so they can feel they belong to something that matters."

"Even you?"

"Sure. What could be crazier than the Army?"

"You're not crazy," Jay said. "So what made you join?"

"It was a group, just like I've been saying—something to belong to. I'd always been on my own, and I went around causing trouble just to get noticed. People are like that. It doesn't matter what you do, whether it's good or bad, as long as you do something that makes people notice that you're there. Nothing's worse than not making any difference to anything." Colman shrugged. "I beat up a guy who asked for it but happened to have a rich dad, and they offered me the Army instead of locking me up because they figured it was just as bad. I jumped at it."

Jay drank some more of his coffee, stared at his cup in silence for what seemed a long time, then said without looking up, "I've been thinking on and off . . . you know, I think I'd like to get into the Army. What would be the best way of going about it?"

Colman stared hard at him for a few seconds. "What do you think you'd get out of it?" he asked.

"Oh, I dunno—some of the things you said, maybe."

"Get away from being caged in at home, be your real self, break out of the straitjacket, and all the rest, huh?"

"Maybe."

Colman nodded to himself and wiped his mouth with a napkin from the dispenser on the table while he tried to form the right answer. He was stuck in the Army but wanted to become a professional engineer; Jay could walk into being an engineer but thought he wanted to be in the Army. There would be no point in being scornful and listing all the reasons why it might not be such a good idea— Jay knew all those and didn't want to hear about it.

Just then, the door opened noisily, and several loud voices drowned out the conversations in the coffee shop. Colman recognized three faces from B Company, Padawski—a tall, wiry sergeant with harsh, thin lips and hard, black eyes set in a long, swarthy face—and two corporals whose names didn't come immediately to mind. They had been drinking, and Padawski could be mean at the best of times. Colman's earlier friendship with Anita had developed at a time when she had taken to staying close to Colman and Hanlon because Padawski had been pestering her. Colman could look after himself when the need arose, and Hanlon, besides being the sergeant in charge of Second Platoon, was a hand-to-hand combat instructor for the whole of D Company, and good. The combination had proved an effective deterrent, and Padawski had nursed a personal grudge ever since.

"Who are they?" Jay asked as he sensed Colman's tensing up.

"Bad news," Colman hissed through his teeth. "Just keep talking. Don't look round."

"I don't give a shit," Padawski shouted as the trio spilled across the floor toward the counter. "I don't give a goddamn shit, I tell ya. If that asshole wants to—" His voice broke off suddenly. "Say, who've we got over here? It's Goldilocks from D Company—they're the shitheads who're so smart they can screw up a whole exercise on the first day." Colman felt the floor vibrate as heavy footfalls approached the booth. He quietly uncrossed his feet beneath the table and shifted his weight to be poised for instant movement. His fingers curled more snugly around the half-full cup of hot coffee. He looked up to find Padawski leering down from about three feet away.

"This is private," he murmured in a voice that was low but menacing. "Beat it."

"Hey, guys, Goldilocks has got a new girlfriend! Take a look. Is there something you wanna tell us, Colman? I've always had my doubts about you." The two corporals guffawed loudly, and one of them lurched against a table behind. The man sitting at it excused himself and left hurriedly. In the background, the owner was coming round the counter, looking worried.

Jay had turned pale and was sitting motionless. Colman's eyes blazed up at Padawski. Padawski's leer broadened. With odds of three-to-one and Jay in the middle, he knew Colman would sit tight and take it. Padawski peered more closely at Jay and blew a stream of beery breath across the table.

"Hey, kid, how do you like—"

"Cut it," Colman grated. "You leave him out of it. If it's me you want, I'll take the three of you, but some other place. He's got nothing to do with this."

The owner bustled forward, twisting a cloth nervously in his hands. "Look, I don't want any trouble. I just wanna sell food to the people, okay? They don't want no trouble either. Now why don't——"

"Oh, so it's trouble them fellas is looking for, is it?" a voice with just a hint of an Irish brogue asked softly from the doorway. Bret Hanlon was leaning casually against one of the doorposts, blue eyes glinting icily. His huge shoulders seeming almost to reach the other side of the door. He looked completely relaxed and at ease, but Colman registered his weight carried well forward on the balls of his feet and his fingers flexing inconspicuously down by his hip. The two corporals glanced at each other apprehensively. Hanlon's appearance altered the odds a bit. Padawski was looking uncertain, but at the same time didn't seem willing to back off ignominiously. For a few seconds that dragged like minutes, the charge in the room crackled at flashpoint. Nobody moved.

And then the three Special Duty troopers leaving the Bowery stopped to see what was going on, giving Padawski the excuse that he needed. "Let's get out of here," he said. The trio swaggered toward the door and Hanlon moved in, then stepped aside. Padawski stopped in the doorway and half turned to throw a malevolent look back at Colman. "Some other time. Next time you won't be so lucky." They left. Outside, the three SD troopers turned away and moved slowly off.

Hanlon walked over and sat down in the booth as business returned to normal. "They knew you were here, Steve. I heard them talking in the back of Rockefeller's. So I thought I'd come back down and hang around."

"I've always said you've got a good sense of timing, Bret."

"So, is this fine young fella the Jay you were telling me about?" Hanlon asked.

"That's Jay. Jay, this is Bret—Bret Hanlon. He runs one of the other platoons and teaches unarmed combat. Don't mess with him."

"Was that why those guys took off?" Jay asked, by now having regained most of his color.

"It probably had something to do with it," Colman said,

grinning. "That's the kind of trash you have to deal with. Still interested?"

"I guess I'll have to think about it," Jay conceded.

Hanlon ordered three hamburger dinners, and the two sergeants spent a half hour talking with Jay about Army life, football, and how Stanislau could crash the protected sector of the public databank. Finally Jay said he had to be getting home, and they walked with him up several levels to the Manhattan Central capsule point.

"Shall we be getting back to the party then?" Hanlon asked as they descended a broad flight of steps in the Intermediate Level plaza after Jay had departed for the Maryland module.

Colman slowed and rubbed his chin. He wasn't in the mood. "You go on, Bret," he said. "I think I'm just gonna wander around. I guess I'd rather be on my own for a while."

Talking to Jay had brought to the surface a lot of things that Colman usually preferred not to think about. Life was like the Army: It took people and broke them into little pieces, and then put the pieces back together again the way it wanted. Except it did it with their minds. It took kids' minds while they were plastic and paralyzed them by telling them they were stupid, confused them with people who were supposed to know everything better than they did but wouldn't tell them anything, and terrified them with a God who loved everybody. Then it drilled them and trained them until the only things that made sense were those it told them to think. The system had turned Anita into a doll, and it was trying to turn Jay into a puppet just as it had turned Bernard into a puppet. It turned people into recording machines that words went into and came out of again and made them think they knew everything about a planetful of people they'd never seen, just as it blew black guys' brains out because they wanted to run their farms and didn't want their kids nailed to walls, and then told the civilians in Cape Town it was okay. And what had it done to Colman? He didn't know because he didn't know how else it might have been.

"Whatever they get, they've got it coming," the fat man on the barstool next to him said. "Kids running around wild, breeding like rabbits—It's disgusting. And making bombs! Savages is what they are—no better than the Chinese. Kalens has got the right idea. He'll teach 'em some decency and respect." Colman drank up and left.

Jesus, he thought, he was sick of the system. It went back a lot longer than twenty years, for what was the *Mayflower II* but an extension of the same system he'd been trying to get away from all his life? Jay was beginning to feel the trap closing around him already. And none of it was going to change—ever. Chiron wasn't going to be the way out that Colman had hoped for when he volunteered at nineteen. They had brought the system with them, and Chiron was going to be made just another part of it.

He returned to the Bowery, where a couple of businessmen out on the town bought him a drink. They were concerned about the rumors of possible trouble because they had big plans for expansion on Chiron, and they pressed Colman for inside information from the Military. Colman said he didn't have any. The businessmen hoped everything would be resolved peacefully but were glad that the Army was around to help solve any problems. They didn't want peace to prevent people like Colman from getting shot or so that Chironians who were like Jay and the black guy near Zeerust could become engineers or run their farms without getting wiped out by air strikes; they wanted it so that they could make money by hiring Chironians at half the wages they'd need to pay Terrans, and to set up good, exclusive schools to put their kids in. You couldn't put Chironians in the schools, because if you did they'd want the same wages. And in any case they'd never be able to afford it. The Chironians weren't really people, after all.

"What does a Chironian computer print when you attempt illegal access?" one of them asked Colman when they had got into their joke repertoires.

"What?"

"HELP! RAPE! Ha-ha, hah-hah!"

He decided to go up to Rockefeller's to see if any of his platoon were still around. On the way his pace slowed abruptly. Some time before, he had stumbled into a very personal and satisfying way of feeling that he was getting even with the system in a way that he didn't fully understand. Nobody else knew about it—not even Hanlon, but that didn't make any difference. He hadn't seen her for a while now, and he was in just the right mood.

To avoid using a compad in not-too-private surroundings, he went to a public booth in the lobby at Rockefeller's to call the number programmed to accept calls only if she was alone. While Colman waited for a response, his mind flashed back six months. He had been standing stiffly at attention in dress uniform alongside a display of a remote-fire artillery control post that was part of the Army's contribution to the Fourth of July celebrations, when she wandered away from a group of VIPs sipping cocktails and stood beside him to gaze admiringly at the screens carrying simulated battlefield displays. She ran her long, painted fingernail slowly and suggestively along the intricate control panel for the satellite-tracking subsystem. "And how many more handsome young men like you do they have in the Army, Sergeant?" she murmured at the displays before her.

"Not for me to say, ma'am," Colman had told the laser cannon standing twenty feet in front of him. "I'm not an expert on handsome men."

"An expert on ladies in need of stimulating entertainment, perhaps?"

"That depends, ma'am. They can lead to a heap of trouble."

"Very wise, Sergeant. But then, some of them can be very discreet. Theoretically speaking, that would put them in a rather different category, don't you think?"

"Theoretically, I guess, yes, it would," Colman had agreed.

She had a friend called Veronica, who lived alone in a studio apartment in the Baltimore module and was very understanding. Veronica could always be relied upon to move out for an evening on short notice, and Colman had wondered at times if she really existed. Acquiring exclusive access to a studio wouldn't have been all that difficult for a

VIP's wife, even with the accommodation limitations of the *Mayflower II*. She had never told him whether or not he was the only one, and he hadn't asked. It was that kind of a relationship.

The screen before him suddenly came to life to show her face. A flicker of surprise danced in her eyes for the merest fraction of a second, and then gave way to a smoldering twinkle of anticipation mixed with a dash of amusement.

"Well, hello, Sergeant," she said huskily. "I was beginning to wonder if I had a deserter. Now, I wonder what could be on your mind at this time of night."

"It depends. What's the situation, company-wise?"

"Oh, very boring for a Saturday night."

"He's not—"

"Wining, dining, and conspiring—no doubt until the early hours."

Colman hesitated for a split second to let the question ask itself. "So . . . ?"

"Well now, I'm sure Veronica could be persuaded if I were to call her and talk to her nicely."

"Say, half an hour?"

"Half an hour." She smiled a promise and winked. Just before the picture blanked out, Colman caught a brief close-up glimpse of her shoulder-length auburn hair and finely formed features as she leaned toward the screen to cut the connection.

Colman's top-echelon, part-time mistress was Celia Kalens.

CHAPTER EIGHT

"ON THIS, THE eve of the last Christmas that we shall be celebrating together before our journey ends, I have chosen as the subject of my seasonal message to you the passage which begins, 'Suffer little children to come unto me.'" The voice of the Mission's presiding bishop floated serenely down from the loudspeakers around the Texas Bowl to the congregation of ten thousand listening solemnly from the terraces. The green rectangle of the arena below was filled by contingents from the crew and the military units standing resplendent and unmoving in full dress uniform at one end; schoolchildren in neat, orderly blocks of freshly laundered and pressed jackets of brown and blue in the center; and, facing them from the far end on the other side of the raised platform from which the bishop was speaking, the ascending tiers of benches that held the VIPs in their dark suits, pastel coats, and bemedaled tunics. The voice continued. "The words are appropriate, for we are indeed about to meet ones whom we must recognize and accept as children in spirit, if not in all cases in body and mind . . ."

Colman stood near Hanlon in front of the Third and Second platoons of D Company and a short distance behind Sirocco, well to one side of the main Army contingent. Only a few of the Company were absent for one reason or another, conspicuous among them Corporal Swyley, who was in Brigade sick bay and looking forward to a turkey dinner; the standing order for a spinach-and-fish diet had mysteriously erased itself from the administration computer's records. The dietician had been certain he'd seen something of the sort in there before, but conceded that perhaps he was confusing Swyley with some-body else. Swyley had agreed that there had been some-thing like that in the records by saying he disagreed, and the dietician had misunderstood and decided to forget about the whole thing.

". . . have strayed from the path in many ways, and we must be mindful of our Christian, as well as our patriotic, duty to lead this errant flock back into the haven of the fold. Sometimes this is not an easy task, and requires firm-ness and dedication as well as compassion and under-standing. . . ."

Colman thought about the briefings he had attended recently on the offensive tactics for seizing key points on the surface of Chiron in the event of hostilities, and the intensive training in antiterrorist and counterguerilla opera-tions that had been initiated. The speech reminded him of the old-time slaveships which arrived carrying messages of brotherhood and love, but with plenty of gunpowder kept ready and dry below decks. Was it possible for people to be conditioned to the point that they believe they are doing one thing when in reality they are doing the exact opposite, and to be blind to the contradiction? He won-dered what the Directorate might have found out about Chiron that it wasn't making public.

"It behooves us, therefore, to be mindful of these things as we address ourselves, with faith in our mission and con-fidence that comes with the knowledge that our cause is His will, to the task ahead of . . ."

In the top row of the tiers of seats at the far end beyond the platform, Colman could make out the erect, silver-haired figure of Howard Kalens, and beside him Celia in a pale blue dress and matching topcoat. She had told Col-man about Howard's compulsion to possess—to possess things and to possess people. He felt threatened by any-thing or anyone that he couldn't command. Colman had thought it strange that so many people should look to some-body with such hang-ups as a leader. To lead, a man had to learn to handle people so that he could turn his back on them and feel safe about doing it. Celia refused to become another of Kalens's possessions, and she proved it to her-

self in the same way that Colman proved to himself that
nobody was going to tell him what he was supposed to
think. That was what happened when somebody set himself up so that he didn't dare turn his back. Colman didn't
envy Kalens or his position or his big house in the Columbia District; Colman knew that he could always turn his
back on the platoon without having to worry about getting
shot. They should issue all the VIPs up in the benches
M32s, Colman thought. Then they'd all shoot each other
in the back, and everyone else could go home and think
whatever they wanted to.

So how did people like Howard Kalens feel about
Chiron? Colman wondered. Did they think they could
possess a whole planet? Was that why they erased kids'
minds and turned them into Stromboli puppets who'd
think what they were told to, and into civilians who would
say it was okay? But why did the people let them do it?
Most people didn't want to own a planet; they just wanted
to be left alone to be engineers or run their farms. Because they played along with the rules that said they were
better if they thought the way the rules said they should,
and no good if they didn't.

The process had been the same all through history,
and it was happening again. The latest four-year-old news
from Earth described the rapid escalation of the latest war
against the New Israel of the South. Only this time the
EAF was getting involved. The Western strategists had
interpreted it as an EAF policy to provoke an all-out war
all across Africa so they could move in afterward and
close up on Europe from the south. Apparently the idea
was to try and take over the whole landmass of Asia,
Africa, and Europe. Why did they want to take over the
whole of Asia, Africa, and Europe? Colman didn't know.
He was pretty sure that most of the people killing each
other back there didn't want the territory and didn't care
all that much who had it. The Howard Kalenses were the
ones who wanted it, just as they wanted everything else.
Perhaps if they'd learn how to get along with people without being scared to turn their backs all the time and how
to make love with their own wives in bed, they wouldn't

need geographical conquests. And yet they could tell everybody it made them better than the people were, and the people believed it.

He remembered Jay's mentioning a physicist from the labs in the Princeton module who said that human societies were the latest phase in the same process of evolution that had begun billions of years ago when the universe started to condense out of radiation. Evolution was a business of survival. Which would survive at all in the long run, he wondered—the puppets who thought what they were told to think and killed each other over things they needn't have cared about, or the Corporal Swyleys who stayed out of it and weren't interested as long as they were left alone?

Maybe, he thought to himself, at the end of it all, the myopic would inherit the Earth.

CHAPTER NINE

ON THE DAY officially designated December 28, 2080, in the chronological system that would apply until the ship switched over to the Chironian calendar, the *Mayflower II* entered the planetary system of Alpha Centauri at a speed of 2837 miles per second, reducing, with its main drive still firing at maximum power. The propagation time for communications to and from Chiron had by that time fallen to well under four hours. A signal from the planet confirmed that accommodations for the ship's occupants had been prepared in the outskirts of Franklin as had been requested.

December 31, 2080
Distance to Chiron 1.9 billion miles; speed down to 1100 miles per second. Progressive phase-down of the main-drive burn was commenced, and slow pivoting of the variable-attitude Ring modules initiated to correct for the effect of diminishing linear force from the reducing deceleration. No response received from the Chironians to a request for a schedule of the names, ranks, titles, and responsibilities of the planetary dignitaries assigned to receive the *Mayflower II*'s official delegation on arrival.

January 5, 2081
Speed 300 miles per second; distance to destination, 493 million miles. Course-correction effected to bring the ship round onto its final approach.

January 8, 2081
At 8 million miles, defenses brought to full alert and advance screen of remote-control interceptors deployed

50,000 miles ahead of ship to cover final approach. Response from Chiron neutral.

January 9, 2081

Communications round-trip delay to Chiron, twenty-two seconds. Formal arrangements for reception procedures still not concluded. Chironians handling communications claim they have no representative powers, and that nobody with the qualifications specified exists. *Mayflower II*'s defenses brought to combat readiness.

January 10, 2081

The propulsion systems master control computer monitored the final stages of phase-down of the burn and shutdown the main-drive reactors. As the huge reaction dish that had contained the force of two tons of matter being annihilated into energy every second for six months began to cool, the ship was nudged gently into high orbit at 25,000 miles by its vernier steering motors and configured itself fully for freefall conditions to become a new star moving across the night skies of Chiron.

The voyage of the *Mayflower II* had ended.

PART TWO

THE
CHIRONIANS

CHAPTER TEN

As THE *Mayflower II* wheeled slowly in space high above Chiron, the outer door of Shuttle Bay 6 on the Vandenberg module separated into four sectors which swung apart like the petals of an enormous metal flower to expose the nose of the surface lander nestling within. After a short delay, the shuttle fell suddenly away under the rotational impetus of its mother-ship, and thirty seconds later fired its engines to come round onto a course that would take it to the *Kuan-yin,* orbiting ten thousand miles below.

"Our orders are to '. . . precede the Ambassador's party through the docking lock to form an honorary guard in the forward antechamber of the *Kuan-yin,* where the formalities will take place,'" Sirocco read aloud to the D Company personnel assigned as escorts at the briefing held early that morning. " 'Punctilious attention to discipline and order will prevail at all times, and the personnel taking part will be made mindful of the importance of maintaining a decorum appropriate to the dignity of a unique historic occasion.' That means no ventriloquized comments to relieve the boredom, Swyley, and the best parade-ground turnout you ever managed, all of you. 'Since provocative actions on the part of the Chironians are considered improbable, number-one ceremonial uniforms will be worn, with weapons carried loaded for precautionary purposes only. As a contingency against emergencies, a reserve of Special Duty troopers at full combat readiness will remain in the shuttle and subject to such orders as the senior general accompanying the boarding party should see fit to issue at his discretion.' "

"Ever get the feeling you were being set up?" Carson of Third Platoon asked sourly. "If anyone gets it first, guess who."

"Didn't you know you were expendable?" Stanislau asked matter-of-factly.

"Ah, but think of the honor of it," Hanlon told them. "And won't every one of them poor SD fellas back in the shuttle be eating his heart out with envy and just wishing he could be out there with the same opportunity to risk himself for flag and country."

"I'll trade," Stanislau offered at once.

Sirocco looked back at the orders and resumed, " 'The advance guard will fan out to form two files, of ten men each, aligned at an angle of forty-five degrees on either side of the access lock and take up station behind their respective section leaders. Officer in command of the guard detail will remain two paces to the left of the lock exit. Upon completion of the opening formalities, the guard will be relieved by a detail from B Company who will position themselves at the exit ramp, and will proceed through the *Kuan-yin* to post sentry details at the locations specified in Schedule A, attached. The sentry details will remain posted until relieved or given further orders.' Are there any questions so far?"

The Ambassador referred to was to be Amery Farnhill, Howard Kalens's deputy in Liaison. Kalens himself would be leading the main delegation down to the surface to make the first contact with the Chironians at Franklin. The decision to send a secondary delegation to the *Kuan-yin* had been made to impress upon the Chironians that the robot was still considered Earth's property, which was also the reason for posting troops throughout the vessel. As a point of protocol, Wellesley and Sterm would not become involved until the appropriate contacts on Chiron had been established and the agenda for further discussion suitably prepared.

The *Kuan-yin* had changed appreciably from the form shown in the pictures he had seen of the craft that had departed from Earth in 2020, Colman noted with interest as he sat erect to preserve the creases of his uniform beneath the restraining belt holding him to his seat and watched the image growing on the wall screen at the forward end of the cabin. The original design had taken the form of a dumbbell, with fuel storage and the thermonuclear pulse engines concentrated at one end, and the computers and sensitive reconnaissance instruments carried at the far end of a long, connecting, structural boom to keep them safely away from drive-section radiation. The modifications added after 2015 for creating and accommodating the first Chironians had entailed extensions to the instrumentation module and the incorporation of auxiliary motors which would spin the dumbbell about its center after arrival in order to simulate gravity for the new occupants while the first surface base was being prepared.

In the years since, the instrumentation module had sprouted a collection of ancilliary structures which had doubled its size, the original fuel tanks near the tail had vanished to be replaced, apparently, by a bundle of huge metal bottles mounted around the central portion of the connecting boom, and a new assembly of gigantic windings surrounding a tubular housing now formed the tail, culminating in a parabolic reaction dish reminiscent of the *Mayflower II*'s main drive, though much smaller because of the *Kuan-yin*'s reduced scale. The *Mayflower II*'s designers had included docking adapters for the shuttles to mate with the *Kuan-yin*'s ports, and the Chironians had retained the original pattern in their modifications, so the shuttle would be able to connect without problems.

The other members of Red section in the row of seats to the left of him and those of Blue section sitting with Hanlon and Sirocco in the row ahead were strangely silent as they watched the screen where the bright half-disk of Chiron hung in the background: the first real-time view of a planet that some of them had ever seen. Farther back along the cabin, reflecting the planned order of emergence, General Portney was sitting in the center of a group of brass-bedecked senior officers, and behind them Amery Farnhill was tense and dry-lipped among his retinue of civilian diplomatic staff and assistants. In the rear, the

SD troops were grim and silent in steel helmets and combat uniforms festooned with grenades, propping their machine rifles and assault cannon between their knees.

Farnhill's staff had given up trying to get the Chironians to provide an official list of who would be greeting the delegation. In the end they had simply advised the *Kuan-yin* when the shuttle would arrive and resigned themselves to playing things by ear after that. The Chironians had agreed readily enough, which was why the orders issued that morning had called for a reduced alertness level. Kalens's delegation had met with an equal lack of success in dealing with Franklin, and had elected finally to go to the surface on the same basis as the delegation to the *Kuan-yin,* but with more elaborate preparations and ceremonies.

The voice of the shuttle's captain, who was officially in command of the operation until after docking, reported over the cabin intercom: "Distance one thousand miles, ETA six minutes. Coming into matching orbit and commencing closing maneuver. Prepare for retardation. *Kuan-yin* has confirmed they will open Port Three."

The image on the screen drifted to one side as the shuttle swung round to brake with its main engines, and then switched to a new view as one of the stern cameras was cut in. Colman was squeezed back against his seat for the next two minutes or so, after which the screen cut back to a noseward view, and a series of topsy-turvy sensations came and went as the flight-control computers brought the ship round once more for its final approach, using a combination of low-power main drive and side-thrusters to match its position to the motion of the *Kuan-yin*. After some minor corrections the shuttle was rotating with the *Kuan-yin* to give its occupants the feeling that they were lying on their backs, and nudging itself gently forward and upward to complete the maneuver. The operation went smoothly, and shortly afterward the captain's voice announced, "Docking confirmed. The boarding party is free to proceed."

"Proceed, General," Farnhill said from the back.

"Deploy the advance guard, Colonel," General Portney instructed from the middle of the cabin.

"Guard, forward," Colonel Wesserman ordered from a row in front of Portney.

"Guard detail, file left and right by sections," Sirocco said at the front. "Section leaders forward." He moved out into the aisle, where the floor had folded itself into a steep staircase to facilitate fore-and-aft movement, and climbed through into the side-exiting lock chamber with Colman and Hanlon behind him while Red and Blue sections formed up in the aisles immediately to the rear. In the lock chamber the inner hatch was already open, and the Despatching Officer from the shuttle's crew was carrying out a final instrumentation check prior to opening the outer hatch. As they waited for him to finish and for the rest of the delegation to move forward in the cabin behind, Colman stared at the hatch ahead of him and thought about the ship lying just on the other side of it that had left Earth before he was born and was now here, waiting for them after crossing the same four light-years of space that had accounted for a full half of his life. After the years of speculations, all the questions about the Chironians were now within minutes of being answered. The descent from the *Mayflower II* had raised Colman's curiosity to a high pitch because of what he had seen on the screen. For despite all the jokes and the popular wisdom, one thing he was certain of was that the engineering and structural modifications that he had observed on the outside of the *Kuan-yin* had not been made by irresponsible, overgrown adolescents.

"Clear to exit," the Despatching Officer informed Sirocco.

"Lock clear for exit," Sirocco called to the cabin below.

"Carry on, Guard Commander," Colonel Wesserman replied from the depths.

"Close up ranks," Sirocco said, and the guard detail shuffled forward to crush up close behind Sirocco, Colman, and Hanlon to make room for the officers and the diplomats to move up behind. Sirocco looked at the Despatch-

ing Officer and nodded. "Open outer hatch." The Despatching Officer keyed a command into a panel beside him, and
the outer door of the shuttle swung slowly aside.

Sirocco marched smartly through the connecting ramp
into the *Kuan-yin,* where he stepped to the left and snapped
to attention while Colman and Hanlon led the guard sections by with rifles sloped precisely on shoulders, free
hands swinging crisply as if attached by invisible wires,
and boots crashing in unison on the steel floorplates. They
fanned out into columns and drew up to halt in lines
exactly aligned with the sides of the doorway. Behind them
the officers emerged four abreast and divided into two
groups to follow Colonel Wesserman to the left and General Portney to the right.

"Present . . . *arms!*" Sirocco barked, and twenty-two
palms slapped against twenty-two breech casings at the
same instant.

Through the gap between the officers, the diplomats
moved forward and came to a halt in reverse order of
precedence, black suits immaculate and white shirtfronts
spotless, and finally the noble form of Amery Farnhill conveyed itself regally forward to take up its position at their
head.

"His Esteemed Excellency, Amery Farnhill," the assistant one pace to the rear and two paces to the right
announced in clear, ringing tones that resonated around
the antechamber of the *Kuan-yin*'s docking port. "Deputy
Director of Liaison of the Supreme Directorate of the
official Congress of the *Mayflower II* and appointed emis-
sary to the *Kuan-yin* on behalf of the Director of Congress . . ." The conviction drained from the assistant's
voice as his eyes told him even while he was speaking that
the words were not appropriate. Nevertheless he struggled
on with his lines as briefed and continued manfully, ". . .
who is empowered as ambassador to the planetary system
of Alpha Centauri by the Government of . . ." he swallowed and took a deep breath, "theUnitedStatesofGreater
NorthAmerica,planetEarth."

The small group of Chironians watching from a short
distance away and the larger crowd gathered behind them

in the rear of the antechamber applauded enthusiastically and beamed their approval. They weren't supposed to do that. It didn't preserve the right atmosphere.

"They're okay," Corporal Swyley's disembodied voice whispered from no definable direction. "We're making ourselves look like jerks."

"Shuddup," Colman hissed.

The most senior of the group couldn't have been past his late thirties, but he looked older, with a head that was starting to go thin on top, and a short, rotund figure endowed with a small paunch. He was wearing an open-necked shirt of intricately embroidered blues and grays, and plain navy blue slacks held up with a belt. His features looked vaguely Asiatic. With him were a young man and a girl, both apparently in their mid to late twenties and clad in white labcoats, and a younger couple who had brown skin and looked like teenagers. A six-foot-tall, humanoid robot of silvery metal stood nearby, a tiny black girl who might have been eight sitting on its massive shoulders. Her legs dangled around its neck and her arms clasped the top of its head.

"Hi," the paunchy man greeted amiably. "I'm Clem. These are Carla and Hermann, and Francine and Boris. The big guy here is Cromwell, and the little lady up top is Amy. Well, I guess . . . welcome aboard."

Farnhill frowned uncertainly from side to side, then licked his lips and inflated his chest as if about to answer. He deflated suddenly and shook his head. The words to handle the situation just wouldn't come. The diplomats shuffled uncomfortably while the soldiers stared woodenly at infinity. A few awkward seconds dragged by. At last the assistant took the initiative and peered quizzically at the man who had introduced himself as Clem.

"Who are you?" he demanded. The formality had evaporated from his voice. "Are you in authority here? If so, what are your rank and title?"

Clem frowned and brought a hand up to his chin. "Depends what you mean by authority," he said. "I organize the regular engineering crew of the ship and supervise the maintenance. I suppose you could say that's authority of a kind. Then again, I don't have a lot to do with some of the special research programs and modifications but Hermann does."

"True," Hermann, the young man in the white labcoat, agreed. "But on top of that, parts of this place are used as a school to give the kids early off-planet experience. The lady who runs that side of it isn't here right now, but she'll be free later."

"She got tied up over lunch trying to answer questions about supernovas and quasars," Francine explained.

"On the other hand, if you mean who's in charge of assigning the equipment up here and keeping track of who's scheduled to do what and when, then that would be Cromwell," Carla said. "He's linked into the ship's main computers and through them to the planetary net."

"Cromwell knows everything," Amy declared from her perch. "Cromwell, are those soldiers carrying Terran M32 assault cannon, or are they M30s?"

"M32s," the robot said. "They've the enhanced fire-selectors."

"I hope they're not going to start shooting each other up here. It would be pretty scary in orbit. They could decompress the whole ship."

"I think they know that," Cromwell said. "They've spent a lot longer in space than the few trips you've made."

"I suppose so."

The assistant's patience snapped at last. "This is ridiculous! I want to know who is in overall authority here. You must have a Director of Operations or some equivalent. Please be kind enough to—"

Farnhill stopped him with a curt wave of his hand. "This spectacle has gone far enough," he said. He looked at Clem. "Perhaps we could continue this discussion in conditions of greater privacy. Is there somewhere suitable near here?"

"Sure." Clem gestured vaguely behind him. "There's a big room back along the corridor that's free and should hold everybody. We could all get some coffee there too. I guess you could use some—you've had a long trip, huh?"

He grinned at the joke as he turned to lead the way. Farnhill didn't seem to appreciate the humor.

"Ahem . . ." General Portney cleared his throat. "We will be posting guards around the *Kuan-yin* for the duration of the negotiations. I trust there will be no objections." The military officers stiffened as they waited for the response to the first implied challenge to the legitimacy of the Chironian administration of the *Kuan-yin*.

Clem waved an arm casually without looking back. "Go ahead," he said. "Can't see as you really need any, though. You're pretty safe up here. We don't get many burglars." Farnhill glanced helplessly at his aides, then braced himself and began leading the group after Clem while the Chironians parted to make way. The military deputation broke formation to take up the rear with Wesserman tossing back a curt "Carry on, Guard Commander" in the direction of Sirocco.

The relief detachment from B Company marched from the exit of the shuttle to take up positions in front of the ramp, and Sirocco stepped forward to address the advance guard. "Ship detail, atten-*shun!* Two ranks in marching order, fall . . . *in!*" The two lines that had been angled away from the lock re-formed into files behind the section leaders. "Sentry details will detach and fall out at stations. By the left . . . *march!*" The two lines clumped their way behind Sirocco across the antechamber, wheeled left while each man on the inside marked time for four paces, and clicked away along the corridor beyond and into the *Kuan-yin*.

Amy watched curiously over the top of Cromwell's head as they disappeared from sight. "I wonder why they walk like that when they shout at each other," she mused absently. "Do you know why, Cromwell?"

"Have you thought about it?" Cromwell asked.

"Not really."

"You should think about things as well as just ask questions. Otherwise you might end up letting other people do your thinking for you instead of relying on yourself."

"Ooh . . . I wouldn't want to do that," Amy said.

"All right then," Cromwell challenged. "Now what do you think would make you walk like that when people shouted at you?"

"I don't know." Amy screwed her face up and rubbed the bridge of her nose with a finger. "I suppose I'd have to be crazy."

"Well, *there's* something to think about," Cromwell suggested.

CHAPTER ELEVEN

CLUMP, CLUMP, CLUMP, *clump, clump, clump, clump, clump.*

"Detail . . . *halt!*"

Clump-Clump!

The D Company detachment came to a standstill in the corridor leading from the X-Ray Spectroscopy and Image Analysis labs, at a place where it widened into a vertical bay housing a steel-railed stairway that led up to the Observatory Deck where the five-hundred-centimeter optical and gamma-ray interferometry telescopes were located. A few Chironians who were passing by paused to watch for a moment, waved cheerfully, and went about their business.

"Sentry detail, detach to . . . *post!*" Sirocco shouted. PFC Driscoll stepped one pace backward from the end of the by-this-time-diminished file, turned ninety degrees to the right, and stepped back again to come to attention with his back to the wall by the entrance to a smaller side-corridor. "Parade . . . *rest!*" Driscoll moved his left foot into an astride stance and brought his gun down from the shoulder to rest with its butt on the floor, one inch from his boot. "Remainder of detail, by the left . . . *march!*"

Clump, clump, clump, clump . . .

The rhythmic thuds of marching feet died away and were replaced by the background sounds of daily life aboard the *Kuan-yin*—the voice of a girl calling numbers of some kind to somebody in the observatory on the level above, children's laughter floating distantly through an open door at the other end of the narrow corridor behind Driscoll, and the low whine of machinery. A muted throb-

103

bing built up from below, causing the floor to vibrate for a few seconds. Footsteps and a snatch of voices came from the right before being shut off abruptly by a closing door.

Driscoll was feeling more relieved. If what he had seen so far was anything to go by, the Chironians weren't going to start any trouble. He'd had to bite his tongue in order to keep a straight face back in the antechamber by the ramp, and it was a miracle that nobody important had heard Stanislau sniggering next to him. The Chironians were okay, he had decided. Everything would be okay . . . provided that ass-faces like Farnhill didn't go and screw things up.

What had impressed him the most was the way the kids seemed to be involved in everything that was going on just as much as the grown-ups. They didn't come across like kids at all, but more like small people who were busy finding out how things were done. In a room two posts back, he had glimpsed a couple of kids who couldn't have been more than twelve probing carefully and with deep frowns of concentration inside the electronics of a piece of equipment that must have cost millions. The older Chironian with them just watched over their shoulders and offered occasional suggestions. It made sense, Driscoll thought. Treat them as if they're responsible, and they act responsibly; give them bits of cheap plastic to throw around, and they act like it's cheap plastic. Or maybe the Chironians just had good insurance on their equipment.

He wondered how he might have made out if he'd had a start like that. And what would a guy like Colman be doing, who knew more about the *Mayflower II*'s machines than half the echelon-four snot-noses put together? If that was the way the computers had brought the first kids up, Driscoll reflected, he could think of a few humans who could have used some lessons.

His debut into life had been very different. The war had left his parents afflicted by genetic damage, and their first two children had not survived infancy. Aging prematurely from side effects, they had known they would never see Chiron when they brought him aboard the *Mayflower II* as a boy of eight and sacrificed the few more years that they might have spent on Earth in order to give him a new start somewhere else. Paradoxically, their health had qualified them favorably in their application to join the Mission since the planning had called for the inclusion of older people and higher-risk actuarial categories among the population to make room for the births that would be occurring later. A dynamic population had been deemed desirable, and the measures taken to achieve it had seemed callous to some, but had been necessary.

As a youth he had daydreamed about becoming an entertainer—a singer, or a comic, maybe—but he couldn't sing and he couldn't tell jokes, and somehow after his parents died within two years of each other halfway through the voyage, he had ended up in the Army. So now, though he still couldn't sing a note or tell a joke right, he knew just how to use an M32 to demolish a small building from two thousand yards, could operate a battlefield compack blindfolded, and was an expert at deactivating optically triggered antiintruder personnel mines.

About all he was good with outside things like that was cards. He couldn't remember exactly when his fascination with them had started, but it had been soon after Swyley, then a fellow private, had taught him to shuffle four aces to the top of a deck and feed them into a deal from the palm. Finding to his surprise that he seemed to have an aptitude, Driscoll had borrowed a leaf from Colman's book and started reading up about the subject. For many long off-duty hours he had practiced top-pass palms and one-handed side-cuts until he could materialize three full fans from an empty hand and lift a named number of cards off a deck eight times out of ten. Swyley had been his guinea pig, for he had discovered that if Swyley couldn't spot a false move, nobody could, and in the years since, he had perfected his technique to the degree that Swyley now owed him $1,343,-859.20, including interest.

But his reputation had put him in a no-win situation at the Friday night poker school because when he won, everybody said he was sharping, and when he didn't, everybody said he was lousy. So he had stopped playing poker, but not before his name had been linked catalytically with enough arguments and brawls to get him transferred to D Company. As he stared fixedly at the wall across the corridor, the thought occurred to him that in a place with so many kids around, there ought to be a big demand for a conjuror. The more he thought about it, the more appealing the idea became. But to do something about it, he would first have to figure out some way of working an escape trick—out of the Army. Swyley should have some useful suggestions about that, he thought.

Clump, clump, clump, clump. His train of thought was derailed by the sound of steady tramping approaching from his left—not the direction in which the detail had departed, which shouldn't have been returning by this route anyway, but the opposite one. Besides, it didn't sound like multiple pairs of regulation Army feet; it sounded like one pair, but heavier and more metallic. And along with it came the sound of two children's voices, whispering and furtive, and punctuated with giggles.

Driscoll turned his eyes a fraction to the side. They widened in disbelief as one of the *Kuan-yin*'s steel colossi marched into view, holding a length of aluminum alloy tubing over its left shoulder and being followed by a brown, Indian-looking girl of about seven and a fair-haired boy of around the same age.

"Detail . . . *stop!*" the girl called out. The robot halted. "Detail . . . Oh, I don't know what I'm supposed to say. Stand with your feet apart and put your gun down." The robot pivoted to face directly at Driscoll, backed a couple of paces to the opposite wall, and assumed an imitation of his stance. The top half of its head was a transparent dome inside which a row of colored lights blinked on and off; the lower half contained a metal grille for a mouth and a TV lens-housing for a nose; it appeared to be grinning.

"Stay . . . *there!*" the girl instructed. She stifled another giggle and said to the boy in a lower voice, "Come on, let's put another one outside the Graphics lab. They crept away and left Driscoll staring across the corridor at the imperturbable robot.

A couple of minutes went by. Nobody moved. The robot's lights continued to wink at him cheerfully. Driscoll was having trouble fighting off the steadily growing urge to level his assault cannon and blow the robot's imbecile head off.

"Why don't you piss off," he growled at last.

"Why don't you?"

For a moment Driscoll thought the machine had read his mind. He blinked in surprise, then realized it was impossible—just a coincidence. "How can I?" he said. "I've got my orders."

"So have I."

"That's different."

"How?"

"You don't have to do this."

"Do you?"

"Of course I do."

"Why?"

Driscoll sighed irritably. This was no time for long debates. "You don't understand," he said.

"Don't I?" the robot replied.

Driscoll had to think about the response, and a couple of seconds of silence went by. "It's not the same," he said. "You're just humoring kids."

"What are you doing?"

Driscoll didn't have a ready answer to that. Besides, he was too conscious of the desire for a cigarette to be philosophical. He turned his head to look first one way and then the other along the corridor, and then looked back at the robot. "Can you tell if any of our people are near here?"

"Yes, I can, and no, there aren't. Why—getting fed up?"

"Would it worry anyone if I smoked?"

"It wouldn't worry me if you burst into flames." The robot chuckled raspily.

"How do you know there's no one around?"

"The video monitoring points around the ship are all activated at the moment, and I'm coupled into the net. I can see what's going on everywhere. Go ahead. It's okay. The round cover on the wall next to you is an inlet to a trash incinerator. You can use it as an ashtray."

Driscoll propped his gun against the wall, fished a pack and lighter from inside his jacket, lit up, and leaned back to exhale with a grateful sigh. The irritability that he had been feeling wafted away with the smoke. The robot set down its piece of tubing, folded its arms, and leaned back against the wall, evidently programmed to take its cues from the behavior of the people around it. Driscoll looked at it with a new curiosity. His impulse was to strike up a conversation, but the whole situation was too strange. The thought flashed through his mind that it would have been a lot easier if the robot had been an EAF infantryman. Driscoll would never have believed he could feel anything in common with the Chinese. He didn't know whether he was talking to the robot, or through it to computers somewhere else in the *Kuan-yin* or even down on Chiron, maybe; whether they had minds or simply embodied some clever programming, or what. He had talked to Colman about machine intelligence once. Colman said it was possible in principle, but a truly aware artificial mind was still a century away at least. Surely the Chironians couldn't have advanced that much. "What kind of a machine are you?" he asked. "I mean, can you think like a person? Do you know who you are?"

"Suppose I said I could. Would that tell you anything?"

Driscoll took another drag of his cigarette. "I guess not. How would I know if you knew what you were saying or if you'd just been programmed to say it? There's no way of telling the difference."

"Then is there any difference?"

Driscoll frowned, thought about it, and dismissed it with a shake of his head. "This is kinda funny," he said to change the subject.

"What is?"

"Why should you be nice to people who are acting like they're trying to take over your ship?"

"Do you want to take over the ship?"

"Me? Hell no. What would I do with it?"

"Then there's your answer."

"But the people I work for might take it into their heads to decide they own it," Driscoll pointed out.

"That's up to them. If it pleases them to say so, why should we mind?"

"The people here wouldn't mind if our people started telling them what to do?"

"Why should they?"

Driscoll couldn't buy that. "You mean they'd be just as happy doing what our people told them to?" he said.

"I never said they'd *do* anything," the robot replied. "I just said that people telling them wouldn't bother them."

Just then, two Chironian girls strolled around the corner from the narrow corridor. They looked fresh and pretty in loose blouses worn over snug-fitting slacks, and had light-weight stretch-boots of some silvery, lustrous material. One of them had brown, wavy hair with a reddish tint to it, and looked as if she were in her midthirties; the other was a blonde of perhaps twenty-two. For a split second, Driscoll felt an instinctive twinge of apprehension at the thought of looking ridiculous, but the girls showed no surprise. Instead they paused and looked at him not unpleasantly, but with a hint of reserve as if they wanted to smile but weren't quite sure if they should.

"Hi," the redhead called, a shade cautiously.

Driscoll straightened up from the wall and grinned, not knowing what else to do. "Well . . . hi," he returned.

At once their faces split into broad smiles, and they walked over. The redhead shook his hand warmly. "I see you've already met Wellington. I'm Shirley. This is my daughter, Ci."

"*She's* your daughter?" Driscoll blinked. "Say, I guess that's . . . very nice."

Ci repeated the performance. "Who are you?" she asked him.

"Me? Oh . . . name's Driscoll—Tony Driscoll." He licked his lips while he searched for a follow-up. "I guess me and Wellington are guarding the corridor."

"Who from?" Ci asked.

"A good question," Wellington commented.

"You're the first Terran we've talked to," Shirley said. She nodded her head to indicate the direction they had come from. "We've got a class of kids back there who are bubbling over with curiosity. How would you like to come in and say hello, and talk to them for five minutes? They'd love it."

"What?" Driscoll stared at them aghast. "I've never talked to classes of people. I wouldn't know how to start."

"A good time to start practicing then," Ci suggested.

He swallowed hard and shook his head. "I have to stay here. This conversation is enough to get me shot as it is." Ci shrugged but seemed content not to make any more of it. "Are you two, er . . . teachers here or something like that?" Driscoll asked.

"Sometimes," Shirley answered. "Ci teaches English mainly, but mostly down on the surface. That is, when she's not working with electronics or installing plant wiring underground somewhere. I'm not all that technical. I grow olives and vines out on the Peninsula, and design interiors. That's what brought me up here—Clem wants the crew quarters and mess deck refitted and decorated. But yes, I teach tailoring sometimes, but not a lot."

"I meant as a regular job," Driscoll said. "What do you do basically?"

"All of them." Shirley sounded mildly surprised. "What do you mean by 'basically'?"

"They do the same thing all the time, from when they quit school to when they retire," Ci reminded her mother.

"Oh yes, of course." Shirley nodded. "That sounds pretty awful. Still, it's their business."

"What do you do best?" Ci asked him. "I mean . . . apart from holding people's walls up for them. That can't be much of a life."

Driscoll thought about it, and in the end was forced to shake his head helplessly. "Not a lot that you'd be interested in, I guess," he confessed.

"Everybody's got something," Shirley insisted. "What do you like doing?"

"You really wanna know?" An intense note had come suddenly into Driscoll's voice.

"Hey, back off, soldier," Ci said suspiciously. "We're still strangers. Later, who knows? Give it time."

"I didn't mean that," Driscoll protested, feeling embarrassed. "If you must know, I like working cards."

"You mean tricks?" Shirley seemed interested.

"I can do tricks, sure."

"Are you good?"

"The best. I can make 'em stand up and talk."

"You'd better mean it," Shirley warned. "There's nothing worse than trying to spend money you don't have. It's like stealing from people."

Driscoll didn't follow what she meant, so he ignored it. "I mean it," he told her.

Shirley turned to look at Ci. "Say, wouldn't he be great to have at our next party? I love things like that." She looked at Driscoll again. "When are you coming down to Chiron?"

"I don't know yet. We haven't heard anything."

"Well, give us a call when you do, and we'll fix something up. I live in Franklin, so there shouldn't be too much of a problem. That's where we usually get together."

"Sounds good," Driscoll said. "I can't make any promises right now though. Everything depends on how things go. If things work out okay, how would I find the place?"

"Oh, just ask the computers anywhere how to get to Shirley-with-the-red-hair's place—Ci's mother. They'll take care of you."

"So maybe we'll see you down there sometime," Ci said.

"Well . . . yeah. Who knows? He was about to say something more when Wellington interrupted.

"Two of your officers are heading this way. I thought you ought to know."

"Who?" Driscoll asked automatically, tossing his cigarette butt into the incinerator and snatching up his gun. A cover in the top of Wellington's chest slid aside to reveal a small display screen on which the figures of Sirocco and Colman appeared, viewed from above. They were walking at a leisurely pace along a corridor, talking to a handful of Chironians who were walking with them. Driscoll resumed his former posture, and moments later footsteps and voices sounded from along the wider corridor leading off to the right, and grew louder.

"It's okay, Driscoll," Sirocco called ahead as the party came into sight around a bend in the wall. "Forget the pantomime. We're back in the Bomb Factory." Driscoll relaxed his pose and sent a puzzled look along the corridor.

"I might have guessed," Colman said, nodding to himself and taking in the two girls as he drew to a halt.

"Very cosy," Sirocco agreed.

"Er . . . Shirley and Ci," Driscoll said. "And that's General Wellington."

"Been having a nice chat, have you?" Sirocco asked.

"Well, yes, actually, I suppose, sir. How did you know?"

Sirocco waved at the corridor behind him. "Because it's happening everywhere else, that's how. Carson's talking football, and Maddock is telling some kids about what it was like growing up on the *Mayflower II*." He sighed but didn't sound too ruffled about it. "If you can't beat 'em, then join 'em, eh, Driscoll . . . for an hour or so, anyway. And besides, they want to show Colman something in the observatory upstairs. I don't understand what the hell they're talking about."

"Steve's an engineer," one of the Chironians, a bearded youth in a red check shirt, explained, indicating Colman and speaking to Ci. "We told him about the resonance oscillations in the G7 mounting gyro, and he said he might be able to suggest a way of damping them with feedback from the alignment laser. We're taking him up to have a look at it."

"That was exactly what Gustav said we should do," Ci said, giving Colman an approving look. "He was looking at it yesterday."

"I know. Maybe we can get Gustav and Steve working on it together."

"Hey, don't get too excited about this," Colman cautioned. "I only said I'd be interested in seeing it. The Army might have different ideas about me getting involved. Don't bet your life savings on it."

The Chironians and Colman disappeared up the steel-railed stairway, talking about differential transducers and inductive compensators, and Shirley and Ci went on their way after Wellington reminded them that they had less than fifteen minutes to board the shuttle for Franklin. Driscoll and Sirocco remained with Wellington in the corridor.

"If you don't mind my saying so, isn't this a bit risky, sir?" Driscoll said apprehensively. "I mean . . . with all this going on? Suppose Colonel Wesserman or somebody shows up."

"No chance with these Chironian robots around. They've got the place staked out." He wrinkled his nose, and his moustache twitched as he sniffed the air. "Take a break while you've got the chance, Private Driscoll," he advised. "And I'll have one of those cigarettes that you've been smoking."

Driscoll grinned and began feeling more confident. "You see, Wellington," he said. "They're not *all* as bad as you think."

"Amazing," the robot replied in a neutral voice.

A party was thrown in the Bowery that night to celebrate the *Mayflower II*'s safe arrival and the end of the voyage. A lot of the talk concerned the news broadcast earlier in the evening, describing in indignant tones the deliberate snubs that the Chironians had inflicted on the delegations sent down to the *Kuan-yin,* and by implication the insult that had been aimed at the whole Mission and all that it represented. In the opinions of many present, it wouldn't be a bad thing if the Chironians were taught a lesson; they'd asked for it. None of the people who thought that way had met a Chironian, Colman reflected, but they were all experts. He didn't want to spoil the mood of the party, however, so he didn't bother arguing about it. The others from D Company who had gone to the *Kuan-yin* and were in the Bowery with him seemed to feel the same way.

CHAPTER TWELVE

HOWARD KALENS WAS not amused.

"A scandalous exhibition!" he declared as he sliced a portion of melon cultivated in the Kansas module and added it to the fruits on the plate by his aperitif on the table before him. "Nobodies and cretins, all of them. Not one of them had any representative powers worth speaking of. Yet it's clear that a governing organization of some kind must exist, though God knows what kind of people it's made up of, judging from the state the town's in . . . a total shambles. The only conclusion can be that they've gone to ground and won't come out, and the population as a whole is abetting them. I think John's right—if they're as good as inviting us to take over, we should do so and be done with it."

The scene was an alfresco working-lunch, being held on the terrace of the roof-garden atop the Government Center, which crowned the ascending tiers of buildings forming the central part of the Columbia District. High above, the shutters outside the module's transparent roof had been opened to admit the almost forgotten phenomenon of natural sunlight, streaming in from Alpha Centauri, as it held a position low in the sky below the nose of the Spindle while the *Mayflower II* rotated with its axis kept steady toward it.

Garfield Wellesley finished spreading liver paté on a finger of toast and looked up. "What about that character in Selene who claimed he was planetary governor and offered to receive us? What happened to him?"

Kalens looked disdainfully down his nose. "My staff contacted him through the Chironian communications system.

114

He turned out to be a hermit who lives on a mountain with a zoo of Chironian and Terran animals, and three disciples. They're all quite insane."

"I see . . ." Wellesley frowned and nibbled off a piece of the toast.

"Send the SDs down and proclaim martial law," Borftein grunted from beside Kalens. "They've had their chance. If they've run away and left it for us, let's take it. Why mess around?"

Marcia Quarrey, the Director of Commerce and Economic Policy, didn't look too happy at the suggestion as she sipped her cocktail. "Obviously that would be possible," she said, setting down her glass. "But would it serve any useful purpose? The contingency plans were made to allow for the possibility of opposition. Well, there hasn't been any opposition. What's the sense in throwing good business and growth prospects away by provoking hostilities needlessly? We can acquire Franklin simply by walking in. We don't have to make a demonstration out of it."

"Exactly what I was thinking," Wellesley commented, nodding. "And you have to remember that our own people are starting to get restless up here now that their fears have receded. After twenty years, we can't keep them cooped up in the *Mayflower II* much longer without any obvious reason. They've got accommodations prepared by the space-base at Franklin. I'm inclined to say we should start moving the first batches down. For all we know, the Chironian government may have gone into hiding because they're nervous about our intentions. It might be a good way of enticing them to come out again."

"I agree," Marcia Quarrey said. She looked at Borftein. "If that's the case, then sending in the SD's would only confirm their fears. It would be the worst thing we could do."

Kalens chewed on a slice of orange but made a face as if the fruit was bad. "But we've been publicly insulted," he objected. "What are you saying—that we should simply forget it? That would be unthinkable. What kind of a precedent would we be setting?"

"You can't be soft with people like this," Borftein said

bluntly. "Give them a yard, and they'll hate you because they want a mile. Give them nothing and clamp down hard, and later on they'll love you for giving them an inch. I've seen it all before."

Quarrey sighed and shook her head. "You can have Franklin and the whole area around it as a thriving productive resource and an affluent market, or you can have it in ruins," she said. "Given the choice, which would you prefer? Well, it's not as if we didn't have the choice, is it? We have."

"A nice sentiment, I agree," Kalens said. "But they still should be taught some manners."

Wellesley raised a hand a fraction. "Be careful you don't allow this to get too personal, Howard," he cautioned. "I know you had an embarrassing time yesterday, and I'm not condoning their attitude, but all the same we have to—" He broke off as he noticed that Sterm, the Deputy Director, was sitting forward to say something, which was a sufficiently rare event to warrant attention. "Yes, Matt?" The others looked toward Sterm curiously.

Sterm brought his fingers together in front of his face—a noble face whose proud, Roman-emperor features crowned by laurels of curly hair combed flat and forward concealed an underlying harshness of line from all but the most discerning—and stared at the center of the table with large, liquid-brown, unfathomable eyes. "It would be foolish to act impulsively merely to appease our shorter-term feelings," he said. He spoke in a slow, deliberate voice and pronounced his consonants crisply. "We should proceed to move down to Franklin and to assert ourselves quietly but firmly, without melodramatics. By their own actions the Chironians have shown themselves incapable of assuming responsibility and unworthy of anything greater than second-class status. Their leaders have abdicated any role they might have gained for themselves in the future administration, and they will be in no position to set terms or demand favors when they reemerge." He paused, and then turned his eyes to Howard Kalens. "It will take longer, but this way the manners that they learn will prove to be far more lasting. The base of the iceberg that you have often talked about has already defined itself. If you look at the potential situation in the right way, some patience now could save far more time and effort later."

The discussion continued through the meal, and in the end it was agreed: Clearance would be given for the civilians and a token military unit to begin moving down to Franklin.

"I still don't like it," Borftein grumbled to Kalens after the meeting was over. "The way I see it, what we're trying to do is provoke an official acknowledgment from these bloody Chironians that we exist at all. If I had my way, I'd soon show them whether we exist or not."

"I'm not sure that I agree as much as I thought," Kalens told him. "Sterm may have a point. We should try it his way to begin with at least. We don't have to stick with the plan indefinitely."

"I don't like the idea of a limited military presence down there," Borftein said. "We're trusting the Chironians too much. I still say they could have strength that they're not showing yet. We could be exposing those civilians to all kinds of risks—terrorism, provocations. What if they get hit by surprise? I've seen it all before."

"Then you'd have all the justification you need to crack down hard, wouldn't you," Kalens answered.

Borftein thought about the remark for a few seconds. "Do you think that could be what Sterm's hoping for?" His tone betrayed that the thought hadn't registered fully until then.

"I'm not sure," Kalens replied distantly. "Trying to elucidate Sterm's motives is akin to peeling an onion. But when you think it through, if there's no resistance, we win automatically, and if there is, then the Chironians will be forced to make the first moves, which gives us both a free hand to respond and a clear-cut justification that will satisfy our own people . . . which is doubly important with the elections coming up. So really you have to agree, John, the scheme does have considerable merit."

CHAPTER THIRTEEN

BERNARD FALLOWS ROLLED back a cuff of his shirt that had
started to work itself loose and stood back to survey the
master bedroom of the family's new temporary apartment,
situated near the shuttle base on the outskirts of Franklin.
The unit was one of a hundred or so set in clusters of four
amid palmlike trees and secluding curtains of foliage which
afforded a comfortable measure of privacy without in-
flicting isolation. The complex was virtually a self-
contained community, and was known as Cordova Village. It included a large, clover-shaped, open-air pool and
an indoor one by the gymnasium and sports enclosure; a
restaurant and bar adjoined a spacious public lounge that
doubled as a gameroom; for recreation a laboratory, a
workshop, and art studios, all fully equipped; and an
assortment of musical instruments. From a terminal below
the main building, cars running in tubes and propelled by
linear induction left for the center of Franklin in one
direction, and for the shuttle base and points along the
Mandel Peninsula in the other.

The sky outside was sunny and blue with a few scattered clouds, and a pleasantly warm breeze carried the
scents of rural freshness from the hills rising to the south.
Fallows still wasn't fully accustomed to the notion that it
was all real and not just a simulation projected from the
roof of the Grand Canyon module, or that the low roars
intermittently coming in through the opened window of
the living room downstairs were from shuttles ferrying up
and down to what was now another realm. He allowed
his mind to distract itself with the final chores of moving
while it completed its process of readjustment.

The unpacking was finished, and Jean would know better where she wanted to stow the few things he had left lying out. The move had gone very quickly and smoothly, mainly because the Chironians had even furnished the place—right down to the towels and the bed linen, which had meant that the Fallowses could leave most of their own things in storage at the base until something more permanent was worked out.

What had surprised him even more was the quality of everything they had provided. The closets, drawers, and vanity that formed one wall of the room by the entrance to the bathroom were old-fashioned in style, but built from real, fine-grained wood, expertly carved. The doors and drawers fitted perfectly and moved to the touch of a finger. The fabrics and drapes were soft and intricately woven rather than having been patterned by laser impregnation; the carpets were of an organic self-cleaning, self-regenerating fiber that felt like twentieth-century Wilton or Axminster; the bathroom fittings were molded from a metallic glazed crystal that glowed with a faint internal fluorescence; the heating and environmental systems were noiseless. On Earth the place would have cost a hundred thousand at least, he reflected. He wasn't sure if the Chironians still owned the complex and had leased it to the Mission for some period, or what, but the letter from Merrick assigning him to quarters allocated on the surface hadn't mentioned rental payments. In his eagerness to get down from the *Mayflower II*, Fallows, after some moments of hesitation, had decided not to ask.

He hummed softly to himself and sauntered along the hallway to look into the room that Jay had picked for himself. Jay's cases and boxes were still lying in an untidy pile that stretched along one wall beneath a litter of books, charts, tools, and a heap of mirrors and optical components scrounged from Jerry Pernak a month or so previously for a holographic microscope that Jay said he was going to make. The carcass of a stripped-down industrial process-control computer was lying on the floor by the bed, along with more boxes, an Army battle helmet and ammunition belt—both souvenirs of Jay's mandatory cadet training on the *Mayflower II*—and assorted junk from a medium-duty fluid clutch assembly, the intended purpose of which was a complete mystery. Jay himself had disappeared early on to go off exploring. Bernard shrugged to himself. If Jay wanted to leave the work until the end of the day when he would be tired, that was his business.

"Bernie, this is too much!" Jean's voice came up from the lounge area below. "I'm never going to get used to this." Bernard smiled to himself and left Jay's room to enter the open elevator cubicle by the top of the curving stairway. Seconds later he walked out again and into the lounge. Jean was standing in the center of the floor between the dining room and the area of sunken floor before the king-size wall screen that formed a comfortable enclave surrounded by a sofa, two large armchairs, and a revolving case of shelves half recessed into the wall; a coffee table of dark-tinted glass formed its centerpiece. She gestured helplessly. "What are we ever going to do with all this space? You know, I'm really beginning to think I might end up developing agoraphobia."

Bernard grinned. "It takes some getting used to, doesn't it. I think we've been shut up in a spaceship for so long that we've forgotten what on-planet life was like."

"Was it ever like this? I certainly don't remember."

"Perhaps not quite, but that was twenty years ago, remember. Times change, I guess."

Marie, who had been exploring the house, emerged from the elevator. "The basement is huge!" she told them. "There are all kinds of rooms down there, and I don't know what they're for. I could have my own room to draw things in. And did you know there's another door down there that leads out to a tunnel? I think it might go through to where the cab stops because it's got a thing like a conveyor running along next to it. Perhaps we needn't have carried all those things over and in through the front door at all."

"I said you were in too much of a hurry," Jean said to Bernard. "Just think, all that work for nothing. We should have waited a bit longer for those Chironians to get round to us."

Bernard shrugged. "What the hell? It's done now. We needed the exercise."

Marie walked across the room and gazed at the large screen. "Does this work?" she asked.

"I don't know. We haven't tried it yet," Bernard answered. He raised his voice a fraction. "Anybody home? What do we have to do to get a computer in this place?" No response.

"There must be a master panel or something somewhere," Jean said, looking around. "How about that?" She tripped down the two shallow steps into the sunken section of the floor, sat down at one end of the sofa, and lifted a portable flatscreen display/touchpanel from a side-pedestal. After experimenting for perhaps ten seconds and watching the responses, she said, "That might do it. Try again."

"Is there a computer in the house?" Bernard called out.

"At your service," a voice replied from the direction of the screen. "I answer to *Jeeves,* unless you want to make it something different." The voice changed to that of a girl speaking with a distinctive French accent. *"Une petite française, possiblement?"* Then it switched to a guttural male—*"Karl, ze Bavarian butler, maybe?"*—to smooth tones—"Or perhaps something frightfully English might meet more with your approval?"—and finally back to its original American. "All planetary communications and database facilities at your disposal—public, domestic, educational, professional, and personal; information storage, computation, entertainment, instruction, tuition, reference, travel arrangements, accommodations, services, goods, and resources, secretarial assistance, and consultancy. You name it, I can handle it or put you in touch with the right people."

Bernard raised his eyebrows. "Well, hello, Jeeves. How about all that? I guess you'd better stay who you are for the time being. How about giving us a rundown on this place for a start? For instance, how do you . . ."

Jean looked away as she heard the front door open. A few seconds later Jay arrived. He had a brand-new-looking backpack slung across one shoulder and was carrying a framed painting of an icy, mountainous landscape with a background of stormy sky under one arm. His expression was vaguely perplexed.

"Jay!" Jean exclaimed. "Did you find anywhere nice? What are those things?"

"Oh." Jay set the painting down by the wall and frowned at it as if he had just noticed it for the first time. "I thought that might look nice in my room." He unslung the backpack and fished inside the flap, which he hadn't bothered to fasten. "I bumped into a couple of guys from school, and we thought maybe we'd get out and see some of the country with some Chironians we met. There's a lot more of it around here than inside the GC module. So I got these." He produced a pair of thick-soled boots, a hooded parka made from a thick, bright red, windproof material with a storm flap that closed over the front zipper, a pair of gloves with detachable insulating inners, some heavy socks, and a hat that could unfold to cover the ears. "We were thinking of going to the mountains across the sea," he explained. "You can get there in a flyer from Franklin in about twenty minutes."

Jean took the boots and turned them over in her hands. Then she picked up the parka, unfolded it, and studied it in silence for a couple of seconds. "But . . . these are *good*, Jay," she said. A concerned expression spread over her face. "Where . . . how did you get them? I mean . . . what's all this going to cost?"

Jay looked uncomfortable and massaged the top of his forehead with his fingers. "I know you're not going to believe this, Ma," he said. "But they're not going to cost anything. Nothing seems to cost anything. I don't understand it either, but—"

"Oh, Jay, don't be silly. Come on now—tell me where all this came from."

"Really—you just walk in and help yourself. That's how they do things here . . . for everything."

"What's the problem?" Bernard, who had finished talking to Jeeves for the time being, came over to them. Marie followed close behind.

Jean looked at him with a worried face. "Jay's come

back with all these things, and he's trying to say he got them all for nothing. He's claiming that anyone can just help themselves. I've never heard such nonsense."

Bernard gave Jay a stern look. "You don't expect us to believe that, surely. Now, tell us where this stuff came from. I want the truth. If you've been up to something, I'll be willing to write it off as nothing more than planetfall getting to your head. Now—are you sure there isn't something you want to tell us?"

"Everything I've said is true," Jay insisted. "There's this big kinda market in town. It's got just about everything, and you just walk in and take what you want. We got talking to some Chironians, and they showed us what you do. I don't understand it either, but that's how things work here."

"Oh, Jay," Jean groaned. "They were probably taking you for a ride to get a laugh out of it. At your age, you should know better."

"They weren't," Jay protested. "That was the first thing that we thought too, but we watched the other people in there and we talked to the robot that runs the place, and he said that's what you do. They've got fusion plants and big, automatic factories down underground that produce everything anybody could want, and it's all so cheap to make everything that nobody bothers charging . . . or something like that. I can't figure it out."

"Is this the truth?" Bernard asked uncertainly with a strong note of suspicion in his voice.

"Of course it is." Jay sighed wearily. "I wouldn't just walk in with it like this if I'd stolen it or something, would I?"

"I bet he did," Marie declared.

"Thanks a lot," Jay said.

"I want to see this place. Is there any reason why you couldn't take me back there right now?"

Jay sighed again. "I guess not. Let's go. It's one stop along the maglev line."

"Can we go too?" Marie asked, evidently having forgotten her previous convictions. "I want to gets *lots* of things."

"Oh, let your father go with Jay, dear," Jean said. "You

can help me finish up here. We can go and see it tomorrow."

"Don't you want to come along?" Bernard asked Jean. "It would get you out and give you a break."

Jean shook her head and indicated Marie surreptitiously with her eyes. "It would be best if you went on your own. We've got plenty to do here." Marie made a face but stayed quiet.

Bernard nodded. "Okay. We'll see you later then. Maybe you'd better leave that stuff here for now, Jay. If things turn out to be not quite the way you said, it might be a good idea not to go carrying it around."

Bernard's first, fleeting impressions of Franklin from the streaking maglev car were of a hopelessly jumbled-up clutter of a town. Unlike the neat and orderly models of urban planning that had replaced the heaps of American rubble during the recovery after the Lean Years—with business, entertainment, industrial, and residential sectors segregated by green belts and tidy landsculpting—everything in Franklin seemed to be intermingled with no discernible rhyme or reason. Buildings, towers, houses, and unidentifiable constructions of all shapes, sizes, and colors were packed together, overlapping and fusing in some places while giving way to clumps of greenery and trees in others. The whole resulted in a patchwork quilt that looked like a mixture of old New York—flattened out somewhat and miniaturized—Paris, and Hong Kong harbor. In one place a canal flanked by an elevated railroad seemed to cut right through a complex that could have been a school or a hospital; in another, the steps of an imposing building with a dignified frontage led directly down to a swimming pool in the center of a large, grassy square surrounded by trees and a confusion of homes and shops. A river opened up as the car crossed through a suspended section of tube, giving a glimpse of a few yachts drifting lazily here and there, a couple of larger ships moored lower down where the mouth widened against a background of open sea, and numerous personal flying vehicles buzzing to and fro overhead; a scene of

robot cranes and earthmovers excavating a site on the far
bank came and went, and then the car plunged into the
lower levels of the metropolis ahead and began slowing
as it approached its destination.

"It's a bit different from taking a cab round the Ring,"
Jay remarked as the car eased to a halt.

"You can say that again," Bernard agreed.

"Is this what the cities back on Earth were like?"

"Well . . . some of them, a long time ago, maybe. But
not modern ones."

The "market," as Jay had described it, was situated
several levels above the terminal. To get to it they used
a series of escalators. A lot of people were milling about,
dressed in all manner of styles and colors and reflecting
the various races of Earth in more or less even proportions,
which was to be expected since the genetic codes carried
by the *Kuan-yin* had comprised a balanced mix of types.
Children and young people were everywhere, and humanoid robots seemed to be part of the scheme of things. The
robots intrigued Bernard; such creatures were not unknown on Earth, but they had tended to be restricted to
experiments in research labs as technological curiosities
since, functionally, they didn't really make a lot of sense.
Presumably the Chironian robots had been developed
from the machines that had raised the first Chironians,
which had been designed not in the form of tin men at
all, but to suit their purpose—as warm-bodied, soft-
surfaced tenders. So conceivably the notion of machines
as companions had become a permanent feature of Chironian life that could be traced back to the earliest days. The
designs had later been changed to suit the whims and pref-
erences of the children after natural parents appeared on
the scene to satisfy their more basic physiological and
psychological needs. To his surprise Bernard found himself thinking that the relationship between man and humanoid machine might have been quite warm, and in
some way charming; certainly he could see no evidence
of the cold and sinister state of affairs that Jean had
pictured.

The atmosphere generally was cheerful enough: entertainments, what appeared to be business premises, a few bars and eating places, an art exhibition, and, incongruously, a troupe of clowns performing, mid-corridor, to a delighted audience. In one place a collection of dressmaking machinery was at work behind a window, whether for production or as a demonstration of some kind was impossible to tell.

Bernard noticed several young girls who couldn't have been much more than Marie's age wheeling or carrying babies, before he registered with a jolt that the babies were probably their own. Mixed with the shock of the realization came a twinge of relief that he had left Jean and Marie at home. Explaining this was going to require some delicate handling. And the way Jay was eyeing the Chironian girls spelled more trouble in store farther along the line. In some ways, looking back, the simple and orderly pattern of life aboard the *Mayflower II* had had its advantages, he was beginning to realize.

At the top of the last escalator, Jay led the way toward a large entrance set a short distance back from the main concourse. Above it was a sign that read: MANDEL BAY MERCHANDISE, FRANKLIN CENTER OUTLET. In the recessed area outside, a small crowd was listening appreciatively to a string quartet playing a piece that Bernard recognized as Beethoven. Suddenly, for a moment, Earth seemed less far away. Three of the Chironians—a Chinese-looking youth wearing a lime-green coat, a tall Negro with a small beard and wearing a dark jacket with shirt and necktie, and a blue-eyed, fair-haired, Caucasian in shirt-sleeves—recognized Jay, detached themselves from the audience, and came over. Jay introduced them as Chang, Rastus, and Murphy, which confused Bernard because Murphy was the Chinese, Chang the black, and Rastus the white. Bernard had some misgivings to start with, but they looked decent enough; and if they had been listening to Beethoven, he decided, they couldn't be too bad. He glanced over his shoulder instinctively before remembering that the *Mayflower II* was twenty thousand miles away, realized that he could afford to loosen up a little, and said, "I, er . . . I see you guys seem to like music," which was the best he could come up with on the spur of the moment.

"That's one of my sisters playing the cello," Murphy informed him. (Was it? Oh, yes—the Chinese was Murphy.) Bernard looked over at the quartet. The cello player was olive-skinned with Mediterranean features.

"Oh . . . she's very good," Bernard said.

Murphy looked pleased. "Don't you think it has a fine tone? It's one of Chang's. He makes them."

"Very," Bernard agreed. He didn't really have a clue.

"These are the guys I was telling you about," Jay said. "The ones who are with the group that's going to the mountains."

"You'd be welcome to come too if you want," Rastus said.

Bernard managed a weak smile. "That's a nice thought, but I've got a job to do. We're still going to be busy for a while. Thanks anyway." He thought for a few seconds. "I hope you're not planning anything too tough out there. I mean, Jay hasn't exactly had a lot of practice at that kind of thing. He's never even seen a planet before." Jay winced under his breath and looked away.

Chang laughed. "It's okay. We won't be going very high, and it'll be more walking than anything else. There won't be anything more risky than maybe a few daskrends showing up."

"You can use a gun, can't you, Jay?" Murphy asked.

"Well, yes, but . . ." Jay looked taken aback.

"We should have mentioned it," Murphy said. "Bring one along. A forty-five or something like that would be best, if you've got one."

"Wait a minute, wa-it a minute," Bernard interrupted, raising a hand in alarm. "Just what the hell is this? What's a das?—"

"Daskrend," Murphy supplied. "Oh, they're a kind of wolf but bigger, and they've got poison fangs. But they're pretty dumb and no big deal to handle. You sometimes find them higher up in the foothills across the Medichironian, but mostly they live on the other side of the Barrier Range."

"We're going to have to talk about this, Jay." Bernard's voice was very serious.

"I was teasing, really," Murphy said. "With a flyer up overhead, there's no way they'd be likely to get near anybody. But it's customary to go armed when you're not in places like Franklin . . . just in case."

"Maybe we shouldn't rush things too much," Bernard suggested. He looked at Jay. "You may want to give yourself time to acclimatize before you get into something like this." His tone said that he was being tactful in his phrasing; Jay wasn't going. For the moment, at least, Jay didn't feel inclined to argue too much.

"It's up to you. Just let us know," Murphy said and dismissed the subject with a slight shrug. "So, have you come back for something else?"

"No. My father just wants to see the store."

"Want to come with us?" Bernard invited.

"Sure," Murphy accepted, and they all began walking. On the way, Jay explained the problem to his three friends.

Inside, a large hall of counters and shelves displayed all manner of products from electronic devices and scientific instruments at one end to rainwear and sports equipment at the other. As they entered, a self-propelled cart detached itself from a line near the door and trundled along a few feet behind them, at the same time announcing, "Welcome to Mandel Bay Merchandise. Did you ever think of laying out your own garden and tending it *manually?* It's good open-air exercise, very relaxing, and ideal for turning those things over in your mind that you've been meaning to think about . . . as well as the soil, ho-ho! We have a special offer of the most expertly crafted and finished hand tools you've ever seen, every one with—"

"Go away," Chang told it. "We're just looking today." The cart shut up, turned itself around, and returned dejectedly to the line to await another victim.

Bernard stopped, frowned, and looked around. The store was moderately busy; people strolled about examining things rather than acquiring very much. An exception was a couple on the far side whom he recognized as Terrans from the *Mayflower II,* conspicuous for the three carts trailing them in convoy and loaded with everything imaginable. The couple were lower-echelon office workers, and

Bernard acknowledged their presence from afar with a faint nod.

"I suppose all this seems a bit strange to you folks," Rastus noted. "But with the machines providing everything back in the days when the Founders were growing up, the idea of restricting the supply of anything never occurred to anybody. There wasn't any reason to. We've carried on that way ever since. You'll get used to it."

"But . . . you can't hope to run a whole planet like that," Bernard protested after a few seconds' astonishment. "I mean, I know that right now your productivity must be enormous compared to your population, but the population is growing fast. You've got to start thinking about some kind of . . . system to regulate things. Your resources are only finite."

Rastus looked puzzled. "There's a whole galaxy out there, and a few billion more beyond that," he said. "It'll take a long time for it to get crowded. Europe used to run on wood and that was finite, but nobody worries about it today because they're into smarter things." He shrugged. "It's the same with everything else. The human mind is an infinite resource, and that's all you need."

Bernard shook his head and gestured in the direction of the couple from the *Mayflower II,* who were glancing furtively around them while a handling machine by the exit unloaded their carts onto a conveyor that looked as if it fed down to the level below. "But look what's happening," he said. "How long can you keep up with that kind of thing? What happens when everyone starts acting like that?"

"Why should they?" Chang asked. He looked across at the couple curiously. "I was wondering what they want with all that stuff. Anyone would think it's about to run out."

"For the status," Jay said. Chang looked at him blankly.

"It's okay," Rastus said. "As long as they pay for it."

"That's my whole point," Bernard told them. "They're *not* paying for it—not a cent's worth of any of it."

"They will," Rastus replied.

"How?"

Rastus looked mildly surprised. "They'll find a way," he said.

Just then Jerry Pernak came around a corner accompanied by his fiancée, Eve Verritty, and two more Chironians. A cart was following them with a few odds and ends inside. He gaped at Bernard and Jay in surprise, then grinned. "Hey! So Jay dragged you out to see the sights, eh? Hello, Jay. Started making friends already?" Introductions were exchanged with smiles and handshakes. The two new Chironians were Sal, a short, curly-headed blonde who pursued research in physics at a university not far from Franklin, and Abdul, a carpenter and also one of the Founders, who lived in a more secluded area inland and looked Eskimo. Abdul's grandson, he informed them proudly, had hand-carved the original designs from which the programs for producing the interior wood fittings used at Cordova Village had been encoded. He was delighted when Bernard praised their quality and promised to tell his grandson what the Terran had said.

"And how about this?" Pernak said. "Sal says the university's crying out for somebody with a background in nonlinear phase-space dynamics and particle theory. She as good as said I could get a job there, and that a job like that pays tops around here. What do you think of that for a break?"

Bernard gave a pained smile. "It sounds good," he agreed. "But the Directorate might have a few things to say."

"I know, but I figured I'd go take a look at the place anyhow out of curiosity. That can't do any harm. Later on, well . . . maybe anything could happen."

"How are they going to pay you?" Jay asked.

"We haven't talked about that yet," Pernak told him.

"That's a personal question, Jay," Bernard cautioned. "Anyhow, it's early yet."

"Jay told us you're an engineering officer on the *Mayflower II*," Chang said, sounding interested. "A specialist in fusion processes."

"That's right." Bernard was surprised and felt a little flattered. "I help look after the main drive systems."

"We could probably arrange a visit for you too," Chang offered. "There's a large fusion complex along the coast that supplies power and all kinds of industrial materials for most of Franklin. Another one's due to be built soon, and they'll be needing people too. I could arrange for you to go and see it, if you think you'd be interested."

It was interesting, certainly. "Well . . . maybe," Bernard replied guardedly. "Who do you know there?"

"I've got a friend whose mother works most of her time there. Her name's Kath."

"And that would be enough to fix something?"

"Sure," Chang said confidently. "I'll give you a call when I've talked to Adam. He's the friend. Would Jay like to go too?"

Bernard hadn't really thought of that. He saw Jay nodding vigorously, and tossed up his hands. "Why not? If you're sure it's okay, then thanks . . . thanks a lot."

"No problem," Chang told him.

Eve looked at the cart, which was waiting patiently, and then back at Pernak. "We're through, really," she said. "Shall we carry on and see the town?"

"Let's do that," Pernak agreed. "I'll take the things."

"They can go on the maglev on their own," Murphy informed them. "The handler at the village terminal will route them through. You pick them up by the elevator in your basement. What's your number there?"

"Ninetey-seven," Pernak replied. He looked at Eve and shook his head.

"That's all," Murphy said, addressing the cart. "Ninety-seven, Cordova Village. On your way."

"One second," a voice said from behind them. They looked round to find a Chironian robot winking its lights at them. It was a short, rounded type, which made it look tubby. "You haven't taken any of our special-offer hand gardening tools. Do you want to grow fat and old before your time? Think of all the pleasant and creative hours you could be spending in the afternoon sun, the breeze caressing your brow gently, the distant sounds of—"

"Aw, cut it out, Hoover," Rastus told the robot. "These people have only just arrived. They've got more than enough to do." He looked at the Terrans. "This is Hoover. He runs the place. Don't pay too much attention or you'll end up buried in junk up to your eyes."

"*Junk?!*" Hoover's lights blazed crimson in unison. "What do you mean, *junk?* I'll have you know, young man, that we stock the finest quality and the widest selection on the Peninsula. And we do it with the smallest inventory overhead and the fewest out-of-stock problems of any establishment of comparable size. Junk indeed! Have you troubled to inspect our—"

"Okay, okay, Hoover." Rastus held up an apologetic hand. "You know I didn't mean it. You do a great job here. And the displays today are very artistic."

"Thank you, and my compliments to you, sir." Hoover acknowledged in a suddenly more agreeable voice. "I hope you all enjoyed your visit and that we'll see you here again soon." The cart rolled away to deliver its load to the handling machine. Hoover escorted the group back to the entrance. "Now, next week we're expecting a consignment of absolutely first-class—"

"Lay off, Hoover," Chang said wearily. "We'll check it out through the net. Okay, maybe we'll see you next week."

In the corridor, the quartet had shifted to Mozart. "Have the robots been kept on as a kind of . . . tradition?" Bernard asked.

"The kids like having them around," Sal confirmed. "And to be honest, I suppose we do too. We've all grown up with them."

"I can remember the one that first taught me to talk," Abdul said. "It's still operating today, up there on the *Kuan-yin*. But the ones you see today have changed a lot."

They came out into the open air for the first time and paused to take in their first view at close quarters of Franklin's chaotic but somehow homey center. "And what about all this?" Eve asked. "Does it go back to the first days too?"

"Yes," Sal replied. "Forty years ago this was just a few domes and a shuttle port. The main base that you came in through was only built about ten years ago. Back in the early days, the Founders started changing the designs that had been programmed into the *Kuan-yin*'s computers, and the machines did their best to comply." She sighed. "And this is what it ended up like. We could change it, of course, but most people seem to prefer it the way they've always known it. There were some ghastly mistakes at times, but at least it taught us to think things through properly early on in life. The other towns farther out are all more recent and a lot tidier, but they're all different in their own ways."

"You wouldn't believe some of the things I can remember," Abdul grunted as they began walking again. "Darned machines . . . always did just what we told 'em. For a time we thought they were pretty stupid, but it turned out it was us."

"How old were you then?" Eve asked curiously.

"Oh, I don't know . . . four, five, maybe. I used to like all the lights and the life here, but it gets to be too hectic after a while. Now I prefer the hills. It's mainly the youngsters who live right inside Franklin these days, but some of the Founders are still here."

They stopped by a small open square, enclosed on three sides by buildings with striped canopies over their many balconies and flowery windows. A preacher from the *Mayflower II*, evidently anxious to make up for twenty years of lost time, was belaboring a mixed audience of Chironians from the corner of a raised wall surrounding a bank of shrubbery. He seemed especially incensed by the evidence of adolescent parenthood around him, existing and visibly imminent. The Chironians appeared curious but skeptical. Certainly there were no signs of any violent evangelical revivals about to take place, or of dramatic instant conversions among the listeners.

"It seems irrational to me to argue one way or another about things there's no evidence for," a boy of about fourteen remarked. "You can make up anything you want if there's no way of testing whether it's true or not, so what's the point?"

"We must have *faith!*" the preacher roared, his eyes wide with fervor.

"Why?" a girl in a pink jacket asked.

"Because the Book tells us we must."

"How do you know it's right?"

"There are some things which we must *accept!*" the preacher thundered.

"That's my point," the boy told him. "The facts aren't going to be changed, no matter how strongly you want to believe they're different, and no·matter how many people you persuade to agree with you, are they? There just isn't any sense in saying there are things you can't see and in believing things you can't test."

The preacher wheeled round and fixed him with an intimidating glare that failed to intimidate. "Do you believe in atoms?"

"Sure. Who doesn't?"

"Aha!" The preacher made an appealing gesture to the audience. "Is there any difference, my friends? Can we *see* atoms? Is this not arrogant insolence?" He looked back at the boy and jabbed an accusing finger at him. "Do you claim to have seen atoms? Tell us that you have, and I will say that you *lie!*" Another appealing flourish. "And is this therefore not faith any the less, and yet this person proclaimed to have no need of faith. Does he not, therefore, contradict himself before us?"

"Your comparison is quite invalid," a girl who was with the boy pointed out. "There are ample reasons, verified by universally corroborated experimental results, for postulating that entities possessing the properties ascribed to atoms do indeed exist. Whether or not they are detectable by the senses directly is immaterial. Where are your comparable data?"

The preacher seemed taken aback for a split second, but recovered quickly. "The world around us," he bellowed, throwing his arms wide. "Is it not there? Do I not see it? Who created it? Tell us. Is that not evidence enough?"

"No," the boy answered after a moment's reflection. "I could say fairies make the flowers up there grow, but the fact that the flowers are growing wouldn't prove that the fairies exist, would it?"

"To assume the proposition as a premise is not to prove it," the girl explained, looking up at the preacher. "Your argument, I'm afraid, is completely circular."

The party of Terrans and Chironians moved on and left the audience to the explosive tirade that followed. "Those were hardly more than children," Eve Verritty murmured.

"You seem surprised," Rastus said to Bernard.

"Those kids," Bernard replied, gesturing behind them. "There are some pretty sharp minds among them. Is everyone here like that?"

"Of course not," Rastus said. "But everyone values what they have. I said the mind was an infinite resource, but only if you don't squander it. Don't you think that makes an interesting paradox?"

CHAPTER FOURTEEN

STILL NO OVERTURE came from the Chironian leaders. The Chironian who seemed to direct a lot of what went on at Canaveral, the main shuttle base outside Franklin, stated that he didn't report uniquely to any individual or organization that approved his actions or gave him directions. So who told him how the place was to be run? It depended. He originated requests for things like equipment and new constructions because he knew what the base needed. How did he know? Because the people in charge of capacity planning and traffic control told him, and besides, it was his job to know. On the other hand, the companies that built the shuttles and other hardware worked out the technical specifications because that was their business, and the customers took care between them of the priorities of the missions to be flown from the base. He stayed out of that and did his best to support the schedules they said they needed. So ultimately, who was in charge? Who told whom to do what, and who did it? It depended. Nothing made any sense.

Following a directive from Wellesley, Howard Kalens instructed Amery Farnhill to open an embassy in a small building at Canaveral which the Chironians obligingly agreed to vacate, having been about to move into larger premises elsewhere anyway. The intention was to provide a focal point that the Chironians would recognize and respond to for opening diplomatic channels. Unfortunately, the natives paid no attention to it, and after two days of sitting at his desk with nothing to do, Amery Farnhill pleaded with Kalens for approval to send out snatch squads from his contingent of SD guards to bring in likely candidates to talk to him. Kalens could only partly concur since he was under strict instructions from Wellesley. "If you can persuade them, then do it," he replied over the communications link from the *Mayflower II*. "A calculated degree of intimidation is acceptable, but on no account are they to use force. I don't like it either, Amery, but I'm afraid we'll have to live with the plan for the time being."

"Hey, you. Stop." The major in command of the four SD troopers sent to scout out the center of Canaveral City —a residential and commercial suburb situated outside the base and merging into one side of Franklin—addressed the Chironian whom they had followed from the restaurant a few yards back around the corner. He was well-dressed, in his midthirties, and carrying an attaché case. The Chironian ignored them and kept walking. Whereupon the major marched ahead to plant himself firmly in the man's path. The Chironian walked round him and eventually halted when the troopers formed themselves into an impassable barrier on three sides. "You're coming to talk to the ambassador," the major informed him.

"No, I'm not. I'm going to talk about air-conditioning for the new passenger lounge in the base."

"Say 'sir' when you talk to me."

"If you wish. Sir when you talk to me." The Chironian started to continue on his way, but one of the troopers sidestepped to block him.

"What's your name, boy?" The major thrust his face close and narrowed his eyes menacingly.

"None of your goddamn business."

"Do you want us to have to drag you there?"

"Do you want to get out of here alive?"

The major's jaw quivered; his face colored. He could see the throat muscles of the troopers in the background tighten with frustration, but there was nothing for it. He had his orders. "On your way," he growled. "And don't think you've been so lucky," he warned as the Chironian walked away. "We've got your face taped. There'll be a next time."

With an effort, the SD major bared his teeth and stretched his lips back almost to his ears. "Excuse me, sir, but do you have a few minutes you could spare?"

"What for?" The Chironian in the purple sweater and green shorts asked.

"Our ambassador would like to talk to you. It's not far —just inside the base."

"What about?"

"Just a friendly chat . . . about your government, how it's organized, who's in it . . . a few things like that. It won't take long at all."

The Chironian rubbed his chin dubiously. "I'm not at all sure that I could be much help. Government of what in particular?"

"The planet . . . Chiron. Who runs it?"

"Runs the planet? Gee . . . I don't know anything about that."

"Who tells you what to do?"

"It depends."

"On what?"

"On what I'm doing." The Chironian looked apologetic. "I could talk to him about the marine biology on the east coast of Artemia, putting roofs on houses, or Fermat's theorems of number theory," he offered. "Do you think he might be interested in anything like that?"

The major sighed wearily. "It doesn't matter. Forget it. Do you know anyone else around here we should try asking?"

"Not really. I guess you guys have got a tough job on your hands. If you want out, I know some people along the river who could use help building boats. Have any of you ever done anything like that?"

The major stared at him as if refusing to believe his ears. "Get outa here," he choked in a weak voice. He shook his head incredulously, "Just . . . get the hell outa here, willya . . ."

"It's impossible!" Amery Farnhill protested to a full meeting of the Directorate in the *Mayflower II*'s Government Center. "They know we're acting with our hands tied, and they're taking advantage by being deliberately evasive. The only way we'll get anywhere is if you allow us to get tougher."

Wellesley shook his head firmly. "Not if you're talking about roughing up people in the streets. It would undo everything we've achieved."

"What have we achieved?" Borftein asked contemptuously.

"We have to do something," Marcia Quarrey insisted. "Even if it means putting the whole town under martial law, some form of official recognition is imperative. This has gone on far too long as it is."

Howard Kalens simmered as he listened. Quarrey had changed her tune when the commercial lobby, whose interests she represented, panicked at the prospect of having to compete in the insane Chironian economic system. The signals coming down the line had told her that she'd better get something done about it and soon, if she wanted to see herself reinstated after the elections, which in turn meant that Kalens had better be seen to back her case if he expected her support in his bid for the Directorship.

"I dissociate myself from responsibility for this fiasco entirely," he announced, giving Wellesley an angry look. "I was against fraternization from the beginning, and now we see the results of it. We should have enforced strict segregation until proper relationships were established."

"It wouldn't have worked," Wellesley countered. "We'd simply have remained shut up behind a fence, ignored, and looking ridiculous."

"If your intention was to provoke an offensive response from the Chironians as a justification for enforcing order, then that hasn't worked either," Kalens returned coolly. "Now we must live with the damage and consider our alternatives."

"What are you suggesting?" Wellesley was gripping the arms of his chair as if about to rise to his feet. "Withdraw that accusation at once!"

"Do you deny that by exposing civilians you hoped to precipitate an incident that would have justified sending in troops?"

Wellesley turned pale, and the veins stood out on his temples. "I deny that! I also deny that you urged segregation. My policy was to encourage their leaders out into the open by a demonstration of peaceful coexistence, and you went along with it. Withdraw your statement."

Kalens looked at him calmly for a few seconds, then nodded. "Very well. I withdraw the statement and apologize."

"Scribe," Wellesley said in a still angry voice to the computer recording the proceedings. "Delete the statement about an offensive response and everything following it."

"Deleted," the machine confirmed. "Last line of entry reads: '. . . shut up behind a fence, ignored, and looking ridiculous.' "

The suggestion had served its purpose. Sterm was watching Kalens curiously, and Marcia Quarrey was looking across the table with new respect. Farnhill shuffled his feet uncomfortably.

"So where do we go from here?" Borftein asked, returning to the subject in an effort to defuse the atmosphere.

Sterm studied his fingers for a moment and then looked up. "Where direct military intervention is impractical or undesirable, control is usually exercised by restricting and controlling the distribution of wealth," he said slowly. "Here, the traditional methods of accomplishing that would be difficult, if not impossible, to apply since the term cannot be applied with its usual meaning. This society must have its pressure points, nevertheless. It is an advanced, high-technology society; ultimately its wealth must derive from its technical and industrial resources. That is where we should look for its vulnerable spots."

A short silence fell while the meeting digested the observation. Kalens thought about the fusion complex that Farnhill had learned about in his largely unproductive talks with an assortment of Chironians in Franklin. Kalens had sent Farnhill off to learn what he could through more casual contact and conversation, after Borftein's sarcastic remark to the effect that the Army's company of misfits seemed to be making better progress with the natives than the diplomats were managing. "Yes . . . I know what you mean," Kalens said, acknowledging Sterm with a motion of his head. "As a matter of fact, we have already begun inquiries along those lines." He turned toward Farnhill. "Amery, tell us again about that place along the coast." .

"Port Norday?"

"Yes—some kind of industrial complex, wasn't it?"

"It's a centralized, fusion-based facility that provides generating capacity for practically this whole area, and a great deal of materials via a variety of interdependent processes," Farnhill informed the meeting. "Primary metals and chemicals are among its major products, as well as electricity."

"Who operates it?" Marcia Quarrey asked.

Farnhill looked uneasy and seemed a trifle awkward. "Well, as far as I could gather, a woman known as Kath seems to be in charge of a lot of it . . . as much as anybody's in charge of anything in this place. I haven't actually met her though."

"That could be a good place to start," Kalens suggested to Wellesley.

Wellesley seemed thoughtful. "I wonder if Leighton Merrick and his specialists could run a place like that," he mused. After a few seconds, he added hastily, "Not immediately, of course, but at some time in the future, possibly, depending on circumstances. As insurance, it would certainly pay us to know something more about it."

"I don't know," Farnhill said. "You'd have to ask Merrick about that."

"He ought to be given a chance to go and look at it," Borftein agreed with a nod. "What would be the best way to arrange something like that?"

Kalens shrugged without looking up from the table. "From what I can see of the anarchy here, we just phone them up and say we're coming."

"Perhaps we could propose a goodwill exchange visit," Sterm suggested. "In return, we might offer to show some of their technical people selected parts of the *Mayflower II*. A legitimate cover would be desirable."

"It's a thought," Wellesley agreed distantly. He cast his eyes round the table. "Does anybody have a better idea?" Nobody did. "So let's get Merrick here and talk to him,"

Wellesley said. He sat back and placed his hands on the edge of the table. "This would be a good time to break for lunch. Scribe, adjourn the session here. We will reconvene in ninety minutes. Contact Leighton Merrick in Engineering, and have him join us then. Also ask him to bring with him two of his more capable officers. Advise me at once if there are any difficulties. That's all."

"Acknowledged," the computer replied.

CHAPTER FIFTEEN

MRS. CRAYFORD, THE plump, extravagantly dressed wife of Vice-Admiral Crayford, Slessor's second-in-command of the *Mayflower II*'s crew, closed the box containing her new set of Chironian silver cutlery and added it to the pile of boxes on the table by her chair. Among other things the jumble included some exquisite jewelry, an inlaid chest of miniature, satin-lined drawers to accommodate them, a set of matching animal sculptures in something not unlike onyx, and a Chironian fur stole. "Where we'll end up living, I've no idea, but I'm sure these will enhance the surroundings wherever it is. Don't you think the silver is delightful? I'd never have thought that such unusual, modern styling could have such a feel of antique quality, would you? I must return to that place the next time I go down to Franklin. Some of the tableware there went with it perfectly."

"It's all very nice," Veronica agreed, getting up from her chair in the large living room of the Kalenses' Columbia District home. "I'm sure you'll find somewhere wonderful." Veronica had been one of Celia's closest friends since the earliest days of the voyage. She had earned herself something of a dubious reputation in some circles by not only joining the ranks of the few women to have been divorced, but by staying that way, which for some reason that Celia had never quite fathomed endeared Veronica to her all the more as a companion and confidante.

"They're priceless," Celia commented dryly from her chair. They had been, literally, but the irony was lost on Mrs. Crayford. Veronica caught Celia's eye with a warning look.

"They must be, mustn't they," Mrs. Crayford agreed blissfully. She shook her head. "In some ways it seems almost criminal to take them, but . . ." she sighed, "I'm sure they'd just be wasted otherwise. After all, those people are obviously savages and quite incapable of appreciating the true value of anything." Celia's throat tightened, but she managed to remain quiet. Mrs. Crayford fussed with her pile of boxes. "Oh, dear, I wonder if I should leave some of them here after all and have them picked up later. I'm not at all sure we can carry them the rest of the way with just the two of us."

"That would be quite all right," Celia said.

"We'll manage," Veronica promised. "They're more awkward than heavy. You worry too much."

Mrs. Crayford glanced at the clock display on the room's companel. "Well, then, I really must be getting along. I did so enjoy the trip and the company. We must do it again soon." She heaved herself to her feet and looked around. "Now, where did I leave my coat?"

"I hung it in the hallway," Veronica said, getting up. She walked ahead and out the door while Mrs. Crayford waddled a few feet behind. "Don't bother bringing anything out, Celia," Veronica's voice called back. "I'll come back in for the things."

Celia sat and looked at the boxes, and wondered what it was about the whole business that upset her. It wasn't so much the spectacle of Mrs. Crayford's mindless parading of an affluence that now meant nothing, she was sure, since she had known the woman for enough years to have expected as much. Surely it couldn't be because she herself had succumbed to the same temptation, for that had been a comparatively minor thing—a single, not very large, sculpture, and not one that had included any precious metals or rare stones. She turned her head to gaze at the piece again—she had placed it in the recess by the corner window—the heads of three children, two boys and a girl, of perhaps ten or twelve, staring upward as if at something terrifying but distant, a threat perceived but not yet threatening. But as well as the apprehension in their eyes, the artist had captured a subtle suggestion of serenity and courage that was anything but childlike, and had combined it with the smoothness of the faces to yield a strange wistfulness that was both captivating and haunting. The piece was fifteen years old, the dealer in Franklin had told them, and had been made by one of the Founders. Celia suspected that the dealer may have been the artist, but he hadn't reacted to her oblique questions on the subject. Were the expressions on those faces affecting her for some reason? Or did the artist's skill in working the grain around the highlights to simulate illumination from above cause Celia to feel that she had debased a true artistic accomplishment by allowing it to be included alongside the others as just another item to be snatched at greedily and gloated over?

Veronica came back into the room and began picking up Mrs. Crayford's boxes. "It's all right. You stay there, Celia. I can manage." She saw the expression on Celia's face and smiled. Her voice dropped to a whisper. "I know—awful, isn't it. It's just a phase. She'll get over it."

"I hope so," Celia murmured.

Veronica paused as she was about to turn toward the door. "I'm beginning to miss being thrown out in the middle of the night. How's your handsome sergeant these days? You haven't finished with him, have you?"

Celia gave her a reproachful look. "Oh, come on . . . you know that was just a diversion. I haven't seen him for a while now, but then, everyone has been so busy. Finished? Not really . . . who knows?" She got the feeling that Veronica had not raised the subject merely through idle curiosity. She was right.

"I've got one too," Veronica whispered, bringing her face close to Celia's ear.

"What?"

"A new lover. What do you think?"

"Anyone I know?"

Veronica had to bite her lip to suppress the beginnings of a giggle. "A Chironian."

Celia's eyes opened wide. "You're kidding!"

"I'm not. He's an architect . . . and gorgeous! I met him in Franklin yesterday and stayed last night. It's so easy— they act as if it's perfectly natural . . . And they're *so* uninhibited!" Celia just gaped at her. Veronica winked and nodded. "Really. I'll tell you about it later. I'd better go."

"You bitch!" Celia protested. "I want to hear about it *now*."

Veronica laughed. "You'll have to eat your heart out wondering. Take care. I'll call you tonight."

When the others had gone, Celia sank back in her chair and started brooding again. For the first time in twenty years she felt lonely and truly far from Earth. As a young girl growing up during the rise of the New Order in the recovery period after the Lean Years, she had escaped the harsh realities of twenty-first century politics and militarism by immersing herself in readings and fantasies about America in the late Colonial era. Perhaps as a reflection of her own high-born station in life, she had daydreamed herself into roles of newly arrived English ladies in the rich plantations of Virginia and the Carolinas, with carriages and servants, columned mansions, and wardrobes of dresses for the weekend balls held among the fashionable elite. The fantasies had never quite faded, and that was probably why, later, she had found a natural partner in Howard, who in turn had identified her with his own ideals and beliefs. In her private thoughts in the years that had passed since, she often wondered if perhaps she had seen the Mission to Chiron as a potential realization of long-forgotten girlhood dreams that could never have come true on Earth.

Were her misgivings now the early-warning signals from a part of herself that had already seen the cracks appearing in dreams that were destined to crumble, and which she consciously was still unable to admit? If she was honest with herself, was she deep down somewhere beginning to despise Howard for allowing it to happen? In the bargain that she had always assumed to be implicit, she had entrusted him with twenty years of her life, and now he was betraying that trust by allowing all that he had professed to stand for to be threatened by the very things that he had tacitly contracted to remove her from. Everywhere Terrans were rushing headlong to throw off everything that they had fought and struggled to preserve and carry with them across four light-years of space, and hurl themselves into

Chironian ways. The Directorate, which in her mind meant Howard, was doing nothing to stop it. She had once read a quotation by a British visitor, Janet Schaw, to the Thirteen Colonies in 1763, who had remarked with some disapproval on the "most disgusting equality" that she had observed prevailing on all sides. It suited the present situation well.

She swallowed as she traced through her thoughts and checked herself. She was rationalizing or hiding something from herself, she knew. Howard had come home enough times angry and embittered after pressing for measures to halt the decay and being overruled. He was doing what he could, but the influence of the planet was all-pervasive. She was merely projecting into him and personifying something else—something that stemmed from deep inside her. Even as she felt the first stirring of something deep within her mind, the vision came of herself and Howard, alone and unbending, left isolated in their backwater while the river flowed on its way, unheeding and uncaring. After twenty years, nothing lay ahead but emptiness and oblivion. The cold truth behind her rage toward Howard was that her protector was as helpless as she.

Now she knew why Earth seemed so far away. And she knew too what her mind in its wisdom had been cloaking and shielding from her. It was fear.

Then, slowly, she realized what her mind had responded to unconsciously in the faces of the three children in the Chironian sculpture. The artist had been not merely an expert, but a master. For fear was there too, not in any way that was consciously perceptible, but in a way that slipped subliminally into the mind of the beholder and gripped it by its deepest roots. That was why she had felt disturbed all the way back from Franklin. But there was still something else. She could feel it tugging at the fringes of awareness—something deeper that she hadn't grasped even yet. She turned her eyes to the sculpture again.

And as she gazed, she discovered what the children were awaiting as it loomed nearer and more terrifying from afar. The realization tightened her stomach. Even from fifteen years ago . . . it was she—for she had come with the *Mayflower II*. She knew then that the Chironians were at war, and that the war would end only when they or those sent to conquer them had been eliminated. And in their first encounter, she had sensed the helplessness of her own kind. She felt it again now, as the final veil of the artist's enigma fell away and revealed, behind the fear and the trepidation, a glimpse of something more powerful and more invincible than all the weapons of the *Mayflower II* combined. She was staring at her own extinction.

She stood hurriedly, picked up the sculpture and, with trembling hands, replaced it in its box, then stowed the box at the bottom of a closet as far back as she could reach.

CHAPTER SIXTEEN

PORT NORDAY WAS twenty-five miles or so north of Franklin, beyond the far headland of Mandel Bay, on a rocky stretch of coastline indented by a river estuary that widened about a large island and several smaller ones. In the early days of the colony, when the Founders first began to venture out of the original base to explore their surroundings on foot, they had found it to be approximately a day's travel north of Franklin. Hence its name.

It had grown in stages from constructions that began toward the end of the colony's first decade, by which time the Founders, having profited from reflections on some of their experiences at Franklin, had been more inclined to follow the blunt admonition offered by the machines, which had amounted to, "It's going to be an industrial complex. If you mess around with it, it won't work." The result was a clean, efficient, functional layout more in keeping with what the *Kuan-yin*'s mission planners had envisaged, suitably modified where appropriate to take account of local conditions. Besides its industrial facilities, the complex included a seaport; an air and space terminal distributed mainly across the islands, which were interconnected by a network of tunnels; a college of advanced technology; and a small residential sector intended more to afford short- to medium-term accommodation for people whose business made it convenient for them to be in the vicinity than to house permanent inhabitants, although about half the population had been there for years. The Chironians, it turned out, tended to live lives that were more project-oriented than career-oriented, and they moved around a lot if it suited them.

149

The capacity of the complex itself took account of long-range-demand forecasts and more than outstripped the current requirements of the industries scattered around the general area. Its primary power source was a one-thousand-gigawatt, magnetically confined fusion system which combined various features of the tokamak, mirror, and "bumpy torus" configurations pioneered toward the end of the previous century, producing electricity very efficiently by blasting high-velocity, high-temperature, ionized plasma through a series of immense magnetohydrodynamic coils. In addition, the fast neutrons produced in copious amounts from this process were harnessed to breed more tritium fuel from lithium, to breed fissionable isotopes of uranium and plutonium from fertile elements obtained elsewhere in the same complex, and to "burn up" via nuclear transmutation the small amounts of radioactive wastes left over from the economy's fission component, the fuel cycle of which was fully closed and included complete reprocessing and recycling of reactor products.

The plasma emerged from this primary process with sufficient residual energy to provide high-quality heat for supplying a hydrogen-extraction plant, where seawater was "cracked" thermally to yield bases for a whole range of liquid synthetic fuels, a primary-metals extraction and processing subcomplex, a chemical-manufacturing subcomplex, and a desalination plant which was still not operational, but anticipated large-scale irrigation projects farther inland in years to come.

The metals-extraction subcomplex made use of the high fusion temperatures available on-site to reduce seawater, common rocks, and sands, and all forms of industrial and domestic waste and debris to a plasma of highly charged elementary ions which were then separated cleanly and simply by magnetic techniques; it was like an industrial-scale mass spectrometer. In the chemicals subcomplex a range of compounds such as fertilizers, plastics, oils, fuels, and feedstocks for an assortment of dependent industries were also formed primarily by recombining reactants from the plasma state under conditions in which the plasma radiation was tuned to peak in a narrow frequency band

that favored the formation of desired molecules and opti-
mized yields without an excess of unwanted by-products,
which was far more efficient than using broad-band thermal
sources of combining energy. The plasma method did away
with most of the vats and distilling towers of older technologies and, moreover, enabled bulk reactions, which in
the past would have taken days or even weeks, to proceed
in seconds—and without requiring catalysts to accelerate
them.

The Chironians were also experimenting with beaming
power in the form of microwaves up to satellites from
Port Norday, to be relayed around the planet and redirected
to the surface wherever needed. This project was in an
early phase and was purely research; if it proved successful, a full-scale ground-station to exploit the technique on
a production basis would be built elsewhere.

Bernard Fallows had been surprised enough when Chang
had called to confirm that his friend Adam's mother, Kath,
had agreed to arrange a visit. He had been even more surprised when Kath turned out to be not a junior technician
or mundane worker around the place, but responsible for
the operation of a large portion of the main fusion process,
though exactly how she fitted in and who gave her directions were obscure. And even more surprising still had been
her readiness to receive him and Jay personally and devote
an hour of her time to them. The comparable prospect of
Leighton Merrick showing Chang and friends round the
main-drive section of the *Mayflower II* was unthinkable. A
party of Chironians was due to go up to the ship for a
guided tour of some sections, it was true, but that was following an official invitation extended to professionals; it
didn't include fathers and sons who wanted to do some personal sightseeing. Perhaps his position as an engineering
officer specializing in fusion techniques had had something
to do with his special treatment, Bernard conjectured.

There didn't seem to be any concept of rank or status
here. Bernard had seen orders being given and accepted
without question, sure enough, but the roles appeared to
be purely functional and capable of being interchanged
freely depending on who was considered best qualified to

take command of the particular subject at issue. This seemed to be decided by an unspoken consensus which the Chironians appeared somehow to have evolved without the bickerings, jealousies, and conflicts that Bernard would have thought inevitable. As far as he could make out there was no absolute, top-down hierarchical structure at all. It was a microcosm of the whole planet, he was beginning to suspect. Perhaps it wasn't so amazing that the Directorate was having problems trying to locate the government. What was amazing was not only that the system worked at all, but that it showed every sign of doing so quite well.

"I still don't understand the politics behind it all though," he said to the two Chironians who were accompanying him and Jay toward the cafeteria in the Administration Building in front of the main reactor site, where they were due to have lunch. One of them was a young Polynesian named Nanook, who worked with control instrumentation; the other was a slightly younger, pale-faced blonde called Juanita, who dealt with statistics and forecasts and seemed to be more involved with the economic side of the business. Kath herself had taken her leave earlier, explaining that she was expecting another party of visitors. Bernard spread his hands in an imploring gesture. "I mean . . . who owns the place? Who decides the policies for running it?"

The two Chironians frowned at each other. "Owns it?" Juanita repeated. Her voice suggested that the notion was a new one. "I'm not all that sure what you mean. The people who work here, I guess."

"But who decides who works here? Who appoints them to their jobs?"

"They do. How could it be up to anyone else?"

"But that ridiculous! What's to stop anyone walking in off the street from giving orders?"

"Nothing," Juanita said. "But why would they? Who'd take any notice of them?"

"So how does anyone know who to listen to?" Jay asked, every bit as mystified as his father.

"They soon find out," Juanita said it as if it explained everything.

They entered the cafeteria, which was fairly busy since

it was around midday, and sat by a window overlooking a parking area for flyers, beyond which lay a highway flanking the near bank of the river. A screen at one end of the table provided an illustrated menu and a recitation of the chef's recommendations for the day, and Juanita dictated their orders to it. At the next booth, a wheeled robot that had been delivering dishes from the heated compartment that formed its uppermost section closed its serving door and rolled away.

Bernard wasn't getting through, he could see. "Take Kath as an example," he said, turning toward Nanook. "A lot of people around here seem to accept her as . . . boss, for want of a better word . . . for a lot of things, anyhow."

Nanook nodded. "Right. I do most of the time."

"Because she knows what she's talking about, right?" Bernard said.

"Sure. Why else?"

"So suppose someone else showed up who thought he knew just as much. What if half the people around here thought so too, and the others didn't? Who decides? How would you resolve something like that?"

Nanook rubbed his chin and looked dubious. "That situation sounds very farfetched," he said after a few seconds. "I can't see how anyone else could walk in with the same experience. But if it did happen, and it was true . . . then I suppose Kath would have to agree with him. She'd be indebted by that amount. And that would decide it for everyone else."

Bernard stared at him in open disbelief. "You're not saying she'd simply back down? That's crazy!"

"We all have to pay our debts," Nanook said unhelpfully.

"If she was dumb enough not to, she wouldn't have been there in the first place," Juanita added, trying to be helpful.

That didn't explain anything. Jay couldn't see it either. "Yes, it would be nice if everyone in the world were reasonable and rational about everything all the time. But they can't be, can they? Chironians have the same mix of genes as everyone else. There can't be anything radically different."

"I never said there was," Nanook answered.

"So what about the nuts?" Jay asked. "What do you do about people who insist on being as unreasonable and obnoxious as they can, just for the hell of it?"

"We get them," Nanook agreed. "But not a lot. People usually get to learn very early on what's acceptable and what isn't. They've all got eyes, ears, and brains."

"But Jay's still got a point," Bernard said, glancing at his son and nodding "What about the people who won't use them?"

"We don't get a lot of those," Nanook told them again. "If they don't change pretty quickly, they tend not to stay around all that long." Juanita looked from Bernard to Jay as if satisfied that everything was now clear. It wasn't.

"Why? What happens with them?" Bernard asked.

Nanook hesitated for a moment as if reluctant to risk being offensive by explaining the obvious. He shrugged. "Well . . . usually somebody ends up shooting them," he replied. "So it never gets to be a real problem."

For a few seconds Bernard and Jay were too stunned to say anything. "But . . . that's crazy," Bernard protested at last. "You can't just let everybody go round shooting anyone they don't like."

"What else can you do?" Juanita asked.

"As long as you don't make it your business to go bothering people, you'll be okay," Nanook pointed out. "So it never affects most people. And when it happens . . . it happens."

After a few seconds of silence Jay conceded, "Okay, I can see how it might be a good way of getting rid of the odd freak here and there. But what do you do when a whole bunch of them get together?"

"How can they when there are hardly any around to start with?" Juanita asked him. "We told you—if they're like that, they don't last very long."

"And in any case, whatever would a bunch like that want to get together for?" Nanook asked.

Jay shrugged. "All the things crazy people usually follow crazy leaders for, I guess."

"Like what?" Nanook asked.

Jay shrugged again. "Protection, maybe."

"What from?"

A good point, Jay admitted to himself. "Security?" he tried. "To get rich . . . Whatever."

"They've already got security," Nanook declared. "And if they're not rich enough already, how is some crazy supposed to help?"

Bernard threw up his hands in exasperation. "Well, hell, let's say because they're just plain crazy. They don't need any reason. Never mind why, but let's say it's happened. What do you do?"

Nanook sighed heavily. "We have had one or two things like that from time to time," he confessed. "But it never lasts. In the end a bigger bunch gets itself together and gets rid of them. It comes to the same thing—they end up getting shot anyhow."

Jay looked worried, and Bernard appalled. "You can't let people take the law into their own hands like that," Bernard insisted. "Unchecked violence—mob rule—God alone knows what else. It's plain uncivilized—barbaric. You're going to have to change the system sooner or later."

"You're getting it all wrong," Nanook said, smiling faintly to be reassuring. "It's not so bad. Things like that don't happen all the time—in fact, hardly ever. Just sometimes . . ."

Juanita saw the expressions on Bernard's and Jay's faces. "Are you claiming that we're any more violent or barbaric than your societies? We've never had a war. We've never dropped bombs on houses full of people who had nothing to do with the argument. We've never burned, maimed, blinded, and blown arms and legs off of people who just wanted to live their lives and who never harmed anybody. We've never shot anyone who didn't ask for it. Can you say the same? Okay, so the system's not perfect. Is yours?"

"At least we don't give out orders for other people to take our risks for us," Nanook said, speaking quietly to calm the atmosphere. Juanita was starting to get emotional. "The people who take the risks are the ones who believe it's worth it. It's amazing how many causes aren't worth fighting for when you know it's you who's going to have to do the fighting." He shook his head slowly. "No, we don't get too much of that kind of thing."

"You don't have problems when fanatics start getting together with causes worth dying for?" Jay asked.

Nanook shifted his eyes and shook his head again. "Fanatics are gullible fools. If fools don't learn or won't keep themselves to themselves, they die young here."

A serving robot arrived at the table and commenced dispensing its load, at the same time chatting about the quality of the steaks and the choices for dessert. Bernard turned to stare out of the window and think. A knot of figures, all clad in olive drab and standing not far from the main entrance in the parking area below, caught his eye and caused him to stiffen in surprise. They were wearing uniforms—U.S. Army uniforms. Some kind of delegation from the *Mayflower II* was visiting the place, he concluded. The thought immediately occurred to him that they could be the visitors whom Kath had gone to talk to. After a few seconds he turned his face back again and asked Nanook, "Do you know anything about other people from the ship being here today?"

Nanook looked mildly surprised. "Sure. I thought you'd know about it. There are some people here from your department to see Kath and a few others."

"My department?"

"Engineering. That's the one you're with, isn't it?"

Bernard frowned suddenly. "Yes, it is. And I didn't know about it." His concern intensified as the implications sank in. "Who are they?"

"Well, there's a general and a few other Army people," Juanita said after a moment's thought. "And from Engineering there's a . . . Merrick—Leighton Merrick, that's right." She looked at Nanook. "And one called Walters, wasn't there . . . and some other guy . . ."

"Hoskins," Nanook supplied.

"Yes, Frank Hoskins," Juanita said. "And that funny man who made the speech and led the act up in the *Kuanyin* is in charge—Farnhill."

Bernard's concern changed to a deep, uneasy suspicion as he listened. Walters and Hoskins were his equals in rank and duties; this could only mean that he had been left out of something deliberately. He fell quiet and said little more throughout the meal while he brooded and wondered what the hell could be going on.

"I bet she does," Stanislau maintained. "They all do. Carson made it last night with a chick at Canaveral."

"Who says?" Driscoll demanded.

"He did. She's got a place in the city—just across from the base."

"Carson doesn't know what to do with it," Driscoll scoffed derisively. "He still thinks it's for playing with."

"I'm just telling you what the guy said."

"Oh, in that case it just has to be true, doesn't it. Now tell me that Swyley's color-blind."

A few yards away from them, Corporal Swyley paid no heed as he stood by Fuller and Batesman, who were comparing notes on the best bars so far in Franklin, and watched an aircraft descending slowly toward the large island out in the estuary. He couldn't see any reason why travel shouldn't come free on Chiron, just like everything else, and wondered what kinds of connections could be made from Port Norday to the more remote reaches of the planet. Interesting. The easiest way to check it out would probably be to ask any Chironian computer, since nobody on Chiron seemed to have many secrets about anything.

Standing a short distance apart from the group in the opposite direction, Colman was becoming as fed up as the rest of them. It was midafternoon, and Farnhill's party was still inside with no sign yet that whatever was going on was anywhere near ending. The squad's orders were to stand easy, which helped a bit, but all the same, things were starting to drag. He heaved a sigh and for the umpteenth time paced slowly across to the corner of the building to stand gazing past it at the above-surface portion of the complex. Behind him, Driscoll and Stanislau stopped talking about Carson's sex life abruptly as two Chironians stopped by on their way to the main entrance.

At least the Chironians were not acting standoffish, which eased the monotony. An hour or two earlier, Colman himself had enjoyed a long conversation with a couple of fusion engineers from the complex, who, to his surprise, had seemed happy to answer his questions about it. They had even offered him a quick tour. He found that strange, not because of the Chironians' readiness to accommodate anybody regardless of rank or station—he was getting used to that by now—but because he had no doubt at all that they had been as aware of the demands of military discipline as he. Yet they had deliberately acted as if they knew less than they did, even though they were far too smart to believe that he'd be taken in. The Chironians did it all the time. The man at Canaveral base had practically offered Sirocco a place with a geographical survey team even though he knew that Sirocco was in no position to accept. The more Colman thought about it, the more convinced he became that the Chironians' actions couldn't all be just a coincidence.

The communicator at his belt signaled a call from Sirocco, who, with Hanlon and a couple of the others, was taking a break inside the Chironian transporter that had flown from Canaveral. "How's it going?" Sirocco inquired when Colman answered. "Are the troops mutinying yet?"

"Grumbling, but not too bad. Any news from inside?"

"Nothing yet. It's about time you took a breather. I'll be out in a few minutes to take a spell with Carson and Young. Tell Swyley and Driscoll to stand down with you. They've been out there the longest."

"Will do. See you in a few minutes."

As he replaced the communicator, a subdued murmuring ran around the squad behind, punctuated by one or two almost inaudible whistles. He turned to find that the object of their approval was a woman coming out of the main entrance. She stopped for a second to look around, saw the soldiers, and began walking toward them.

She was in her late thirties—evidently one of the Founders—and carried herself with a stately elegance that was proud and upright without crossing the boundary into haughtiness. Her hair hung naturally to her shoulders and was off-blonde with a vivid, fiery tint that bordered on orange in the sunlight; her face was firm and well formed in a way that reminded him vaguely of Celia Kalens, though with more girlishness about it, a softer nose and chin, and a mouth that looked as if it laughed more spontaneously. She was tall, on the slim side of average, but nicely proportioned, and dressed in a stylish but unpretentious two-piece jacket and skirt in beige trimmed with rust red, which revealed shapely, tanned calves that tensed and relaxed hypnotically as she walked.

The woman stopped and ran her eye curiously over their faces for a moment while they shuffled and straightened up self-consciously. "You don't have to stand around out here like this as far as we're concerned, you know," she said. "You can come on inside if you want. How about a coffee, and maybe something to eat?" The faces turned instinctively toward Colman as he rejoined them.

He started to grin automatically. "That's a nice thought, ma'am, but we're under orders and have to stay here. We appreciate it though." And then he frowned. It was happening again. She knew damn well they had to stay there.

Her eyes rested momentarily on his chevrons. "Are you Sergeant Colman—the one who's interested in engineering?"

Colman stared hard at her in surprise. "Yes, I am. How—"

"I've heard about you." It could only have been from the Chironians he had talked with earlier. Why would they mention his name to her? Who was she? She came nearer and smiled. "My name is Kath. I have some connection with the technical aspects of what goes on here. From what I've heard, I'd imagine you'd find this an interesting place. Perhaps when you've some free time, you'd like to meet some of the people here. If you like, I could mention it to them."

Colman was nonplussed. He shook his head as if to clear it. "What—What exactly do you do around here?"

Kath's smile became impish, as if she were amused by his confusion. "Oh, you'd be surprised."

Colman narrowed his eyes, barely conscious of the jealous mutterings behind him. "Well . . . sure," he said cautiously. "If it wouldn't be any trouble to anyone. You must have talked to the two guys who were here earlier."

Kath nodded. "Wally and Sam. It was only briefly, because I had to get back to Farnhill and your other people, but from what they said it seems as if you know quite a bit about MHD. Where did you study?"

"Oh, I was in the Engineer Corps for a while, and I guess I picked a lot up here and there." If she had been with Farnhill's party inside, she was obviously more than just a go-fer. Why in hell did she come out to the parking lot to be nice to the troops?

"How many other engineers do you have here?" she inquired lightly, looking around the rest of the squad. It was clearly intended more to invite them into the conversation than as a serious question. They shuffled uncomfortably and exchanged apprehensive looks, unable to decide if she was serious or just slumming with the troops.

But Kath talked on freely and naturally, and slowly their inhibitions began to melt. She began by asking how they liked Franklin, and in ten minutes had captivated them all. Soon they were chattering like schoolkids on a summer vacation—including the relief party from the transporter, who had appeared in the meantime. The detail due for a break seemed to have forgotten about it. Something very strange was going on, Colman told himself again.

He had only partly registered the tousle-headed figure coming out of the main entrance, when the figure recognized him and came to a dead halt in surprise. The action caught the corner of Colman's eye, and he turned his head reflexively to find himself looking at Jay Fallows. Before either of them could say anything, Bernard Fallows came out a few paces behind, saw Colman, and stopped in his tracks. It was too late for him to go back in, and impossible to walk on by. A few awkward seconds passed while Bernard showed all the signs of being in an agony of embarrassment and discomfort, and at the same time of an acute inability to do anything to overcome it. Colman didn't feel he had any prerogative to make a first move. Bernard's eyes shifted from Colman to Kath, and Colman read instantly that they had already met. Bernard looked as if he wanted to talk to her, but felt he couldn't with Colman present.

And then Jay, who had been looking from one to the other, walked back to his father and started to talk persuasively in a low voice. Bernard hesitated, looked across at Colman again, and then took a deep breath and came haltingly across with Jay beside him. "It's been a long time," he mumbled. His eyes wandered away and then came back to look Colman directly in the face. "Look, Steve, about that time up on the ship in the pump bay. I, er . . . I—"

"Forget it," Colman interrupted. "It happens to everyone. Let's leave it with all the other stuff that's best left up there."

Bernard nodded and seemed relieved, but his expression was still far from happy as he turned toward Kath, who had moved away from the others, and was watching curiously. Bernard seemed to want to say something that he didn't know how to begin.

Jay was evidently developing a feel for Chironian directness. "We're kind of curious about the people inside," he said. "Especially my dad. It's funny that he wasn't told anything about it."

Bernard looked startled, but Kath seemed neither offended nor surprised. "I thought you might be," she said, nodding half to herself. "Nanook told me about that." She looked at Bernard. "We don't have a lot of time for secrets," she told him. "Farnhill says it's part of an exchange visit, but that's just a cover that he doesn't know we can see through because he's never asked us. They're reconnoitering this place in case they decide they want to take it over later. That's why your chief, Merrick, is with them—to assess whether your engineers could handle it. He's picked Walters and Hoskins to put in here if the Directorate goes ahead with the idea."

Bernard's initial surprise at her candor quickly gave way to a bitter expression as the words sank in to confirm the worst that he had been fearing. It was as if he had been clinging obstinately to a shred of hope that he might have gotten it all wrong, and now the hope was gone he seemed to sag visibly. Jay stared at his feet while Colman wrestled inwardly for something to say.

Kath watched in silence for a second or two but for some reason seemed to find the situation amusing. Bernard stared with a mixture of uncertainty and resentment. "I think I know what's going through your mind," she told him. "But don't worry about it. We don't take orders from Farnhill or Merrick here. Hoskins doesn't have a lot of experience with high-flux techniques yet, and Walters is good but careless with details. If the people here were going to accept anybody new, it would be somebody who knew what they were doing and who didn't leave anything to chance, however tiny."

"Just . . . what are you getting at?" Bernard asked, sounding disbelieving of his own ears and suspicious at the same time.

Kath switched on her impish smile again. "That's all I'm prepared to say," she replied. "For now, anyway. I just thought you'd like to hear it." She turned to Jay to change the subject. "Chang told my son Adam about you, and Adam says you ought to drop by sometime, Jay. He lives in Franklin, so it wouldn't be far. Why don't you do that?"

"Sounds great. I will. How do I get directions—from the net?"

"You've got it." Kath smiled.

Jay glanced at Colman, then looked at Bernard. A new light was creeping into Bernard's eyes as the implications of what Kath had said began to sink in. Jay hesitated, then decided that his father was in the right mood. "You know, this is a bit of a risky place, Dad," he said in an ominous voice. "People getting shot all over the place and stuff like that. I could run into all kinds of trouble on my own. I'm sure you'd feel a lot happier if I had some professional protection."

Bernard looked at him suspiciously. "Just what are you up to now?"

Jay grinned, just a trifle sheepishly. "Er . . . would you get mad if I asked Steve to come along too?"

"I'm sure Adam would be more than happy," Kath interjected. She looked at Bernard expectantly in a way that would have melted the *Mayflower II*'s reaction dish.

Bernard looked from Kath, to Colman, to Jay, and then back to Colman. He was beaten, and he knew it. But after Kath's cryptic statement, he wasn't inclined to argue too much. "Hell, it's not so bad. He doesn't need anyone to stop him from getting shot," he replied. Beside him, Jay's face dropped. Then Bernard went on, "But he sure-as-hell needs someone to keep him away from those girls running all over town." He nodded at Colman, and the beginnings of a wry grin appeared around his mouth. "Keep a good eye on him, Steve. He's crafty." He turned his head and stared resignedly at his son. "And you," he grunted. "Get home on time, and don't say anything about this to your mother."

CHAPTER SEVENTEEN

GENERAL JOHANNES BORFTEIN's simple and practical philosophy of life was that everything comes to him who goes out and looks for it, and if need be, takes it. Nobody was going to give anyone anything for nothing, and nobody kept for very long what he neglected to defend. The name of the game was Survival. He hadn't made up the rules; they had been written into Nature long before he existed.

Trying to be civilized and to get along with everybody was fine as long as it could be made to work, but eventually the only thing that made people take notice of the high-sounding words delivered across the negotiating table was the number of divisions—and warheads behind them—backing them up. And if, when all else failed, the only way left for a nation to look after its interests was to defend them by force, then the best chance for survival lay with promoting the cause totally and using every expedient that came at hand; half measures were fatal.

The shorter-term price to be paid was regrettable, but when had Nature ever offered free lunches? And in the longer term, what did it mean anyway? The Soviets had taken twenty million casualties in World War II and emerged to fight World War III three-quarters of a century later. And in that conflict the U.S. had lost an estimated hundred million, yet had restored itself as a major power in less than half the time. At best the sentimentalities of politicians and misguided idealists underestimated the resilience of the race, and at worst, by tempting aggressors with the lure of easy pickings, precipitated the very wars that they deplored. Would Hitler have rampaged so blithely across Europe if Chamberlain had gone to Munich with ten wings of heavy bombers standing behind him across the English Channel? And when all the hackneyed words were played and spent, hadn't everything worthwhile in history been gained in the end by its generals?

Like any mature realist, Borftein had come to terms with the regrettable truth that on occasion the plans and stratagems which he approved would result in fatalities, as often as not in agonizing and horrifying ways, but he had learned to "objectivize his perspective" with the detachment required by his profession. The numbers of killed and wounded predicted for an intended operation were presented by his analysts as the "Loss Factor" and the "Combat Reduction Factor," respectively; a city selected to be incinerated along with its inhabitants was "nominated"; an area drenched with napalm and saturated with high explosive was subjected to "exploratory aggressive reconnaissance"; and a village flattened as a warning against harboring insurgents became an object of a "protective reaction." Such were the rules.

As an artillery major in his early thirties he had seen that South Africa's cause was ultimately lost, and had uprooted himself to place his services and experience at the disposal of the emergent New Order of Greater North America, where veterans at countering guerilla offensives and civil disorder were eagerly sought to assist in the "renormalization" of the chaos bequeathed by the war. Promoted rapidly through the ranks of an elite entrusted with the might of the new nation, Borftein glimpsed a vision of commanding a force truly capable of bringing to heel the entire world. But the vision had been short-lived. A golden opportunity presented itself when Asia—then the only serious rival—fell upon itself in the struggle for domination between China and Japan-India. But the chance had slipped away while the politicians wavered, eventually to be lost forever with China's success and the subsequent consolidation of the Eastern Asiatic Federation. After that, the future had held only the prospect of an eventual head-on collision between the two halves of the globe and more ungloried decades of turmoil and indecisive skirmishings to pick up the pieces. Conditions for launching a worldwide Grand

Design would not come again in his lifetime. And so he had left to seek a more rewarding destiny with the *Mayflower II*. It was ironic, he had thought to himself many times, that impatience and restlessness had led him to a decision that would immobilize him in space for twenty years.

His impatience was asserting itself again now, as Borftein sat in the chambers of Judge William Fulmire, the *Mayflower II*'s Supreme Justice, listening to Howard Kalens and Marcia Quarrey argue over the finer points of the Mission's constitution, while on the surface the troops were fraternizing openly with what could become the enemy, and two years away in space the EAF starship daily drew nearer. The news from Earth told of a three-cornered conflict sweeping through eastern Africa, black nations clashing against Arabs in the north and whites in the south, Australian forces landing in Malagasay, and the Europeans maneuvering desperately to quell the flames while the EAF fanned them gleefully. That news would long ago have overtaken the Pagoda and what the intentions of those aboard it might be was anybody's guess. It wasn't a time to be fussing over ambiguous syntax and legal niceties.

Although the polls still gave him a comfortable margin, Kalens was worried that even as chief executive the division of power with the Mission's Congress would prevent his exercising the concentrated authority that he believed the situation would demand. Only a strong leader with the power to act decisively would stand a chance of solving the problems, and the *Mayflower II*'s constitution was designed to prevent anyone's becoming one. Its spirit was an anachronism inherited from antiquity when a newly founded Federation had sought to guard itself against a renewed colonialism, and the governing system embodied that spirit quite effectively. That was the problem.

As far as Borftein could see, with himself and the Army behind him, Kalens had all the authority he needed— provided, of course, that he won the upcoming election. But after talking to Sterm about it, Kalens had accepted that an attempt to impose authority over Chiron overtly would risk alienating the Mission's population. A more subtle approach was called for. "Ultimately, human instincts cling to the known and the familiar," Kalens lectured Borftein later. "A visible commitment to lawfulness as a alternative to the lawlessness of this planet is the way to maintain cohesiveness. We can't afford to jeopardize that." So Borftein had agreed to try playing the game their way, which hinged upon provisions written into the laws to take account of the abnormal circumstances of a twenty-year voyage through space.

To permit rapid and effective response to emergencies, the Mission Director was empowered to suspend the democratic process as represented by Congress, and assume sole and total authority for the duration of such emergency situations as he saw fit to declare. Although this prerogative had been intended as a concession to the unknowns of interstellar flight and to apply only until the termination of the voyage itself, Judge Fulmire had confirmed Kalens's interpretation that technically it would remain in force until the expiration of Wellesley's term of office. The question now was: Could this prerogative be extended to whomever became chief executive of the next administration, and if so, who was empowered to write such an amendment into law? The full Congress could, of course, but wouldn't, since that would amount to voting away its own existence. Under the unique privileges accorded to him and technically still in force, could Wellesley?

Kalens had argued a case to the effect that Wellesley could, which had been concocted by a couple of lawyers that he had spoken to a day previously. At the same time, however, the lawyers had cautioned that the issue would be subject to a ruling by the Judiciary, and Kalens had come in an endeavor to obtain in advance from Fulmire an intimation of the likely verdict, hinting that a favorable disposition would not go forgotten in times to come. The endeavor had backfired spectacularly.

"I will not be a party to such shenanigans!" the Judge exclaimed. "This is all highly irregular, as you well know. A ruling must be subject to all due process, and only to all due process. There the matter must remain. What you are asking is inexcusable."

"Our own people have a right to expect the protection

of a properly constituted legal system, and this planet fails even to possess one," Kalens argued. "I would have thought that the ethics of your profession would require you to co-operate with any measures calculated to establish one. The purpose of this provision is precisely that."

"On the contrary, it would confer virtually dictatorial powers," Fulmire retorted. "There can be no validity in a legality established by illegal means."

"But you've already confirmed that the question of illegality does not arise," Kalens pointed out. "The emergency clauses apply until the elections have been held."

"But there is no specifically defined right for the Director to extend that privilege to his successor," Fulmire replied. "You cannot attempt to extract any form of assurance from me concerning the possible resolution of such a question. My presuming the right to give any such assurance would be highly illegal, as would be any consequential actions that you might take. I repeat, I have no more to say."

"Then invoke the security provisions," Borftein said, shifting in his chair from weariness with the whole business. "It's a security matter, isn't it? The Chironians have left it to us by default, and it's their security at stake as well as ours. The Pagoda's only two years away. Somebody's got to take the helm in all this."

Fulmire gestured over the books and documents spread across his desk. "The security provisions provide for Congress to vote exceptional powers to the Directorate in the event of demonstrable security demands, and for the Directorate to delegate extraordinary duties to the chief executive once *they* are voted that power. They do not provide for the chief executive to assume such duties for himself, and therefore neither can he do so for his successor."

A short silence fell, and the deadlock persisted. Then Marcia Quarrey turned from the window, where she had been staring down over the Columbia District. "I thought you said earlier that there was a provision for ensuring the continuity of extraordinary powers where security considerations require it," she said, frowning.

"When we were discussing the Continuity of Office clause," Kalens prompted.

Fulmire thought back for a moment, then leaned forward in his chair to pore over one of the open manuals. "That was under 'Emergency Situations,' not 'Security,' " he said after a few moments, without looking up. "Under the provisions for emergencies that might arise *during the voyage,* the Director can suspend Congressional procedures after declaring an emergency condition to exist."

"Yes, we know that," Quarrey agreed. "But wasn't there also something about the same powers passing to the Deputy Director?"

Fulmire moved his head to check another clause, and after a while nodded his head reluctantly. "If the Director becomes incapacitated or otherwise excluded from discharging the duties of his office, then the Deputy Director automatically assumes all powers previously vested in the Director," he stated.

Kalens raised his head sharply. "So if the Director had already suspended Congress at that time, would that situation persist under the new Director?" He thought for a moment, then added, "I would assume it must, surely. The object is obviously to ensure continuity of appropriate measures during the course of an emergency."

Fulmire looked uneasy but in the end was forced to nod his agreement. "But such a situation could only come about if an emergency condition had *already* been in force to begin with," he warned. "It could not be applied in any way to the present circumstances."

"You don't think that a ship full of Asiatics coming at us armed to the teeth qualifies as an emergency?" Borftein asked sarcastically.

"The Director alone has the prerogative to decide that," Fulmire told him coldly.

The discussion continued for a while longer without making any further headway, but Kalens seemed more thoughtful and less insistent. Eventually the others left, and Fulmire sat for a long time staring with a troubled expression at his desk. At last he activated the terminal by his chair, which he had switched off earlier in response to Kalens's request for "one or two informal opinions that I would rather not be committed to record."

"Which service?" the terminal inquired.

"Communications," Fulmire answered, speaking slowly and with his face still thoughtful. "Find Paul Lechat for me and put him through if he's free, would you. And route this via a secured channel."

CHAPTER EIGHTEEN

"THE THING I still can't understand is what motivates these people," Colman remarked to Hanlon as they walked with Jay to Adam's house. "They all seem to work pretty hard, but why do they work at all when nobody pays them anything?"

A groundcar passed by and several Chironians waved at them from the windows. "It can't be quite like that," Jay said. "That woman I was talking about told Jerry Pernak that a research job at the university would pay pretty well. That must have meant something."

"Well, it sure doesn't pay any money." Colman turned his head toward Hanlon. "What do you say, Bret?"

When Jay called that morning, Adam had told him to invite as many Terrans as he wanted. Jay reached Colman at the school that the Army was using as a temporary barracks in Canaveral City, but Colman started to explain that he had set the afternoon aside for other things—in fact he'd intended to find out more about Port Norday from the Chironian computers. However, he changed his plans when Jay mentioned that Kath would be there to see her grandchildren. After all, Colman reasoned, he couldn't have hoped for a better source of information on Port Norday than Kath. As Hanlon was off duty, Colman had invited him along too.

"I hope you're not expecting an answer," Hanlon said. "It makes about as much sense to me as Greek. . . ." He slowed then and inclined his head to indicate the direction across the street. "Now, there's the fella you should be asking," he suggested.

The other two followed his gaze to a Chironian wearing

coveralls and a green hat with a red feather in it, painting the lower part of a wall of one of the houses. Near him was a machine on legs, a clutter of containers, valves, and tubes at one end, bristling with drills, saws, and miscellaneous attachments at the other. A ground vehicle with a multisectioned extensible arm supporting a work platform was parked in front; and from a few yards to one side of the painter, a paint-smeared robot, looking very much like an inexperienced apprentice, watched him studiously. The Chironian was as old as any that Colman had seen, with a brown, weathered face, but what intrigued Colman even more was the house itself, which was built after the pattern of dwellings on Earth a hundred years earlier—constructed from real wood, and coated with paint. It was not the first such anachronism that he had seen in Franklin, where designs three centuries old coexisted quite happily alongside maglev cars and genetically modified plants, but he hadn't had an opportunity to stop and study one before.

The painter glanced across and noticed them watching. "Nice day," he commented and continued with his work. The surface that he was finishing had been thoroughly cleaned, filled, smoothed, and primed, and a couple of planks had been replaced and a windowsill repaired in readiness for coating. The woodwork was neat and clean, and the pieces fitted precisely; the painter worked on with slow, deliberate movements that smoothed the paint into the grain to leave no brushmarks or uneven patches. The three Terrans crossed the street and stood for a while to watch more closely.

"Nice job you're doing," Hanlon remarked at last.

"Glad you think so." The painter carried on.

"It's a pretty house," Hanlon said after another short silence.

"Yep."

"Yours?"

"Nope."

"Someone you know?" Colman asked.

"Kind of." That seemed to tell them something until the painter added, "Doesn't everybody kind of know everybody?"

Colman and Hanlon frowned at each other. Obviously they weren't going to get anywhere without being more direct. Hanlon wiped his palms on his hips. "We, ah . . . we don't mean to be nosy or anything, but out of curiosity, why are you painting it?" he asked.

"Because it needs painting."

"So why bother?" Jay asked. "What's it to you if somebody else's house needs painting or not?"

"I'm a painter," the painter said over his shoulder. "I like to see a paint job properly done. Why else would anyone do it?" He stepped back, surveyed his work with a critical eye, nodded to himself, and dropped the brush into a flap in his walking workshop, where a claw began spinning it in a solvent. "Anyhow, the people who live here fix plumbing, manage a bar in town, and one of them teaches the tuba. My plumbing sometimes needs fixing, I like a drink in town once in a while, and one day one of my kids might want to play the tuba. They fix faucets, I paint houses. What's so strange?"

Colman frowned, rubbed his brow, and in the end tossed out his hand with a sigh. "No . . . we're not making the right point somehow. Let's put it this way—how can you *measure* who owes who what?" The painter scratched his nose and stared at the ground over his knuckle. Clearly the notion was new to him.

"How do you know when you've done enough work?" Jay asked him, trying to make it simpler.

The painter shrugged. "You just know. How do you know when you've had enough to eat?"

"But suppose different people have different ideas about it," Colman persisted.

The painter shrugged again. "That's okay. Different people value things differently. You can't tell somebody else when they've had enough to eat."

Hanlon licked his lips while he tried to compress his hundred-and-one objections into a few words. "Ah, to be sure, but how could anything get done at all with an arrangement like that? Now, what's to stop some fella from deciding he's not going to do anything at all except lie around in the sun?"

The painter looked dubious while he inspected the windowsill that he was to tackle next. "That doesn't make much sense," he murmured after a while. "Why would somebody stay poor if he didn't have to? That'd be a strange kind of way to carry on."

"He wouldn't get away with it, surely," Jay said incredulously. "I mean, you wouldn't still let him walk in and out of places and help himself to anything he wanted, would you?"

"Why not?" the painter asked. "You'd have to feel kinda sorry for someone like that. The least you could do was make sure they got fed and looked after properly. We do get a few like that, and that's what happens to them. It's a shame, but what can anybody do?"

"You don't understand," Jay said. "On Earth, a lot of people would see that as their big ambition in life."

The painter eyed him for a moment and nodded his head slowly. "Mmm . . . I kinda figured it had to be something like that," he told them.

Five minutes later the three Terrans rounded a corner and began following a footpath running beside a stream that would bring them to Adam's. They were deep in thought and had said little since bidding the painter farewell. After a short distance Jay slowed his pace and came to a halt, staring up at a group of tall Chironian trees standing on the far side of the stream alongside a number of familiar elms and maples that were evidently imported— genetically modified by the *Kuan-yin*'s robots to grow in alien soil. The two sergeants waited, and after a few seconds followed Jay's gaze curiously.

The trunks of the Chironian trees were covered by rough overlapping plates that resembled reptilian scales more than bark, and the branches, clustered together high near the tops in a way reminiscent of Californian sequoias, curved outward and upward to support domed canopies of foliage like the caps of gigantic mushrooms. The foliage was green at the bottoms of the domes but became progressively more yellow toward the tops, around which several furry, cat-sized, flying creatures were wheeling in slow, lazy circles and keeping up a constant chattering among themselves. "You wouldn't think so, but that yellow stuff up there isn't part of those trees at all," Jay said, gesturing. "Jeeves told me about it. It's a completely different species—a kind of fern. Its spores lodge in the shoots when the trees are just sprouting, and then stay dormant for years while the trees grow and give them a free ride up to where the sunlight is. It invades the leaf-buds and feeds through the tree's vascular system."

"Mmm . . ." Colman murmured. Botany wasn't his line.

Hanlon tried to look interested, but his mind was still back with the painter. After a few seconds he looked at Colman. "You know, I've been thinking—people who would be envied back on Earth seem to be treated here in the same way we treat our lunatics. Do you think we're all crazy to the Chironians?"

"It's a thought," Colman replied vaguely. The same idea had crossed his mind while the painter was talking. It was a sobering one.

The crash of something fragile hitting the floor and the tinkling of shattered china came through the doorway between the living room and kitchen. Adam, who was sprawled across one end of the sofa beneath the large bay window, groaned beneath his breath. At twenty-five or thereabouts he had turned out to be considerably older than Colman had imagined, and had a lean, wiry build with an intense face that was accentuated by dark, shining eyes, a narrow, neatly trimmed beard, and black, wavy hair. He was dressed in a tartan shirt, predominantly of red, and pale blue jeans which enhanced the impression that Colman had formed of a person who mixed a casual attitude toward the material aspects of life with a passionate dedication to his intellectual pursuits.

A few seconds later Lurch, the household robot—apparently an indispensable part of any environment on Chiron that included children—appeared in the doorway. "It slipped," it announced. "Sorry about that, boss. I've wired off an order for a replacement."

Adam waved an arm resignedly. "Okay, okay. Never

mind the sackcloth-and-ashes act. How about cleaning it up?"

"Oh, yes. I should have thought of that." Lurch about-faced and lurched back to the kitchen. The sound of a door opening and the brief clatter of something being fumbled from a closet floated back into the room.

"Does it do that a lot?" Colman asked from his chair, which had been cleared of a pile of books and some stuffed birds to make room for him when they had arrived an hour or so earlier.

"It's a klutz," Adam said wearily. "It's got a glitch in its visual circuits somewhere . . . something like that. I don't know."

"Can't you get it fixed?" Colman asked.

Adam threw up his hands again. "The kids won't let me! They say it wouldn't be the same any other way. What can you do?"

"We couldn't let him do that, could we?" Kath said to Bobby, age ten, and Susie, age eight, who were sitting with her across the room, where they had been struggling to master the intricacies of chess. "Lurch is half the fun of coming here."

"You don't have to live with it, Mother," Adam told her.

Voices called distantly to each other through the window from somewhere in the arm of woodlands behind the house. Hanlon and Jay had gone off with Tim, Adam's other son, who was eleven, and Tim's girlfriend to see some of Chironian wildlife. Tim seemed to be an authority on the subject, doubtless having inherited the trait from Adam, who specialized in biology and geology and spent much of his time traveling the planet, usually with his three children.

Or, at least, the three that lived with him. Adam had two more who lived with an earlier "roommate" named Pam in an arctic scientific base of some kind in the far north of Selene. Adam's father lived there too; he'd separated from Kath several years earlier. Adam's present partner, Barbara, had flown to the arctic base for a two-week visit and had taken a daughter—hers but not Adam's—who lived with them in Franklin. Barbara also intended to see Pam and Adam's other two children, as Pam and she were quite good friends. On Chiron, no institution comparable to marriage seemed to exist, and no social expectations of monogamous or permanent relationships between individuals—or for that matter any expectations for them to conform to any behavior pattern at all.

Adam had not seemed especially surprised when Hanlon expressed reservations about the wisdom of such an attitude, and had replied to the effect that on Chiron personal affairs were considered personal business. Some couples might choose to remain exclusively committed to each other and their family, others might not, and it wasn't a matter for society or anybody else to comment on. As far as he was concerned, Adam had said, the notion of anybody's presuming to decree moral standards for others and endeavoring to impose them by legislation was "obscene."

Adam also had an older sister—to the surprise of the Terrans—who designed navigation equipment for spacecraft at an establishment located inland from the Peninsula, a twin brother who was an architect and rumored to be getting friendly with a lively redhead from the *Mayflower II* whom Colman couldn't place, a younger sister who lived with two other teenagers somewhere in Franklin, and a still younger half-brother, not a son of Kath's, who was with their father in Selene. It was all very confusing.

"But doesn't this kind of thing upset the kids when it happens?" Hanlon had asked uneasily.

"Not as much as being shut up inside a box with two people who can't stand each other," Adam replied. "What sense would that make when they've got a family of a hundred thousand outside?"

"We're dying to meet your sister, Jay," Tim's girlfriend had said, an arm slipped through Tim's on one side and Adam's on the other.

"Her mother's dying too," Jay had replied dryly.

Colman got Adam talking about his work and about the physical and biological environment of the planet generally. Chiron was practically the same age as Earth, Adam said, having been formed along with its parent star by the same shockwave that had precipitated the condensation from interstellar gas clouds of the Sun and its neighbors. It was an intriguing thought, Adam suggested, that the bodies of the people being born now on Chiron and on Earth all included heavy elements that had been formed in the same first-generation star—the one that had triggered the shock wave when it exploded as a supernova. "We might have been born light-years apart," he told Colman. "But the stuff we're made of came from the same place."

Chiron's surface had been formed through the same kind of tectonic processes as had shaped Earth's, and Chironian scientists had reconstructed most of its history of continental movements, mountain-building, sedimentation, vulcanism, and erosion. Like Earth, it possessed a magnetic field which reversed itself periodically and which had written a coherent story onto the moving seafloors as they spread outward and cooled from uplifts along oceanic ridges; the complicated tidal cycle induced by Chiron's twin satellites had been unraveled to yield the story of previous epochs of periodic inundation by the oceans; and analysis of the planet's seismic patterns had mapped its network of active transform faults and subduction zones, along which most of its volcanos and earthquake belts were located.

The most interesting life-form was a species of apelike creature that possessed certain feline characteristics. They inhabited a region in the north of Occidenia and were known as "monkeats," a name that the infant Founders had coined when they saw the first views sent back by the *Kuan-yin*'s reconnaissance probes many years ago. They were omnivores that had evolved from pure carnivores, possessed a highly developed social order, and were beginning to experiment with the manufacture of simple hand tools. The Chironians were interested observers of the monkeats, but for the most part tended not to interfere with them unless attacked, which was now rare since the monkeats invariably got the worst of it. Other notable dangerous life-forms include the daskrends, which Jay had already told Colman about, various poisonous reptiles and large insects that were concentrated mainly around southern Selene and the isthmus connecting it to Terranova, though some kinds did spread as far as the Medichironian, a flying mammal found in Artemia which possessed deadly talons and a fanged beak and would swoop down upon anything in sight, and a variety of catlike, doglike, and bearlike predators that roamed across parts of all four continents to a greater or lesser degree.

Colman remembered what Jay had said about the Chironian custom of going armed outside the settlements, and guessed that it traced back to the days when the Founders had first ventured out of the bases. Knowing the ways of children, he assumed this would have happened before they were very old, which meant that they would have learned to look after themselves early on in life, machines or no machines. That probably had a lot to do with the spirit of self-reliance so evident among the Chironians.

"How else could it be?" Adam said when Colman asked him about it. "Sure they had to learn how to use a gun. You know what kids are like. The machines couldn't be everywhere all the time. Ask my mother about it, not me."

Kath smiled on the other side of the room. "I was from the first batch to be created. There were a hundred of us. Leon—he's Adam's father—was another. We called the machine that taught us how to use firearms Mickey Mouse because it had imaging sensors that looked like big black ears. I shot a daskrend when I was six . . . or maybe less. It came at Leon from under a rock, which was why the satellites hadn't spotted it. He's still got a limp today from that." She emitted a soft chuckle. "Poor Leon. He reminds me of Lurch."

Colman's eyes widened for a moment as he listened. "I'd never really thought about it," he admitted. "But I guess, yes . . . it'd have to have been like that. Your kids today don't seem to have changed all that much either."

"How do you mean?" Kath asked.

Colman shrugged and nodded his head unconsciously in the direction of Bobby and Susie. "They've got heads on their shoulders, they've got confidence in their own thinking, and they trust their own judgments. That's good."

"Well, I'm pleased to hear that at least one Terran thinks so," Bobby said. "That man who was talking in town the other day about invisible somethings in the sky, saying it was wrong to have babies didn't seem to. He said we'd suffer forever after we were dead. How can he know? He's never been dead. It was ridiculous."

"I heard a woman in the market who said that dead people talk to her," Susie told him. "That's even more ridiculous."

"They're not all like that, are they?" Bobby asked, looking hopefully at Colman.

"Not all, I guess," Colman replied with a grin. He turned to Adam and then Kath. "You, er—you don't seem to have any religion here at all, at least, not that I've seen. Is that right?" Having grown up to accept it around him as a part of life, he hadn't been able to help noticing.

Adam seemed to think about it for a long time. "No . . ." he said slowly at last. "We're on our own on a grain of dust somewhere in a gas of galaxies. Inventing guardian angels for company won't change it. Whether we make it or not is up to us. If we mess it up, the universe out there won't miss us." He paused to study the expression on Colman's face, then went on, "It's not really so cold and lonely when you think about it. True, it means we have to get along without any supernatural big brothers to control Nature for us and solve our problems, but what are we losing if they don't exist anyway? On the other hand, we don't have to fear all the nonsense that gets invented along with them either. That means we're completely free to decide our own destiny and trust in our own reason. To me that's not such a bad feeling."

Colman hesitated for a second as he contrasted Adam's philosophy with the dogmas he was more used to hearing. "I, ah—I know a few people who would say that was pretty arrogant," he ventured.

"Arrogant?" Adam smiled to himself. "They're the ones who are so sure they 'know,' not me. I'm just making the best interpretation I can of the facts I've got." He thought for a moment longer. "Anyhow, arrogance and pride are not the same thing. I'm proud to be a human being, sure."

"They'd tell you modesty was a better virtue too," Colman said.

"It is," Adam agreed readily. "But modesty and self-effacement aren't the same thing either."

Colman looked unconsciously toward Kath for her opinion.

"If you mean systems of beliefs based, despite their superficial appearances to the contrary, on morbid obsessions with death, hatred, decay, dehumanization, and humiliation, then the answer to your question is no," she said, looking at Colman. She glanced at her grandchildren. "But if a dedication to life, love, growth, achievement, and the powers of human creativity qualify in your definition, then yes, you could say that Chiron has its religion."

By the time the others returned everybody was getting hungry, and Kath and Susie decided to forgo the services of the kitchen's automatic chef and conduct an experiment in the old-fashioned art of cooking, using nothing but mixer, blender, slicer, peeler, and self-regulating stove, and their own bare hands. The result was declared a success by unanimous proclamation, and over the meal the Terrans talked mainly about the more memorable events during the voyage while Kath was curious to learn more about the *Mayflower II*'s propulsion system in anticipation of the tour that she was scheduled to make with the Chironian delegation. Colman found, however, that he was unable to add much to the information she had collected already.

Then came the question of what to do with the rest of the evening. "Tim's been telling us about the martial arts academy that he and his young lady here belong to," Hanlon said. "It sounds like quite a place. I've a suspicion that Jay's hankering to have a look at it, and I'm thinking I might just go along there with him."

"Me?" Jay exclaimed. "I'll come long, sure, but I thought it was you who couldn't resist it."

"Bret's an unarmed-combat instructor with the Army," Tim explained.

Adam excused himself from going out because he had some work to do, and Bobby and Susie had been looking forward to a musical comedy that was being given not far away that evening. Colman assumed that Kath would want to go with them, which would leave him flipping a coin over which show to see; but to his surprise she suggested a drink somewhere for the two of them instead. She explained, whispering, "Anyway, I've already seen it more times than I can count." So who was he to turn it down? Colman asked himself. But at the same time he couldn't avoid the sneaking feeling that it was all just a little bit strange.

Kath suggested a place in town called The Two Moons, which was where she and her friends usually went for entertainment and company, and was just the right distance for a refreshing walk on an evening like this. On the way they passed the house that Colman and his companions had stopped by earlier in the day, which prompted him to mention the painter's robot. "It looked as if it was learning the trade," Colman said.

"Very probably it was," Kath replied. "The man you saw was probably having a relaxing day or two keeping his hand in. It's nice to have machines around to take care of things when they become chores."

"People don't worry about being replaced by a chip?"

"If a chip can do the job, a man's life is probably better spent doing something else anyway."

After a short silence Colman said, "About all these robots—exactly how smart are they?"

"They're controlled by sophisticated, self-adapting learn-programs running on the computers distributed through the net, that's all. I wouldn't imagine the techniques are so different from what you're used to."

"So they're not anywhere near intelligent . . . self-aware, anything like that?"

Kath gave a short laugh. "Of course not . . . but they're deceptive, aren't they. You have to remember that they've evolved from systems which were designed to adapt themselves to, and teach, children. You project a lot of yourself into what you think they're saying."

"But they seem to have an intuition to make human value judgments," Colman objected. "They know too much about how people think."

Kath laughed again. "Do they? They don't really, you know. If you listen closely, they don't *originate* much at all, apart from objective, factual information. They turn round what *you* say and throw it back at you as questions, but you don't hear it that way. You think they're telling you something that they're not."

"Catalysts," Colman said after a few seconds of reflection. "You know, you're right, now that I think about it. All they do is make you exercise the brains you never knew you had."

"You've got it," Kath said lightly. "Isn't that what teaching children is all about?"

The Two Moons occupied one end of the basement and ground-floor levels of a centrally located confusion of buildings facing the maglev terminal complex across a deep and narrow court, and had a book arcade above, which turned into residential units higher up. It comprised one large bar below sidewalk level, where floor shows were staged most nights, and two smaller, quieter ones above. Kath suggested one of the smaller bars and Colman agreed, permitting himself for the first time the thought that a pleasantly romantic interlude might develop, though why he should be so lucky was something he was far from comprehending. If it happened, he wasn't going to argue about it.

Of course, Swyley, Stanislau, Driscoll, and Carson had to be there. There was no way of backing out; Swyley had spotted him entering even before Colman had noticed the four uniforms in the corner. "Small world, chief," Driscoll remarked with a delighted leer on his face.

"It is, isn't it," Colman agreed dismally.

Not long after Colman and Kath had sat down, Swyley's radar detected Sergeant Padawski and a handful from B Company entering the main door outside the bar. They were talking loudly and seemed to be a little the worse for drink. Colman noticed Anita and another girl from Brigade with them, clinging to the soldiers and acting brashly. He shook his head despairingly, but it wasn't really his business. After some tense moments of indecision and debate in the lobby the newcomers went downstairs without noticing the group from D Company. Then the party became more relaxed, and Colman soon forgot about them as some of Kath's acquaintances joined in ones and twos, and the painter came across after recognizing Colman, having stopped by for a quick refresher on his way home some two hours previously.

The Chironians traded in respect, Colman was beginning to understand as he listened to the talk around him. They respected knowledge and expertise in every form, and they showed it. Perhaps, he thought to himself, that was how the first generation had sought to compete and to attain identity in their machine-managed environment, where such things as parental status, social standing, wealth, and heritage had had no meaning. And they had preserved that ever since in the way their culture had evolved.

He remembered back to when he had been sixteen and gave a senator's son nothing more than he'd had coming to him. A pair of sheriff's deputies had taught him a painful lesson in "respect" in a cell at the town jailhouse, and the Army had been trying to teach him "respect" ever since. But that had been Earth-style respect. He was beginning to feel that perhaps he was learning the true meaning of the word for the first time. True respect could only be earned; it couldn't be extorted. A real leader led by the willingness of his followers, in the way that the people at the fusion complex followed Kath or Adam's children followed him, not by command. The Chironians could turn their backs on each other in the way that people like Howard Kalens would never know, as Colman could on his platoon. These were his kind of people. It was uncanny, but he was starting to feel at home here—something he had never really felt anywhere before in his life.

Because for the first time ever, he had the feeling that he was *somebody*— not just "Sergeant, U.S. Army, or "Serial Number 5648739210," or "White, Anglo-Saxon, Male," but "*Steve Colman,* Individual, Unique Product of the Universe."

It was a nice feeling.

CHAPTER NINETEEN

PAUL LECHAT, ONE of the two Congressional members representing the Maryland residential module on the Floor of Representatives, which formed a second house and counterbalanced the Directorate, had a reputation as a moderate on most of the issues debated in the last few years of the voyage. Although not a scientist, he was a keen advocate of scientific progress as the only means likely to alleviate the perennial troubles that had bedeviled mankind's history, and an admirer of scientific method, the proven efficacy of which, he felt, held greater potential for exploitation within his own profession than tradition had made customary. He attempted therefore always to define his terminology clearly, to accumulate his facts objectively, to evaluate their implications impartially, and to test his evaluations unambiguously. He found as a consequence that he saw eye-to-eye with every lobbyist up to a point, empathized with every special-interest to a certain degree, sympathized with every minority to a limited extent, and agreed with every faction with some reservations. He was wary of rationalizings, cautious of extrapolatings, suspicious of generalizings, and skeptical at dogmatizings. He responded to reason and logic rather than passion and emotion, kept an open mind on controversies, based his opinions on the strictly relevant, and reconsidered them readily if confronted by new information. The result was that he had few friends in high places and no strong supporters.

But he did have strong principles and a disposition to discretion and not being impetuous, which was why Judge Fulmire had felt safe in confiding his misgivings about the

185

situation that he suspected was shaping up behind the scenes, politically.

Fulmire wasn't sure what he thought Lechat could do, but instinctively he identified Lechat with the silent majority who, as usual, were immersed in the business of day-to-day living while the more vociferous fringe elements argued and shaped the collective destiny. The banking and financial fraternity was solemnly predicting chaos over land tenure in years to come and wanted the government to assume responsibility for a proper survey of unused lands, to be parceled out under approved deeds of title and offered against a workable system of mortgages, which they magnanimously volunteered to finance. The manufacturing and materials-industry lobbies agreed with the bankers that a monetary system would have to be imposed to check the "reckless profligacy of inefficiency and waste" and to promote "fair and honest" competition; they disagreed with bankers over the mortgage issue, however, claiming that development land on Chiron had already been deemed up for grabs "by virtue of natural precedent"; they disagreed with each other about prices and tariffs, the manufacturers pushing for deregulation of cheap (i.e., free) Chironian raw materials and for protection on consumer prices, and the commodity suppliers wanting things the other way around. The educational and medical professions were anxious to discharge their obligations to teach the Chironians when they were well and treat them when they were not, but were more anxious for a mechanism to raise the taxes for funding them, while the legal profession pressed for a properly constituted judicial system as a first move, ostensibly to facilitate collecting the taxes. The other groups went along with the taxes as long as each secured better breaks than the others, except the religious leaders, who didn't care since they would be exempt anyway. But *they* clashed with the teachers over a move to place ministers in the schools in order to "strangle at its roots the evil and decay which is loose upon this planet," with the doctors over whether the causes were cultural or spiritual, with the lawyers over the issue of making the Chironian practice of serial, and at times parallel, polygamy and polyandry illegal, and with everybody over the question of "emergency" subsidies for erecting churches. And so it went.

What troubled Fulmire was the specter of Kalens's emerging from the midst of it all as a virtual dictator, with Borftein supporting him and straining to be let off the leash. Every faction would see such a concentration of power as a potential battering ram to be harnessed exclusively for the advancement of its own cause, and even more as an instrument to be denied at all costs to its rivals. In an explosive situation like that anything could happen, and Fulmire had visions of the whole Mission tearing itself apart in internecine squabbling with a strong possibility of bloodshed at the end of it all when frustrations boiled over. The only force that he could see with any potential for exerting a stabilizing influence was the more moderate consensus as represented by the *Mayflower II*'s population as a whole; and Lechat, possibly, could provide a means of mobilizing it before things got out of hand.

Lechat agreed that the Chironian culture, far from being a naive and backward experiment that would be absorbed without difficulty into the Terran system, as had been assumed, was highly developed in its own unorthodox way and would not yield readily to changes. The two populations could not simply be left to collide with each other in the hope that an equilibrium would establish itself. Something, somewhere, would blow up before that happened.

The Chironians had both complied with the *Mayflower II*'s advance request for surface accommodation and anticipated their own future needs at the same time by developing Canaveral City and its environs in the direction of Franklin to a greater degree than their own situation then required. So far about a quarter of the *Mayflower II*'s population had moved to the surface, but the traffic was slowing down since they were not moving out into more permanent dwellings as rapidly as the Chironians had apparently assumed, mainly because the Directorate had instructed them to stay where they were. Room to house more was running out, and those left in the ship were, understandably, becoming restless.

Lechat told Fulmire that he no longer thought it advis-

able to attempt setting up a Terran community alongside
the totally unfamiliar experience of Franklin—at least,
not immediately. The Terrans would need time to read-
just, and in the meantime they would cling to their own
familiar ways and customs. The proximity of Franklin
would only cause tensions. Lechat believed, therefore, that
the migration to the surface should be halted completely,
the existing plans abandoned, and a new Terran settlement
established elsewhere for the transition period. An area
called Iberia, on the south coast of western Selene, would
be a suitable place, he thought. Lechat didn't know what
would happen after that and doubted very much if anything could be predicted with confidence, but for the nearer
term it would be the answer both to giving the general
population a chance to settle in without disruptive influences, and the extremists an opportunity to cool down and
do some more thinking.

Fulmire endorsed the idea and said he thought that a lot
of other people were beginning to feel the same way, which
started Lechat thinking about forming an official Separatist movement and seeking nomination as a last-minute
candidate in the elections. Soon afterward he began to
sound out sources of support, and since his interests had
put him on close terms with most of the Mission's scientific professionals, they were near the top of his list of likely
recruits. Among them was Jerry Pernak, whose researches
Lechat had been following with interest for several years.
Accordingly, Lechat invited Pernak and Eve Verritty to
dinner with him one evening in the Françoise, a restaurant
in the Columbia District frequented mainly by political
and media people, and explained his situation.

"I don't think it could work," Pernak said, shaking his
head after Lechat had finished. "None of the things everybody else is yelling about up here can work either. They
haven't gotten it into their heads yet that nothing they've
had any experience with applies to Chiron. This is a whole
new phenomenon with its own new rules."

"How do you mean, Jerry?" Lechat asked across the
table. He was a slightly built man of average height, in his

late forties, with thinning hair and a dry, pinkish complexion. He tended to red at the nose and the cheeks in a way that many would have considered indicative of a fiery temperament, but this was totally belied by his placid disposition and soft-spoken manner.

Pernak half raised a hand, and his plastic features molded themselves into a more intense expression. "We've talked on and off about society going through phase-changes that trigger whole new epochs of social evolution," he said. "Well, that's exactly what's happened down there. You can't extrapolate any of our rules into this culture. They don't apply. They don't work on Chiron."

Lechat didn't respond immediately. Eve Verritty elaborated. "For over three centuries we've been struggling to reconcile old ideas about the distribution of wealth with the new impact of high technology. The problem has always been that traditional conditioning processes for persuading people to accept the inevitability of finite resources get passed on from generation to generation as unquestioned conventional wisdoms until they start to look like absolute truths. Wealth was always something that had to be competed and fought for. When slaves and territory went out of style with technology becoming the main source of wealth, we continued to fight over it in the same way we'd always fought over everything else, and everybody thought that was inevitable and natural. They couldn't separate the old theories from the new facts." Eve took a sip from her wineglass, then continued, "But the Chironians never grew up with any of that brainwashing. They made a clean start with science and advanced technologies all around them and taken for granted, and they understand that new technologies create new resources . . . without limit."

Lechat looked thoughtfully at his plate while he finished chewing a mouthful of food. "You make them all sound like millionaires," he commented.

"That's exactly what they are," Pernak said. "In the material sense, anyway. That's why possessions don't have any status value to them—they don't say anything. That's why you won't find any absolute leaders down there either."

"How come?" Lechat asked, puzzled.

"Why do people follow leaders?" Pernak replied. "For collective strength. What do you need collective strength for? Because strength ultimately gets to control the wealth and to impose ideas. But why does a race of millionaires need leaders if it already has all the material wealth it needs, and isn't interested in imposing ideas on anyone because nobody ever taught it to? The Chironians don't. There isn't anything to scare them with. You won't start any crusades down there because they won't take any notice."

Lechat thought for a while as he continued to eat. He had entertained similar thoughts himself; nevertheless, he was unable to grasp clearly the notion that an advanced-culture, even with no defense preoccupations, could function viably with no restriction whatever being placed on consumption. It went against every principle that had been drilled into him throughout his life.

Even as he thought that, Eve's words about brainwashing came back to him. Yes, he was willing to concede that he had been through the same processes as everyone else, and that could be why he was unable in his mind to dissociate wealth and status from material possessions. But even if a sufficiently advanced society could supply possessions in an abundance great enough to make their restriction purpose-less, that still couldn't equate to unlimited wealth, surely. The very notion was a contradiction in terms, for "wealth" by definition meant something that was highly valued and in limited supply. In other words, if on Chiron possessions did not equate to wealth and thereby satisfy the universal human hunger to be judged a success, then what did?

"I can see your point to a degree," Pernak said eventually. "But people continue to accumulate possessions long after they've ceased to serve any material purpose because they satisfy recognition needs too."

"That's so true," Eve agreed.

Lechat looked puzzled. "That's my point—how do the Chironians satisfy them?"

"You've already said it," Eve told him. She studied the expression on his face for a few seconds and then smiled. "You can't see it yet, can you, Paul?"

Pernak waited for a moment longer, then put down his

fork and leaned across the table. "On Chiron, wealth is *competence!*" he said. "Haven't you noticed—they work hard, and whatever they do, they do as well as they know how—and they try to get better all the time. It doesn't matter so much *what* they do as long as it's good. And everybody appreciates it. That's their currency—*recognition,* as you said . . . recognition of competence." He shrugged and spread his hands. "And it makes a lot of sense. You just told us that's what everyone wants anyway. Well, Chironians pay it direct instead of indirectly through symbols. Why make life complicated?"

The suggestion was too extraordinary for Lechat to respond instantly. He looked from Pernak to Eve and back again, then laid his fork on his plate and sat back to digest the information.

"When did you see a shoddy piece of workmanship on Chiron . . . a door that didn't fit, or a motor that wouldn't start?" Eve asked him. "Have you ever come across anything like that anywhere there? It makes what we're used to look like junk. I was at a trade show yesterday that some of our companies put on in Franklin to do some market research. The Chironians thought it was a joke. You should have seen the kids down there—they thought our ideas of design and manufacturing were hilarious. Our guys had to give it up as a dead loss."

"That's how they get rich," Pernak said. "By being good at what they do and getting better. Who but a crazy would do anything and stay poor by choice?"

"You mean by reputation, or something like that?" Lechat asked, beginning to look intrigued.

"That's part of it," Pernak replied, nodding. "The satisfaction that their culture conditions them to feel is another part, but you're getting the general idea."

Lechat picked up his fork again. "I never looked at it in quite that way. It's an interesting thought." He began eating again, then stopped and looked up. "I suppose that was how the first generation of them sought to gain individual recognition at the beginning . . . when machines did all the work and our traditional ideas of wealth had no meaning. And it's become embedded in their basic thinking." He nodded slowly to himself and reflected further. "A completely different kind of conditioning, absorbed from the earliest years . . . based on recognizing individual attributes. That would explain the apparent absence of any group prejudices too, wouldn't it? They've never had any reason to feel threatened by other groups."

"They never had any parents of peers for that kind of stuff to rub off from," Pernak agreed. "Classes, echelons, black, white, Soviet, Chinese . . . it's all the same to them. They don't care. It's what *you* are that matters."

"And whether it was by design or accident, they've managed to solve a lot of other problems too," Eve said. "Take crime for instance. Theft and greed are impossible, because how can you steal another man's competence? Oh, you could try and fake it, I suppose, but you wouldn't last long with people as discerning as Chironians. They can see through a charlatan as quickly as we can spot ourselves being shortchanged. In fact to them that's just what it is. They have their violent moments, sure, but nothing as bad as what's coming in from Africa on the beam right now, or what happened in 2021. But it never turns into a really big problem. There's no motivation for anyone to rally round a would-be Napoleon. He wouldn't have anything to offer that anybody needs."

After another short silence Lechat said, "It's a strange system of currency though, isn't it. I mean, it's not additive at all, or subject to any laws of arithmetic. You can pay what you owe and still not be any poorer yourself. It sounds —I don't know—impossible somehow."

"It's not subject to finite arithmetic," Pernak agreed. "But why does it have to be? Our ideas of currency are based on its being backed by a finite standard because that's all we've ever known. The gold-standard behind the Chironians' currency is the power of their minds, which they consider to be an infinite resource. Therefore they do their accounting with a calculus of infinities. You take something from infinity, and you've still got infinity left." He shrugged. "It's consistent. I know it sounds crazy to us, but it fits with the way they think."

"It certainly puts a new light on things," Lechat conceded. He sat back again, looked from one to the other, and spread his hands resignedly. "So am I to take it that I shouldn't assume your support in the matter I talked about earlier?"

"It's nothing personal, Paul. We think you're a great guy. . . ." Pernak frowned and sighed apologetically. "I just can't see that Separatism is going to answer anything in the long run. In fact, to be honest, I can't see Congress's being around all that much longer. On that planet down there, it's a dodo already."

"You could be right, but that's long-term," Lechat replied. "I'm more worried about what might happen in the shorter term. I need help to do something about it."

"Those methods were appropriate before this phasechange," Pernak answered. "They don't have any place now."

"What other way is there?" Lechat asked.

Pernak shrugged. "Just let the system die naturally."

"It might not want to die that easily," Lechat pointed out. "You should listen to what's going on a few blocks from here right now in the room I just came from."

"They won't stop anything, Paul," Pernak said. "They're up against the driving force of evolution. Canute had the same problem."

"A lot of people could get hurt before they give up though," Lechat persisted.

Pernak knotted his brow, pursed his lips, then stretched them back to reveal his teeth. "Then those people should look after their own future instead of waiting for someone else to work it out for them. That's the old way. They have to learn to think the Chironian way." After a second of hesitation he added, "That's what Eve and I are going to do."

"What do you mean?" Lechat asked, although in the same instant he thought he knew.

Pernak glanced at Eve for a moment. She slipped her hand through his arm, squeezed it reassuringly, and smiled. They both looked back at Lechat. "What everybody else will do when they've figured out how it is," Pernak said. He grinned, almost apologetically. "That's why we won't be able to help much, Paul. You see, we're leaving."

"I see . . ." Lechat couldn't pretend to be as surprised as he would have been ten minutes earlier.

Pernak tossed up his hands. "I've been to take a look at their university and what they do there. You wouldn't believe it. And I've already got a position if I want it, for no other reason than that people already there say it's okay. You get a house, for nothing . . . a good one. Or they'll build you one however you want it. How can you say no? We're going to become Chironians. And so will everybody else when they've gotten over the voyage. Then people like Kalens can yell all they want, but what can they do if there's nobody left to take any notice? It's as I said—you have to start thinking like Chironians."

"They've still got the Army . . . and a lot of nasty hardware up here," Lechat reminded him.

Pernak twisted his face through a few contortions, then sighed again. "I know. That crossed my mind too, but what is there to provoke any real trouble? There may be one or two flareups before it's all over, but this state of affairs can't last." He shook his head. "We're convinced this is the only way to go. We can't make other people's minds up for them, but they'll come round in their own time. Anything else would cause worse problems."

Lechat nodded reluctantly. "Well, it sounds pretty final, I guess."

Pernak spread his hands and nodded. "Yes. Sorry and all that kind of thing, Paul, but that's how it is."

Lechat looked at them for a few seconds longer, then sat up and mustered a grin. "Well, what can I say? Good luck to the pair of you. I hope everything works out."

"Thanks," Pernak acknowledged.

"I trust we'll all stay friends and keep in touch," Eve said.

"You'd better believe it," Lechat promised.

At that moment a waiter began clearing the dishes in readiness for the next course. "Have you heard the news from the surface?" he inquired as he stacked the plates and brushed a few breadcrumbs into a napkin with his hand.

"News?" Lechat looked up, puzzled. "When? We've been here for the last hour. There wasn't anything special then."

"It came in about fifteen minutes ago," the waiter said. He shook his head sadly. "Bad news. There's been a shooting down there . . . in Franklin somewhere. At least one dead—one of our soldiers, I think. It was at some place called The Two Moons."

CHAPTER TWENTY

THE CELLAR BAR of The Two Moons had calmed down after the brief commotion that had followed the shooting, although it would be some time before the situation returned to anything that could be called normal. Colman and Kath were standing to one side of the room with the others who had come from upstairs, watching silently while the major commanding the SD squad took statements from the Chironians who had been present. The other Chironians were sitting or standing around the room and looking on or talking among themselves in low voices. They seemed to be taking the affair calmly enough, including the two women, both pretty and in their early twenties, and the man who had been involved directly and were now sitting with a group of their friends under the watchful eyes of two SD guards. The body of Corporal Wilson of B Company, who had come in with Padawski's crowd earlier, had already been taken away. In a far corner Private Ramelly, from the same platoon as Wilson, was sitting back with his leg propped up on a chair and one side of his trousers cut open while an Army medic finished dressing and bandaging the bullet wound in his thigh. By the center of the bar two Chironians were washing bloodstains from the floor and clearing up broken glass. Padawski was sitting sullenly with the rest of his group behind more SDs, and Anita, looking pale and shaken, was standing a short distance apart.

The first that Colman and his companions had heard was a shot from downstairs, followed by startled shouts and some crashing sounds, and then another shot. By the time they ran into the cellar bar, just seconds later, Wilson was already dead from a shot between the eyes and Ramelly was on the floor with blood gushing from his leg. Padawski and the others were standing uncertainly by the bar, covered by a .38 automatic that one of the young Chironian women was holding. Several other weapons had appeared around the room. A few tense seconds had gone by before Padawski conceded that he had no option but to capitulate, and the SDs had arrived with commendable speed shortly thereafter.

Apparently some of Padawski's friends had the idea that the Chironian women were among the things that could be had for the taking on Chiron, and two of them had persisted in pressing lewd advances upon the two girls at the bar despite their being told repeatedly and in progressively less uncertain terms that the girls weren't interested. The soldiers, who had been drinking heavily, became angry and even more unpleasant, paying no attention to dour warnings from around the room. An argument developed, in the course of which Ramelly grabbed one of the women and handled her roughly. She produced a gun and shot him in the leg. There would probably have been no more to it than that if Wilson hadn't seized the gun and turned it on the Chironians who were about to intervene, at which point another Chironian had shot him dead from the back of the room.

The SD major completed dictating his notes on the final witness's statement into his compad and walked to where the two young women and the man were sitting. Their expressions as they looked up at him were not apprehensive or apologetic, but neither were they defiant. The deed was unfortunate but it had been necessary, the faces seemed to say, and there was nothing to feel guilty about. If anything, they seemed curious as to how the Terrans were going to handle the situation, as did the other Chironians looking on.

"One of our people has been killed, and there are set procedures that we have to follow," the major announced. "My orders require me to take you three back with us. It would make things a lot easier for everybody if you complied. I'm sorry, but I don't have any choice."

"Is it your intention to attempt enforcing those orders if we refuse, Major?" the Chironian who had killed Wilson asked. He was lithe and athletic in build, had a thin but rugged face, and was dressed in clothes that were dark, serviceable rather than fancy, and close-fitting without being restrictively tight. He reminded Colman of the bad guy in an ancient Western movie. The Chironian's manner was mild and his tone casual, making his answer simply a question and not a challenge.

The major met his eye firmly. "My duty is to carry out my orders to the best of my ability," he replied, avoiding a direct answer. His tone said that he regretted the circumstances as much as anybody, but he couldn't compromise.

The display of tact seemed to do the trick. The Chironian held his eye for a moment longer, and then nodded. "Very well." Inwardly Colman breathed a sigh of relief. The women were evidently willing to allow the man to speak for them too. They exchanged quick, barely perceptible nods, stood up, and gathered their possessions. Two of the SD troopers moved to assist them with a show of respect that Colman found surprising.

The major hesitated for a second, and then said, "Ah . . . in view of the circumstances, it would be better if you permitted us to carry your guns back for you. Would you mind?"

"Are you telling us we're prisoners?" the Chironian man asked.

"I would prefer not to use that term," the major answered. "The legal ramifications are not for me to comment on. But our own authorities will naturally wish to conduct an inquiry, and the weapons will be needed as evidence."

"By *your* customs," the Chironian observed.

"It was one of *our* people," the major said.

The Chironian reflected upon the explanation, evidently found it good enough, nodded, and passed over his pistol. The girl who had wounded Ramelly followed suit. Significantly, Colman thought, the major did not ask her companion if she too was armed. As the guards began motioning Padawski and his group to their feet, the major marched over to where Colman and the others from D Company were standing with the Chironians who had been upstairs with them. He had already taken their names and established that they had not witnessed the incident first-hand. "You guys are free to go," he informed them. "If there's a hearing, you might be called in to testify. If so, the appropriate people will contact you."

"They know where to find us," Colman said.

Kath's pocket communicator buzzed, and she took it out to answer. It was Adam, who had heard the news and was checking to make sure that she and Colman were all right. Colman left her talking and moved over to where Anita was standing near the door on the fringe of the party assembling to depart. "Why'd you ever get mixed up with that bunch?" he murmured. "Wise up when it's all over. Get out of it."

There was no repentance or remorse in her eyes when she looked at him. "It's none of your business anymore," she hissed. "How I choose to have fun is my affair and my life."

Colman snorted derisively. "You call that fun?"

"You know what I mean. They weren't doing anything. They'd just had a bit too much to drink. Those two bitches didn't have to do something like that."

"Maybe you should try looking at it their way," Colman said.

Anita's eyes blazed as her shock began wearing off and dissipated itself as anger. "Why should I? Bruce just got killed and Dan's got a hole in his leg, and you're telling me to see it *their* way? What kind of a man are you any-how?" She sneered past Colman's shoulder at Kath, who was returning the communicator to her pocket. "I can see why. It didn't take *you* long, did it. Is she good?"

Colman ignored the remark. "Just think about it," he muttered. "For your own sake."

"I told you once already, it's none of your business anymore. Leave me alone. I don't want to talk to you. Just—go away and leave me alone."

Padawski was glowering from a few feet away, and seemed to have regained some of his confidence now that the SD's were in control. "You stay away from her, Goldilocks," he spat. "Stick with your nice, murdering friends. We won't forget you either." He turned his head back to glare at the whole room before turning for the door. "And that goes for all of you," he warned in a louder voice. "We won't forget. You'll see."

"On your way." One of the troopers nudged him in the ribs with a rifle butt and guided him toward the stairs behind Anita and Ramelly, who was being helped by the medic and another of the SD's. Colman watched until they had all left, then returned to the others.

"Is she a friend of yours?" Kath inquired.

"From a while back. But not anymore, I guess, by the look of it."

"She's a good-looking girl. What does she do?"

"A communications specialist at Brigade."

Kath's eyebrows lifted approvingly. "Smart as well, eh?"

"She could do a lot better than waste herself with those bums. She's the kind that prefers the easy road . . . for as long as it lasts, anyhow."

"That's a shame," Kath said.

Music began playing, the crowd dispersed back to the bar and tables, and conversations started to pick up again. Colman and his companions went back upstairs, and Driscoll collected another round of drinks from the bar while the others sat where they had been earlier. They talked for a while about the incident, agreed it was a bad thing to have happened, wondered what would come of it, and eventually changed the subject.

"I guess you have to learn moderation in this place," Stanislau remarked, studying his half-emptied glass of dark, frothy Chironian beer. He shook his head slowly. "You know, this sounds crazy but sometimes I wish they would make us pay for it."

"I know exactly what you mean," Carson said. Driscoll nodded his mute assent also.

"I'm not so sure I agree," Swyley said, which meant that he did.

Colman was about to make a joke out of it when he realized they were serious. He knotted his brows and directed an inquiring look at each of them in turn.

"It's this whole business of not paying for anything," Stanislau said at last. "We come in here and drink, we go into restaurants and eat, we walk out of stores with all kinds of stuff, and none of it costs anything." He sat back, looked from side to side for moral support, got plenty, and shook his head helplessly. "It seemed too good to be true at first, but that soon wears off. It's not funny anymore, chief. It's getting to all of us."

"We feel we owe something, and we want to pay our way," Driscoll confirmed. "We don't want any free rides. But all we get are pieces of paper that aren't any good for anything here. What can you do?"

"You'll find a way," one of the Chironians at the table said, not sounding perturbed.

"Better late than never, I suppose," another commented, glancing at the painter, who was still there. The painter nodded but didn't reply.

"What does that mean?" Driscoll asked, looking at the Chironian who had spoken.

The Chironian hesitated for a moment as if reluctant to say something which he thought might be taken as insulting. Kath caught his eye and nodded reassuringly. "Well," the Chironian began, then paused again. "Most people here start to feel that way by the time they're about ten. I'm not trying to offend anyone—but that's the way it is."

Carson frowned and thought about the implications, then shook his head. "It's impossible," he said. "No system could work like that."

An intrigued and thoughtful look came over Swyley's face as he listened. He said nothing, which meant that he didn't agree.

CHAPTER TWENTY-ONE

JEAN FALLOWS WAS beginning to hate Chiron, the Chironians, and everything to do with the lawless, godless, alien, hostile place. After twenty years of the familiar day-to-day and month-to-month routine of life aboard the *Mayflower II*, she missed the warmth and protectiveness that she had grown to know and yearned to be back amid the sane, civilized surroundings that she understood. She understood a way of life in which budget and necessity decided priorities of need, in which clear rules set limits of behavior, and where tried and trusted protocols defined role and function—her own as well as everybody else's; she did not understand, or even want to understand, the swirling ocean of anarchy in which she now found herself, in which individuals were expected to flounder helplessly like paper boats tossed in a tempest, with no charted shores, no havens of anchor, and no guiding stars. She had no place in it, and she desired no place in it. Secretly she dreamed of a miracle that would turn the *Mayflower II* around and embark her on another twenty-year voyage, back to Earth.

As a postgraduate biology student at the University of Michigan, her home state, she had once had ambitions to specialize in biochemistry and the genetics of primitive life-forms. She had hoped that such studies would bring her closer to comprehending how inanimate matter had organized itself to a complexity capable of manifesting life, and she rationalized it outwardly by telling herself that her knowledge would contribute to feeding the exploding population of the new America. And then she had met Bernard, whose youthful zeal and visions of the

Reformation that would sweep the world had awakened her political awareness and carried her along with him into a whole new dimension of human relationships and motivations which until then she had hardly recognized as existing at all. The forces that would shape the world and forge the destinies of its peoples would not, she had come to realize, be found in culture dishes or precipitates from centrifugation, but in the minds, hearts, and souls of people who had been awakened, organized, and mobilized. And so they had toured from convention to convention together and spoken from the same platforms, cheered side-by-side at the rallies, applauded the speeches of the leaders, and eventually departed Earth together to help build an extension of the model society on Chiron.

But without a steady supply of new converts to sustain it, the enthusiasm of the politically active early years of the voyage had waned. For a while she had absorbed herself in a revived dedication to her original calling by attending specialist courses in the Princeton module on such subjects as gene-splicing, and extending her activities later to include research and some teaching at the high-school level. Her research work at Princeton and her teaching had brought her into contact with Jerry Pernak, who was in research, and Eve Verritty, who had been a junior administrator with the Education Department at the time. In fact it was Jean who had first introduced them to each other.

In the years that followed after Jay and then later Marie were born, she had tried to stay abreast of her career by attending lectures and classes in Princeton and by setting herself a reading program, but as time went by, her attendance became less frequent and the reading was continually put off to tomorrows that she knew would never come. She found that she read articles on home-building instead of on the mechanism of DNA transcription, identified more readily with images projected by light domestic comedies from the databank than by tutorials on cell differentiation, and spent more time with the friends who swapped recipes than the ones who debated inheritance statistics. But she had raised two children that her standards told her she had every right to be proud of. She was entitled to rewards for the sacrifices she had made. And now Chiron was threatening to steal the rewards away.

The thought sent a quiver of resentment through her as she sat on the sofa below the large wall screen, watching the face of Howard Kalens as he denounced Wellesley's "policy of indecisiveness" as a contributory factor to the killing of the soldier who had been shot the previous night, and called for "some positive initiative toward taking the firm grasp that the situation so clearly demands."

"A boy of twenty-three," Kalens had said a few minutes previously. "Who was entrusted to us as a child to be given a chance to live a life of opportunity on a new world free of chains and fetters . . . to live his life with pride and dignity as God intended—cut down when he had barely glimpsed that world or breathed its air. Bruce Wilson did not die yesterday. His life ended when he was three years old."

Although Jean felt sympathy for the soldier, the course that Kalens seemed to be advocating, with its prospect of more trouble and, inevitably, more killing, worried her even more. Why did it always have to be like this? she asked herself. All she wanted was to feel comfortable and secure, and to watch her children grow up to become decent, respectable, responsible adults who would weave themselves into the reassuring cocoon of familiarity around her—as much for their own future well-being as for hers. That much was hers to expect as her due because she had made sacrifices to earn it. It threatened nobody. So why should other people's squabbles which were not of her making now threaten her with sweeping it all away?

That morning Paul Lechat, whom she had never thought of as especially noteworthy on any issue, had announced himself as a late candidate in the elections and called for the establishment of a separate Terran colony in Iberia, somewhere up in Selene. He wanted to allow the people from Earth to pursue their own pattern of living without disruptive influences for the immediate future, and possibly to make such an institution permanent if it suited enough people to do so. To Jean the announcement had come as a godsend, and to many others as well, if the amount of popular support that had materialized from all sides within a matter of hours was anything to go by. Why couldn't everybody see it that way? she wondered. It was so obvious. Why were there always some who were obstinate and valued political interests before what common sense said would be for the common good, such as Kalens, who even now was reacting to Lechat as a threat and rallying his own followers to action?

"Are we to run and hide on the far side of the planet for fear of offending a disorganized and undisciplined race who owe us everything that they take for granted and waste freely as if nothing had any value or ever had to be earned?" Kalens was asking from the screen. "Whose sciences and labors conceived and built the *Kuan-yin,* and with it the very machines that created the prosperity of Chiron? Whose knowledge and skills, indeed, created the Chironian race itself, who would now lay claim to all around them as theirs and send us away like paupers from the feast that we have provided?" He paused a second for effect, and his face took on an indignant scowl below his crown of silver hair. "I say no! I will not be driven away in such fashion. I will not even contemplate such an action. I say, publicly and without reservation, that any such suggestion can be described only as a surrender to moral cowardice that is beneath contempt. Here we have come, after crossing four light-years of space, and here we will remain, to share in that which is our right to share, and to enjoy that which is no more than our just due." A thunder of applause greeted the exhortation. Jean had heard enough and told Jeeves to turn off the screen.

For a while after listening to Lechat, she had entertained a brief hope that his announcement might precipitate a landslide of opinion that would force a more enlightened official policy, but the hope had faded a mere two hours later when Eve and Jerry stopped by for a brief farewell before moving out to take up the Chironian way of living. Apparently many people were doing the same thing, and there were even rumors of desertions from the Army. Jean had been unable to avoid feeling that Eve and Jerry were somehow deserting her too, but she had managed to keep a pleasant face and wish them well. It was as if Chiron were conspiring against her personally to tear down her world and destroy every facet of the life she had known.

The house around her was another part of it. She no longer saw it as the dream it had been on the day they moved down from the *Mayflower II,* but instead as another part of the same conspiracy—a cheap bribe to seduce her into selling her soul in the same way as a university research post and the lure of a free home had seduced Eve and Jerry. Chiron didn't want to let her be. It wanted her to be like it. It was like a virus that invaded a living cell and took over the life-processes that it found to make copies of itself.

She shivered at the thought and got up from the sofa to find Bernard. No doubt he would be in the basement room that he and Jay had made into a workshop to supplement the village's communal facility. Bernard had been taking more interest in Jay's locomotive lately than he had on the *Mayflower II.* Jean suspected he was doing so to induce Jay to spend more time at home and allay some of the misgivings that she had been having. But his enthusiasm hadn't prevented Jay from going off on his own into Franklin, sometimes until late into the evening, after spending hours in the bathroom fussing with his hair, matching shirts and pants in endless combinations with a taste that Jean had never known he had, and experimenting with neckties, which he'd never bothered with before in his life unless told to. Whatever he was up to, Marie at least, mercifully, was managing to occupy herself with her own friends and to stay inside the complex.

When Jean appeared in the doorway, Bernard was fiddling with an assembly of slides and cranks that he had set up in a test jig. She watched while he pushed a tiny rod which in turn caused all the other pieces to slide and turn in a smooth unison, though what any of them did or what the whole thing was for were mysteries to Jean. Bernard pulled the rod back again to return all the pieces to their original positions, then looked up and grinned. "I have to take my hat off to Army training," he said. "I'll say one thing for Steve Colman—he sure knows what he's doing. Our son has produced some first-class work here." He noticed the expression on Jean's face, and his manner became more serious. "Aw, try and snap out of it, hon. I know everything's a bit strange. What else can you expect after twenty years? You'll need time to get used to it. We all will."

"You don't mind, do you? Here . . . the way things are . . . it doesn't bother you. You're like Eve and Jerry." Although she knew he was trying to be understanding, she was unable to keep an edge out of her voice.

"Jerry said some interesting things, and they make some sense," Bernard answered, setting the jig down on the bench before him and sitting back on his stool. "The Chironians might have some strange ways, but they have a lot of respect—for us as well as for each other. That's not such a bad way for people to be. Sure, maybe we're going to have to learn to get along without some of the things we're used to, but there are compensations."

"Was it respect they showed that boy who was killed last night?" Jean asked bitterly. "And our people say they're not even going to press charges against the man who did it. What kind of a way is that to live? Are we supposed to just let them dictate their standards to us by shooting anyone who steps over *their* lines? Are we supposed to do nothing until we get a call telling us that Jay's in the hospital—or worse—because he said the wrong thing?"

Bernard sighed and forced his voice to remain reasonable. "Now, come on . . . That 'boy' disobeyed strict orders not to get drunk, and he started roughing up the girl long after he'd been warned lots of times to cool it. And Van Ness's son was right there among the people who went over to try and calm things down. Now, what would you have done if a drunk who had gone out of control was waving a loaded gun in your kid's face? What would anybody have done?"

"How do you know?" Jean challenged. "You weren't there. And that's not the way it sounded when Kalens was talking just now. And a lot of people seemed to agree with him."

"He's just playing on emotion, Jean. I had it on down here for a few minutes but couldn't stand it. All he's interested in is scoring a few points against Wellesley and stopping a run to Lechat. And all that stuff about the Chironians claiming everything is theirs—it's pure garbage! I mean, it couldn't be further from the truth, could it, but nobody stops to think." He frowned to himself for a moment. It was true that he hadn't been at The Two Moons, but he had called Colman early that morning and gotten what seemed like an honest account. But with Jean acting the way she was, he didn't want to mention that. "Anyhow, the facts about the shooting are on record," he said. "All you have to do is ask Jeeves."

Jean seemed to dismiss the subject from her mind. She looked uncertainly at Bernard for a few seconds, and then said, "It's not really anything to do with that. It's—oh, I can't put this any other way—it's you."

Bernard didn't seem as surprised as he might have been. "Want to spit it out?"

Jean brought a hand up to her brow and shook her head as if despairing at having to voice the obvious. "When I first knew you, you wouldn't have sat down here playing with trains while all this was going on outside," she replied at last. "Don't you understand? What's happening out there, right now, is *important*. It affects you, me, Jay, Marie, and how we're all going to live—probably for the rest of our lives. Twenty years ago you—both of us—we'd have *done* something. Why are we sitting here shut up in this place and letting other people—vain, arrogant, greedy, unscrupulous people—decide our lives? Why aren't we doing something? It's that. I can't stand it."

Bernard made no reply but let his eyebrows ask the question for him.

Jean raised her hands in an imploring gesture. "Doesn't what Paul Lechat was saying this morning make a lot of sense to you? Isn't it the only way? Well, he's going to need *help* to do it. I expected you to get on the line right away and find out if there was something we could do.

But you hardly even talked about it. Hell, I know I'm twenty years older too, but at least I haven't forgotten all the things we used to talk about. We were going to help build a new world—our world, the way it ought to be. Well, we've arrived. The ride's over. Isn't it time we started thinking about earning the ticket?"

Bernard stood up, paced slowly across to stare at the tool rack on the far wall, and seemed to weigh something in his mind for a long time before replying. Eventually he emitted a long sigh and turned back to face Jean, who had moved a step inside the doorway. "We can still build it," he said. "But it doesn't quite work the way we thought then. Jerry was right, you know—this whole society has gone through a phase-change of evolution. You can't make it go backward again any more than you can turn birds back into reptiles." Bernard came a pace nearer. His voice took on a persuasive, encouraging note. "Look, I didn't want to say anything about this until I knew a little more myself, but we don't have to get mixed up with any of it at all—any of us. Kalens and the rest of them belong to everything we've left behind now. We don't need them anymore. Don't you see, it can't last?"

"What are you talking about, Bernard?"

"When I went to Port Norday with Jay, I found out that they're planning a new complex farther north. They're going to need engineers—fusion engineers. They practically told me I'd have no problem getting in there, to a top job maybe. Think of it—our own place just like we've always said, and no more crap from Merrick or any of them!" Bernard threw his hands high. "I could be *me* for the first time in my life . . . and so could you, all of us. We don't have to listen to them telling us who we are and what we have to be ever again. Doesn't that . . ." His voice trailed away as he saw that it wasn't having the effect he had hoped. Jean was backing away through the door, shaking her head in mute protest.

"It's getting to you too," she whispered tightly. "Just as it's already gotten to Eve and Jerry. Oh, how I hate this place! Can't you see what it's doing to us all?"

"But, hon, all I—"

Jean spun round and ran back to the elevator. Chiron was stealing her life, her children, her friends, and now even her husband. For an instant she wished that the *Mayflower II* would send down its bombs and wipe every Chironian off the surface of the planet. Then they would be able to begin again, cleanly and decently. Ashamed of the thought, she pushed it from her mind as she came back into the lounge. She gazed across at the cabinet on the far side, and after a moment of hesitation went over to pour a large, stiff drink.

CHAPTER TWENTY-TWO

"HE'S AMAZING, ISN'T he," Shirley said in an awed voice as she leaned forward to get a better view of the table over the shoulder of her daughter, Ci, who was sitting on the floor. "It must be a genetic mutation that makes sticky fingers or something."

"Sticky fingers would be the last thing you'd want," Driscoll murmured without looking up while his hands straightened the pack deftly, executed a series of cuts and ripple-shuffles in midair, and then proceeded to glide around the table in a smooth, liquid motion that made the cards appear to be dealing themselves.

"Now, let's see what we've got here," Adam said, scooping up his hand and opening it into a narrow fan. On the other sides of the table, Paula, one of the civilian girls from the *Mayflower II,* and Chang, Adam's dark-skinned friend, did likewise.

"There's no need to look," Driscoll told him nonchalantly. "You've got a pair of kings." Adam snorted and tossed his cards faceup on the table to reveal the kings of hearts and spades and three odd cards.

"What about me?" Ci asked, looking at Driscoll. She leaned to one side to let her mother see the hand she was holding.

Driscoll stared at her. "Three queens, and I could beat it," he said. Ci and Shirley exchanged baffled looks.

Paula was looking at him impishly. "Do you think you could beat mine?" she asked in a curious voice.

"Sure," Driscoll told her. His eyes twinkled just for an instant. "If you want to know how, I'd beat you with aces."

"Are you sure, Tony? Paula asked. "You wouldn't want

211

to bet on that, now, would you?" Paula turned her head to smile slyly at her friend, Terry, also from the *Mayflower II*, who was watching from behind.

Driscoll met her eyes calmly. "I'd risk it," he said. "Sure, if this was for real, I'd put money on it."

"How much?" Paula asked.

Driscoll shrugged. "What would you stake?"

"Twenty?"

"Sure, I'd cover that."

"Fifty?"

"I'm still with you.'

"A hundred?'

"A hundred."

Paula slapped down four aces gleefully. "You *lose!* Hey, how about that? I just cleaned him out. See, I knew he had to be bluffing."

"Bluffing, hell." Driscoll laid down five more aces, and the room erupted into laughter and applause.

"Hey, you haven't asked me," Chang said. "I beat that."

"You do?" Driscoll looked surprised.

Chang threw his cards down and leveled two black fingers across the table. "A Smith and Wesson beats five aces." He grinned and stood up. "Everybody set for another drink?" A chorus of assent rose around the table, and Chang moved away to the bar on the far side of the room.

Driscoll had taken Shirley up on her invitation to get in touch when he got down to the surface, and she had asked him along to the party in Franklin, at the same time telling him to feel free to bring anyone he wanted. So Driscoll had invited Colman, Swyley, Maddock, and Stanislau, who among them had persuaded Sirocco to come too, and Sirocco had suggested bringing some of the girls from the *Mayflower II*. Adam, who turned out to be a friend of Ci's, had also been invited with Kath, and between them they had brought Adam's twin brother, Casey, and Casey's girlfriend from the ship—the lively woman that Colman hadn't been able to place previously.

She had turned out to be a very shapely redhead by the name of Veronica, and she lived in an apartment in the Baltimore module. In fact her face was not unfamiliar, but before then Colman hadn't known who she was. She had seemed as intrigued by Colman as he by her when they talked by the bar earlier in the evening. "Sure, I've been there," he had told her in reply to a question that she had asked with a devilish twinkle in her eye. "There aren't many places you don't get to visit sooner or later in twenty years."

"Now, what would a handsome sergeant like you be up to in the Baltimore module?"

"Why would anybody be interested?"

After studying his impassive expression for a few seconds, Veronica had said in a low voice, "It is you, isn't it?"

"Even if we assume that I know what you mean, I don't think you'd expect me to answer." So now they both knew, and knew that the other knew. Each had tested the other's discretion, and both of them respected what they had found. Nothing more needed to be said.

With all public bars having been put off-limits to the *Mayflower II*'s soldiers after the shooting, the party couldn't have come at a better time, Colman reflected as he leaned against the bar and nursed his glass while gazing around the room. Swyley and Stanislau were behind him in a corner with a mixed group of Chironians and seemed interested in the planet's travel facilities; Sirocco was with another group in the center of the room discussing the war news with another group, and Maddock, looking slightly disheveled, was sprawled along a couch in an alcove on the far side with his arm draped around Wendy, another girl from the *Mayflower II*, who seemed to be asleep. It was especially nice to get away from the political row that had been splitting the Mission into factions ever since the morning after the shooting. Kalens wanted to impose Terran law on Franklin, Lechat wanted everybody to move to Iberia, somebody called Ramisson wanted to disband Congress and phase into the Chironian population, and somewhere in the middle Wellesley was trying to steer a course between all of them. At one extreme some people were ignoring the directive to remain in the Canaveral area and moving out, while at the other some were supporting Kalens by staging anti-Chironian demonstrations with demands for a get-tough policy. Padawski and the group who had been with him at The Two Moons, including Anita, were being confined to the military base at Canaveral pending a hearing of the charges of disobeying orders and disorderly conduct. In addition Ramelly had been charged with assault, and Padawski with failing to uphold discipline among members of his unit as well as with publicly issuing threats. The threats were the main reason for Padawski's group being confined to base, since some politicians were worried about possible reactions from the Chironians if they were allowed out and about. Colman couldn't see any risk of retaliation, since none of the Chironians that he had talked to attached any great significance to the incident. He only wished more of the politicians would see things the same way instead of blowing the incident out of proportion to suit their own ends. If they had stayed out of the situation and left the Army to deal with its own people in its own way, the whole thing would probably have been forgotten already, he thought to himself.

Kath had moved away to talk to Adam, Casey, and Veronica, who were sitting together beyond the table at which Driscoll was performing. Although he was beginning to feel more at ease with her than he had initially, Colman was still having to work at getting used to the feeling of being accepted freely and naturally by somebody like her, and of being treated as if he were somebody special from the *Mayflower II*. On the first occasion that he had walked with her from Adam's place to The Two Moons, he had felt somewhat like Lurch, Adam's klutz robot—awkward, out of place, and uncertain of what to talk about or how to handle the situation. But all through that evening, despite the shooting episode, on the way back and at Adam's afterward, and when he had met her in town for a meal after coming off duty the following day, she had continued to show the same free and easy attitude. Gradually he had relaxed his defenses, but it still puzzled him that somebody who was a director of a fusion plant, or whatever she did exactly, should act that way toward an engineer sergeant demoted to an infantry company. Why would she do something like that? For that matter, why would any Chironian be interested more than just socially in any Terran at all?

"Because she's seducing you," a voice murmured from behind him.

Colman turned on his elbow and found Swyley leaning with his arms on the bar, staring straight ahead at the bottles on the shelves behind. Colman raised his eyebrows. Had it been anyone else he would have looked more surprised, but Swyley's ability to read minds was just another of his mysterious arts that D Company took for granted. After a few seconds Swyley went on, "They're seducing all of us. That's how they're fighting the war."

Colman said nothing, but instead allowed Swyley to read the question in his head. Sure enough, Swyley explained, "They don't make bombs or organize armies. It's too messy, and too many of the wrong people get hurt. They go for the grass roots. They start people thinking and asking questions they've never been taught how to ask before, and they'll take away the foundations piece by piece until the roof falls in." He paused and continued staring at the wall. "You're an engineer, and she runs part of a fusion complex. If you want out, you've got a place to go. That's what she's telling you."

Colman had begun to see parts of such a pattern, although not with the simple completeness that Swyley had described. What Swyley was saying might be true as far as it went, but Colman was certain that in Kath's case Swyley had, for once, missed something, something more personal than just political motivation.

A hand descended on his arm and slid upward to tease the back of his neck. He turned round to find that Kath had come back. "You're starting a bachelors' party here," she said. "I have to break that up before the idea catches on."

Colman grinned. "Good thinking. We were starting to talk shop." He inclined his head to where Veronica was still talking animatedly between Kath's twin sons and evidently enjoying herself. "Somebody seems to be quite a hit over there."

"Isn't she a lot of fun," Kath agreed. "She's talking Casey into teaching her to be an architect. She could do it too. She's an intelligent woman. Have you known her long?"

Colman smiled to himself. "I've only seen her around. This may sound crazy, but I never really met her before tonight."

"After twenty years on the same ship? That's not possible, surely."

Colman shrugged. "Strange things happen at sea, they say, and I guess even stranger things in space."

"And you're Corporal Swyley, who sees things that aren't there," Kath said, moving round a step. "Your Captain Sirocco told me about your ability. I like him. He told me about the way you ruined the exercise up on the ship too. I thought it was wonderful."

"If you're going to lose anyway, you might as well win," Swyley replied. "If you win the wrong way, you lose, and if you lose either way, you lose. So why not enjoy it?"

"What happens if you win the right way?" Kath asked him.

"Then you lose out to the system. It's like playing against Driscoll—the system makes it's own aces."

At that moment one of the Chironian girls from the group in the corner took Swyley lightly by the arm. "I thought you were getting some more drinks," she said. "We're all drying up over there. I'll give you a hand. Then you can come back and tell us more about the Mafia. The conversation was just getting interesting."

Colman's eyes widened in surprise. "Him? What in hell does he know about the Mafia?"

The girl gave Colman a funny look. "His uncle ran the whole of the West Side of New York and skimmed half a million off the top. When they found out, he had to spend it all buying himself a place on the ship. You didn't know?"

For a second Colman could only gape at her. He'd known that Swyley had been brought on to the *Mayflower*

II as a kid by an uncle who had died fifteen years into the voyage from a heart condition, but that was about all. "Hey, how come you never told us about that part?" he asked as the girl led Swyley away.

"You never asked me," Swyley answered over his shoulder.

He turned back, shaking his head despairingly, and looked at Kath again. Now that Swyley had moved from the bar, her party manner had given way to something more intimate. Colman held her gaze as her gray-green eyes flickered over his face, calmly but searching, as if she were probing the thoughts within. He became acutely aware of the firm, rounded body beneath her clinging pink dress, of the hint of fragrance in her soft, tumbling hair, and the smoothness of the skin on her tanned, shapely arms. Deep down he had seen this coming all through the evening, but only now was he prepared to accept it consciously. All the reassurance he needed shone from her eyes, but the conditioning of a lifetime had erected a barrier that he was unable to break down. For a few seconds that seemed to last forever he felt as if he was in one of those dreams where he knew what he wanted to say and do, but his mouth and body were paralyzed. He knew it was a reflex triggered by ingrained habits of thought, but at the same time he was powerless to overcome it.

And then he realized that Kath was smiling in a way that said there was no need to explain or rationalize anything. Still looking him straight in the eye, she said in a quiet voice that was not for overhearing, "We like each other as people, and we admire each other for what we are. There isn't anything to feel hung up about on Chiron. People who feel like that usually make love, if that's what they want to do." She paused for a second. "Isn't that what you'd like to do?"

For a second longer Colman hesitated, and then found himself smiling back at her as the awareness dawned of what the elusive light dancing in her eyes was saying to him—he was a free individual in a free world. And suddenly the barrier crumbled away.

"Yes, it is," he replied. There was nothing more to say.

"I only live at Port Norday during the week," Kath said. "I've got a place in Franklin as well. It's not far from here at all."

"And I am on early duty tomorrow," Colman said.

He grinned again, and she smiled back impishly, "So why are we still here?" they asked together.

CHAPTER TWENTY-THREE

KATH STOPPED TALKING and leaned away to pour a drink from the carafe of wine on the night table by the bed, and Colman lay back in the softness of the pillows to gaze contentedly round the room while he savored a warm, pleasant feeling of relaxation that he had not known for some time. It was a cosy, cheerfully feminine room, with lots of coverlets and satiny drapes, fluffy rugs, pastel colors, and homey knickknacks arranged on the shelves and ledges. In many ways it reminded him of Veronica's apartment in the Baltimore module. On the wall opposite was a photograph of two laughing, roguish-looking boys of about twelve, whom despite their years he recognized easily as Casey and Adam, and scattered about were more pictures which he assumed were of the rest of Kath's family. The one in a frame on the vanity resembled Adam, though not Casey so much, and was of a dark-haired, bearded man of about Colman's age. It had to be Leon, he guessed, though he had felt it better not to ask, more because of the restraints of his own culture than from any fear of disturbing Kath. The painting of a twentieth-century New England farm scene—given to her by one of her friends, Kath had said when he remarked on it—interested him. Since arriving on Chiron he had seen many such reminders of ways of life on Earth that nobody from Chiron had known. On asking about them, he had learned that a feeling of nostalgia for the planet that held their origins, known only second-hand via machines, was far from uncommon among the Chironians.

Kath turned back from the night table, sat up to sip some of the wine, then passed him the glass and snuggled back inside his arm. "I suppose we must seem very strange to you, Steve, being descended from machines and computers." She chuckled softly. "I bet there are lots of people on your ship who think we're really aliens. Do they think we walk like Lurch and talk in metallic, monotone voices?"

Colman grinned and drank from the glass. "Not quite that bad. But some of them do have pretty funny ideas— or did have, anyway. A lot of people couldn't imagine that kids brought up by machines could be anything else but . . . 'inhuman,' I guess you'd call it—cold, that kind of thing."

"It wasn't like that at all," she said. "Although, I suppose, I shouldn't really say too much since I've had nothing to compare it with. But it was"—she shrugged— "warm, friendly . . . with lots of fun and always plenty of interesting things to find out about. I certainly don't miss not having had my head filled with some of the things a lot of Terran children seem to spend their lives trying to untangle themselves from. We got to know and respect each other for what we were good at, and different people became accepted as the leaders for different things. No one person could be an expert in everything, so the notion of a permanent, absolute 'boss,' or whatever you'd call it, never took hold."

"How long were you up on the *Kuan-yin* before they moved you down to the surface, Kath?"

"I was very young. I'm not sure I can remember without checking the records. Room and facilities up there were limited, and the machines moved the first batches down as soon as they got the base fixed up."

"The ship's changed a lot since then though," Colman remarked. "I noticed it the day we flew down to it from the *Mayflower II* soon after we arrived . . . when Shirley and Ci met Tony Driscoll. The front end must be at least twice as big as it used to be."

"Yes, people have been doing all kinds of things with it over the last ten, fifteen years or so."

"What are all the changes around the back end?" Colman asked curiously. "It looks like a whole new drive system."

"It is. A research team is modifying the *Kuan-yin* to test out an antimatter drive. In fact the project is at quite an advanced stage. They're doing the same kind of thing back on Earth, aren't they?"

Colman's eyebrows arched in surprise. "True, but—wow! I had no idea that anything here was that advanced." Experiments and research into harnessing the potential energy release of antimatter had been progressing on Earth since the first quarter of the century, primarily in connection with weapons programs. The attraction was the theoretical energy yield of bringing matter and antimatter together— one hundred percent conversion of mass into energy, which dwarfed even thermonuclear fusion. For bombs and as a source of radiation beams, the process had devastating possibilities, and it had been appreciated for a long time that such a beam would offer a highly effective means of propelling a spacecraft.

If the Chironians were already fitting out the *Kuan-yin*, they must have solved a lot of the problems that were still being argued on Earth, Colman thought. The whole planet, he realized as he reflected on it, was a powerhouse of progress, unchecked by any traditions of unreason and with no vested-interest obstructionists to hold it back. If the pattern continued until Chiron became a fully populated world, it would effectively leave Earth back in the Stone Age within a century. "Have you actually flown it anywhere yet?" he asked, turning his head toward Kath. "The *Kuan-yin* . . . has it been anywhere since it arrived in orbit here?"

She nodded. "To both the moons, and we've sent missions to all of Alpha's other planets. But that was quite a while ago now. With the original drive. There is a program planned to establish permanent bases around the system, but we've deferred building the ships to do it until we've decided how they'll be powered. That's why the *Kuan-yin*'s being made into a test-bed. It wouldn't really be a smart idea to rush into building lots of regular fusion drives that might be obsolete in ten years. There's plenty to do on Chiron in the meantime, so there's no big hurry." She turned her face toward him and rubbed her cheek along his shoulder. "Anyhow, why are we talking about this? You told me I had to stop you from talking shop. Okay, I just did. Quit it."

Colman grinned and stroked her hair. "You're right. So what do you want to hear about?"

She wriggled closer and slid an arm across his chest. "Tell me about Earth. I've told you how I grew up. What was it like with you?"

Colman smiled ruefully. "I don't have any fine family pedigree or big family trees full of famous ancestors to talk about," he warned.

"I'm not interested in anything like that. I just want to hear about someone who lived there and came from there. Where did you come from?"

"A city called Chicago, originally. Heard of it?"

"Sure. It's on the lakes."

"That's right—Michigan. I think I was something of a not-very-welcome accident. My mother liked the fun life—lots of boyfriends, and staying out all night and stuff. I guess I was in the way a lot of the time."

"Was your father like that too?"

"I never found out who he was. For all I know, nobody else did either."

"Oh, I see."

Colman sighed. "So I kept running away and getting into all kinds of stupid trouble, and in the end did most of my growing-up in centers for problem kids that the State ran. Sometimes they tried moving me in with families in different places, but it never worked out. The last ones tried pretty hard. They adopted me legally, and that's how I got my name. Later we moved to Pennsylvania . . . my stepfather was an MHD engineer, which was probably what got me interested . . . but there was some trouble, and I wound up in the Army."

"Was that where you learned about engineering?" Kath asked.

"That came later—after I'd been on the ship for some time. At first I was with the infantry . . . saw some combat in Africa. I spent most of the voyage in the Engineer Corps though . . . up until about a year or two back."

"What made you sign up for the trip?"

Colman shrugged. "I don't know. I guess there didn't seem much risk of making any worse a mess of things than I had already."

Kath laughed and rolled back to stare up at the ceiling. "You're just like us, aren't you," she said. "You don't know where you came from either."

"That happened with a lot of people," Colman told her. "Things were so messed up after the war. . . . Does it matter?"

"I suppose not," Kath said. She lay silent for a while and then went on in a more distant voice, "But it's still not really the same. I mean, it must be wonderful to have actually been born there . . . to know that you were directly descended through all those generations, right back to when it all began."

"What?"

"Life! Earth life. You're a part of it. Isn't that an exciting feeling? It has to be."

"So are you," Colman insisted. "Chironian genes were dealt from the same deck as all the rest. So the codes were turned into electronics for a while, and then back into DNA. So what? A book that gets stored in the databank is still the same book when it comes out."

"Technically you're right," Kath agreed. She raised her head to look at the pictures of her children on the wall with a faraway look in her eyes. "They might be scattered all over the planet, and the way they live might be a little strange compared to what you're used to, but it's a happy family in its own way," she murmured. "But it's still not really the same. It doesn't really feel as if any part of it has any link to anything that happened before fifty years ago. Don't you think it's . . . oh, I don't know, kind of a shame somehow?"

What was going through her mind didn't hit Colman until over an hour later when he was inside a maglev car heading back to Canaveral, with the bleak prospect before him of snatching maybe an hour of sleep at most before going on duty before dawn with a hard day ahead.

Family?

Earth?

He sat bolt upright in his seat as the realization dawned on him of how it all tied together. Maybe Swyley did have it all figured out after all.

So *that* was why somebody from Chiron would want to get mixed up with a Terran!

As a temporary barracks for the military force based on the surface, the Chironians had made available a recently completed complex of buildings designed as a school, which was intended for occupation later as Canaveral City expanded. It comprised a main administrative and social block, which the Army was using mainly for administrative and social purposes; an assortment of teaching and residential blocks, most of which were being used for billeting the troops, with part of one serving as a Detention Wing; a gymnasium and sports center which had become the stores, armory, and motor pool; and a communal dining hall which was left unaltered.

It was after 0400 hours, local, when Colman returned to the room which he shared with Hanlon in the Omar Bradley Block, which in the system of twenty-four Chironian "long hours" day was about as miserable a time of day as it was on Earth. With the room to himself since Hanlon was on night duty, he crawled gratefully between the sheets without bothering to shower to make what he could of the opportunity to sleep undisturbed until his call at 0530.

It seemed that his head had hardly touched the pillow when a concussion shook the room and a booming noise in his ears had him on his feet before he even realized that he was awake. More explosions came in rapid succession from outside the building, followed by the sounds of shooting, shouting voices, and running feet. Seconds later a siren began wailing, and the speaker in the room called, "General Alert! General Alert! A breakout is being attempted from the Detention Wing. All officers and men report to General Alert stations."

What followed was a General Foul-up.

Colman found Sirocco in the Orderly Room, acting on

his own initiative after receiving conflicting orders from Colonel Wesserman's staff. Sirocco ordered most of the D Company personnel to secure the block against intrusion and cordoned off the routes past it toward the outside. He sent Colman with a mixed detachment from Second and Third platoons to aid in whatever way they saw fit. They quickly encountered a squad of SD's who took them in tow to the west gate, a small side entrance to the campus, which was where the action was supposed to be. Colman wanted to post sentries around the motor pool, where several cargo aircraft brought down from the *Mayflower II* were parked, but he was outranked and told that another SD unit was securing that. Then all the lights went out.

Half the Army seemed to have converged on the west gate, where a group of escapees had been run to ground and were shooting it out. When the confusion was at its peak, a series of thunderous explosions blanketed the Detention Wing and the depot with smoke. When the smoke cleared, one of the transporters was gone. No one had been guarding the motor pool.

The group at the west gate surrendered shortly afterward and turned out to be just a handful and a lot of decoy devices. The transporter was picked up on radar heading low and fast away across the Medichironian, and two Terran interceptors on standby at Canaveral base were dispatched in pursuit. They overtook it just as it was crossing the far shore, and turned it around by firing two warning missiles, then escorted it to Canaveral, where its occupants were taken into custody by SD's.

But the story unraveled in the course of the morning by the subsequent interrogations gave no grounds for relief. Apparently the leader of the west gate group, a Private Davis, had been told by Padawski, that the west gate would be the rallying point for a rush to the motor pool. Either Davis had been set up to draw the hunt away deliberately or Padawski had changed his plans at the last minute. Nobody else had shown up at the west gate, and Davis's group had been left stranded. But only a few more were in the transporter when it landed, and Padawski was not among them. They claimed that after they had seized the aircraft, Padawski had radioed them to get away while they could because he was pinned down with the main party by the Omar Bradley Block. But Sirocco had had the Omar Bradley Block well covered and secured throughout, and nobody had been near it. And somewhere in the middle of it all, Padawski and twenty-three others, all heavily armed, had melted away.

Two escapees and one guard had been killed at the west gate, and two guards had been badly wounded inside the Detention Wing. Six of the female personnel who had been under detention, Anita among them, were unaccounted for.

"It was one glorious fuck-up from start to finish," Sirocco declared, tugging at his moustache as he and Colman discussed the events late that evening. "Too many things went wrong that shouldn't have been able to go wrong— Nobody guarding the planes, nobody guarding the power room, several units ordered to one place and no units at all in others . . . And how did they get hold of the guns? I don't like it, Steve. I don't like it at all. There's a very funny smell to the whole business."

CHAPTER TWENTY-FOUR

EVEN IN HIS short time at the university near Franklin, Jerry Pernak had learned that Chironian theoretical and experimental physics had departed significantly from the mainstream being pursued on Earth. The Chironian scientists had not so much advanced past their terrestrial counterparts; rather, as perhaps was not surprising in view of the absence on Chiron of traditional habits of thought or authorities whose venerable opinions could not be challenged until after they were dead, they had gone off in a totally unexpected direction. And some of the things they had stumbled across on their way had left Pernak astounded.

Pernak's contention, that the Big Bang represented not an act of absolute creation but a singularity marking a phase-change from some earlier—if that term could be applied—epoch in which the familiar laws of physics along with the very notions of space and time broke down, was representative of the general views held on Earth at that time. Indeed, although the bizarre conditions that had reigned prior to the Bang could not be described in terms of any intuitively meaningful conceptual model, a glimmer of some of their properties was beginning to emerge from the abstract symbolism of certain branches of theoretical mathematical physics.

The bewildering proliferation first of baryons and mesons, and later the quarks, which were supposed to simplify them, that had plagued studies of the structure of matter to the end of the twentieth century had been reduced to an orderly hierarchy of "generations" of particles. Each generation contained just eight particles: six quarks

227

and two leptons. The first generation comprised the "up" and "down" quarks, each appearing in the three color-charge variants peculiar to the strong nuclear force to give six in all; the electron; and the electron-type neutrino. The second generation was made up of the "strange" and "charmed" quarks, each of them again appearing in three possible colors; the muon; and the muon-type neutrino. The third generation contained the "top" and "bottom" quarks; the tau; and the tau-type neutrino; and so it went on.

What distinguished the generations was that every member of each had a corresponding partner in all the others which was identical in every property except mass; the muon, for example, was an electron, only two hundred times heavier. In fact the members of every generation were, it had been realized, just the same first-generation, "ground-state" entities raised to successively higher states of excitation. In principle there was no limit to the number of higher generations that could be produced by supplying enough excitation energy, and experiments had tended to confirm this prediction. Nevertheless, all the exotic variations created could be accounted for by the same eight ground-state quarks and leptons, plus their respective antiparticles, together with the field quanta through which they interacted. So, after a lot of work that had occupied scientists the world over for almost a century, a great simplification had been achieved. But were quarks and leptons the end of the story?

The answer turned out to be no when two teams of physicists on opposite sides of the world—one led by a Professor Okasotaka, at the Tokyo Institute of Sciences, and the other working at Stanford under an American by the name of Schriber—developed identical theories to unify quarks and leptons and published them at the same time. It turned out that the sixteen entities and "anti-entities" of the ground-state generation could be explained by just two components which in themselves possessed surprisingly few innate properties: Each had a spin angular momentum of one-half unit, and one had an electrical charge of one-third while the other had none. The other properties which had been thought of as fundamental, such as quark color charge, quark "flavor," and even mass, to the astonishment of some, became seen instead as consequences of the ways in which combinations of these two basic components were *arranged,* much as a melody follows from an arrangement of notes but cannot be expressed as a property of a single note.

Thus there were two components, each of which had an "anticomponent." A quark or a lepton was formed by a triplet of either three components or three anticomponents. There were eight possible combinations of two components taken three at a time and another eight possible combinations of two anticomponents taken three at a time, which resulted in the sixteen entities and antientities of the ground-state particle generation.

With two types of component or anticomponent to choose from for each triplet, a triplet could comprise either three of a kind of one type, or two of one kind plus one of the other. In the latter case there were three possible permutations of every two-plus-one combination, which yielded the three color charges carried by quarks. The three-of-a-kind combinations could be arranged in only one way and corresponded to leptons, which was why leptons could not carry a color charge and did not react to the strong nuclear force.

Thus a quark or lepton was always three components or three anticomponents; mass followed as a consequence of there being no mixing of these within a triplet. Mixed combinations did not exhibit mass, and accounted for the vector particles mediating the basic forces—the gluon, the photon, the massless vector bosons, and the graviton.

Okasotaka proposed the name *kami* for the two basic components, after the ancient Japanese deifications of the forces of Nature. The Japanese gods had possessed two souls—one gentle, *nigi-mi-tama*; and one violent, *ara-mi-tama*—and, accordingly, Okasotaka christened his two species of *kami* "nigions" and "araons," which a committee on international standards solemnly ratified and enshrined into the officially recognized nomenclature of physics. Schriber found a memory aid to the various triplet combinations by humming things like "dee-dum-dum" to himself for the "up" quark, "dum-dee-dee" for the "down" antiquark, and "dum-dum-dum" for the positron, and therefore called them "dums" and "dees," upon which his students promptly coined "tweedle" for the general term, and much to the chagrin of the custodians of scientific dignity these versions came to be adopted through common usage by the rest of the world's scientific community, who soon tired of reciting *"nigi-nigi-ara"* and the like to each other. The scientists were less receptive to Schriber's claim that Quandum Mechanics had at last been unified with Relatividee.

Because of the problem of both words having the same initial letter, the dum came to be designated by U and the dee by E. The dum carried a one-third charge, and the dee carried none. Two dums and a dee made the up quark, its three possible color charges being represented by the three possible permutations, UUE, UEU, and EUU. Similarly two dees and a dum yielded the down antiquark in its three possible colors as UEE, EUE, and EEU; in the same way two "antidums" and an "antidee" gave the up antiquark; and two antidees and an antidum, the down quark. Three dums together carried unit charge but no color and resulted in the positron, designated $\bar{U}\bar{U}\bar{U}$, and three antidums, each one-third "anticharge," i.e., negative, made up the normal electron, UUU. Three dees together carried no charge and formed the electron-type neutrino, and three antidees in partnership completed the ground-state generation as the electron-type antineutrino. It followed that "antitweedles" didn't necessarily give an antiparticle, and tweedles didn't always make a particle. Tweedles predominated over antitweedles, however, in the constitution of normal matter; the proton, for example, comprising two up quarks and a down quark, was represented by a trio of "tweeplets" such as UUE; UEU; $\bar{U}\bar{E}\bar{U}$, depending on the color charges assigned to the three constituent quarks.

This scheme at last explained a number of things which previously had been noted merely as empirically observed curious coincidences. It explained why quarks came in three colors: Each one-plus-two combination of dums and dees had three and only three possible permutations. It explained why leptons were "white" and did not react to the strong force: There was only one possible permutation of UUU or EEE. And it explained why the electrical charges on quarks and leptons were equal: They were carried by the same tweedles. Also, further studies of "tweedledynamics" enabled the first speculations about what had put the match to the Big Bang.

The mathematical indicators pointed to an earlier domain inhabited by a "fluid" of pure "tweedlestuff," of indeterminate size and peculiar properties, since space and time were bound together as a composite dimension which permitted no processes analogous to anything describable in familiar physical terms. There were grounds for supposing that if an expanding nodule of disentangled space and time were introduced arbitrarily through some mechanism—pictured by some people as a bubble appearing in soda water, although this wasn't really accurate—the reduced "pressure" inside the bubble would trigger the condensation of raw tweedlestuff out of "tweedlespace" as an explosion of tweedles and antitweedles, the tweedles preserving the "timelike" aspect, and the antitweedles the "antitimelike" aspect of the timeless domain from which they originated. Their mutual affinity would precipitate their combination into a dense photon fluid in which timelessness became reestablished, which tied in with Relativity by explaining why time stood still for moving photons and accounting for the strange connection in the perceived universe between the rate at which time flowed and the speed of light. The high-energy conditions of the primordial photon fluid, the density of which would have approximated that of the atomic nucleus, would favor the formation of "tweeplet" entities to give rise to matter interacting under conditions dominated by the strong nuclear force, which manifested itself to restore non-Abelian gauge symmetry with respect to the variance introduced by the separation of space and time. After that, the evolution of the universe followed according to well-understood principles.

The theories currently favored on Earth attributed the

domination of matter, as opposed to antimatter, in the universe to a one-part-per-billion imbalance in the reactions occurring in the earliest phase of the Bang, in which the energy available produced copious numbers of exotic particles not found in the present universe, whose decay patterns violated baryon-number conservation. In the present universe they appeared rarely, only as transient "virtual particles" and were responsible for the almost immeasurable, but measured, 10^{31}-year mean lifetime of the proton.

It was believed virtual particles were virtual because the conditions of the present universe could not supply the energy necessary to sustain tweeplets. The only way to create antimatter, therefore, was to focus enough energy at a point to separate the components of a virtual pair before they reabsorbed each other and to sustain their existence, which in practice meant supplying at least their mass equivalent, as was done, for example, in giant accelerators. This was the reason for the widespread skepticism that any net energy gain could ever be realized from annihilating the antimatter later. At best it was felt to be an elaborate storage battery, and not a very efficient one at that; the power poured into the accelerator would be better applied directly to whatever the antimatter was wanted for.

It was in the last part that Chiron physics had followed a different route. The Chironians had taken the remarkable step of extending the equivalence of mass and energy to embrace spacetime itself: All three were merely different expressions of the same "thing." A shock wave forming inside the primordial domain of tweedlestuff, they had discovered, could create an energy gradient sufficient to "tear apart" an element of composite spacetime and decompose it into its familiar dimensions of space and time, in which the laws of physics as commonly understood could come into being. Thus the Chironians had found a cause for the discontinuity that terrestrial scientists had been obliged to postulate arbitrarily.

The subsequent expansion of space followed directly from the Chironian mass-energy-space equivalence relationship: The cooling photon fluid actually transformed into space as well as matter tweeplets, the ratio depending on the temperature and shifting from one favoring tweeplets to one favoring space as the universe cooled down. Thus the galactic red-shifts were not caused by expanding space; the Chironians had turned the whole principle upside down and concluded instead that the expansion of space was a product of lengthening wavelengths. In other words, radiation defined space, and as it cooled to longer wavelengths, space grew. Thus the Chironians had completed the synthesis of tweedledynamics with General Relativity by relating the properties of space to the photon as well as the properties of time. The "islands" of matter tweeplets left behind from the cooling photon fluid remained dominated internally by the strong force while gravitation became the dominant influence in the macroscopic realm created outside, and in many ways they continued to behave as microcosms of the domain from which they had originated.

Even more remarkable was another prediction that followed from the Chironian symmetry relationships, which required the creation of an "antiuniverse" along with the universe, populated by antimatter and consisting of an extraordinary realm in which "antitime" ran backward and "antispace" contracted from an initial volume of zero. Universes, like particles, were created in pairs. And it was the duality of universes, each exhibiting a spacetime decomposed into two discrete dimensions, which gave rise to the two-way duality manifested by tweedles and antitweedles: Dums, dees, antidums, and antidees were simply spacelike, timelike, antispacelike, and antitimelike projections of the same fundamental entity existing in the timeless, spaceless domain of tweedlespace.

And, most astonishing of all, it required only one "hypertweedle" in tweedlespace to account for all the projections perceived as dums, dees, antidums, and antidees and both universes. A universe provided, in effect, a screen upon which the same projections were repeated over and over again as a consequence of the separation of the space and time dimensions of the screen itself, which of course was why every dum was the same as every other dum, and every dee the same as every other dee. It was as if a typewriter created paper as it typed on, leaving the planar inhabitants of the flat universe that it had brought into being to ponder why all the characters encountered serially in their own "flat-time" should have exactly the same form.

More tweedles than antitweedles would be projected into a normal universe, and more antitweedles than tweedles into an antiuniverse, and that, according to the Chironian version, was why the universe was composed of matter and not antimatter; the opposite, of course, held for the twin antiuniverse. The way to obtain antimatter, they therefore reasoned, would be to make a small part of the universe look like an antiuniverse so that tweedlespace could be "fooled" into projecting antitweedles instead of tweedles into it. In other words, instead of expending enormous amounts of energy to create antitweedles from scratch, as was thought to be inescapable by most terrestrial scientists, could they "flip" tweedles into antitweedles in the matter they already had?

To the astonishment of even themselves, they found that they could. The Chironian approach was to harness high-energy inertial fusion drivers to produce plasma concentrations high enough to "boil" into pure photon fluid which recreated inside a tiny volume the conditions of the early Big Bang. Within this region, space and time recoupled and contracted inward with the imploding core to simulate for an instant the bizarre, inverted conditions of an antiuniverse, and in that instant a large portion of the tweedles liberated in the process transformed into antitweedles which, under the prevailing high-energy conditions, combined preferentially into antiquarks and antileptons rather than radiation. Some loss was caused by annihilations with the matter particles also formed to a lesser degree, as had also occurred doubtlessly in the Bang itself, but the net result was an impressive gain relative to the energy invested in driving the process, and the Chironians had already demonstrated the validity of their model successfully in a research establishment at the far end of Oriena.

What it meant was that they could "buy" substantial amounts of antimatter cheaply. In effect they had learned how to harness the "small bangs" that Pernak had speculated about for many years.

The theory opened up whole new realms, Pernak was beginning to appreciate as he sat back in his office to give his mind a rest from absorbing the information being presented on the wall screen opposite. What he was starting to glimpse hadn't just to do with the physics; it was the completely new philosophy of existence that came with the physical interpretation.

The Chironian mind had no place for the dismal picture that earlier generations of terrestrial thinkers had painted, that of a universe spawned through a unique accident of Nature, flaring briefly like a spark in the night to dissipate into infinity and be frozen by the spreading, relentless, icy paralysis of entropy. To the Chironian, the universe was but one atom of a possibly infinite Universe of sibling universes, every one of which coexisted at every point in space with the source-realm that had procreated its family with the profligacy of a summer stormcloud precipitating raindrops. Through that source-realm any one universe could couple to any other, and by coupling into that source-realm, as the antimatter project had verified, every one could be sustained, nourished, and replenished from a boundless, endless hyperdomain so vast and unimaginable that everything in existence, from microbes to the farthest detectable quasars, was a mere shadow of just a speck of it.

Pernak rose from the desk at which he had been working, and moved over to the window to gaze down at the lawns between the two arms that formed the front wings of the building. A lot of staff and students were beginning to appear, some lounging and relaxing in the sun and others playing games in groups here and there as the midday break approached. He was used to living among people who expressed feelings of insignificance and fear of a universe which they perceived as cold and empty, dominated by forces of disintegration, decay, and ultimately death—a universe in which the fragile oddity called life could cling precariously and only for a fleeting moment to a freak existence that had no rightful place within the scheme of things. Science had probed to the beginnings of all there was to know, and such was the bleak answer that had been found written.

The Chironian, by contrast, saw a rich, bright, vibrant universe manifesting at every level of structure and scale of magnitude the same irresistible force of self-ordering, self-organizing evolution that had built atoms from plasma, molecules from atoms, then life itself, and from there produced the supreme phenomenon of mind and all that could be created by mind. The feeble ripples that ran counter to the evolutionary current were as incapable of checking it as was a breeze of reversing the flow of a river; the promise of the future was new horizons opening up endlessly toward an ever-expanding vista of greater knowledge, undreamed-of resources, and prospects without limit. Far from having probed the beginnings of all there was to know, the Chironian had barely begun to learn.

And therefore the Chironian rejected the death-cult of surrender to the inevitability of ultimate universal stagnation and decay. Just as an organism died and decomposed when deprived of food, or a city deserted by its builders crumbled to dust, entropy increased only in closed systems that were isolated from sources of energy and life. But the Chironian universe was no longer a closed system. Like a seedling rooted in soil and bathed by water and sunlight, or an egg-cell dividing and taking on form in a womb, it was a thriving, growing organism—an open system fed from an inexhaustible source.

And for such a system the universal law was not death, but life.

Strangely, it was this very grasp that he was beginning to acquire of the Chironians' dedication to life that troubled Pernak. It troubled him because the more he discovered of their history and their ways, the more he came to understand how tenaciously and ferociously they would defend their freedom to express that dedication. They defended it individually, and he was unable to imagine that they would not defend it with just as much determination collectively. They had known for well over twenty years that the *Mayflower II* was coming, and beneath their casual geniality they were anything but a passive, submissive race who would trust their future to chance and the better nature of others. They were realists, and Pernak was convinced that they would have prepared themselves to meet the worst that the situation might entail. Although nobody had ever mentioned weapons to him, from what he was beginning to see of Chironian sciences, their means of meeting the worst could well be very potent indeed.

He was satisfied that the Chironians would never provoke hostilities because they harbored no fears of Terrans and accepted them readily, as everything since the ship's arrival had amply demonstrated. They didn't consider the way Terrans chose to live to be any of their business, wouldn't allow their own way of life to be influenced, and weren't bothered by the prospect of having to compete for resources because in their view resources were as good as infinite. But he felt less reassured about the Terrans—at least some of them. Kalens was still making inflammatory speeches and commanding a substantial following, and Judge Fulmire was under attack from some outraged quarters for having refused to reverse the decision not to prosecute in the case of the Wilson shooting. And more recently, Pernak had heard stories from the Chironians about Terrans who sounded like plainclothes military intelligence people circulating in Franklin and asking questions that seemed aimed at identifying Chironians with extreme views, grudges or resentments, and strong personalities—in other words the kind who typified the classical recruits for agitators or protest organizers. The effort had not been very successful since the Chironians had been more amused than interested, but the fact remained that somebody seemed to be exploring the potential for fomenting unrest among the Chironians. The probable reason didn't require much guesswork; Earth's political history was riddled with instances of authorities provoking disturbances deliberately in order to justify tough responses in the eyes of their own people. If some faction, and presumably a fairly powerful one, was indeed maneuvering to bring about a confrontation, and if what Pernak was beginning to glimpse of the Chironians was anything to go by, then that faction might well be in for some nasty surprises. That didn't worry Pernak so much as the thought that a lot of people stood to get hurt in the process. Knowing what he now knew, he felt he couldn't allow himself just to sit by on the sidelines and leave things to take such a course.

Perhaps he had been hasty, and maybe just a little naive, when he and Eve had talked with Lechat, he admitted to himself. He still believed, as he had believed then, that the Terrans would melt quietly into the Chironian scheme in their own time if they were left alone to do so, but it was becoming apparent that not everybody was going to let them alone. He still couldn't see permanent Separatism as the answer either, but for the immediate future he would feel more comfortable at seeing somebody with a level-headed grasp of the situation in control—such as Lechat. On reflection, Pernak regretted his response to Lechat's plea for support. But it was far from too late for him to be able to change that. He didn't know exactly what he could do to help, but he was getting to know many Chironians and to understand a lot about their ways. Surely that knowledge could be put to some useful purpose.

Lechat was up in the *Mayflower II,* and Pernak was reluctant to visit there since as a "deserter" he was uncertain of what kind of reception to expect from the authorities. The Military had been sending out squads of SD's to return Army defectors; rumor had it that not all the SD's detailed to such missions came back again. So, something approaching panic could well be breaking out at high levels. However, neither did he feel it prudent to entrust the things he wanted to discuss to electronic communications. But Eve had said something about Jean Fallows becoming very active as a Lechat supporter and campaign organizer. . . . That would be a good place to begin.

He nodded to himself. That was what he would do. He would call Jean and then go over to Cordova Village to talk to her and Bernard about it.

CHAPTER TWENTY-FIVE

LEIGHTON MERRICK FORMED his fingers into a fluted column to support the Gothic arch of his brows and stared down at the desk while he chose his words. "Ah, I've been looking over your record, Fallows," he said when he looked up. "It shows a consistent attention to detail that is very pronounced . . . everything thorough and complete, and properly documented. It's commendable, very commendable . . . the kind of thing we could do with more of in the Service."

"Thank you, sir." It was obviously a softener. Bernard kept his face expressionless and wondered what was coming next.

Merrick allowed his hands to drop down to his chest. "And how are you settling in? Is your family adjusting well?"

"Very smoothly, considering that it's been twenty years." Bernard permitted a faint smile. "Jean's finding some things a bit strange, but I'm sure she'll get over it."

"Good, very good. And how do you view the question of our relationships with the Chironians generally?"

"I find them a refreshingly honest and direct people. You know where you stand with them." Bernard gave a slight shrug. "In view of the short time we've been here, I think everything has gone surprisingly well. Certainly it could have been a lot worse."

"Hmm . . ." The reply didn't seem quite what Merrick hoped for. "Not quite everything, surely," he said. "What about the shooting of Corporal Wilson a week ago?"

"That was unfortunate," Bernard agreed. "But in my opinion, sir, he asked for it."

"That may be, but it's beside the point that I was try-ing to make," Merrick said. "Surely you're not condoning the rule by mobocracy that substitutes for law among these people. Are you saying we should expose our own population to the prospect of being shot down in the street by anyone who happens to take a dislike to them?"

Bernard sighed. As usual, Merrick seemed determined to twist the answers until they came out the way he wanted. "Of course not," Bernard replied. "But I think people are exaggerating the situation. That incident was not representative of what we should expect. The Chironians act as they're treated. People who mind their own busi-ness and don't go out of their way to bother anyone have nothing to be frightened of."

"So everyone becomes a law unto himself," Merrick concluded.

"No, the law is there, implicitly, and it applies to every-one, but you have to learn how to read it." Bernard frowned. That hadn't come out the way he had intended. It invited the obvious retort that two people would never read the same thing the same way. The difference was that the Chironians could make it work. "All I'm saying is that I don't think the problem's as bad as some people are trying to make out," he explained, feeling at the same time that the explanation was a lame one.

"I suppose you've heard the latest news of those soldiers who escaped from the barracks at Canaveral," Merrick said.

"Yes, but that situation can't last. If the Army doesn't get them soon, the Chironians will."

Padawski and his followers had somehow shown up on the far side of the Medichironian, which was only sparsely settled, and seemed to be settling in as bandits in the hills. What a bandit would hope to achieve on a world like Chiron was hard to see, but revenge against Chironians seemed to have a lot to do with it; two isolated homes had been invaded, ransacked, and looted, in the course of which five Chironians and one soldier had been killed. Three Chironians, including a fifteen-year-old girl, had been raped. The Army was scouring the area from the air and with search parties on foot, but so far without success —the renegades were well trained in the arts of concealment. Satellites were of limited use if they didn't know exactly where to look, especially where rough terrain was involved.

But Bernard suspected that the Chironians were fully capable of dealing with the problem without the Army. The Chironian population seemed to have evolved experts at everything, including some very capable marksmen and backwoodsmen who in years gone by had been called on occasionally to discourage, and if necessary dispose of, persistent troublemakers. Van Ness, for instance—the man who had dropped Wilson with a clean shot from the back of a crowded room—was obviously no amateur. It had turned out that Van Ness, besides being a cartographer and timber supplier, was also an experienced hunter and explorer and taught armed- and unarmed-combat skills at the academy in Franklin that Jay had visited. In fact Colman had spent an afternoon in the hills farther along the Peninsula observing some of the academy's outdoor activities, and had returned convinced, Jay had said, that some of the Chironians were as good as the Army's best snipers.

But Merrick didn't seem inclined to pursue that side of the matter. "Nevertheless Chironians are getting killed," he said. "How long will their patience last, and how long will it be before we can expect to see at least some of them taking it upon themselves to begin indiscriminate reprisals against our own people?—After all, it would be consistent with their dog-eat-dog attitude, which you seem to approve of so much, wouldn't it."

"I never said anything of the kind. The whole point is that they are *not* indiscriminate. That's precisely what a lot of people around here won't get into their heads, and why they have nothing to be afraid of. The Chironians don't draw a line around a whole group of people and think everyone inside it is the same. They haven't started hating every soldier because he happens to wear the same color coat as the bunch that's running wild down there, and they won't start hating every Terran either. They don't think that way."

Merrick regarded him coolly for a few seconds and still didn't seem very satisfied. "Well, all I can say is that not everyone shares your enviable faith in human nature—myself included, I might add. The official policy conveyed to me from the Directorate, which it is your duty as well as mine to support irrespective of our own personal views, is that the possibility of violent reaction from the Chironians cannot be dismissed. Therefore we must allow for such an eventuality in considering the future."

Bernard spread his hands resignedly. "Very well, I can see the sense in being prepared. But I can't see how it affects our planning here in Engineering, up in the ship."

Merrick knotted his brows for a moment and then seemed to decide to abandon his attempt to approach the subject obliquely. "Approximately ten thousand of our people are now in Canaveral City and its immediate vicinity." He looked straight at Bernard. "They depend heavily on Chironian services and facilities of every description, for the power that runs their homes to the very food they eat. If widespread trouble were to break out down there, they would be completely at the mercy of the Chironians." He raised a hand to stifle any objection before Bernard could speak. "Clearly we cannot tolerate such a state of affairs. It has been decided therefore that, purely as a precautionary measure to protect our own people if the need should arise, we must be able to guarantee the continuity of essential services if circumstances should demand. Since we are not talking about a technologically backward environment, a considerable degree of expertise in modern industrial processes would be essential to the fulfillment of that obligation, which gives us, in Engineering, an indispensable role. I trust you see my point."

Bernard's eyes narrowed a fraction. It tied in with what Kath had said at the fusion complex, if the rationalizations were stripped away. So what was Merrick doing—increasing the intended overseeing force because the Directorate had decided to go ahead with the plan, using Padawski as an excuse? "I'm not sure that I do," he replied. "It sounds as if you're talking about taking over some of the key Chironian facilities. Wouldn't that only make any trouble worse?"

"I made no mention of taking over anything. I'm merely saying we should be sufficiently familiar with their operations to be able to guarantee services if we are required to. Now that we've had an opportunity to look at Port Norday and a few other installations, I am reasonably confident we could manage them. I didn't want to take up too much of everybody's time before, but since the whole thing now seems feasible I'd like you to have a look at what's at Norday. You should take Hoskins with you. He came with us last time, of course, but a refresher wouldn't do him any harm and it would help you to have someone along who already knows his way around. That was really what I wanted to talk to you about." Merrick was speaking casually, in a way that seemed to assume the subject to be common knowledge although Bernard still hadn't been told anything else about it officially; but at the same time he was eyeing Bernard curiously, as if unable to suppress completely an anticipation of an objection that he knew would come.

Bernard decided to play along to see what happened. "I'm sorry—how do you mean, last time? I must be missing something."

Merrick's eyebrows shot up in an expression of surprise that was just a little too hasty. "The last time we went to see the complex at Port Norday." Bernard stared blankly at him. Merrick seemed pained. "Don't tell me you didn't know. I went there with Walters and Hoskins a while ago. Didn't Walters tell you about it?"

"Nobody told me anything."

Merrick's pained expression deepened into a frown. "Tch, tch, that's inexcusable. How unfortunate. Let me see now—I can't remember exactly when it was, but you were on duty. That was why I couldn't include you at the time." That was an outright lie; Bernard had been there on his day off, with Jay. "But anyway, we can soon put that straight. You'll find the place fascinating. A woman runs most of the primary process—a remarkable lady—so I can promise you some interesting company as well as interesting surroundings. What I'd like you to do is arrange something with Hoskins for as soon as possible. I'm afraid I'll be tied up for the next couple of days."

Obviously something unusual was going on. Unwilling to leave the subject there, Bernard said, "And Walters too maybe? Perhaps he could use a refresher too."

Merrick drew a long breath, and his expression became grave. "Mmm . . . Walters. That brings me to the other thing I have to tell you," he said in a heavy voice. "Officer Walters is no longer with us. He and his family disappeared from Cordova Village two days ago and have not been heard of since. He failed to report for duty yesterday. We must assume that he has absconded. He shook his head sadly. "Disappointing, Fallows, most disappointing. I credited him with more character."

So that was it! Merrick's blue-eyed boy had let him down, and he needed a replacement. Merrick didn't give a damn about Bernard's qualities as an engineer; he was interested only in extricating himself from what was no doubt an embarrassing predicament. As Bernard thought back over the deviousness that he had listened to since he sat down, his memory of Kath's frankness and openness, even to a stranger, came back like a breath of fresh air. "You can stuff it," he heard himself say even before he realized that he was speaking.

"*What?*" Merrick sat up rigidly in his chair. "What did you say, Fallows?"

"I said you can stuff it." Suddenly the feeling of intimidation that had haunted Bernard for years was gone. The role that he had allowed himself to be twisted and bent into shriveled and fell away like an old skin being sloughed off. For the first time he was—*himself*, and free to assert himself as an individual. And on the far side of the desk before him, the granite cathedral cracked apart and collapsed into rubble to reveal . . . nothing inside. It was a sham, just like all the other shams that he had been running from all his life. He had just stopped running.

Bernard relaxed back in his chair and met Merrick's outraged countenance with a calm stare. "Nobody's going to shut that complex down, and you know it," he said. "Save the propaganda. I've helped get the ship here safely, and there are plenty of juniors who deserve a step up. I've done my job. I'm quitting."

"But you can't!" Merrick sputtered.

"I just did."

"You have a contractual agreement."

"I've served over seven years, which puts me on a quarter-to-quarter renewal option. Therefore I owe you a maximum of three months. Okay, I'm giving it. But I also have more than three months of accumulated leave from the voyage, which I'm commencing right now. You'll have that confirmed in writing within five minutes." He stood up and walked to the door. "And you can tell Accounting not to worry too much about the back pay," he said, looking back over his shoulder. "I won't be needing it."

Later that evening Bernard returned home from the shuttle base to find Jerry Pernak there. Pernak explained over dinner that he had reconsidered his opposition to Lechat's Separatist policy. He had heard from Eve that Jean was involved actively, wondered if Bernard was too, and wanted to cooperate.

Bernard couldn't see why Pernak had changed his mind. "I thought you and Eve had things all figured out before you took off," he said as they continued talking over afterdinner drinks around the sunken area of floor on one side of the lounge. "Look what's happening—you've left, other people are leaving all over. You were right. Just leave the situation alone and let it straighten itself out."

"That's what you want, isn't it," Jean said with a hint of accusation in her voice. "You'd like us to be the way they are. But have you really thought about what that would mean? No standards, no order to anything, no morality . . . I mean, what kind of a way would that be for Jay and Marie to grow up?"

Jay and Marie were her latest weapons. Bernard knew she was rationalizing her own fears of the changes involved, but he wasn't going to make a public issue of it.

"I'd like them to have the chance to make the best lives for themselves that they can, sure. They've got that chance right here. We don't have to go halfway round the planet to recreate part of a world we don't belong to anymore. It couldn't last. That's all over now. You have to bring yourself to face up to it, hon."

"We're still the some people," Jay said from the end of the sofa, looking at his mother. "That's not going to change. If you're going to act dumb, you can do that anywhere." To Bernard's mild surprise Jay had shown a lively interest in the conversation all through dinner and had elected to sit in afterward. About time too, Bernard thought to himself.

Jean shook her head, still refusing to contemplate the prospect. "But why does it have to be over?" She looked imploringly at Bernard. "We were happy all those years in the ship, weren't we? We had our friends, like Jerry and Eve, we had the children. There was your job. Why should this planet take it all away from us? They don't have the right. We never wanted anything from them. It's—it's all wrong."

Bernard felt the color rising at the back of his neck. The pathos that she was trying to project was touching a raw nerve. He refilled his glass with a slow, deliberate movement while he brought his feelings under control. "What makes you so sure I found it all that wonderful?" he asked. "Aren't you assuming the same right to tell me what I ought to want?" He put the bottle down on the table with a thud and looked up. "Well, I didn't think it was so wonderful, and I don't want any more of it. Today I told Merrick to stuff his job up his ass."

"You what?" Jean gasped, horrified.

"I told him to stuff it. It's over. We can be us now. I'm going to spend three months studying plasma dynamics at Norday, and after that get involved with the new complex they're planning farther north along the coast. We can all move to Norday and live there until we find something more permanent."

Jean shook her head in protest. "But you can't . . . I won't go. I want to move to Iberia."

"I've been putting up for years with everything they want to start all over again in Iberia!" Bernard thundered suddenly, slamming down his glass. His face turned crimson. "I hated every minute of it. Who ever asked me if that was what I wanted? Nobody. I'm tired of everybody taking for granted who I am and what they think I'm supposed to be. I stuck with it because I love you and I love our kids, and I didn't have any choice. Well, now I have a choice, and this time *you* owe *me*. I say we're going to Norday, and goddamnit we're going to Norday!"

Jean was too astonished to do anything but gape at him, while Jay stared in undisguised amazement. Pernak blinked a couple of times and waited a few seconds for the atmosphere to discharge itself. "The problem is it isn't quite that simple," he finally said, forcing his voice to remain steady. "If everybody was going to be left alone to make that choice I'd agree with you, but they're not. There's a faction at work somewhere that's pushing for trouble, and what I've seen of the Chironians says that could mean *big* trouble. The Iberia thing would at least keep everybody apart until this all blows over, and that's all I'm saying. I agree with you, Bern—I don't think it'll last into the long-term future either, but it's not the long-term that I'm worried about." He glanced at Jean apologetically. "Sorry, but that's how I think it'll go."

Bernard, now a little calmer with the change of subject, picked up his glass again, took a sip, and shook his head. "Aren't you overreacting just a little bit, Jerry? Exactly what kind of trouble are you talking about? What have we seen?" He looked from side to side as if to invite support. "One idiot who should never have been allowed out of a cage got what he asked for. I'm sorry if that sounds like a callous way of putting it, but it's what I think. And that's all we've seen."

"Have you seen the news this evening?" Jean asked. "Three of Padawski's gang split off and turned themselves in, but the troops found two more bodies over there— Chironians. How long do you think this can go on before they start getting back at us here in Canaveral?"

Bernard shook his head in a way that said he rejected

the suggestion totally. "They won't. They're not like that. They just don't think that way."

"But how can you be so sure?"

"I'm getting to know them."

"And I'm getting to know them better," Pernak told both of them. Something in his tone made them turn their heads toward him curiously. He spread his hands above his knees. "It's not exactly that kind of trouble I'm bothered about. But if this goes further than that . . . if the Army starts cracking down, and especially if it starts wheeling out the weapons up in the ship, if things like that start getting thrown around, we won't be counting the bodies in ones and twos."

Bernard looked at him uncertainly. "I'm not with you, Jerry. Why should it escalate to anything like that? The Chironians don't have anything in that league anyway."

"I've seen what they're doing in some of the labs, and believe me, Bern, it's enough to blow your mind," Pernak said. "Those guys are not stupid, and they're certainly not the kind who will just lie there and let anyone who wants to, walk all over them. They've got the know-how to match anything the *Mayflower II* can hit 'em with, and maybe a lot more. They've known for well over twenty years what to expect. Well, figure the rest out yourself."

Bernard stared at his glass for a few seconds, then shook his head again. "I can't buy it," he said. "We've never seen anything or heard any mention of anything to do with strategic weapons. Where are they supposed to be?"

"We've only seen Franklin," Pernak replied. "There's a whole planet out there."

"Ghosts in your head," Bernard said. "Come on, Jerry, you're a scientist. Where's your evidence? Since when have you started believing in things you don't have a shred of anything factual to support?"

"Gut-feel," Pernak told him. "The weapons have to exist. I tell you, I know how these people's minds work."

Jay stood up and left the room quietly. Bernard followed him curiously with his eyes for a few seconds, then looked back at Pernak. "But it's a hell of a thin case for shipping everyone off to Iberia, isn't it? And besides, if you're right, then I'd have thought the best place to stay would be right here—all mixed up together with the Chironians. That way nobody's likely to start throwing any big bombs around, right?" He turned his head to grin briefly at Jean. "I think Jerry made my point."

Pernak remained unsmiling. "What about that ship sitting twenty thousand miles out in space?" he said.

Before Bernard could reply, Jay came back in carrying the landscape painting he had brought back from Franklin after his first expedition out exploring. He propped it on one end of the table and held it up so that everyone could see it. "Do you notice anything unusual about that?" he asked them.

Pernak and Jean looked at each other, puzzled. Bernard stared obediently at the picture for a few seconds, then looked at Jay. "It looks like a nicely done painting of mountains," he said. "Is this supposed to have something to do with what we're talking about?"

Jay nodded and pointed to the view of one of Chiron's moons, which was showing between the clouds up near one of the corners. "That's Remus," he said. "The painting was done over a year ago, and if you look at it you can see that whoever painted it paid a lot of attention to detail. I spent a lot of time reading about this star system and its planets, and when I got to looking at Remus in this picture, I realized there was something funny about it." Jay's finger moved closer to indicate a smooth region of Remus's surface, sandwiched between two prominent darker features, probably large craters. "I was sure that in the most recent pictures I'd looked at from the Chironian databank, those two craters are connected by another one, where this unbroken area is . . . a big one, several hundred miles across. When I checked, I found I was right—there's a huge crater right here, and it wasn't there a year ago."

Bernard frowned as the implication of what Jay was suggesting sank in. "Did you ask Jeeves about it?" he inquired.

"Yes, I did. Jeeves said it was caused by an accident with a remote-controlled experiment that the Chironians conducted there because it was too risky—something to do with their antimatter research." Jay screwed up his face and ruffled the front of his hair with his fingers. "But that's the kind of thing you'd expect somebody to say, isn't it . . . and Chironians don't make a lot of mistakes." He looked around the circle of appalled faces staring back at him. "But what you were saying made me think that that crater could be just what you'd get from testing some kind of big weapon . . ."

Bernard, Pernak, and Jean stared at the picture for a long time. Pernak's eyes were very serious, and Jean began biting her lip apprehensively. At last Bernard nodded and looked at the other two. "Okay, I'm with you," he told them. "Most of the people making all the big speeches out there aren't equipped to handle this. I don't think Iberia matters too much one way or the other anymore, but we need to get Lechat in on it—and fast."

CHAPTER TWENTY-SIX

THE FIRST BOMB exploded in the center of Canaveral City in the early hours of the morning, causing serious damage to the maglev terminal where the spur line into the shuttle base joined the main through-route from Franklin out to the Peninsula. Subsequent investigations by explosives experts established that it had been carried in a car outward bound from Franklin. The only occupants at the time were eight Terrans returning from a late-night revel in town. They were killed instantly.

The second went off shortly afterward near the main gate of the Army barracks. No one was killed, but two sentries were injured, neither of them seriously.

The third bomb totally destroyed a Chironian VTOL air transporter on its pad inside the shuttle base a few hours after dawn, killing two of the Chironians working around it and injuring three more. Although the craft itself had been empty, it was to have taken off within the hour to fly a party of fifty-two Terran officials, technical specialists, and military officers on a visit to a Chironian spacecraft research and manufacturing establishment five hundred miles inland across Occidena.

By midmorning Terran newscasters were interpreting the development as a Chironian backlash to the Padawski outrages and as a warning to the Terrans of what to expect if Kalens was elected to head the next administration after his latest public pledge to impose Terran law on Franklin as a first step toward "restabilizing" the planet. Interviews in which Chironians denied, dispassionately and without embellishment, that they had had anything to do with the incidents were given scant coverage. Reactions among the

Terrans were mixed. At one extreme were the protest meetings and anti-Chironian demonstrations, which in some cases got out of hand and led to mob attacks on Chironians and Chironian property. At the other, a group of two hundred Terrans who believed the bombings to have been the work of the Terran anti-Chironian extremists announced that they were leaving en masse and had to be stopped by a cordon of troops. Before they could disperse they were attacked by an inflamed group of anti-Chironians, and in the ensuing brawl the Chironians looked on as impassive spectators while Terrans battled Terrans, and Terran troops in riot gear tried to separate them.

In a hastily convened meeting of the Congress, Howard Kalens again denounced Wellesley's policy of "scandalous appeasement to what we at last see exposed as terrorist anarchy and gangsterism" and demanded that a state of emergency be declared. In a stormy debate Wellesley stood firm by his insistence that alarming though the events were, they did not constitute a general threat comparable to the in-flight hazards that the emergency proviso had been intended to cover; they did not warrant resorting to such an extreme. But Wellesley had to do something to satisfy the clamor from all sides for measures to protect the Terrans down on the surface.

Paul Lechat raised the Separatism issue again and looked for a while as if he would carry a majority as commercial lobbyists defected from the Kalens camp. But the timing of the moment was not in Lechat's favor, and Borftein torpedoed the motion fresh off the launching ramp with a scathing depiction of them all allowing themselves to be chased off across the planet like beggars from somebody's back door. Ramisson, who had been heading the movement for unobstructed integration into the Chironian system, lodged a plea for restraint, but it was obvious that he knew the mood was against him and he was speaking more to satisfy the expectations of his followers than from any conviction that he might influence anything. The assembly listened dutifully and took no notice.

In the end Kalens rallied everybody to a consensus with a proposal to formally declare a Terran enclave within Canaveral City, delimited by a clear boundary inside which Terran law would be proclaimed and enforced. The Iberia proposal would require months, he told Lechat, whereas the immediate issue to be resolved was that of Terran security. In any case, it could hardly be carried out without an electorial mandate. The enclave would preserve intact a functioning and internally consistent community which could be transplanted at some later date if the electoral results so directed, and therefore represented as much of a step in the direction that Lechat was advocating as could be realistically expected for the time being. Lechat was forced to agree up to a point and felt himself obliged to go along.

Kalens had evidently been working on the details for some time. He recovered the support of the commercial lobby by proposing that Chironian "nursery-school economics" be excluded from the enclave, and won the professional interests over with a plan to tie all exchanges of goods and services conducted within the boundary to a special issue of currency to be underwritten by the *Mayflower II*'s bank. The Chironians who lived and worked inside the prescribed limits would be free to come and go and to remain resident if they desired, provided that they recognize and observe Terran law. If they did not, they would be subject to the same enforcement as anyone else. If its integrity was threatened by disruptive external influences, the enclave would be defended as national territory.

Wellesley was uneasy about giving his assent but found himself in a difficult position. After backing down and conceding the state-of-emergency issue, Kalens came across as the voice of reasonable compromise, which Wellesley realized belatedly was probably exactly what Kalens had intended. Wellesley had no effective answer to a remark of Kalens's that if something weren't done about the desertions, Wellesley could well end his term of office with the dubious distinction of presiding over an empty ship; the desertions had been as much a thorn in Wellesley's side as anybody's.

That touched at what was really at the bottom of it all. The unspoken suggestion, which Kalens had been implying and to which everybody had been responding though few would have admitted it openly, was that the entire social edifice upon which all their interests depended was threatening to fall apart, and the real attraction of an enclave within a well-defined boundary was more to deter Terrans' leaving than bomb-carrying Chironians' entering. Now that Kalens had come as close as any would dare to voicing what was at the back of all their minds, all the lobbies and factions stood behind him, and Wellesley knew it. If Wellesley opposed, he stood to be voted out of office. So he concurred, and the resolution was passed all but unanimously.

Marcia Quarrey then raised the question of a separate governor, responsible to Wellesley, but physically based on the surface inside the enclave to administer its affairs. Perhaps the division of authority between the members of the Directorate sitting twenty thousand miles away in the ship had contributed to the difficulties experienced since planetfall, she suggested, and delegating it to one person who had the advantages of being on the spot would remedy a lot of defects. Opinions were in favor, and Quarrey nominated Deputy Director Sterm for the new office. Sterm, however, declined on the grounds that a large part of the job would involve policymaking connected with Terran-Chironian relationships, and since a Liaison Director existed to whom that responsibility was already entrusted, the sensible way to avoid possible conflicts was to unify the two functions. He therefore nominated Howard Kalens; Quarrey seconded, and the vote was carried by a wide margin.

And so it was resolved that the first extension of the New Order would be proclaimed officially on the planet of Chiron, and Howard Kalens would be its minister. He had gained the first toehold of his empire. "It's the beginning," he told Celia later that night. "Ten years from now it will have become the capital of a whole world. With a whole army behind me, what can a rabble of ruffians with handguns do to stop me now?"

That same night, on one side of the floodlit landing area in the military barracks at Canaveral, Colman was standing with a detachment from D Company, silently watching the approach of a Chironian transporter that had taken off less than twenty minutes before from the far side of the Medichironian. Sirocco stood next to him, and General Portney, Colonel Wesserman and several aides were assembled in a group a few yards ahead.

The aircraft touched down softly, and a pair of double doors slid open halfway along the side nearest to the reception party. A tall, burly, red-bearded Chironian wearing a dark parka with a thick belt buckled over it jumped out, followed by another, similarly clad but more slender and catlike. More figures became visible inside when the cabin light came on. Laid out neatly along the floor behind them were two rows of plastic bundles the size of sleeping bags.

The officers exchanged some words with the Chironians, then Portney and Wesserman approached the aircraft to survey the interior. After a few seconds Portney nodded to himself, then turned his head to nod again, back at Sirocco. Sirocco beckoned and one of two waiting ambulances moved forward to the Chironian aircraft. Two soldiers opened its rear doors. Four others climbed inside the aircraft and began moving bodies. As each body bag was brought out, Sirocco turned the top back briefly while an aide compared the face to pictures on a compack screen and another checked dogtag numbers against a list he was holding, after which the corpse was transferred to the ambulance.

Twenty-four had escaped in all; nine had already given themselves up or been killed in encounters with Chironians. Anita had not been among them. Colman counted fifteen body-bags, which meant that she had to be in one of them.

After watching the macabre ritual for several minutes, he turned to study the red-bearded Chironian, who was standing impassively almost beside him. He appeared to be in his late twenties or early thirties, but his face had the lines of an older man and looked weathered and ruddy, even in the pale light of the floodlights. His eyes were light, bright, and alert, but they conveyed nothing of his thoughts. "How did it happen?" Colman murmured in a low voice, moving a pace nearer.

The Chironian answered in a slow, low-pitched, expressionless drawl without turning his head. "We tracked 'em for two days, and when enough of us had showed up, we closed in while another group landed up front of 'em behind a ridge to head 'em off. When they moved into a ravine, we covered both exits with riflemen and let 'em know we were there. Gave 'em every chance . . . said if they came on out quiet, all we'd do was turn 'em in." The Chironian inclined his head briefly and sighed. "Guess some people never learn when to quit."

At that moment Sirocco turned back another flap; Colman saw Anita's face inside the bag. It was white, like marble, and waxy. He swallowed and stared woodenly. The Chironian's eyes flickered briefly across his face. "Someone you knew?"

Colman nodded tightly. "A while back now, but . . ."

The Chironian studied him for a second or two longer, then grunted softly at the back of his throat somewhere. "We didn't do that," he said. "After we told 'em they were cooped up, some of 'em started shooting. Five of 'em tried making a break, holding a white shirt up to tell us they wanted out. We held back, but a couple of the others gunned 'em down from behind while they were running. She was one of those five." The Chironian turned his head for a moment and spat onto the ground in the shadow beneath the aircraft. "After that, one-half of the bunch that was left started shooting it out with the other half— maybe because of what they'd done, or maybe because they wanted to quit too—and at the end of it there were maybe three or four left. We hadn't done a thing. Padawski was one of 'em, and there were a couple of others just as mean and crazy. Didn't leave us with too much of a problem."

* * *

Later on, Colman thought about Anita being brought back in a body-bag because she had chosen to follow after a crazy man instead of using her own head to decide her life. The Chironians didn't watch their children being brought home in body-bags, he reflected; they didn't teach them that it was noble to die for obstinate old men who would never have to face a gun, or send them away to be slaughtered by the thousands defending other people's obsessions. The Chironians didn't fight that way.

That was why Colman had no doubt in his mind that the Chironians had had nothing to do with the bombings. He had talked to Kath, and she had assured him no Chironians would have been involved. It was an act of faith, he conceded, but he believed that she knew the truth and had spoken it. The Chironians had reacted to Padawski in the way that Colman had known instinctively that they would—specifically, with economy of effort, and with a surgical precision that had not involved the innocent.

For that was how they fought. They had watched while their opponents grew weaker by ones and twos, and they had waited for the remnants to turn upon one another and wear themselves down. Then the Chironians had moved.

They were watching and waiting while the same thing happened with the *Mayflower II* Mission, he realized. When and how would they move? And, he wondered, when they did, which side would he be on?

PART THREE

PHOENIX

CHAPTER TWENTY-SEVEN

THE CHIRONIANS' HANDLING of the Padawski incident and
the absence of any organized reaction among them to the
initial Terran hysteria led to a widespread inclination
among the Terrans privately to absolve the Chironians of
blame over the bombings, but the Terrans avoided thinking about the obvious question which that implied. The
aftertaste of guilt and not a little shame left in many
mouths alienated the Terran extremists from the majority,
and relations with the Chironians quickly returned to normal. Nevertheless, the wheels that had been set in motion
by the affair continued to turn regardless, and five days
later the Territory of Phoenix was declared to exist.

Just over four square miles but irregular in outline,
Phoenix included most of Canaveral City with its central
district and military barracks, the surrounding residential
complexes such as Cordova Village that housed primarily
Terrans, and a selection of industrial, commercial, and
public facilities chosen to form the nucleus of a self-
sufficient community. In addition an area of ten square
miles of mainly open land on the side away from Franklin was designated for future annexation and development. Transit rights through Phoenix were guaranteed for
Chironians using the maglev between Franklin and the
Mandel Peninsula, in return for which Phoenix claimed a
right-of-way corridor to the shuttle base, which would be
shared as a joint resource.

Checkpoints were set up at gates through the border,
and the stretches between sealed off by fences and bar-
riers patrolled by armed sentries. Terran laws were proclaimed to be in force within, and the unauthorized carry-

ing of weapons was prohibited, all permanent residents were required to register; all persons duly registered and above voting age were entitled to participate in the democratic process, thus conferring upon the Chironians the right to choose the leaders they didn't want, and an obligation to accept the ones they ended up with anyway.

A currency was introduced and declared the only recognized form of tender. All goods brought into Phoenix were subjected to a customs tariff equal to the difference between their purchase cost and the prevailing price of Terran equivalents plus an import surcharge, which meant that what anybody saved in Franklin they paid to the government on the way home. Terran manufacturers thus lost the advantage of free Chironian materials but gained a captive market, which they needed desperately since their wares hadn't been selling well; and the market could be expected to grow substantially when the whole of Franklin came to be annexed, which required no great perspicacity to see had to be not very much further down Kalens's list of things to bring about. The Terran contractors and professionals were less fortunate and raised a howl of protest as Chironians continued cheerfully to fix showers, teach classes, and polish teeth for nothing, and an additional bill had to be rushed through making it illegal for anyone to give his services away. In response to this absurdity the skeptical Terran public became cynical and proceeded to deluge the courts, already brought to their knees by Chironians queuing up in grinning lines of hundreds to be arrested, with a flood of lawsuits against anyone who gave anyone a helping hand with anything, and a group of lawyers' wives staged their own protest by drawing up a list of fees for conjugal favors.

Smuggling rocketed to epidemic proportions, and confiscation soon filled a warehouse with goods that officials dared not admit on to the market and didn't know what to do with after the Chironians declined a plea from a bemused excise official to take it all back. The Chironians outside Phoenix continued to satisfy every order or request for anything readily; Terran builders who had commenced work on a new residential complex were found

to be using Chironian labor with no references appearing
in their books; every business became convinced that its
competitors were cheating, and before long every session
of both houses of Congress had degenerated into a bedlam
of accusations and counteraccusations of illegal profiteer-
ing, back-door dealing, scabbing, and every form of skul-
duggery imaginable.

Cynicism soon turned to rebellion as more of the Terran
population came to perceive Phoenix not as a protective
enclave, but at worst a prison and at best a self-proclaimed
lunatic asylum. Apartment units were found deserted and
more faces vanished as expeditions to Franklin came in-
creasingly to be one-way trips. Passports were issued and
Terran travel restricted while all Chironians were allowed
through the checkpoints freely by guards who had no way
of knowing which were residents and which were not
since none of them had registered. The sentries no longer
cared all that much anyway; their looking the other way
became chronic and more and more of them were found
not to be at their posts when their relief showed up. An
order was posted assigning at least one SD to every guard
detail. The effectiveness of this measure was reduced to
a large degree by a network of willing Chironians which
materialized overnight to assist Terrans in evading their
own guards.

Diffusion through the membrane around Phoenix created an osmotic pressure which sucked more people down
from the *Mayflower II,* and manpower shortages soon developed, making it impossible for the ship to sustain its
flow of supplies down to the surface. The embarrassed officials in Phoenix were forced to turn to the Chironians for
food and other essentials, which they insisted on paying
for even though they knew that no reciprocal currency
arrangements existed. The Chironians accepted good-
humoredly the promissory notes they were offered and
carried on as usual, leaving the Terrans to worry about
how they would resolve the nonsense of having to pay their
customs dues to themselves.

Nobody talked any more about annexing Franklin.
Howard Kalens's chances of being elected to perpetuate

the farce plummeted to as near zero as made no difference, and Paul Lechat, recognizing what he saw as a preview of the inevitable, dropped his insistence for a repeat-performance in Iberia; at least, that was the reason he offered publicly. Ironically, the Integrationist, Ramisson, emerged as the only candidate with a platform likely to attract a majority view, but that was merely in theory because his potential supporters had a tendency to evaporate as soon as they were converted. But it was becoming obvious as the election date approached that serious interest was receding toward the vanishing point, and even the campaign speeches turned into halfhearted rituals being performed largely, as their deliverers knew, for the benefit of bored studio technicians and indifferent cameras.

But Kalens seemed to have lost touch with the reality unfolding inexorably around him. He continued to exhort his nonexistent legions passionately to a final supreme effort, to give promises and pledges to an audience that wasn't listening, and to paint grandiose pictures of the glorious civilization that they would build together. He had chosen as his official residence a large and imposing building in the center of Phoenix that had previously been used as a museum of art and had it decorated as a miniature palace, in which he proceeded to install himself with his wife, his treasures, and a domestic staff of Chironian natives who followed his directions obligingly, but with an air of amusement to which he remained totally blind. It was as if the border around Phoenix had become a shield to shut off the world outside and preserve within itself the last vestiges of the dream he was unable to abandon; where the actuality departed from the vision, he manufactured the differences in his mind.

He still retained some staunch adherents, mainly among those who had nowhere else to turn and had drawn together for protection. Among them were a sizable segment of the commercial and financial fraternity who were unable to come to terms with an acceptance that their way of life was finished; the *Mayflower II*'s bishop, presiding over a flock of faithful who recoiled from abandoning themselves to the evil ways of Chiron; many from every sector of society whose natures would keep them hanging on to the end regardless. Above all there remained Borftein, who had nowhere else to attach a loyalty that his life had made compulsive. Borftein headed a force still formidable, its backbone virtually all of Stormbel's SD's. Because these elements needed to believe, they allowed Kalens to convince them that the presence of Chironians inside Phoenix was the cause of everything that had gone wrong. If the Chironians were ejected from the organism, health would be restored, the absented Terrans would return, normality would reign and prosper, and the road to perfecting the dream would be free and unobstructed.

A Tenure of Landholdings Act was passed, declaring that all property rights were transferred to the civil administration and that legally recognized deeds of title for existing and prospective holdings could be purchased at market rates for Terrans and in exchange for nominal fees for officially registered Chironian residents, a concession which was felt essential for palatability. Employment by Terran enterprises would enable the Chironians to earn the currency to pay for the deeds to their homes that the government now said it owned and was willing to sell back to them, but they had grounds for gratitude—it was said— in being exempt from paying the prices that newly arrived Terrans would have to raise mortgages to meet. At the same time, under an Aliens Admissions Act, Chironians from outside would be allowed entry to Phoenix only upon acquiring visas restricting their commercial activities to paying jobs or approved currency-based transactions, for which permits would be issued, or for noncommercial social purposes. Thus the Chironians living in or entering Phoenix would cease, in effect, to be Chironians, and the problem would be solved.

Violators of visa privileges would face permanent exclusion. Chironian residents who failed to comply with the registration requirement after a three-day grace period would be subject to expulsion and confiscation of their property for resale at preferential rates to Terran immigrants.

Most Terrans had no doubts that the Chironians would

take no notice whatsoever, but they couldn't see Kalens enforcing the threat. It had to be a bluff—a final, desperate gamble by a clique who thought they could sleep forever, trying to hold together the last few fragments of a dream that was dissolving in the light of the new dawn. "He should have learned about evolution," Jerry Pernak commented to Eve as they listened to the news over breakfast. "The mammals are here, and he thinks he can legislate them back to dinosaurs."

Bernard Fallows leaned alongside the sliding glass door in the living room and stared out at the lawn behind the apartment while he wondered to himself when he would be free to begin his new career at Port Norday. He had broached the subject to Kath, as he now knew she had guessed he would, and she had told him simply that the people there who had met him were looking forward to working with him. But he had agreed with Pernak and Lechat that a nucleus of people capable of taking rational control of events would have to remain available until the last possibility of extreme threats to the Chironians went away, and that Ramisson's Integrationist platform, to which Lechat had now allied himself, needed support to allow the old order to extinguish itself via its own processes.

Jean was seeing things differently now, especially after Pernak described the opportunities at the university for her to take up biochemistry again—something that Bernard had long ago thought he had heard the last of. He turned his head to look into the room at where she was sitting on the sofa below the wall screen, introducing Marie to the mysteries of protein transcription—diagrams courtesy of Jeeves—and grinned to himself; she was becoming even more impatient than he was. Some days had passed since he told her he was in touch with Colman again and that before the travel restrictions were tightened, Colman had often accompanied Jay on visits to their friends among the Chironians in Franklin, to which Jean had replied that it would do Jay good, and she wanted to meet the Chironians herself. Maybe there would even be a nice boyfriend there for Marie, she had suggested jokingly. "A *nice* one," she had added in response to Bernard's astonished look. "Not one of those teenage Casanovas they've got running around. The line stays right there."

Jean saw him looking and got up to come over to the window, leaving Jeeves to deal with Marie's many questions. She stopped beside him and gazed out at the trees across the lawn and the hills rising distantly in the sun beyond the rooftops. "It's going to be such a beautiful world," she said. "I'm not sure I can stand much more of this waiting around. Surely it has to be as good as over."

Bernard looked out again and shook his head. "Not until that ship up there is disarmed somehow." After a pause he turned to face her again. "So it doesn't scare you anymore, huh?"

"I don't think it ever did. What I was afraid of was in my own head. None of it was out there." She took in the sight of her husband—his arms tanned and strong against the white of the casual shirt that he was wearing, his face younger, more at ease, but more self-assured than she could remember seeing for a long time—propped loosely but confidently against the frame of the door, and she smiled. "Kalens may have to hide himself away in a shell," she said. "I don't need mine anymore."

"So you're happy you can handle it," Bernard said.

"*We* can handle anything that comes," she told him.

CHAPTER TWENTY-EIGHT

CELIA KALENS STRAIGHTENED the kimono-styled black-silk top over her gold lamé evening dress, then sat back while a white-jacketed steward cleared the dinner dishes from the table. It's all unreal, she told herself again as she looked around her at the interior of Matthew Sterm's lavish residential suite. Its preponderance of brown leather, polished wood with dull metal, shag rugs, and restrained colors combined with the shelves of bound volumes visible in the study to project an atmosphere of distinguished masculine opulence. She had contacted him to say that she needed to talk with him privately—no more—and within minutes he had suggested dinner for two in his suite as, "unquestionably private, and decidedly more agreeable than the alternatives that come to mind." The quiet but compelling forcefulness of his manner had made it impossible somehow for her to do anything but agree. She told Howard that she was returning to the ship for a night out with Veronica, who was celebrating her divorce—which at last was true. Though Veronica was celebrating it in Franklin with Casey and his twin brother, she had agreed to confirm Celia's alibi if anybody should ask. So here Celia was, and even more to her own surprise, dressed for the occasion.

Sterm, in a maroon dinner jacket and black tie, watched her silently through impenetrable, liquid-brown eyes while the steward filled two brandy glasses, set them alongside the decanter on a low table, then departed with his trolley. Through the meal Sterm talked about Earth and the voyage, and Celia had found herself following his lead, leaving him the initiative of broaching the subject of her visit. Finally, he stood, came around the table, and moved her chair back for her to rise. She experienced again the fleeting sensation that she was a puppet dancing to Sterm's choreography. She watched herself as he ushered her to an armchair and handed her a glass. Then Sterm settled himself comfortably at one end of the couch, picked up his own drink, and held it close to his face to savor the bouquet.

"To your approval, I trust," he said. Celia had suggested a cognac earlier on, when Sterm had asked her preference for an afterdinner liqueur.

She took a sip. It was smooth, warm, and mellowing. "It's excellent," she replied.

"I keep a small stock reserved," Sterm informed her. "It is from Earth—the Grande Champagne region of the Charante. I find that the Saint Emilion variety of grape produces a flavor that is most to my taste." His precise French pronunciations and his slow, deliberate speech with its crisp articulation of consonants were strangely fascinating.

"The white makes the best brandies, I believe," Celia said. "And isn't the amount of limestone in the soil very important?"

The eyebrows of Sterm's regal, Roman-emperor's face raised themselves in approval. "I see the subject is not unfamiliar to you. My compliments. Regrettably, rareness of quality is not confined to grapes."

Celia smiled over her glass. "Thank you. It's rare to find such appreciation."

Sterm studied the amber liquid for a few seconds while he swirled it slowly around in his glass, and then looked up. "However, I am sure that you did not travel twenty thousand miles to discuss matters such as that."

Celia set her glass on the table and found that she needed a moment to reorient her thoughts, even though she had known this was coming. "I'm concerned over this latest threat to evict Chironians from Phoenix. It's not the bluff that many people think. Howard is serious."

Sterm did not appear surprised. "They have merely to comply with the law to avoid such consequences."

"Everyone knows they won't. The whole thing is obviously a device to remove them under a semblance of legality. It's a thinly disguised deportation order."

Sterm shrugged. "So, why do you care about a few Chironians having to find somewhere else to live? They have an entire planet, most of which is empty. They will hardly starve."

It wasn't quite the answer that Celia had been prepared for. She frowned for a second, then reached for her glass. "The reaction that it might provoke worries me. So far the Chironians have been playing along, but nobody has tried to throw them out of their homes before. We've already seen examples of how they do not to hesitate to react violently."

"That frightens you?"

"Shouldn't it?"

"Hardly. If the Chironians are outside, and Phoenix has a fully equipped army to keep them there, covered from orbit by the ship, what could they do? Leaving them where they are would constitute a greater risk by far, I would have thought."

"True, once they're separated," Celia agreed. "But how many more killings would we have to see before that was achieved?"

"And that bothers you?"

"Well—of course."

"Really?" Sterm's one word conveyed all the disbelief necessary; its undertone suggested that she reconsider whether she believed her answer either. "Come now, Celia, the realities of life are no strangers to either of us. We can be frank without fear of risking offense. The people live their lives and serve their purpose, and a few more or less will make no difference that matters. Now tell me again, who are you really worried about?"

Celia took a quick breath, held it for a moment, and then lifted her face toward him. "Very well. I've seen what happened to the corporal and to Padawski. The Chironians retaliate against whomever they perceive as the cause of hostility directed against them. If the evictions are enforced

. . . well, it's not difficult to see who the next target would be, is it."

"You want me to prevail upon Howard to prevent his destroying himself."

"If you want to put it that way."

"What makes you imagine that I could?"

"You could talk to him. I know he listens to what you say. We've talked about things."

"I see." Sterm studied her face for what seemed like a long time. At last he asked in a strangely curious voice, "And if I did, what then, Celia?"

Celia was unable to reply. The answer lay behind a trapdoor in her mind that she had refused to open. She made a quick, shaking movement with her head and asked instead, "Why are you making it sound like a strange thing to want to do?"

"Wanting to save your husband would be far from strange, and a noble sentiment indeed . . . if it were true. But is it true?"

Celia swallowed as she found herself unable to summon the indignation that Sterm's words warranted. "What makes you think it isn't?" She avoided his eyes. "Why else would I be here?"

Sterm stared at her unblinkingly. "To save yourself."

"I find that insulting, and also unbecoming."

"Do you? Or is it that you are unable, yet, to accept it?"

Celia forced as much coldness into her voice as she could muster. "I don't like being told that I'm interested in protecting my own skin."

Sterm was unperturbed, as if he had been expecting such an answer. "I made no mention of your wanting to save yourself physically. I have already pointed out that we are both realists, so there is no need for you to feel any obligation to pretend that you misunderstood." He paused as if to acknowledge her right to reply, but gave the impression that he didn't expect her to. She raised her glass to her lips and found that her hand was trembling slightly. Sterm resumed. "The dream has crumbled away, hasn't it, Celia. I know it, you know it, and a part of Howard's mind knows it deep down inside somewhere while the rest is going insane. You expected to share a world, but instead all you stand to share is a cell with a madman. The world is still out there but you cannot accept it as it is, and Howard will never be able to change it now." Sterm extended a hand expressively. "And the future awaits you." He paused again, watched as Celia lowered her eyes, and nodded. "Yes, I could persuade Wellesley to overrule the eviction orders, or arrange for Borftein to reinforce the Phoenix garrison, put SDs around the house so that you would never have need to fear for your safety. But is that what you want me to do?"

Celia looked down at the glass in her hand and bit nervously at her lip. "I don't know," was all she could whisper. Sterm watched her impassively. In the end she shook her head. "No."

Sterm allowed a few seconds for her admission to settle. "Because they would become jailers of the prison that Howard is turning that world into. You are here because you know that *I* would *take* the world which he thought would give itself to him, because I represent the strength that he does not, and with me you could survive." Celia looked up again, but Sterm's eyes had taken on a faraway light. "Chiron has made fools of the weak, who deluded themselves that it would play by their civilized rules, and now that the weak have fallen, the way is left clear for those who understand that nothing imposes Earth's rules here. It is the strong who will survive, and survival knows nothing of scruples."

Celia's eyes widened as many things suddenly became clearer. "You . . ." Her voice caught somewhere at the back of her throat. "You knew this was going to happen— Howard, Phoenix . . . everything. You were manipulating all of them from the beginning, even Wellesley. You knew what would happen after the landing but you endorsed it."

Sterm looked back at her and smiled humorlessly. "Hardly what I would call manipulating. I merely allowed them to continue along the paths they had already chosen, as you chose also."

"But you saw where the paths led."

"They would never have listened if I had told them. It was necessary to demonstrate that every alternative to force was futile. Now they will understand, just as you have come to understand."

"How—how could you justify it?"

"To whom do I have to justify anything? Those rules belong to Earth. I make my own."

"To Congress, the people."

Sterm snorted. "I need neither. The same forces that will subdue Chiron will subdue the people also." His eyes flickered over Celia's body momentarily. "And they will submit because they, like you, have an instinct to survive."

Celia found herself staring into eyes that mirrored for a split second the calm, calculated ruthlessness that lay within, devoid of disguise or apology, or any hint that there should be any. A chill quivered down her spine. But she felt also the trapdoor in her mind straining as a need that lay imprisoned behind it, and which she was still not ready to face, responded. Sterm's eyes were challenging her to deny anything that he had said. She was unable to make even that gesture.

Howard had sought to possess, and she had refused to become a possession. Sterm sought not to possess but to dominate Chiron. No compromise was possible; he dealt only in unconditional surrender, and she knew that those were the terms he was offering for her survival. Perhaps she had known it even before she arrived.

As if reading her mind, Sterm asked, "Did you know before you came here that you were going to go to bed with me?" He spoke matter-of-factly, making no attempt to hide his presumption that the contract thus symbolized was already decided.

"I . . . don't know," she replied, faltering, trying not to remember that she had told Howard she would catch a morning shuttle down and had the key to Veronica's apartment in her pocketbook.

"Does he expect you tonight?" Sterm inquired curiously, although Celia couldn't avoid a feeling that he already knew the answer. She shook her head. "Where are you supposed to be?"

"With a friend in Baltimore," she told him, thus making her capitulation total. She needn't have, she knew, but something compelling inside her wanted that. She knew also that it was Sterm's way of forcing her to admit it to herself. The terms were now understood.

"Then there is no reason for us to allow unseemly haste to lower the quality of the evening," Sterm said, sitting forward and reaching with a leisurely movement of his hand for the decanter. "A little time ripens more than just fine cognac. Will you join me in a refill?"

"Of course," Celia whispered and passed him her glass.

CHAPTER TWENTY-NINE

"WE'LL TAKE CARE of that." Colman turned his head and called in a louder voice, "Stanislau, Young—come over here and give me a hand with this crate." Rifles slung across their backs, Stanislau and Young stepped away from the squad standing on the sidewalk and helped Colman to heave the crate into the truck waiting to leave for the border checkpoint, while the Chironian who had been struggling to lift it with his teenage son watched. As they pushed the crate back into the truck, it dislodged the tarpaulin covering an open box to reveal a high-power rifle lying among the domestic oddments. The Chironian saw it and lifted his head to look at Colman curiously. Colman threw the tarp back over the box and turned away.

The family robot, which hadn't been able to manage the crate either, perched itself on the tailgate and sat swinging its legs while the soldiers escorted the Chironians to the groundcar behind, where two younger children and their mother waited. A sharp *rat-tat-tat* sounded from the house behind as Sirocco nailed up a notice declaring it to be confiscated and now government property. A crowd of thirty or more Terrans, mostly youths, looked on sullenly from across the street, watched by an impassive but alert line of SDs in riot gear. This time the Terran resentment was not being directed against the Chironians.

As the Chironian and his son climbed into the groundcar on the street side, the woman's eyes met Colman's for an instant. There was no malice in them. "I know," she said through the window. "You've got a job that you have to do for a little while longer. Don't worry about it. We can use the vacation. We'll be back." Colman managed the shadow

275

of a grin. Seconds later the truck moved away, the robot sitting in the rear, and the groundcar followed, two wistful young faces pressed against the rear window.

Angry murmurs were heard from the Terran civilians. Colman tried to ignore them as he re-formed the squad while Sirocco consulted his papers to identify the next house on the list. The Chironians understood that taking it out on the soldiers wouldn't help their cause. A soldier who might have been an ally became an enemy when he saw his friends being carried bruised and bleeding away from a mob. Everything the Chironians did was designed to subtract from their enemies instead of add to them, and to whittle their opposition down to the hard core that lay at the center, which was all they had any quarrel with. He could see it; Sirocco could see it, and the men could see it. Why couldn't more of the Terrans see it too?

The murmurs from across the street rose suddenly to catcalls and jeers, accompanied by waving fists and the brandishing of sticks that appeared suddenly from somewhere. Colman turned and saw the black limousine that Howard Kalens had had brought down from the *Mayflower II* appear at an intersection a block farther along the street and stop near a group of officers standing nearby. Major Thorpe detached himself from the group and walked across. Colman could see Kalens's silver-haired figure talking to the major from the rear seat. Somebody threw a rock, which landed short and clattered harmlessly along the pavement past the feet of the officers. More followed, and several Terrans moved forward threateningly.

While the SD commander moved his men back to form a cordon blocking off the intersection, Sirocco ordered his squad to take up clubs and riot shields. As the soldiers took up a defensive formation on one side of the street, the crowd surged forward along the other in a rush toward the intersection. Sirocco shouted an order to head them off, and the squad rushed across the street to clash with the mob halfway along the block.

Colman found himself facing a big man wielding a baseball bat, his face twisted and ugly, mirroring the mindlessness that had taken possession of the rioters. The man swung the bat viciously but clumsily. Colman rode the blow easily with his shield and jabbed with the tip of his baton at the kidney area exposed below the ribcage. His assailant staggered back with a scream of pain. Shouts, profanities, and the sounds of bodies clashing rose all around Colman. Something hard bounced off his helmet. Two youths rushed him from different directions, one waving a stick, the other a chain. Colman jumped to the side to bring the two in line for a split second's cover, feinted with his baton, then sent the first cannoning into the second with a shove from his shield with the full weight of his shoulder behind it, and both rioters went down into a heap. Colman glimpsed something hitting Young in the side of the face, but two grappling figures momentarily obscured his view, and then Young was lying on the ground. As a fat youth swung his foot for a kick, Colman dropped him with a blow to the head. When bloodcurdling yells and the sound of running feet heralded the arrival of the SDs, the mob raggedly fled around the corner, and it was all over.

Young had a gash on his cheek that was more messy than deep and a huge bruise along his jaw to go with it, and four rioters were left behind with sore heads or other minor injuries. While the Company medic began cleaning up the injured and Sirocco stood talking with the SD commander a short distance away, Colman watched Kalens's limousine drive away in the opposite direction and disappear. That was how it had always been, he could see now. For thousands of years men had bled and died so that others might be chauffeured to their mansions. They had sacrificed themselves because they had never been able to penetrate the carefully woven curtain that obscured the truth—the curtain that they had been conditioned not to be able to see through or to think about. But the Chironians had never had the conditioning.

The inverted logic that had puzzled him had not been something peculiar to the military mind; it was just that the military mind was the only one he had ever really known. The inversions came from the whole insane system that the Military was just a part of—the system that fought wars to protect peace and enslaved nations by liberating them;

that turned hatred and revenge into the will of an all-benevolent God and programmed its litanies into the minds of children; that burned and tortured its heretics while preaching forgiveness, and made a sin of love and a virtue of murder; and which brought lunatics to power by demanding requirements of office that no balanced mind could meet. A lot of things were becoming clearer now as the Chironians relentlessly pulled the curtain away.

For the curtain that was falling away was the backcloth of the stage upon which the dolls had danced. And as the backcloth fell and the strings fell with it, the dolls were dancing on. The dolls were dancing without the strings because there were no strings. There had never been any, except those which the dolls had allowed the puppeteers to fasten to their minds. But those strings had held up the puppeteers, not the dolls, for the puppeteers were falling while the dolls danced on.

Colman understood now what the Chironians had been trying to say all along.

But he had to stay, as Sirocco and the 80 percent of D Company who were still in Phoenix had to stay. After Swyley went, Driscoll went, and many of the others went, Sirocco had called the rest together and reminded them about the weapons in the *Mayflower II.* "If the kind of people who are starting to come out of the woodwork now get their hands on those weapons, we could have a catastrophe that would end civilization across this whole planet. You've all seen what's happening back on Earth. Well, the same mentalities are here too, and they're panicking. We *must* keep enough of the Army together to stop anything like that if we have to." And so they had stayed.

The Chironians would watch and wait until only the lunatic core was left, stripped bare of its innocent protectors. Eventually only two kinds would be left: There would be Chironians, and there would be Kalenses. And Colman no longer had any doubts as to which he would be.

In the D Company Orderly Room in the Omar Bradley barracks block, Hanlon secured his ammunition belt, put on his helmet, and took his M32 from the rack. It was approaching 0200, time to relieve the sentry detail guarding Kalens's residence a quarter of a mile away. "Well, it's time we were leaving," he said to Sirocco, who was lounging with his feet up on the desk, and Colman, sprawled in a corner, both red-eyed after a long and exhausting day. "I'll try to shout quietly. I'd hate to be disturbing His Honor in his sleep."

Sirocco smiled tiredly. "You're excused from taking off your boots," he murmured.

"Are we still invited to the Fallowses tonight, Steve?" Hanlon asked, stopping at the door to look back at Colman.

Colman nodded. "I guess so. I'll probably be asleep when you come off duty. Better give me a call."

"I will indeed. See you later." Hanlon left, and they heard him forming up the relief guard outside.

"Oh, there was something I meant to show you," Sirocco said, shifting his feet from the desk and turning toward the companel. "It come in earlier this evening. Want a laugh?"

"What?" Colman asked him.

Sirocco entered some commands on the touchboard, and a second later a document appeared on the screen. Colman got up and came across to study it while Sirocco sat back out of the way. It was a communication from Leighton Merrick, the Assistant Deputy Director of Engineering in the *Mayflower II*, routed for comment via Headquarters and Brigade. It advised that, due to an unexpectedly high rate of promotions among junior technicians, Engineering was now able to give "due reconsideration" to the request for transfer filed by Staff Sergeant Colman. Would the Military please notify his current disposition? "Looks like they're running out of Indians," Sirocco remarked. "What do you want me to say?"

"What do you think?" Colman answered, and went back to his chair. Sirocco casually entered NEGATIVE, and cut the display.

"So what will you do?" Sirocco inquired, propping his feet back on the desk. "Figured it out yet?"

"Oh, there's a lot of studying I've got listed—general

engineering with a lot of MHD, then maybe I'll see if I can get into something at Norday for a while. Later on I might move out to the new place they're talking about."

"Will Kath fix it up for you?"

Colman nodded. "To start with, anyhow. Then, I guess, it's a case of how well you make out. You know how things operate here." After a pause he asked, "How about you?"

Sirocco tweaked his moustache pensively. "It's a problem knowing where to start. You know the kind of thing I'd like —to get out and see the whole planet. The Barrier Range is as big as the Himalayas, there's Glace . . . a Grander Canyon out in Oriena . . . there's so much of it. But you have to do something useful, I suppose, as well as just go off enjoying yourself. But I think there's a lot of survey work waiting to be done yet. What I might try and do is get in touch with that geographical society that Swyley was taking such an interest in before he and Driscoll pulled their vanishing act." Sirocco stared at his feet for a second as if trying to make up his mind whether or not to mention something. "And then of course there's Shirley," he added nonchalantly.

"Shirley? . . . You mean Ci's mother?"

"Yes."

"What about her?"

Sirocco raised his eyebrows in what was obviously feigned surprise. "Oh, didn't I tell you? She wants me to move in. It's surprising how a lot of these Chironian women have a thing about Terrans to . . ." he frowned and scratched his nose while he searched for the right words ". . . assist with their future contribution to procreation." He looked up. "She wants my kids. How about that, Steve? Come on, I bet it's the same with Kath." Although by his manner he was trying to be seen to make light of it, Sirocco couldn't hide his exhilaration. Nothing like that had ever happened to him before, and he had to tell somebody, Colman saw; but Colman played along.

"You sly bastard!" he exclaimed. "How long has this been going on?" Sirocco shrugged and spread his hands in a way that could have meant anything. Then Colman grinned. "Well, what do you know? Anyhow—good luck."

Sirocco resumed twiddling his moustache. "Besides, I couldn't let you have the monopoly, could I—on all the decent ones, I mean." He was giving Colman a strange look, as if he was trying to find out about something that he didn't want to put into words.

"What are you getting at?" Colman asked him.

Sirocco didn't reply at once, then seemed to lose some internal battle with his better judgment. "Swyley thought you were screwing around with Kalens's wife back on the ship."

Colman kept a poker face. "What made him think that?"

Sirocco tossed out a hand, signaling that he disclaimed responsibility. "Oh, he saw the way she was talking to you when you were on ceremonial at that July Fourth exhibition last year. That was one thing. Do you remember that?"

Colman went through the motions of having to think back. "Yes . . . I think so. But I don't remember Swyley being around."

"Well, he must have been there somewhere, mustn't he?"

"I guess so. So what was the rest of it?"

Sirocco shrugged. "Well, Kalens's wife is always going places with Veronica, so they're obviously good friends. Swyley noticed something funny between you and Veronica at that party we went to at Shirley's, and that was the connection he figured out." Sirocco shrugged again. "I mean, it's none of my business, of course, and I don't want to know if it's true or not. . . ." He paused and looked at Colman hopefully for a second. "Is it?"

"Would you expect me to say so if it was?" Colman asked.

"I suppose not." Sirocco conceded, deflating with a disappointed sigh. After a second he looked up sharply again. "I'll do a deal with you though. Tell me after this is all over, okay?"

Colman grinned. "Okay, chief. I will." A short silence fell while they both thought about the same thing. "How long do you think it'll be?" Colman asked at last.

"Who can say?" Sirocco answered, picking up the more serious tone. "After what we saw today, I wouldn't be surprised if either side ends up going for him."

"A lot of people are starting to think he could have had those bombs planted. What do you think?"

Sirocco frowned and rubbed his nose. "I'm not convinced. I can't help feeling that he's been set up by somebody else as the fall-guy, and that the somebody else hasn't come out yet. I think the Chironians believe that too."

Colman nodded thoughtfully to himself and conceded the point. "Any ideas?"

Sirocco shrugged. "I'm pretty sure it can't be Wellesley. He's tried to play it straight, it's all sweeping him way out of his depth. Anyhow, what would he have to gain? All he wants to do is to be put out to pasture; he's only got a few days left. Ramisson obviously wouldn't be involved in something like that, and the same goes for Lechat. But as for the rest, if you ask me, they're all crazy. It could be any of them or all of them. But that's who the Chironians are really after."

"So it could take a while," Colman said.

"Maybe. Who knows? Let's just hope there aren't too many of them in the Army."

At that moment the emergency tone sounded shrilly from the companel. Sirocco jerked his legs off the desk, cut the alarm, and flipped on the screen. It was Hanlon, looking tense.

"It's happened," Hanlon told him. "Kalens is dead. We found him inside the house, shot six times. Whoever did it knew what they were doing."

"What about the sentries?" Sirocco asked curtly.

"Emmerson and Crealey were at the back. We found them unconscious in a ditch. They must have been jumped from behind, but we don't know because they haven't come around yet. They look as if they'll be okay though. The others didn't know a thing about it."

Colman was listening grimly. "What about his wife?" he muttered to Sirocco.

"How is Kalens's wife?" Sirocco asked Hanlon.

"She isn't here. We've checked with transportation, and she was booked onto a shuttle up to the ship earlier this

evening. She must have left before it happened." Beside
Sirocco, Colman breathed an audible sigh of relief.

"Well, that's something, anyway," Sirocco said. "Stay
there, Bret, and don't let anyone touch anything. I'll get
onto Brigade right away. We'll have some more people over
there in a few minutes." He returned to Colman. "Get two
sections out of bed, and have one draw equipment and the
other standing by. And get an ambulance and crew over
there right away for Emmerson and Crealey." Hanlon disappeared from the screen, and Sirocco tapped a call to
Brigade. "It looks as if the fall-guy has gone down, Steve,"
he murmured while Colman called the ambulance dis-
patcher on another panel. "Let's see who steps out from
the wings now."

CHAPTER THIRTY

THE STRAIN THAT had been increasing since planetfall and the shock of the most recent news were showing on Wellesley's face when he rose to address a stunned meeting of the *Mayflower II*'s Congress later that morning. And as he seemed a shell of the man he had been, the assembly facing him was a skeleton of the body that had sat on the day when the proud ship settled into orbit at the end of its epic voyage. Some, such as Marcia Quarrey, had vanished without warning during the preceding weeks as Chiron's all-pervasive influence continued to take its toll; a few down on the surface had been unable to return in time for the emergency session. Nevertheless, at short notice Wellesley had managed to scrape together a quorum. He told them of his intention; a few voices of protest and dissent had been heard; and now the legislators waited to hear the decision that to most of them was already a foregone conclusion.

"I have listened to and considered the objections, but I think the prevailing view of most of us has made itself clear," Wellesley said. "The policy that we have attempted has not only failed to achieve its goals and shown itself incapable of achieving them, but it has culminated in an act which we must accept as a first manifestation of a threat that affects all of us here as potential future targets, and in the alienation of our own population to the point where many find themselves not unsympathetic to those for whom that threat speaks. Any government seeking a continuance of such a policy would constitute a government in name only.

"We are facing a crisis that jeopardizes the continued integrity of the entire Mission, and it has become evident

284

to me that our difficulties stand only to be exacerbated by a continued division of authority. Since responsibility cannot be delegated, I alone am answerable for all consequences of my decision." He paused to look around the room, and then took a long breath. "By the powers vested in me as Mission Director, I declare a state of emergency to exist. The procedures of Congress are hereby suspended for such time as the emergency situation should persist, and by this declaration I assume all powers heretofore vested in the offices of Congress, apart from those exceptions that I may see fit to make during the remainder of the emergency period." After a short pause he added in a less formal tone, "And I ask the cooperation of all of you in making that period as short as possible."

Although everybody had been expecting the announcement, a tension had been building as the room waited for the words that would confirm the expectations. Now that the words had been said, the tension released itself in a ripple of murmurs accompanied by the rustle of papers, and the creaks of chairs as bodies unfolded into easier postures.

Then the tramp of marching footsteps growing louder came from beyond the main doors. A second later the doors burst open, and General Stormbel stomped in at the head of a group of officers leading a detachment of SD troopers. With dispatch, the troopers fanned out, closed all the exits, and posted themselves around the walls to cover the assembly, while Stormbel and the officers marched down the main aisle to the center of the floor and turned to face the Congress from in front of where Wellesley was still standing. Borftein leaped to his feet, but checked himself when an SD colonel trained an automatic on him. He sank into his seat, a dazed expression on his face.

Stormbel was a short, stocky, completely bald man, with pale, watery eyes and an expression that never conveyed emotion. A thin moustache pencil-lined his upper lip. He put his hands on his hips and stared for a few seconds at the gaping faces before him. "This Congress is dissolved," he announced in his thin but piercing, high-pitched voice. "The Mission is now under the direct command of the Military." He turned his head to Borftein. "You are relieved of command of both the regular and Special Duty forces. Those functions are now transferred to me."

"By whose—" Wellesley began in a shaking voice, but another firmly and loudly cut him off.

"By *my* authority." Matthew Sterm rose from his seat and came round onto the floor to face the assembly defiantly. "This prattling has continued for too long. I have no eloquent speeches to make. Enough time has been wasted on such futilities already. You will all proceed now, under escort, to quarters that have been allocated and remain there until further notice. We have business to attend to." He nodded at Stormbel, who motioned at the guards. "I would like Admiral Slessor to remain behind to discuss matters concerning the continued well-being of the ship."

As the guards started forward and the members continued to sit in paralyzed silence, Ramisson rose and walked haltingly to the center of the main aisle to face Sterm. "I will not submit to such intimidation," he said in a harsh whisper. "Remove your men from that door." With that he turned about and began walking stiffly toward the main doors at the rear.

Stormbel drew his automatic and leveled it at Ramisson's back. "You have one warning," he called out. Ramisson kept walking. Stormbel fired. Ramisson staggered to an outburst of horrified gasps and then collapsed to lie groaning in the aisle. Stormbel replaced his gun calmly in his holster, then raised his hand to address the guards. "Remove that man, and see to it that he receives medical attention." Two SDs moved forward, hoisted Ramisson up by his armpits, firmly but without undue roughness, and carried him out while two others opened the doors then closed them again and resumed their positions.

"Are there any more objectors?" Sterm inquired. Behind him Wellesley, white faced and haggard, slumped into his chair.

"Stop this now," Borftein advised grimly. "How much of the Army do you think will follow you?"

Stormbel gave him a contemptuous look. "How much of *your* Army is left?" he asked. "Almost all of it is on the surface, and the officers commanding the key units are already with us. Besides, *we* control the ship, which is the most important thing."

"For now," Sterm added. "The rest comes later."

Borftein licked his lips and thought frantically. As Stormbel was about to repeat the order to clear the room, Borftein looked at Sterm, closed his eyes for a moment, and then raised a hand and shook his head. Sterm looked at him questioningly. "I . . . I'm not sure I even know what's happened," Borftein said. "It's been too sudden. Just what do you think you're going to do?" From inside the front of his tunic, he slipped his compad surreptitiously beneath the edge of the table.

Sterm emitted a sigh of sorely tried patience. "I will endeavor to spell it out in simple terms," he replied. "This act of clowns has been . . ."

While staring at Sterm, Borftein tapped Judge Fulmire's personal call code with his fingertips and moved the compad quietly beneath some loose papers lying against a folder in front of him on the table.

Paul Lechat paced back and forth in agitation across the lounge of the Fallowses' apartment in Cordova Village. "I didn't think the Chironians would go that far," he said. "I thought they would react only against direct violence. Why couldn't they have just let everything die a natural death?"

"Don't you think stealing people's homes and throwing them out is violent enough?" Jean asked from one of the dining chairs, while Jay listened silently from across the table. "What were they supposed to do? They ignored the soldiers and settled it with the man responsible. He should have been expecting it."

Lechat shook his head. "It wasn't necessary. In a few more days Ramisson would have been elected, almost certainly. Then everything would have worked itself out smoothly and tidily. This action complicates everything again. Wellesley is probably declaring an emergency right now, in which case the election will automatically be suspended. It puts everything back weeks, maybe months."

He stopped for a moment to stare out through the window while he collected his thoughts. Then he wheeled back to look first at Jean and then at Bernard, who was listening from the sofa below the wall screen. "Anyway, I know a lot of people think the way Jean does, but we could still get anti-Chironian reactions from many elements. That's what worries me. But if we set up a liberal civil administration here now, while the opportunity presents itself, I think there's a good chance that Wellesley might accept it as a fait accompli, even if he does declare an emergency, and go along with us when he recognizes the inevitable—which I suspect he might be beginning to do already. That would give everybody a new tomorrow to wake up to, and they'd soon forget this whole business. But there isn't much time. That's why I skipped the meeting. Now you two can help, pretty much in the ways we've discussed. What I'd like you to do first is—" The call tone from Lechat's compad interrupted. He looked down instinctively at the breast pocket of his jacket. "Excuse me for a moment."

The others watched as he pulled the unit out, accepting the call with a flip of his thumb. Judge Fulmire peered from the miniature screen. "Are you alone, Paul?" Fulmire asked without preamble. His voice was clipped and terse.

"I'm with company, but they're safe. What—"

"Stay off the streets and keep out of sight," Fulmire said. "Sterm and Stormbel have pulled a coup. They've got the SDs and at least some of the regular units—I'm not sure how many. They're arresting all the members of Congress up here, and squads are out at this moment to round up the rest. I'm probably on the list too, so this will have to be quick. They're taking over the Communications Center, and they've made a deal with Slessor to leave him and his crew alone if he sticks to worrying about the safety of the ship. Get out of Phoenix if you can. I don't know if—" The picture and the voice cut out suddenly.

"Who was that?" Jean gasped, her eyes wide with disbelief.

"Judge Fulmire." Lechat frowned and tapped in a code to reconnect. The unit returned a "number unobtainable" mnemonic. He rattled in another code to alert a communications operator. The same thing happened. "The regular net seems to have gone down," he said. "Even the standby channels."

"Oh, God . . ." Jean whispered. "They're going to bring out those bombs."

Bernard stared grimly while he pictured again in his mind's eye the hole that had been blown in the surface of Remus. "We've got to stop it," he breathed. "We've got to get a message up there somehow . . . to Sterm . . . telling him what he's up against. Thousands of people are still up there."

"He wouldn't believe us," Lechat said bleakly. "It sounds like the first bluff anyone would try."

Jean shook her head. "There must be something—the Chironians! He'd have to believe them. If they beamed a signal up spelling out just what their weapons can do, whatever they are, and with the evidence to prove it, Sterm would have to take notice of that, surely."

"But we don't even know which Chironians to talk to," Lechat pointed out.

Bernard fell silent for a few seconds. "Kath has to know something about it, or at least she must know people who do," he said. "After all, there aren't billions of people on Chiron. And Jerry said that she has a lot to do with the people working on the antimatter project at the university. Let's start with her."

Jean glanced at the screen and then looked at Bernard. "Should we try calling her through Jeeves . . . via the Chironian net? It shouldn't be affected, should it?"

"I'm not sure I'd trust any electronics," Lechat cautioned.

"Could be risky," Bernard agreed after a second's reflection. "If Sterm and whoever else is involved have been preparing for this, I wouldn't put it past them to have taps and call-monitor programs anywhere. Someone will have to go there."

"Who," Jean asked.

"Well, Paul can't show his face outside. You heard what Fulmire said." Bernard replied. "So I guess I'll have to."

"But what about the border guards?" Jean looked alarmed. "We don't know who we can trust. Fulmire didn't know which side how much of the Army is on. There could be fighting out there at any minute. You don't know what you'll be walking into."

Bernard shrugged helplessly. "I know. It's a chance—but what else is there?"

A tense silence fell. Then Jay said, "I know at least one person in the Army who we can trust." The others looked at him in surprise.

Bernard snapped his fingers. "Of course, Colman! Why the hell didn't I think of that?"

"Who's Colman?" Lechat inquired.

"A family friend, in the Army," Jean said.

"Ye-es," Bernard said slowly, nodding to himself. "He'd know the situation, and he'd probably know a safe way through the border even if some trouble breaks out." He began nodding more strongly. "And we certainly know we can trust him."

"I could go and see if I can find him," Jay offered. "I don't think I'd attract much attention. Even if the SDs are out, they're not going to be looking for me."

Bernard looked at Lechat. Lechat frowned and seemed about to object. Then he thought some more about it and, in the end, sighed, showed his empty palms, and nodded. Bernard turned back to Jay. "Okay, see what you can do. If you do find him, ask him to get over here as soon as he can make it."

Jay jumped up and ran to a closet for a jacket. He looked at Jean as he pulled it on. "Yes, Mother, I'll be careful."

Jean forced a smile. "Just remember that," she said.

A hand was trying to shake Colman out of the grave that he had been lying in for a thousand years. "Sarge, wake up," the Voice of Judgment boomed from above, sounding uncannily like Stanislau. "Hanlon wants you over at the main gate."

"Wha—huh? . . . Who? . . ." Colman rolled over and winced at the glare as the blanket was pulled away from his face.

The Angel Stanislau descended from the radiance and assumed Earthly form beside the cot. "Hanlon's got someone over at the main gate who wants to talk to you. Says it's urgent."

Colman sat up and rubbed his eyes. "Why didn't he put a call through?"

"Regular comm channels are all down, to the ship . . . everywhere. They have been for over an hour," Stanislau said. "Emergency channels are restricted to priority military traffic." Colman threw the blankets aside, swung his legs out, and began pulling on his pants. "Strange things happening everywhere," Stanislau told him, handing him his boots. "Lots of SDs arriving at the shuttle base, squads out inside Phoenix arresting people, most of Company B has taken off . . . I don't know what it's all about."

"Is Sirocco around?" Colman moved over to the washbasin to rinse his face.

"In the Orderly Room. Hanlon got him up earlier. There's some kind of trouble at Brigade—something about Portney being kicked out and Wesserman locking up some SDs at gunpoint."

Colman wiped his face with a towel, tossed the towel to Stanislau, and snatched a shirt from a closet. "Do me a favor and straighten out this mess," he said. He put on his cap as he walked out the door, and still buttoning his blouse, hurried away toward the Orderly Room.

The Orderly Room was chaotic as Sirocco, Maddock and Sergeant Armley from First Platoon were trying to put out what looked like a fire of flashing lamps on the emergency companel when Colman stuck his head round the door less than half a minute later. "What the hell's going on?" he asked them.

"Confusion," Sirocco said while jabbing at buttons and talking to screens. "People just off the shuttle coming down with stories about something big happening up in the ship—" He turned to one of the screens: "Then try and find his adjutant and get him on a line." Then back to Colman: "I'm trying to find someone to confirm the rumors."

"Hanlon wants me at the gate for something," Colman said. "Talk to you in a few minutes."

"Okay. Get back here when you're through."

Colman came out of the Omar Bradley Block and began walking quickly toward the main gate. Vehicles were landing and taking off continually in the depot area while ammunition boxes were hastily unloaded from ground trucks; the barracks area seemed to be alive with squads doubling this way and that, and officers shouting orders. Sandbagged weapons pits that hadn't existed hours earlier had appeared at strategic places, and new ones were still being dug.

The guard had been doubled at the main gate. Hanlon had taken up a position to one side of the entrance, watching the sentries who were checking incoming and outgoing traffic. Jay Fallows was standing just outside, by the wall of the sentry post. Hanlon saw Colman approaching and sauntered across to meet him. "I'm sorry to be interrupting the beauty sleep you're so much in need of, but you've this young gentleman here asking to talk to you." Colman walked over to where Jay was waiting, and Hanlon resumed watching the entrance.

Jay began speaking earnestly and in a low voice. "My father asked me to find you. It's urgent. One of the people the SDs are looking for is at the house. Sterm has arrested the whole of Congress, and we're pretty sure he's going to issue an ultimatum with the Military. If they do, the Chironians will take out the whole ship. Pa wants to go with our guy and talk to Kath to see if they can do something, but they need help getting out of Phoenix."

Colman's face creased into a frown. "Take the ship out with what?"

"I don't know," Jay said. "It's a lot to go into now, but we're certain they've got the capability. It's really that urgent, Steve. When can you get over?"

"Oh, Christ . . ." Wearily, Colman brought a hand up to his brow. "Okay. Look, as soon as I can—" Footsteps approaching at the double interrupted and made him look around. It was Sergeant Armley, from the Orderly Room.

Armley stopped in front of Colman and beckoned Hanlon over. "Sirocco wants you both back right away," he said breathlessly. "I'll take over at the gate. There's trouble at the shuttle base. Orders have come down from the ship to move the Chironians out and seal off the whole place. Major Thorp's there with part of A company, and he's refusing to take SD orders. We've been ordered to send two platoons. Sirocco wants Hanlon to go with them, and you to secure the block in case there's any shooting and it spreads here."

Colman groaned to himself. Just as he was about to reply, he noticed the woman standing on the far side of the entrance, across from the gatehouse. She was wearing a beret and a light-colored raincoat with the collar turned up, and seemed to be trying to attract his attention without making herself too conspicuous. "Oh, Jesus—" He looked at the two. "Look, I need a few minutes. Jay, stay right there." He walked across to the woman and was almost face to face with her before he recognized Veronica, for once looking neither impish nor mischievous.

"I've just come down from the ship, Steve." She drew him close to the gatepost.

"Aren't the boarding gates being checked?" Colman murmured, surprised.

"Of course they are. It's all a mess up there."

"Then how—"

"I know Crayford and his wife. One of the crew got me through. That can wait. It's about Celia."

It wasn't a moment to be keeping up pretenses. Colman's frown deepened. "What about her? Is she okay?"

Veronica nodded her head quickly a couple of times. "She's not hurt or anything like that, but she's in a lot of trouble. She's gotten herself mixed up with Sterm, and she can't make a move without being watched. She could be in real danger, Steve. She has to get away from there."

Colman nodded but tossed up his hands. "Okay, but how can she?"

"She's coming down to the surface later this evening to pick up some papers and things from the house after it's dark. But she'll be under escort. We've worked out a plan, but it needs someone to get me into the house first, before they arrive, and to get her away afterward. Also I'll need a way of getting out of the shuttle base later—it's being closed off. You're the only person she'll trust. Can you get away inside the next hour, say?"

Colman looked away in a daze. Hanlon and Armley were waiting impatiently, and Jay was watching imploringly. He thought furiously. Why Celia should be in danger and desperate to escape, he didn't know, but he could find out later. If he said he had to get away for a few hours, Sirocco would cover for him, so that was okay. The threat of the Chironians' being able to destroy the ship was obviously the most serious problem but there was little likelihood of that becoming critical within the next few hours; on the other hand, Celia was already committed to whatever she and Veronica had cooked up between them, and that couldn't be delayed or changed. So Celia would have to come first. Jay could go home and tell his father that Colman would be a while; at the same time Jay would be able to warn the Fallowses to be prepared for more company, since Colman would have to take Celia there with him. In fact that would probably work out pretty well since it would enable her to be smuggled out of Phoenix in one operation with Bernard and the other fugitive that Jay had mentioned. Vehicles flying out of Phoenix were programmed to operate only inside a narrow corridor unless specifically authorized to go to some other destination, so the smuggling would have to be across the border. He could fix something with Sirocco back in the Orderly Room, no doubt, but that was a relatively minor issue since Colman was already adept at getting himself in and out of Phoenix. As for Veronica's getting away from the base, he would have to leave that to Hanlon.

"We can probably figure out a way to get you into the house, Veronica. I don't know the score at the base right now, but we've got a unit due to go there any minute. That means you'll have to trust some other guys too. Okay?"

"If you say so. Do I have a choice?"

"No." Colman turned his head and waved Hanlon over. "Bret, this is Veronica. Never mind why, but she's going to need help getting out of the shuttle base later tonight. What do you think?"

"We'll work out something. Where and when?" Hanlon said. Colman looked over at Veronica.

"A shuttle's lifting off from Bay Five at 2130," she said. "I'll be coming off it about thirty minutes before it leaves. All I need is to get over into Chironian territory. I can make it on my own from there."

"Where to?" Colman asked her.

"Casey's, I suppose," Veronica replied.

"Does Casey know?" Colman asked. Veronica shook her head. Colman thought for a few seconds. "I don't like the sound of what's going on around there," he said. "Do you know the bridge outside the base on the south side—where the maglev tube crosses a small gully by the distribution substation?"

"I think so. I can find it anyway."

"Make for the bridge and wait there," Colman told her. "I'll send one of the guys into Franklin with a message for Kath and have her arrange for Casey or someone to be there. SD patrols could be prowling around, or anything. Best not to risk it." Veronica nodded her assent.

"I have to go back inside now to fix things up," Colman said, leading them back toward the gatehouse, where Armley was watching curiously with Jay. "Mike," Colman said to him as they stopped by the door. "Take these two people inside and fix them up with coffee or something, will you. Jay, wait inside with Veronica. I have to get back in with Bret, but I'll be back in a few minutes. Don't worry. It'll be okay."

Ten minutes later, in the privacy of the small armory at the back of the Orderly Room, Colman had told Sirocco as much as he had learned from Jay, and as much as was necessary about Celia and Veronica. Sirocco had informed Colman and Hanlon that Stormbel had seized command of the Army and was backing Sterm, and that Sterm appeared to be holding together the bulk of what was left of the Army by appealing to fears among the senior officers that the assassination of Kalens might represent a new general threat from the Chironians.

"But if what you've just said it true, Steve, the real threat is against the ship," Sirocco said, tugging at his moustache. "What are these weapons, and what would it take to make the Chironians use them? I've got to have more information."

Colman could only shake his head. "I don't know. Neither did Jay. That's what Fallows and whoever this other guy is want to find out."

"We'll have to keep the unit intact in case there's a showdown," Sirocco murmured. "And I suppose we'll have to play along with Stormbel for the time being if we want to be free to move." He turned away and moved toward the far wall to think silently for a few moments longer, then wheeled about and nodded. "Okay. Bret, you have to leave for the base right away. Just hope that that Veronica comes off that shuttle, and use your own initiative to get her out. That's all you have to worry about. So, on your way." Hanlon nodded and disappeared back through the Orderly Room. "Steve," Sirocco said. "Pick anyone you want to send to Franklin, and we'll just have to leave the rest of that side of things to Kath. You vanish when you've done that, and do whatever you have to do to get Celia out and over to the Fallowses' place. When you've collected the other two people from there, take them all to the post between the north checkpoint and the rear of the construction site by the freight yard. Maddock's section will be manning that sector from midnight to 0400. They know how to distract the SDs, and I'll make sure they're expecting you." Colman nodded and turned to follow in the direction which Hanlon had gone. "Oh, and Steve," Sirocco called as a new thought struck him. Colman stopped at the door and looked back. "You say you know Fallows fairly well?"

"For a long time," Colman said.

"Don't leave them at the post," Sirocco said. "Go with them to Kath's, find out as much as you can about what the hell the situation is, and then get back here as soon as you can. That way, maybe we'll be able to figure out what needs to be done."

CHAPTER THIRTY-ONE

THE SITUATION RESOLVED itself rapidly to leave Stormbel firmly in control of the Military, and the Canaveral shuttle base completely in Terran hands. Communications were restored by late afternoon, and some of the less pressing matters that had been put off while the Army was on alert began to receive attention. Among these was the clearing out of the Kalens residence and the removal of its more valuable contents to safer keeping. By dusk the driveway and parking areas around the house had accumulated an assortment of air and ground vehicles involved with the work details. Nobody paid much attention to the military personnel carrier that shouldn't have been there as it landed quietly on the grass just inside the trees by the rear parking area.

Inside, Stanislau shut down the flight-control systems, then walked into the passenger compartment without turning on the cabin lights to join Colman, Maddock, Fuller, and Carson, who were sitting with a large picture-crate propped between them, and a pile of cartons, tools, and packing materials around their feet. Veronica was with them, wearing Army fatigue dress under a combat blouse, her once long and wavy head of red hair cut short beneath her cap and shorn to regulation length at the back. Maddock climbed over the litter to open the door, and then climbed out with Carson and Fuller; Stanislau stayed inside to help in the unloading. Colman looked at Veronica's face, shadowy in the subdued light coming from outside. "Feel okay?" he asked.

She nodded, then after a few seconds said, "Casey will have a fit."

Her attempt at humor was a good sign. Colman grinned and heaved himself from his seat. "Then let's go," he grunted.

When they were all outside, Carson and Maddock took the picture-crate, Stanislau a toolbox, Fuller assorted ropes and fasteners, and Colman some papers and inventory pads. Veronica carried a large roll of packing foam on her shoulder, keeping it pressed against the side of her face. Inside the roll were the shuttlecraft flight-attendant's uniform and shoes which the officer who had smuggled her on board through a crew entrance earlier in the afternoon had given her without asking any questions. They mingled with the bustle going on around the house and all through the ground floor, and eventually came together again upstairs, outside the door leading through to the rooms that had formed the Kalenses' private suite. Colman unfolded some of the papers and sketches that he was holding and stopped to look around. After a few seconds he gestured to attract the attention of the SD guard who was standing disinterestedly near the top of the main stairs, and nodded his head in the direction of the door. "Is that the way into the bedroom and private quarters?" he asked.

"It is, but nothing in there's to be touched until Mrs. Kalens has been back to get some stuff," the guard answered. "She should be on her way down just about now."

"That's okay," Colman said. "We just have to take some measurements." Without waiting for a reply he walked over to the door, opened it, poked his head in, called back to Stanislau, "This is it. Where's Johnson?" and went inside. Stanislau put down the toolbox and followed, then Colman came back out and squatted down to rummage inside it for something. Veronica appeared and went in with the packing roll, Stanislau came out, Colman went back in with a measure, and a few yards away along the corridor Carson and Maddock managed to get the picture-crate stuck across an awkward corner. While the SD was half watching them, Fuller came up the stairs to ask where Johnson was, Stanislau waved in the direction of the doorway, and Fuller went in while Colman came out. Carson dropped his end of the crate, Stanislau went in with a compad, Maddock started yelling at Carson, and Fuller came out.

In the bathroom through the far door of the bedroom behind the lounge, Veronica was already stripping off her fatigues and boots, which she then stowed beneath the towels in the linen closet. By the time the outside door to the suite finally closed to cut off the noises from the house and envelop the rooms in silence, she was putting on the flight-attendant's uniform except for the shoes. After that she used Celia's things to attend to her makeup.

Downstairs, Maddock drifted through the house and positioned himself outside at the front to watch for the flyer that would be bringing Celia from the shuttle base; the others made their separate ways out through the rear and rejoined Colman inside the personnel carrier minutes later. They settled themselves down to wait, and Fuller and Carson lit cigarettes. "Still think it'll go okay, Sarge?" Stanislau asked. "I could do a quick hair-job in there." He had brought the things with him, just in case.

Colman shook his head. "There shouldn't be any need. Celia's hair is a lot shorter. There'll be fewer people around later. It'll be okay . . . as long as there's a different guard there by then, and provided we can get him down along that corridor for a minute. And anyhow, they'll be expecting people to be going in there then."

"If you say so," Stanislau said.

"How long before the flyer shows up?" Carson asked.

Colman looked at his watch. "About half an hour if it's on schedule."

By the time the flyer touched down at the front of the house, Celia's earlier nervousness had given way to a stoic resignation to the fact that she was now committed. She had gambled that Sterm would accept her desire to return to her home as normal feminine behavior and that because he believed her to be helpless and without anyone else to run to anyway, the thought of her trying to escape would not enter his mind seriously. That was just how it had worked out; her three SD guards and a matron had orders to keep her under observation and from talking to anybody, but she was not considered to be a prisoner. Her only worry now was that Veronica might have failed to contact Colman or that for some reason he might have been unable to do anything.

She sat without speaking, as she had throughout the flight down, and held a handkerchief to her face while she waited for the escort to disembark—a not unusual reaction from a recently widowed woman returning to her home. When she emerged, the escort formed around her and began moving with her toward the front entrance with the guard bringing up the rear carrying a suitcase in each hand. Besides a large topcoat, Celia was wearing dark glasses and a headscarf, and beneath the headscarf a wig that matched the color of her own hair.

The party ascended the main staircase, at the top of which the two leading guards took up positions outside the door to the suite while the one with the suitcases accompanied Celia and the matron inside. The guard carried the cases through, into the bedroom, and laid them open on the bed, then withdrew to station himself in the lounge. While Celia began selecting and packing items from the drawers and closets, the matron went to the door at the back to look into the bathroom, swept her eyes round in a perfunctory check for windows or other exits, and then came away again to assume a blank-faced, postlike stance inside the lounge door, moving only when Celia went through to collect some papers and other items from the desk beyond. Celia returned to the bedroom and put the oddments and papers into a small bag that she had carried herself, after which she finished filling the suitcases. Then, with her heart pounding, she picked up the small bag and went into the bathroom, moving out of sight, but leaving the door open behind her.

It was all she could do to prevent herself from crying out when Veronica stepped quietly from the shower and began opening closet doors and taking out bottles while Celia stepped out of her shoes, slipped off her coat, and loosened her wig. There was no time for smiles or reassuring gestures. Veronica put Celia's shoes on her feet and the flight-attendant's shoes in Celia's bag; the wig went into place easily over her new haircut; the coat went over her uniform, and she tied the scarf over the wig while Celia took over the job of putting bottles, jars, brushes, and tubes into the bag to keep up the background noise. Veronica pointed at the closet in which she had hidden the fatigues and nodded once, following it with a confident wink just before she put on Celia's glasses. Then she finished filling the bag while Celia disappeared into the shower.

The matron didn't gave Veronica a second glance when she came out of the bathroom with Celia's bag on one hand and holding Celia's handkerchief to her face with the other. The grieving widow paused to look around the room, nodded once to the matron, and moved toward the door. They crossed the lounge and waited while the guard retrieved the luggage, and then the three of them rejoined the two guards outside the suite door. The party then reformed and began descending the stairs.

Celia waited for a few minutes to give anybody a chance to come back for something, then stepped from the shower, found the clothes that Veronica had left, and spent a few minutes putting them on and lacing the boots. Her hair was already tied high from wearing the wig, but she spent a while studying the cap in the mirror and making some adjustments before she considered herself passable. She was just walking back into the bedroom to wait when she heard the door on the far side of the lounge open, and immediately the suite was filled with the sounds of bodies moving around and voices calling to each other. A few seconds later Colman appeared in the doorway from the lounge. Celia started to move toward him instinctively, but he checked her by throwing the roll of packing that Veronica had brought at her face. "You're in the Army," he said gruffly as she caught it. "Move your ass."

It was the right thing to do. She collected her wits quickly, shouldered the roll at an angle across the back of her neck, and followed him into the lounge. Colman went ahead to stand peering through the doorway from one side while soldiers came and went in bewildering confusion and then he motioned her out suddenly. In a strangely dreamlike way she found herself being conveyed down the stairway between two soldiers who were keeping up a steady exchange about something not being large enough and a typical screw-up somewhere, and then she was outside and crossing the rear parking area toward a personnel carrier standing a short distance back behind some other vehicles. Suddenly, without really remembering getting in, she was sitting in the cabin. Figures materialized swiftly and silently from the darkness and jumped in after her. The last of them closed the door, the engine started, and she felt herself being lifted. Only then did she start shaking.

"Never say you don't get anything back for your taxes." Colman was sitting next to her, grinning faintly in the brief glow as one of the others lit a cigarette. But she had gone for so much of the day without speaking that she was unable to answer immediately. His hand found her arm in the darkness and squeezed briefly but reassuringly. "It'll be okay," he murmured. "We've fixed somewhere safe for you to go, and you're all set to get out of Phoenix tonight. I'll be coming with you into Franklin."

"What about Veronica?" she whispered.

"One of our units at the base is expecting her. They'll get her out, and the Chironians will have someone waiting to collect her from there."

Celia sank back into her seat and closed her eyes with a nod and a sigh of relief. One of the figures in the darkness wanted to know how come somebody called Stanislau knew how to fly something like this. Another voice replied that his father used to steal them from the government.

Colman stared at Celia for a few seconds longer. He still didn't know why Celia should have been so anxious to get away from Sterm or why she should have been in any danger. Life couldn't have been much fun with somebody like Howard, he could see, so the thought of her gravitating toward a strong, protective figure like Sterm wasn't so strange. And it didn't seem so unnatural that she should have stayed near Sterm after Howard was killed. In such circumstances it would have been normal to provide her with an escort down to the surface too, for her own security; but having her watched all the time and not allowing her contact with anybody made no sense. Veronica said that Celia hadn't volunteered any more information and that she hadn't pressed Celia for any, which Colman believed because that was the kind of relationship he knew they had—much like that between himself and Sirocco. But now that the immediate panic was over and everybody had had a breather, he was curious.

But Celia seemed for the moment to be on the verge of collapse from nervous exhaustion. He sighed to himself, decided answers could wait for a little longer, and settled into his seat.

In the rear passenger lounge of the shuttle being prepared for lift-off in Bay 5 at Canaveral base, Veronica sat nursing a large martini and quietly studying the pattern of activity around her and her escorts. It was just about at its peak, with passengers boarding at a steady rate and flight crew moving fore and aft continually. But most of the faces had not yet had time to register. The matron had evidently not considered it part of her duties to assist in packing or carrying anything, but had maintained her distance as a purely passive observer; there was no reason why she should change that role now.

Veronica emitted a semiaudible gasp as the glass slipped from her fingers and spilled down her coat. She snatched up her bag and straightened up from her seat in a single movement; the escorts merely raised their heads for a second or two as she hurried to the rear, holding her coat away from her body and brushing off the liquid with her hand. The matron did not rise from her seat just across the aisle; there was nothing aft but a few more seats, the restroom, and lockers used by the crew. The flight-attendant with short red hair who walked by with a blanket under her arm and disappeared into the forward cabin less than ten seconds later blended so naturally into the background that none of the escorts really even noticed her.

CHAPTER THIRTY-TWO

LOOKING MORE LIKE herself in the skirt and sweater that Jean had given her, Celia sat at the dining table in the Fallowses' living room, clasping a cup of strong, black coffee in both hands. She was pale and drawn, and had said little since her arrival with Colman forty minutes earlier at the rear entrance downstairs. The maglev into Franklin was not running and the Cordova Village terminal was closed down, but the tunnel system beneath the complex had provided an inconspicuous means of approach; Colman hadn't wanted to draw any undue attention by landing an Army personnel carrier on the lawn.

"Starting to feel a little better?" Jean asked as she refilled Celia's cup. Celia nodded. "Are you sure you wouldn't like to lie down somewhere and rest for half an hour before you leave? It might do you a lot of good." Celia shook her head. Jean nodded resignedly and replaced the pot on the warmer before sitting down again between Celia and Marie.

Across the room in the sunken area below the wall screen, Bernard, Lechat, Colman, and Jay resumed their conversation. "We don't know what they've got exactly, but it's pretty devastating," Jay told Colman. "We figure they've already tested it. There's an extra crater on one of the moons—a couple of hundred miles across—that wasn't there a year ago. Imagine if whatever did that was to hit the ship."

"You think that's really a possibility?" Colman asked, looking concerned and doubtful at the same time.

"It's how the Chironians have been working all along," Lechat said. "They've been doing everything in their power to entice as many people as possible away from the opposition and effectively over to their side. Haven't they done it with us? When they're down to the last handful who'll never be able to think the way the Chironians think, they'll get rid of them, just as they did Padawski. That's how their society has always worked. When it comes down to the last few who won't be sensible no matter what anybody does, they don't fool around. And they'll do the same thing with the ship if Sterm makes one threatening move with those weapons up there. I'm convinced of it. The Chironians took out their insurance a long time ago. That would be typical of how they think too."

Colman frowned and shook his head with a sigh as he thought about it. "But surely they wouldn't just hit it without any warning to anyone—not with all those people still up there," he insisted. "Wouldn't they say something first . . . let Sterm know what he's up against?"

"I don't know," Bernard said dubiously. "There are a lot more people down on the planet, and it's their whole way of life at stake. Maybe they wouldn't. Who knows exactly how the Chironians think when all the chips are down? Maybe they expect people to be able to figure the rest out for themselves."

Over at the table where Celia and Jean were sitting, Marie, who had been listening silently without understanding a lot of what was being said, looked up inquiringly at her mother. Jean smiled and squeezed her hand reassuringly.

"So what is it they've got?" Colman asked again. "Missiles wouldn't be any use to them, and they know it. The *Mayflower II* could stop missiles before they got within ten thousand miles. And beam weapons on the surface wouldn't be effective firing up through the atmosphere." He spread his hands imploringly. "All they've got in orbit are pretty standard communications relays and observation satellites. The moons are both out of range of beam projectors. So what else is there?"

"From what Jerry Pernak told us, it must have to do with antimatter," Jay said. "The Chironians are into a whole new world of particle theory. That means they can produce lots of antimatter economically. With that they could make matter–antimatter annihilation bombs, super-

intense radiation sources, guided antimatter beams, maybe
. . . who knows? But it has to be something like that."

The mention of antimatter reminded Colman of something. He sat back on the sofa and cast his mind back as
he tried to pinpoint what. It reminded him of something
Kath had said. The others stopped talking and looked at
him curiously. And then it came to him. He cocked his
head to one side and looked at Bernard. "Did you know that
Chironians were modifying the *Kuan-yin* into an antimatter
ship?" he asked.

Bernard sat forward, his expression suddenly serious.
"No, I didn't," he said. "Is that what they've been doing to
it? How did . . ." His voice trailed away silently.

Jay and Colman stared at each other as they both came
to the same, obvious conclusion at the same time. "That's
it," Jay murmured.

Bernard's expression was grave and distant. "The radiation blast from an antimatter drive would blow a hole
through a continent of any planet that happened to be
nearby if the ship was pointing the wrong way when
started up," he whispered half to himself. "It's been up
there in orbit, right under our noses all the time. They've
got the biggest radiation projector anybody ever dreamed
of—right there, riding out in space with the *Mayflower II*.
They put kids and comic robots on it, and we never even
noticed it."

A long silence went by while they took it all in. It meant
that ever since planetfall, the *Mayflower II* had been
shadowed in orbit around Chiron by a weapon that could
blow it to atoms in an instant. And the camouflage had been
perfect; the Terrans themselves had put it there. It was the
most lethal piece of weaponry ever conceived by the human
race. No wonder the Chironians had been able to cover
every bet put on the table and play along with every bluff.
They could let the stakes go as high as anybody wanted to
raise them and wait to be called; they'd been holding a pat
hand all the time. Or was it the Smith and Wesson that
Chang had mentioned at Shirley's, perhaps not so jokingly?

"We might not be the only ones who've noticed there's an

extra hole on Remus," Jay said at last. "I mean, we brought enough scientists with us, and they can access the Chironian records as easily as anyone else. The Chironians aren't exactly secretive about their physics."

"They could have," Bernard agreed. "But have they? It doesn't add up to the way Sterm's acting."

Jay shrugged. "Maybe he figures he's got a better than even chance of outshooting them. Maybe he's just crazy."

Lechat had digested the implications by now and appeared worried. "Maybe the Chironians have given a warning, but nobody realized it. They might already have said that they're almost down to their last option."

"How do you mean?" Colman asked.

Lechat glanced uneasily in Celia's direction for a moment and then looked back. "Howard Kalens," he said in a lower voice. "Couldn't that have been a final warning? Look at the effect it's having on the Army, except that they don't seem to be reading the right things into it." He looked at Jay. "I can't see that they've got it all figured out. They can't have."

Bernard sat back and drew a long breath. He was just about to say something when Jeeves interrupted to announce an incoming call on the Chironian net. It was Kath, calling from her place in Franklin. "I've heard from Casey," she said when Bernard accepted. "He's collected his package with Adam, and they're on their way home with it. I just thought you'd like to know."

Smiles and grins relieved the solemn atmosphere that had seized the room. From the direction of the table, Jean emitted an audible sigh of relief. Bernard grinned up at the screen. "Thanks," he said. "We're all glad to hear it. Talk to you again soon." Kath gave a quick smile and vanished from the screen.

"Veronica made it!" Jean exclaimed delightedly. "Steve, I don't know how you handled it all."

"It pays to have friends," Colman grunted.

"Congratulations, Steve," Bernard said, still smiling. "I wonder what those guards are doing right now."

"I'm very pleased," Lechat murmured. Jay grinned, and Marie smiled at what was evidently good news.

Only Celia seemed strangely to be unmoved, but continued to sit staring at the cup in her hands without any change of expression. Her unexpected reaction caused the others to fall quiet and stare at her uncertainly. Then Jean said in a hesitant voice, "You don't seem very excited, Celia. Is there something wrong?"

Celia didn't seem to hear. Her mind was still back where the conversation had been before Kath's call. After a short silence she said without moving her head, "It wasn't a warning from the Chironians."

The others exchanged puzzled looks. Jean shook her head and looked back at Celia. "I'm sorry, we're not with you. Why—"

"The Chironians didn't kill Howard," Celia said. "I did."

A silence descended like steel doors slamming down around the room. Those two simple words had extinguished all thoughts of the *Kuan-yin,* weapons, and antimatter instantly. Every head turned disbelievingly to Celia as she sat staring ahead. Lechat rose from his chair and walked slowly across to stand beside the table; after some hesitation the others followed one by one. Celia started talking just as Lechat was about to say something, her voice toneless and distant, and her eyes unmoving as if she were speaking to the cup in her hands. "I couldn't have spent my life with a man who had closed his mind to reality. You can't know what it was like. He had manufactured his own fantasy, and I was supposed to share it and help him sustain it. It was impossible." She paused to gulp some of the coffee. "So, the thing with Sterm . . . happened . . . Howard learned about it . . ." Celia closed her eyes as if she were trying to shut out a memory that she was seeing again. "He lost control of himself completely . . . there was a fight, and . . ." She left the rest unsaid. After a few seconds she opened her eyes and stared blankly ahead again. "Maybe I wanted him to find out—provoked him to it. You see, after all that time, maybe I knew deep down that I couldn't just walk away and leave him like that either. What other way was there?" Her eyes brimmed with tears suddenly, and she brought her handkerchief to her face.

Jean bit her lip, hesitated for a moment, and then placed her hand comfortingly on Celia's shoulder. "You mustn't think like that," she urged. "You're trying to take all the guilt upon yourself and—"

Celia raised her head suddenly to look up at Lechat. "But I only shot him twice, not six times as the soldiers found. And the house hadn't been broken into when I left. Don't you see what that means?"

Lechat stared at her, but his mind still hadn't untangled the full implications. Beside him Colman's jaw clamped tight. "Somebody faked it to look like the Chironians did it," Colman grated.

Bernard's jaw dropped. "Sterm?" he gasped, then looked down at Celia. "You did tell him?"

Celia nodded. "That evening, as soon as I got up to the ship. I think I must have been hysterical or something. But . . . yes, I told him."

Lechat was nodding slowly to himself. "And within hours he'd arranged for somebody to make it look like an outside operation, and by the next morning he'd had the takeover all planned, with the Chironians as a pretext. Everything fits. But who would have done it?"

"SDs," Colman said at once. "It was a professional job."

"Would they accept a job like that?" Jean asked, sounding dubious.

Colman nodded. "Sure. They're selected and trained to obey orders and not ask questions. Some of them would shoot their own mothers if the right person said so. And Stormbel was in on it. It fits." He thought for a second longer, and then looked at Lechat and Bernard. "There were a lot of suspicious things about Padawski breaking out too. It couldn't have happened the way it did without inside help. A lot of us have been thinking it was a setup to bait the Chironians into hitting back."

Lechat's brows lifted and then creased into an even deeper frown. "And then there were those bombings . . ." He looked down at Celia. "Was Sterm behind those things too?"

"I don't know, but it wouldn't surprise me," Celia answered. "I just know the true story about Howard because . . . because . . ."

"Does anyone else know about Howard?" Colman asked. "Veronica, for instance?"

Celia shook her head. "Nobody until now."

Colman exhaled a long breath. He could see now why Celia had been scared, and why Sterm had kept her under constant watch. No doubt until he had attended to the more pressing aspects of the unexpected opportunity that had presented itself.

"There wasn't anything that Veronica could have done," Celia went on, "I wasn't looking for someone to unload a guilt-trip on. What I had to say was a lot bigger than that. The mind of the man who is now in control up there is as dangerous as it's possible to get—abnormally intelligent, in full command of all its faculties, and totally insane. Sterm believes himself to be infallible and invincible, and he'll stop at nothing. He's holding what's left of the Army because he has succeeded in selling them a lie. And I was the only person who could expose that lie. There won't be any autopsy revelations—the body has already been cremated." Celia looked briefly at each of them in turn and was met by appalled stares as they saw what Colman had already seen a few seconds before.

"Yes, I knew I was in danger, but that was secondary," Celia told them. "I still can expose the lie. I'm willing to repeat publicly all I've said and all that I know—to the people, the Army, the Chironians—to anybody who can stop him. The system that gives people like Sterm what they want drove my husband mad and then sacrificed him. There must be no more sacrifices. That was why I had to get away."

CHAPTER THIRTY-THREE

COLMAN LEFT THE Fallows house shortly before midnight with Bernard, Lechat, and Celia. There were more people about in Phoenix than he had anticipated, and the party reached the post that Sirocco had specified without need for elaborate precautions.

On their arrival, they learned from Maddock that there was little need for them to have bothered making the arrangements with Sirocco. Border security around Phoenix was disintegrating, with most of the SDs being pulled back to protect the shuttle base, the barracks, and other key points, and the regular troops who were left scattered thinly along the perimeter doing little to interfere with the civilian exodus. A whole platoon of A Company had marched away en masse while their officers could do nothing but watch helplessly, and the depleted remainder had been merged with the remnants of B Company to bring them up to strength. More SDs were disappearing too. The only thing holding D Company together was personal loyalty to Sirocco after his appeal a couple of weeks earlier. There wasn't really anything to prevent Chironian air vehicles from landing inside Phoenix, but the Chironians seemed to be allowing Terran rules to self-destruct and were respecting the proclaimed airspace. Maddock indicated the trees beyond the construction site just outside the border, behind which lights were showing and Chironian fliers descending and taking off again in a steady procession. "No need for you to walk very far," he told them. "I can call Kath and have her send a cab over. What's her number?"

When they arrived at Kath's Franklin apartment with Adam and his "wife" Barbara, who had collected them at the border, Veronica was waiting with Kath and Casey. Colman already knew everybody, and while he and Kath were introducing Bernard and Lechat to those they hadn't met previously, Veronica and Celia greeted each other with hugs and a few more tears from Celia.

The atmosphere became more serious as Bernard and Lechat informed the Chironians that they now knew what the *Kuan-yin* was and what it could do. "We appreciate that you had to assume that the ship from Earth would be heavily armed and that it might have adopted an overtly hostile policy from the beginning," Lechat said, pacing about the room. "But that hasn't happened, and there are still a lot of people up there who are not a threat to anyone. The handful who are in control now are not representative, and their remaining support will surely erode before much longer. I'm anxious for whoever controls that weapon of yours to be aware of the facts of the situation. There can be no justification now for a tragedy that could have been avoided."

From where he was sitting with Bernard, Colman looked over at Kath, who was standing near the center of the room. "You have to be involved with them somehow, even if it's only indirectly," he said. "You must know these people, even if you're not one of them yourself."

"What would you wish them to do?" Kath asked, implying that Colman was correct in at least one of his assumptions without giving any hint of which. She had reacted to the subject with calmness and composure, almost as if she had been expecting it, but there was a firmness in her expression that Colman had not seen on any previous occasion. Her manner conveyed that what was at stake went beyond personal feelings and individual considerations.

"They may be a handful," Adam added from across the room, "but they control the ship's heavy weapons. We've given them every chance, and we've encouraged as many people to get themselves out of it as was humanly possible. Our whole world is at stake. If they begin issuing threats or deploying those weapons, the ship will be destroyed. There can be no changing that decision. It was made a long time ago."

Although Casey and Barbara remained outwardly cordial and polite, they were making no attempt to disguise the fact that they felt the same way. Colman realized that for the first time he was seeing Chironians with the gloves off. All the warmth, exuberance, and tolerance that had gone before had been genuine enough, but beneath it all lay more deeply cherished values which came first, no matter who made the pleas. On that, there could be no concessions.

"That's true," Bernard agreed. "But the risk of Sterm trying anything with those weapons has to be greater if he thinks he can blackmail a defenseless planet. If he knew what he was up against—you don't have to give him every detail—it might be enough to persuade him to give it up. That's all we're asking. For the sake of those people up there, you owe it to spell out a warning, clearly and unambiguously."

"Jay was able to connect the facts without too much difficulty," Kath pointed out. "We didn't try to hide them. Haven't the scientists on the ship done the same?"

"I don't know," was all that Bernard could reply. "If they have, they haven't published it. But does it seem likely? Would Sterm be moving the way he is if they had? But you have nothing to lose by spelling it out to them. It has to be worth a try."

Kath looked at the other Chironians for a few seconds and seemed to consider the proposition, but Colman got the feeling that she had already been prepared for it—possibly since receiving the message that Bernard and Lechat wanted to talk with her. Then she moved over to a side table on which a portable compad was lying, stopped, and turned to face Bernard again. "It isn't a matter for me to decide," she said. "But the people concerned are waiting to talk to you." Bernard and Lechat exchanged puzzled looks. Kath seemed to hesitate for a second, and then looked at Lechat. "I'm afraid we have been taking an unpardonable liberty with you. You see, this was not entirely unexpected. The people you wish to speak with have been monitoring our discussion. I hope you are not too offended."

She touched a code into the compad, and at once the large screen at one end of the room came to life to reveal head-and-shoulder views of six people. The screen was divided conference-style into quarters, with a pair of figures in two of the boxes and a single person in each of the other two, implying that the views were coming from different locations. Kath noted the concerned look that flashed across Bernard's face. "It's all right," she told him. "The channels are quite secure."

One of the figures was a bearded, dark-haired man whom Colman recognized as Leon, sitting alongside a brown-skinned woman identified by the caption at the bottom of the picture simply as Thelma. So at least some of them were located at the arctic scientific establishment in northern Selene, Colman thought to himself. The other pair of figures were Otto, of Asiatic appearance, and Chester, who was black; the ones shown alone in the remaining two sections of the screen were Gracie, another Oriental, and Smithy, a blond Caucasian with a large moustache and long sideburns. From their ages they were all evidently Founders. Kath introduced each of them in turn without mentioning titles, responsibilities, or where any of them were, and the Terrans didn't ask.

Otto seemed to be the spokesman. He seemed anxious to reassure them. "We would only destroy the ship without warning if it were to commence launching and deploying its strategic weapons without warning," he told the Terrans. "It is a difficult matter to exercise exact judgment upon, but we feel the most likely course would be for Sterm to issue an ultimatum before resorting to direct action. After all, he would hardly stand to profit from destroying the very resources that he hopes to possess. Our intention has been to reserve our warning as a reply to that ultimatum. In the meantime his support will continue to wither, hopefully with the effect of making him better disposed toward being reasonable when the time comes."

"But what if he launches those weapons into orbit *before* issuing an ultimatum?" Bernard asked.

Leon nodded gravely from his section of the screen. "That is a risk," he agreed. "As Otto said, it is difficult to judge exactly. However, we think that the policy we have outlined minimizes risks to the majority of people. Nothing will eliminate the risks completely." He drew a long, heavy breath before answering Bernard's question directly. "But there can be no alteration of our resolution."

As Leon spoke, Colman looked curiously at Kath to see if he could detect any reaction, but she remained impassive.

Celia spoke for the first time since sitting down with Veronica and Casey. Until now she had not been fully aware of the reason for Bernard and Lechat's visit. "Either way a warning won't do any good," she said. "Whether you issue one now or later is academic. He would defy it. You don't know him. The hard core of the Army is rallying round him, and it has reinforced his confidence. He thinks he is unbeatable."

Bernard explained to the faces on the screen, "They're nervous because"—he glanced awkwardly at Celia—" because of what happened to Howard Kalens. Sterm is playing on that."

"That was unfortunate, but it was beyond our control," Leon said. "I hope you do not believe that we were responsible." Bernard shook his head.

After a long silence Otto looked up. "Then I'm afraid we can offer no more."

There seemed to be no more to say. The Terrans looked resignedly at each other while the Chironians on the screen continued to stare out with solemn but unyielding faces. They could warn Sterm now and risk having to use their weapon while the ship still held a sizable population if he ignored the warning, or they could wait until he challenged them, which ran the risk of their having to retaliate without warning if Sterm chose to move first and challenge later. Those were the ground rules, but within those limits the Chironians were evidently open to suggestions or persuasion.

Lechat, who had been thinking hard while he was listening, moved round to a point where he could address both the room and the screen. "Perhaps there is something else we can do," he said. Everybody looked at him curiously and waited. He raised his hands briefly. "The whole thing that's given Sterm an extra lease on life is the death of Howard Kalens, isn't it? Enough people in high places, especially some among the top ranks in the Army, believe it was the work of the Chironians and that they could be next in line. So they're clustering around Sterm for mutual preservation. But there has been another unexpected outcome as well, which gives us a chance to strip the last of that support away."

"What kind of outcome?" Thelma asked from beside Leon.

Lechat hesitated and looked uncertainly in Celia's direction. She returned an almost imperceptible nod. Lechat looked back at the screen. "Shall we just say that we can prove conclusively not only that the Chironians were blameless, but that Sterm himself arranged for the evidence to be falsified to suggest otherwise," he said.

"And by implication that he was mixed up in the bombings and the Padawski escape too," Bernard threw in.

The Chironians suddenly appeared intrigued. "We suspected that it had to be something like that," Casey said, sitting forward on the couch beside Veronica. "But how can you prove it?"

An awkward silence hung over the room. Then Celia said, "Because I killed him. The rest was faked after I left the house. Only Sterm knew about his death."

Murmurs of surprise came from the screen. In the living room, the Chironians were staring at Celia in amazement. Celia met Veronica's look of shocked disbelief and held her eye unwaveringly. Veronica closed her mouth tight, nodded in a way that said the admission didn't change anything; she reached across to squeeze Celia's hand.

Lechat didn't want to see Celia dragged through an ordeal again. He raised his arms to attract attention back to himself. "But don't you see what it means," he said. The voices on the screen and inside the room died away. "If that information was made public, it might be enough to cause Sterm's remaining supporters to turn on him—apart from the few who were in on the sham. Surely if that happened he'd have to see that it was all over. He's hanging on by the thread of a lie, and we possess proof of the truth that can cut that thread. That gives us an option to try before resorting to last, drastic measures. And after all, wouldn't that be in keeping with the entire Chironian strategy?"

Kath looked apprehensively at Celia. Celia nodded in answer to the unvoiced question. "Yes, that's the way I want it," she said. Kath nodded and accepted the situation at that.

"Exactly what are you asking us to do?" Otto asked from the screen.

Lechat tossed up his hands and began pacing again. "Anything to publicize what we've said . . . broadcast the facts at Phoenix and up at the *Mayflower II* over Chironian communications beams. At least some of the population would hear it . . . the word would soon be spread. . . . I don't know . . . whatever would bring word to the most people in the shortest time for greatest effect."

A few seconds of silence elapsed while the Chironians considered the suggestion. Their expressions seemed to say it couldn't do any harm, but it probably wouldn't change very much. "Is the case strong enough to turn the whole Army round in a moment?" Kath asked doubtfully at last. "We have no proof about Padawski and the bombings. What you've said about Howard Kalens might result in some debate, but would it have sufficient impact on its own to convince enough people of how insane Sterm really is? Now, if we could *prove* all the incidents, all at the same time—"

"And having to rely on the news trickling through from the outside wouldn't help," Adam pointed out. "There have been so many rumors already. It would be more likely to just fizzle out."

"It's an idea," Bernard said, looking up at Lechat. "But it needs more of what Kath said—*impact*."

"I agree, I agree," Lechat told them. "But we only know what we know, and we can only do what we can do. Surely doing so is not going to make things any worse. Will you try it?"

Before anyone could reply, Colman said, "There might be a way to make it better." Everyone looked at him. He swept his eyes around quickly. "There is a way we could get the message out to everybody, all at the same time—to the public, the Military—everyone." He looked around again. The others waited. "Through the Communications Center up in the ship," he said. "Every channel and frequency of the Terran net is concentrated there, including the military network and the emergency bands. We could broadcast from there on all of them simultaneously. You couldn't make much more impact than that." He sat back and looked around again to invite reactions.

Bernard was nodding but with evident reservations. "True," he agreed. "But it's up in the ship, not down here. And it must be strongly protected. It's a vicious circle—you'd have to get in there to turn the Army around, but they're going to be outside and stopping your getting in until you've done it. How can you break out of it?"

"And from what we've heard, their command structure is all a shambles anyway," Adam commented. "Could a penetration operation like that be organized now?"

Colman had been expecting something like that. "I know one unit of the Army that could do it," he said. "And they operate best when nobody's trying to organize them."

"Which one is that?" Leon asked from the screen, sounding dubious but also interested.

Colman grinned faintly and gestured across the room. "The same one that brought you Veronica and Celia."

A gleam of hope had come into Lechat's eyes. "Do you really think they might be able to pull something off?"

"If anyone could, they could," Veronica said from across the room. "That bunch could clean out Fort Knox without anyone knowing."

"She's right," Celia agreed simply.

Everybody looked at Colman again, this time with a new interest. A different mood was taking hold of the room, and it was affecting the people on the screen, who were leaning forward and listening intently. So far it was just an idea, but already it was beginning to hook all of them.

Bernard was rubbing his lip slowly as he thought about it. He caught Lechat's eye and appeared worried. "The message would have to go out live from there," he said slowly. "With active opposition around, you wouldn't want to go risking complications with remote links into it." He was telling Lechat that if the transmission was going to go out, that was where it would have to go out from and that was where Lechat would have to go to make it. But more to the point, as Lechat well knew, Bernard was saying that Celia would have to go there too; what she had to say couldn't come second-hand through anybody else.

Lechat pursed his lips for a second, and then nodded curtly. "I'll do it," he said simply. He averted his eyes for a moment longer, and then looked across at Celia. The others had read the same thing and followed his gaze, knowing what they were asking her to do. Colman could see the torment in her eyes as she looked back at Lechat. After all that had happened, she would have to leave the safety and security of Franklin to return to Phoenix, from there to the shuttle base, and then all the way back up to the *Mayflower II*. There was no other way.

Celia was already prepared for it. She nodded. Nothing remained to be said. The room had become very quiet.

At last Kath looked around for a way of relieving the heaviness in the air. "How will you get them up to the ship?" she asked Colman.

"I'll leave that to Sirocco," he replied. "He'll know more about the score at the base. We've had a unit there this evening, but they're probably back by now."

"How do you know he'll go along with it?" Barbara asked.

"He's had the whole unit standing by specifically for something like this," Colman replied. "He's waiting for news right now. That's why I'm here."

Celia had become very thoughtful in the last few seconds. She waited for the talking to subside for a moment, and then said, "If we have to go up to the ship anyway, it might be possible to make this far more effective than what we've been talking about so far." She paused, but nobody interrupted. "I know where the people who have been arrested are being held. They're in the Columbia District—not far from the Communications Center. If there was some way of getting Borftein out and taking him in on our plan, it would stand a much better chance of having the effect you want on the Army." Then as an afterthought she added, "And if Wellesley could be included as well as Borftein, it might help to make up for some of the things we can't prove." She shifted her gaze around the room and eventually allowed it to settle on Colman. "But I don't know if something like that would be possible."

"What do you think?" Bernard asked Colman after a short silence. "Could it be done?"

"I don't know. It depends on the situation. Maybe. That's something else we'll have to leave to Sirocco to decide."

Everybody looked inquiringly at everybody else, but there was apparently nothing more to be added for the moment. At last Colman rose to his feet. "Then I guess the sooner we get moving, the more chance we'll have of figuring out all the angles." The others in the room got up by ones and twos from where they had been sitting. Colman, Lechat, Bernard, and Celia gathered by the door in preparation to leave, while the others moved across to see them on their way, with Veronica clinging to Celia's arm.

"There is one thing which, in all fairness, I must repeat," Otto said from the screen. They turned and looked back at him. "We cannot alter our basic decision in any way. If Sterm becomes threatening, we will be forced to react. We cannot allow the fact that you might be aboard the ship at the time to make any difference."

Lechat nodded. "That was already understood," he replied grimly.

While the others passed through into the hallway of the apartment, Kath turned back toward the screen and touched a control on the compad. All of the views vanished except that of Leon, which expanded to fill the whole screen just as Thelma moved away out of the picture to leave him on his own. "We ought to commence evacuating the *Kuanyin*," Kath said. "It looks as if it could be dangerous up there very soon."

"I had already come to that conclusion," Leon replied. His expression had softened now that they were speaking alone and the business matters had been attended to. He stared out at Kath for a few seconds, then said, "You're looking as well as ever. Are the children keeping fine too?"

"As ever," Kath told him and smiled. "And yours, Lurch?"

Leon grinned. "Mischievous, but they're fun." He paused for a moment. "He seems to be a good man. You should be very happy until whenever. I hope nothing happens to them. They are all brave people. I admire them."

"I hope so too," Kath said with feeling. "I ought to go now and see them off. Take care, Leon."

"You too." The image vanished from the screen.

Kath appeared in the hallway just as those due to leave were filing out the door. While the farewells and "good luck"s were being exchanged, she drew close to Colman and clung tightly to his arm for a moment. "Come back," she whispered.

He returned the squeeze reassuringly. "You'd better believe it."

"I wish I felt as confident as you sound. It seems risky."

"Not when you've got the best outfit that the Army ever produced on your side," he told her.

"Oh, is that what it is? I never realized. You never told me you were with a special unit."

"Classified information," Colman murmured. Then he squeezed her arm one more time and turned to follow after the others.

CHAPTER THIRTY-FOUR

OUTSIDE DAWN WAS creeping into the sky as Stanislau sat before a portable communications panel in one corner of the mess hall of the Omar Bradley Block, frowning at the mnemonics appearing on the screen and returning coded commands with intermittent movements of his fingers. Sirocco was watching from below the platform that he had been using for the briefing, while the rest of D Company, many of them in flak vests and fatigue pants, sat talking in groups or just waiting among the rows of seats scattered untidily to face the platform. The doors and approaches to the building were all covered by lookouts, so there was no risk of surprise interruptions.

Sirocco had devised a plan for getting the Company up to the ship and into the Communications Center, but it hinged on Stanislau's being able to alter the orders posted for the day, which were derived from schedules held in one of the military logistics computers. Lechat, who was standing nearby with Celia and Colman, had called for a test-run to make sure that Stanislau could do it, since if that part of the scheme didn't work none of the rest could. Sirocco had suspended the briefing to resolve the issue there and then.

Bernard was watching with interest over Stanislau's shoulder. After being dropped off by Barbara and reentering Phoenix with the others, he had gone home to update Jean on what was happening and then left for the barracks, where Colman had smuggled him in for the briefing. It was just as well that he had; the scheme that Sirocco finally evolved required some familiarity with the *Mayflower II*'s electrical systems, and while Colman had been prepared to have a crack at that part of it, Bernard was the obvious

322

choice. So Bernard was going up to the *Mayflower II* too. He would explain everything to Jean later, he decided.

Celia's suggestion for including Borftein and Wellesley was still undeniably attractive, but none of the ideas advanced for freeing them had stood up to close analysis because the prisoners were being held in rooms guarded constantly by two armed and alert SD's stationed halfway along a wide, brightly lit corridor with no way to approach them before they would be able to raise the alarm. Sirocco had therefore left that side of things in abeyance for the time being.

Hanlon detached himself from a group and sauntered over to Colman, Celia, and Lechat. Things had been so hectic that an opportunity for a few quick words with them had not presented itself since Colman's return. "Well, I see there's no need to ask how things went on your side, Steve. I take it that Veronica's in safe hands now."

Colman nodded. "Her friends showed up, and she's in Franklin. It all went fine." He turned his head to Celia. "This is Bret. He got Veronica off the base."

Celia managed a smile. Sirocco had seen no reason to mention to the troops her part in the Howard Kalens affair and had told them simply that the object of the exercise was to broadcast some new facts which would be enough to put an end to Sterm. "I'm not sure what I'm supposed to say," she told Hanlon. "I'll never be able to thank you both enough. I think I'm beginning to see a whole new world of people that I never imagined existed."

"Ah, well, it's not over yet," Hanlon said. His eyes twinkled for a second as he remembered something else. "Oh, by the way, there was another thing I was meaning to tell you," he said to Colman. "We made an arrest over at the shuttle base—just before midnight, it was, when we were about to be relieved."

"Really? Who?" Colman asked.

"Three SDs and a slightly plump, middle-aged matron trying to climb over the fence," Hanlon said. "The woman was stuck on the top and making quite a fuss. Now, what do you imagine they could have been trying to run away from?"

"I have no idea," Colman said, grinning. Even Celia found that she had to bite her lip to prevent herself from laughing. "So what happened? Did you send them back up?"

Hanlon shook his head. "Ah, why be vindictive? We got her off and sent them all on their way. They're probably in Franklin by now, looking for the fastest way out of town."

At that moment Stanislau emitted a triumphant shout, and Bernard straightened up behind him to look across at Colman. "He's done it!" Bernard exclaimed. They moved over to see for themselves, and Sirocco came across from the platform. The rest of the mess hall quieted down. The screen in front of Stanislau was showing the day's duty roster for the entire infantry brigade.

"Is that just a copy file, or are you displaying the master schedule?" Lechat inquired.

"It's the master," Bernard said. "He's got overwrite privileges too. I just watched him try it."

"This looks like what we want, chief," Stanislau said to Sirocco, and pointed to one of the entries. Sirocco leaned closer to peer at the screen.

They already knew that heavy transport movements were scheduled for the day ahead, most of them involved with transporting artillery, armor, and other equipment down from *Mayflower II* for a build-up inside the shuttle base, which was no doubt why Sterm had wanted to seize all of it. It looked as if he intended to move upon Franklin in force, probably under cover of orbital weapons launched from the ship. With the coup in the *Mayflower II* now accomplished and the ship evidently considered secure, the SDs who had been concentrated there were being moved down to strengthen what was to become a fortified base for surface operations, and some regular units were being moved up to take over duties aloft. Stanislau had identified an order for C company to embark at 1800 hours that evening for transfer to the *Mayflower II*, which was just the kind of thing that Sirocco had been hoping for. Sirocco was willing to gamble that with a busy day ahead and lots to do, nobody would have time to question a late change in the orders.

"Let's see you overwrite it," Lechat said.

Stanislau touched in some commands, and immediately all references to C Company were replaced by references to D Company. Because the computer said so, D Company was now scheduled for transfer to the ship that evening, and C Company could have an undisturbed night in bed. Stanislau promptly reset the references to their original forms. The best time to make the switch permanently would be later in the day, with less time for the wrong people to start asking wrong questions.

Lechat nodded and seemed satisfied. "That gets us up there," he said. "Now what about getting into the Communications Center?"

Stanislau entered more commands. A different table of information appeared on the screen. "SD guard details and timetable for posts inside the Columbia District tonight," Stanislau said. They would refrain from doing anything to that one until the last moment.

"Good enough?" Sirocco asked, cocking an eyebrow at Lechat.

Lechat nodded. "It's amazing," he murmured.

"Well done, Stanislau," Sirocco said. "Let's hope that the repeat performance will be as good later today."

"You can count on it, sir," Stanislau said.

Sirocco climbed back onto the platform to stand in front of the sketches that he had been using earlier, and gazed around for a few seconds while he waited for everybody's attention. "Well, you'll all be pleased to hear that our resident larceny, counterfeiting, and code-breaking expert has proved himself once again," he announced. "Phases one and four appear to be feasible, as we discussed." To one side and below the platform, Stanislau turned with a broad, toothy grin and clasped his hands above his head to acknowledge the chorus of murmured applause and low whistles, rendered enthusiastically, but quietly enough not to attract undue attention to the block at that time of the morning.

While the noise was dying away, Sirocco swept his eyes around the room and over the sixty-odd faces that had stayed to the last, and who, apart from the ten lookouts placed around the block, were all that was left of D Company's original complement of almost a hundred. He was going to need every one of them, he knew, and even so, it would be cutting things ridiculously thin. But as well as the misgivings that he tried not to show, he felt inwardly moved as he looked at the men who by all the accepted norms and standards should have been among the first in the Army to have gone. But apart from the SD units, D Company's record was second to none. It was a tribute to him personally, expressed in the only common language that meant anything to the mixture of oddballs and misfits that fate had consigned to his charge. But Sirocco had always seen them not as misfits but as individuals, many of them talented in their own peculiar and in some cases bizarre ways, and had accepted them for what they were, which was all they had ever really wanted. But the term misfit was a relative one, he had come to realize. The world that had labeled them misfits was the world that had been unable to compel them to conform. Chiron was a world full of individualists who could never be compelled to conform and who asked only to be accepted for what they were or to be left alone. Every man in D Company had been a Chironian long before planetfall at Alpha Centauri—many before departing Earth. The highest form of currency that a Chironian could offer was respect, and these Chironians were paying it to him now, just by being there. Their respect meant more than medals, citations, or promotions, and Sirocco permitted himself a brief moment of pride. For he knew full well that, whatever the outcome of the operation ahead of them all, it would be the last time they would formally be assembled as D Company.

"Very well," he said. "Stanislau has had his encore. Now let's get back to business.

"First, let's recap the main points. The primary object is to get into the Communications Center and secure it while the transmission goes out, and after that to hold it and hope that enough of the Army reacts quickly enough to take the pressure off. Okay?" There were no questions, so Sirocco continued. "The big risk is that SD reinforcements will be brought up from the surface. If that happens, they'll have to dock at the Vandenberg bays, and that's why we've got Armley's section there to stop them. What do you do if you can't hold them, Mike?" Sirocco asked, looking down at the front row.

"Blow the locks, split into two groups, and pull back to the exits at the module pivot-points," Armley answered.

"Right. The other—yes, question?"

"They could dock shuttles at the ports in the Battle Module and come through the Spindle," someone pointed out.

"Yes, I was about to come to that," Sirocco replied. He lifted his head a fraction to address the whole room again. "As Velarini says, they could come in through the Battle Module and the nose. The Battle Module is the main problem. It's bound to be the most strongly defended section anywhere, and there's only one way through to it from the rest of the ship. Therefore we assault it directly only if all else fails. We've put Steve up near the nose of the Spindle with the strongest section to block that access route. Steve's task is to stop any SD's getting out and, more important, to stop Sterm and his people from getting in if things go well and they realize they can't hold the rest of the ship. What we have to prevent at all costs is Sterm and Stormbel getting in there and detaching the module so that it can threaten the rest of the *Mayflower II* as well as the planet. Yes, Simmonds?"

"It could still detach, even without Sterm."

"That's a gamble we'll have to take," Sirocco said. "Sterm will hardly order them to fire on the rest of the ship if he's in it."

"Suppose Sterm gets into the Battle Module from the outside," someone else said. "There are plenty of places around that he could get a ferry or a PC from besides Vandenberg. He's only got to hop across a couple of miles. It wouldn't need a surface shuttle."

Sirocco hesitated for a moment, then nodded reluctantly. "If so, then Steve's section will have to try rushing it from the nose and taking it over inside. But that's only as a last resort, as I said." He looked across at Colman, who returned a heavy nod.

"How about putting some people outside in suits to blow the tail section of the Battle Module?" Carson suggested from the second row back.

"We're looking into that. It will depend on how many people Steve can spare. Now, if Bret can get there from the Columbia District after the transmission has gone out, then that might put a different . . ." Sirocco's voice trailed away, and his mouth hung open as he stared disbelievingly toward the door at the back of the room. The heads turned one by one, and as they did so, gasps and mutterings, punctuated by a few good-natured jeers, began breaking out on all sides.

Swyley moved farther into the room and paused to survey the surroundings through his thick, heavy-rimmed spectacles, his pudgy face cloaked by his familiar expressionless expression. Driscoll was with him, and more were marching in behind them. Sirocco blinked and swallowed hard as they dispersed among the empty seats at the back and began sitting down. Harding, Baker, Faustzman, Vanderheim . . . Simpson, Westley, Johnson—all of them. They were all back. "We heard you could use some help, chief," Driscoll announced. "Couldn't leave it all to the amateurs." Ribald comments and hoots of derision greeted the remark.

Sirocco watched for a second longer, and then pulled himself together quickly. "Enjoy your vacation, Swyley?" he inquired with a note of forced sarcasm in his voice. "Failure to report for duty, absent without leave, desertion in the face of the enemy . . . the whole book, in fact. Well, consider yourselves reprimanded, and sit down. There's a lot to go over, and we're all going to need some rest today. The situation is that—" Sirocco stopped speaking and looked curiously at the figure that he hadn't noticed before —an unfamiliar face by the side of Swyley, who was still standing. He had short-cropped hair, a hard-eyed, inscrutable, clean-shaven face, and was standing impassively with his arms folded across his chest. "Who's this?" Sirocco said. "He's not from D Company."

"Ex-sergeant Malloy of the SDs," Swyley said. "He decided he'd had enough and quit over a month ago. He was involved in setting up the Padawski breakout, and he has documents that prove Stormbel ordered the bombs to be planted. He wants to go public." Swyley shrugged. "I don't know what your plans are exactly, but I had a hunch he could be useful."

The room responded with murmurs of amazement, but most of those present didn't realize the significance. Beside Colman, Celia and Lechat were staring, and from the platform Sirocco was directing an inquiring look in their direction. Celia turned her head to look at Colman. "I don't believe this," she whispered. "Who is that corporal?"

"D Company's resident miracle worker," Colman answered, but his voice was distant as he fitted the new pieces into the picture in his head. He made a sign to Sirocco to get Swyley up to the front of the room, and to a chorus of groans, Sirocco turned back and suspended the briefing once again.

Five minutes later Swyley and Malloy had gone into conference in a corner with Celia and Lechat, and Colman stood apart with Sirocco and Hanlon, discussing tactical details. "We might have enough now to put a demolition squad outside to take out the Battle Module drive section like Carson suggested," Hanlon said. "Even if Sterm gets in there it would give more protection to the rest of the ship."

"I'll have to keep that option open until we see how things shape up," Colman said. "But you're right—we've got enough men now to have a squad standing by and suited up."

"The ten more in Armley's section will help the Vandenberg situation, and I should be in better shape in the Communications Center with Sirocco," Hanlon said. "So where does that leave us?"

"All set, except for springing Borftein and Wellesley," Colman said. "Now that we've got Malloy, those two would make the whole thing cast-iron." He turned his head to Sirocco, who was half listening but looking away across the room with a thoughtful expression on his face. "Had any more thoughts about that?" Colman asked.

"Mmm? . . ." Sirocco responded distantly.

"Borftein and Wellesley."

"I've been thinking about that . . ." Sirocco continued to

gaze across the room at Driscoll, who was recounting his experiences to Maddock and a group of others. "He's pretty good, isn't he," Sirocco said, still half to himself.

It took a second for Colman to realize what Sirocco was talking about. "Yes . . . Why? What are you—"

"Come over for a second. I want to ask him something." Sirocco led Colman, and Hanlon followed. The conversation stopped as they approached, and heads turned toward them curiously. "Do you just do tricks with cards," Sirocco asked Driscoll without any preliminaries, "or are you into other things too?"

Driscoll looked at him in surprise. "Well, it depends on what you mean," he said cautiously. Then after a second he nodded. "But, yes—I can do other things too, a pretty diversified act, you might say."

Sirocco turned his head towards Hanlon. "Get a couple of pistol belts and sidearms from the Armory, Bret," he said. "Let's find out just how good this character really is. I think he might be able to help us solve our problem."

CHAPTER THIRTY-FIVE

GENERAL KAZIMIERA STORMBEL did not make mistakes, and he was not accustomed to being held responsible for the mistakes of others; people under him tended to find out early on that they did not make mistakes. Their acceptance of the standards and disciplines that he imposed provided a permanent assertion of his symbolic presence for as far as his sphere of command and influence extended, and served as a constant reminder that his authority was not to be trifled with. Displays of laxness represented an acknowledgment that was less than total, and signified lapses of mindfulness of the ominipresence that his authority projected—as if people were beginning to forget that what he said mattered. Stormbel didn't like that. He didn't like people acting as if he didn't matter.

The bureaucrats who had mismanaged the sprawling politicomilitary machine that had come to dominate the North American continent had been unable or unwilling to recognize his worth and dedication while they heaped honors and favors on sons of spineless sycophants and generals' blue-eyed protégés groomed to the movie image at West Point, and he felt no compassion for them now as the laser link from Earth brought news of nuclear devastation across the length and breadth of Africa, and of titanic clashes between armies in Central Asia. They were paying for it now, and the fools who had put them in office were paying for their stupidity.

Wellesley and the Congress had tried to perpetuate the same injustices by eclipsing him with Borftein because he hadn't graduated from the right places or possessed the right family credentials. They had tried to fob him off with the command of what they had seen as a proficient but small and unimportant corps of specialists. They had all paid too. Now they all knew who he was and where they stood. He had no regrets about Ramisson's death; it underlined the lesson more forcefully than any words could have done. He was only sorry he hadn't made a cleaner sweep by shooting them all.

Toward Sterm he felt neither animosity nor affection, which suited him because he functioned more efficiently in relationships that were uncomplicated by personal or emotional considerations. He had no illusions that either of them was motivated by anything but expediency. Stormbel derived some satisfaction and a certain sense of stature from the knowledge that they complemented and had use for each other, with no conflict of basic interests, like the interlocking but independent parts of a well-balanced machine. Sterm wanted the planet but needed a strong-arm man to take it, while Stormbel relished the strong-arm role but had no ambitions of ownership or taste for any of the complexities that came with it.

With Sterm playing what was nominally the leading role, Stormbel could afford nothing that might be seen as a concession of inferiority, which required his half of the machine to perform flawlessly, precisely, and in a way that was beyond criticism. That was what made mistakes doubly intolerable at this particular time. But what made the whole thing completely baffling and all the more galling was that the escorts and their charge had not only checked in on time, but had actually boarded the return shuttle—having passed safely through all the riskier parts of the agenda—before vanishing without a trace. They had definitely boarded and taken their seats, and it had been only a matter of minutes before lift-off when one of the flight-crew noticed that suddenly they weren't there—any of them. The SD guards at the boarding gate had all known what Celia Kalens looked liked, and they had been under special instructions to watch for her, but none of them had seen her when the escorts came out of the shuttle after somehow losing her; and shortly after that, the escorts had disappeared into the base and were never seen again. Nobody remembered seeing them around the base later; nobody had seen them at the perimeter; nobody had flown them out; and an intensive search carried on all through the night had failed to locate them anywhere. It was impossible, but it had happened.

Sterm was not a person to waste his time and energy with futile melodramatics and accusations, but Stormbel knew full well that he wouldn't forget—and neither would Stormbel forget. The Chironians were behind it, he was certain, just as they had been behind the subversion of the Army and even of some of Stormbel's own troopers. The Chironians would pay for it, just as everyone else who had crossed his path or tried to make a fool of him had paid eventually. They would pay the moment someone offered resistance when his troops moved into Franklin. His orders were quite explicit.

"The build-up at Canaveral is proceeding on schedule and will be completed before midnight," he informed Sterm at a midday staff meeting in the Columbia District's Government Center. "The greater part of Phoenix is being abandoned as we assumed would be unavoidable, but the key points are secure and the wastage among the regular units has been checked. Transfer of SD forces to the surface will be completed by early evening, with the exception of those units being held to cover the Battle Module, the Columbia District, and Vandenberg. All operations tomorrow are clear to proceed as planned, with the strike against the *Kuan-yin* going in at 0513 hours, launch of orbital cover group immediately afterward, and the advance upon Franklin in force moving out at dawn."

Sterm nodded slowly as he ticked off the points one by one in his mind, looking at Stormbel coolly, then turned to Gaulitz, one of the senior scientists, who was sitting with some advisers to one side of the room. "Let us be certain about the *Kuan-yin*," he said. "The success of the entire operation is at stake. You are quite sure?"

Gaulitz nodded emphatically. "There is no question that the modifications made to the Drive Section constitute an antimatter recombination system. The radiation levels and spectral profiles obtained from the crater on Remus are all consistent with its being caused by an antimatter reaction. The evidence of gamma-induced transmutations, the distribution of neutron-activated isotopes, the pattern of residual—"

Sterm held up a hand. "Yes, yes, we have been through all that."

Gaulitz nodded hastily and touched a control to bring a view of the *Kuan-yin* onto the room's main display screen. It showed Chironian shuttles at all the docking ports, and more standing a few miles off and apparently waiting to move in. "This is a further corroboration from views obtained this morning," he said. "All indications are that the Chironians have evacuated the vessel, which supports the contention of its being cleared for action."

Sterm studied the view in silence. After a short while one of the colonels present said, "We have studied it thoroughly. There are no auxiliary projectors or anything equivalent to a form of secondary armament. The only direction that it can fire in is sternward from the tail-dish. With eight missiles the odds of at least one getting through would be better than ninety-eight percent. With sixteen the chances of failure are about as near zero as you can get."

The *Kuan-yin*'s lower orbit put it out of synchronism with the *Mayflower II* and resulted in the two vessels being shielded from each other by Chiron's mass for a period of thirty-two minutes every three-and-a-quarter hours. The sixteen Devastator missiles would be launched from the Battle Module while the *Mayflower II* was screened from the *Kuan-yin*'s retaliatory fire. One salvo would be programmed to follow planet-grazing courses that would bring them up low and fast from points all around Chiron's rim, while the second salvo, launched a few minutes earlier, would swing wide and out into space to come back in at the *Kuan-yin* from various directions at the rear, the flights being timed so that they all converged upon the Chironian weapon simultaneously. A mass the size of the *Kuan-yin* could not maneuver rapidly, and the worst-case simulations run on the computers had shown an overwhelming margin in favor of the attack, whatever defensive tactics might be employed.

"The calculations and simulations have been verified?" Sterm said, looking at Gaulitz.

"Thoroughly and repeatedly. There is no risk that the *Mayflower II* might be exposed at any time," Gaulitz answered.

There were no more major points to discuss. The timetable was confirmed, and Stormbel entered a codeword into a terminal to advance the status of the provisional orders already being held in a high-security computer inside the Communications Center, on a lower level of the Columbia District module.

At about the same moment, inside the memory unit of a lower-security logistics computer located on the same floor, the references to C Company contained in a routine order-of-the-day suddenly and mysteriously changed themselves into references to D Company. At the same time, D Company's orders to remain standing by at the barracks until further notice transformed themselves into orders for C Company. Ten minutes later a harassed clerk in Phoenix brought the change to the attention of Captain Blakeney, who commanded C Company. Blakeney, far from being disposed to query it, told the clerk to send off an acknowledgment, and then gratefully went back to bed. Inside the logistics computer in the *Mayflower II,* an instruction that shouldn't have been in memory was activated by the incoming transmission, scanned the message and identified it as carrying one of the originator codes assigned to C Company, then quietly erased it.

CHAPTER THIRTY-SIX

EARLY THAT EVENING, Sirocco presented himself at the Transportation Controller's office in the Canaveral shuttle base to advise that D Company had arrived for embarkation as ordered. Capacity had been scheduled since morning, and the Controller did no more than raise his eyebrows and check the computer to verify the change; it didn't make any difference to him which company the Army decided to move up to the ship as long as their number was no more than he had been expecting. An hour later the company marched off the shuttle in smart order, and after clearing the docking-bay area in Vandenberg, dispersed inconspicuously to their various destinations around the *Mayflower II*. Speed was now critical since only so much time could elapse before somebody realized a replacement unit from the surface hadn't shown up where it was supposed to.

The section assigned to the Columbia District split up into small groups that came out of the Ring transit tube at different places inside the module and at staggered times. Colman, Hanlon, and Driscoll got off with Lechat, who was dressed to obscure his appearance since he was presumably still high on Sterm's wanted list. They rendezvoused with Carson and three others a few minutes later, then they headed via a roundabout route for the Françoise restaurant, which was situated on a public level immediately below the Government Center complex.

All entrances into the Center itself were guarded. Sirocco had proposed dressing a squad in SD uniforms and marching Lechat and Celia openly up to the main door and brazening out an act of bringing in two legitimate

fugitives after apprehending them. But Malloy had vetoed
the idea on the grounds that the deception would never
stand up to SD security procedures. Then Lechat had
suggested a less dramatic and less risky method. As a
regular customer of the Françoise for many years, he was
a close friend of the manager and had spent many late
nights discussing politics with the staff until way after
closing. They all knew Lechat, and he was sure he could
rely on them. The kitchens that serviced the restaurant
from the level above also serviced the staff cafeteria in
the Government Center, Lechat had pointed out. There
had to be service elevators, laundry chutes, garbage ducts—
something that connected through from the rear of the
Françoise.

The party arrived at the little-used connecting passage
running behind the Françoise and its neighboring estab-
lishments, and the soldiers waited among the shadows of
the surrounding entrances and stairways while Lechat
tapped lightly on the rear door of the restaurant. After a
few seconds the door opened and Lechat disappeared inside. Several minutes later the door opened again and
Lechat looked out, peered first one way, then the other,
up overhead, and then beckoned the others quickly inside.

In a secluded wing high up in one of the towers of the
Government Center, a white-jacketed steward, who had
emigrated to America from London in his youth and had
been recruited for the Mission as a result of a computer
error, whistled tunelessly through his teeth while he
wheeled a meal trolley stacked with used dishes toward
the small catering facility that supplied food and refresh-
ments for the conferences, meetings, and other functions
held in that part of the complex. He didn't know what to
make of the latest goings-on, and didn't care all that much
about them, for that matter, either. It was all the same to
him. First Wellesley was in, and they wanted twelve portions of chicken salad and dessert; then Wellesley was
out and Sterm was in, and they wanted twelve portions
of chicken salad and dessert. It didn't make any difference
to him who—

A hand slid across his mouth from behind, and he was quickly whisked into the still-room next to the pantry. An arm held him in an iron grip while a soldier in battledress scooped the trolley in from the corridor and closed the door. There were more of them in there, with a civilian. They looked mean and in no mood for fooling around.

The hand over his mouth loosened a fraction after the door was closed. "Gawd! Wot's goin' on? Who—?" Somebody jabbed him in the ribs. He shut up.

"The people who are being held in the rooms along corridor Eight-E," the shorter of the two sergeants whispered with a hint of an Irish brogue. "You take their food in?" The steward gulped and nodded vigorously. "When is the evening meal due?"

"Abaht ten minutes," the steward said. "I'm supposed ter collect it next door any time nah." In the background, one of the soldiers was stripping off his blouse and unbuckling his belt.

"Start taking off the jacket and the vest," the Irish sergeant ordered. "And while you're doing it, you can tell us the routine."

Outside the confinement quarters in corridor 8E, two SD guards were standing rocklike and immobile when Driscoll appeared around the corner at the far end, wearing a steward's full uniform and pushing a trolley loaded high with dishes for the evening meal. Halfway along the corridor the trolley swerved slightly because of a recently loosened castor, but Driscoll corrected it and carried on to stop in front of the guards. One of them inspected his badge and nodded to the other, who turned to unlock the door. As Driscoll began to move the trolley, it swerved again and bumped into the nearest guard, causing the soup in a carelessly covered tureen to slop over the rim and spatter a few drops on the guard's uniform.

"Oh, Christ!" Driscoll began fussing with a napkin to clean it off, in the process managing to trail a corner of it through the soup and brush it against the hem of the second guard's jacket as he turned back from the door. Driscoll moaned miserably and started dabbing it off, but was shoved away roughly. "Get off, you clumsy asshole," the guard growled. Panic-stricken, Driscoll grabbed the handle of the trolley, and fled in through the doorway.

Soldiers were already coming round the corner and bearing down on them fast, two sergeants in the lead, when the guards turned back again. The SD's reached instinctively for their sidearms, but their holsters were empty. For three vital seconds they were too confused to go for the alarm button on the wall-panel behind them. Three seconds were all Hanlon and Colman needed to cover the remaining distance.

Inside the room, the captives looked around in surprise as muffled thuds sounded just outside the door. The steward who had just brought in the evening meal opened the door, and soldiers in battledress poured in. Wellesley gasped as he saw Lechat with them. "Paul!" he exclaimed. "Where have you been hiding? You're the only one they didn't pick up. What—"

Lechat cut him off with a wave of his hand. "Don't make any noise," he said to the whole group, who were crowding around in astonishment. "Everything is okay." He signaled Borftein over with another wave of his hand. Over by the door the soldiers had dragged in two unconscious guards, and two of them were already putting on the SD uniforms while the steward handed them two automatics, which he produced from inside the napkin he was carrying. "There isn't a lot of time," Lechat advised Wellesley and Borftein. "We have to get you downstairs and into the Communications Center. Now listen, and I'll give you a quick rundown on the situation . . ."

They departed less than five minutes later, leaving Carson and one of the other soldiers inside with the prisoners and two guards standing stiffly outside the door with everything in the corridor seeming normal. Hanlon took Wellesley, Borftein, and Lechat to a storeroom near the Communications Center where they could remain out of sight. Colman followed Driscoll to a machinery compartment on the lowermost level where an emergency bulkhead door, unguarded but sealed from the outside and protected by alarm circuits, led through to the motor room of an elevator bank in the civic offices adjoining the Government Center. Colman traced, checked, and neutralized the alarms. Then he double-checked what he had done, and nodded to Driscoll, who was waiting by the door; Driscoll opened the latches and swung the door outward while Colman held his breath. The alarms remained inactive. Sirocco was waiting on the other side with Bernard Fallows, who was wearing engineer's coveralls and carrying a toolbox.

"Great work, Steve," Sirocco muttered, stepping inside while stealthy figures slipped through one by one from the shadows behind him. "How did the Amazing Driscoll go over?"

"His best performance ever. Everything okay out there?"

"It seems to be. How about Borftein and Wellesley?" Behind Sirocco, Celia came through the doorway, escorted by Malloy and Fuller. Stanislau was behind, carrying a field compack.

Colman nodded. "Gone to the storeroom with Hanlon and Lechat. Everything was quiet upstairs when we left."

Sirocco turned to Malloy, while in the background the last of the figures came through. "Okay, you know where to go. Hanlon should be there now with the others." Malloy nodded. "We'll make a soldier out of you yet," Sirocco said to Celia. "You're doing fine. Almost there now." Celia returned a thin smile but said nothing. She moved away with the others toward the far side of the compartment. Meanwhile Stanislau had set up the compack and was already calling up codes onto the screen. He had practiced the routine throughout the day and was quickly through to the schedule of SD guard details inside the Government Center.

The next part was going to be the trickiest. The information obtained by Stanislau had confirmed that the outside entrances to the complex, which had already been bypassed, were the most strongly guarded, and the three inner access points to the Communications Center itself—the main foyer at the front, the rear lobby, and a side entrance used by the staff—were covered by less formidable, three-man security teams. The problem with these security teams lay not so much with the physical resistance they might offer, but with their ability to close the Communications Center's electrically operated, armored doors and raise the alarm at the first sign of anything suspicious, which would leave Sirocco's force shut outside with no hope of achieving their objective and facing the bleak prospect of either fighting it out or surrendering to the guard reinforcements that would show up within minutes. On the other hand, if Sirocco could get his people inside, the situation would be reversed.

Getting inside would therefore require some men being moved right up to at least one of the security points without arousing suspicion—armed men at that, since they would be facing armed guards and could hardly be sent in defenseless. Malloy had again discouraged ideas of attempting to impersonate SD's. The only alternative came from Armley—a bluff, backed up with information manufactured by Stanislau, to the effect that regular troops were being posted to guard duties inside the complex as well as SD's, and providing reliefs from D Company. Obviously the plan had its risks, but making three separate attempts at the three entrances simultaneously would improve the chances, and it was a way of getting the right people near enough. In the end, Sirocco agreed. Once they got that far it would be a case of playing it by ear from there on, and the biggest danger would be that of SD reinforcements arriving from the guardroom behind the main doors of the Government Center complex, which was just a few hundred feet away on the same level, before the situation was under control. That was the part that Bernard Fallows had come along to handle.

Stanislau stood back from the compack and announced that the changes were completed. Sirocco peered at the screen, checked the entries in the revised schedule that Stanislau had produced, and nodded. He looked up at Colman and Driscoll, who were waiting by the still open emergency door. "Okay, the last ball's rolling," he told them. "On your way. Good luck."

"You too," Colman said. He and Driscoll left for the forward section of the Spindle to join Swyley, who, if all was going well, would already be organizing the men drifting in from various parts of the ship to block off the Battle Module.

Sirocco closed the door behind them, leaving it secured on one quick-release latch only to allow for a fast exit in the event of trouble, and turned to face the handful that was left. "Let's go," he said.

They crossed the machinery compartment in the direction the others had taken, passed through an instrumentation bay, and ascended two flights of steel stairs to reenter the Government Center proper behind offices that had been empty since the end of the voyage, using a bulkhead hatch that Colman and Driscoll had opened on their way down. There was no sign of the others who had gone ahead. Here the group split three ways.

Stanislau and two others, moving carefully and making use of cover since they were now in a part of the complex that was being used, headed for the storeroom near the front foyer of the Communications Center to join Hanlon's group, which by now should have been swollen by the arrival of Celia, Malloy, and Fuller; Sirocco took three more to where another group was assembling near the approaches to the rear lobby; and Bernard with his toolbox strolled away casually on his own toward the corridor that connected the Communications Center to the main entrance of the complex.

Fifteen minutes later, inside an office that opened onto a passageway to the rear lobby of the Communications Center, an indignant office manager and two terrified female clerks were sitting on the floor with their hands clasped on the top of their heads, under the watchful eye of one of the soldiers who had burst in suddenly brandishing rifles and assault cannon. "What do you think you're trying to do?" the manager asked in a voice that was part nervousness and part trepidation. "We don't want to get mixed up in any of this."

"Just shut up and keep still, and you won't," Sirocco murmured without moving his eye from the edge of the almost-closed door. "We're just passing through." After a short silence Sirocco tensed suddenly. "Here they come . . . just two of them with a sergeant," he whispered. "Get ready. There are two guys talking by the coffee dispenser. We'll have to grab them too. Faustzman, you take care of them." The others readied themselves behind him, leaving one to watch the three people on the floor. Outside in the passageway, the SD detail on its way to relieve the security guards at the rear lobby was almost abreast of the door.

"*Freeze!*" Sirocco stepped out in front of them with his automatic drawn and Stewart beside him holding a leveled assault cannon. Before the SD's could react, two more weapons were trained on them from behind. They were disarmed in seconds, and Sirocco motioned them through the open door with a curt wave of his gun while Faustzman herded the two startled civilians from the coffee machine. Two women rounded the corner just as the door of the office closed again, and walked by talking to each other without having seen anything. Moments later Sirocco left the office again with two privates. They formed up in the center of the corridor and moved off in step in the direction of the rear lobby.

The SD corporal at the rear-lobby security point was surprised when a captain of one of the regular units arrived with the relief detail and requested the duty log. "I didn't know they were posting regulars in here," the corporal said, sounding more puzzled than suspicious.

Sirocco shrugged. "Don't ask me. I thought it was because a lot of SD's are shipping down to Canaveral. I just do what the orders say."

"When was it changed, Captain?"

"I don't know, Corporal. Recently, I guess."

"I better check those orders." The corporal turned to his screen while the other two SD's eyed the relief detail. After a few seconds the corporal raised his eyebrows. "You're right. Oh, well, I guess it's okay." The other two SD's relaxed a fraction. The corporal called up the duty log and signed his team off. "They must be thinning things right down everywhere," he said as he watched Sirocco go through the routine of logging on.

"Looks like it," Sirocco agreed. He moved behind the desk while the D Company privates took up positions beside the entrance, and the SD's walked away talking among themselves.

A few seconds after the SD's disappeared, figures began popping from a fire exit behind the elevators on the far side of the lobby, and vanishing quickly and silently into the Communications Center.

Meanwhile, the SD sergeant at the main foyer was being conscientious. "I don't care what the computers say, Hanlon. This doesn't sound right to me. I have to check it out." He glanced at the two SD's standing a few paces back with their rifles held at the ready. "Keep an eye on 'em while I call the OOD." Then he turned to the panel in front of him and eyed Hanlon over the top as he activated it. "Hold it right where you are, buddy." Hanlon tensed but there was nothing he could do. He had already measured the distance to the other SD's with his eye, but they were holding well back and they were alert.

Suddenly, from the outer entrance to the foyer behind Hanlon, a firm, authoritative voice ordered, "Stop that!" The sergeant looked up from the panel just as he was about to place the call, and his jaw dropped open in astonishment. Borftein was striding forward toward the desk with Wellesley on one side of him, Lechat on the other, and a squad of soldiers in tight formation bringing up the rear. Celia and Malloy were between them. The two SD guards glanced uncertainly at each other.

The SD sergeant half rose from his seat. "Sir, I didn't— I thought—"

Borftein halted and stood upright and erect before the desk. "Whatever you thought was mistaken. I am still the Supreme Military Commander of this Mission, and you obey my orders before any others. Stand aside."

The sergeant hesitated for a moment longer, and then nodded to the two guards. Borftein and his party marched through, and Hanlon began posting men to secure the entrance. Another section of D Company materialized from a stairwell to one side of the foyer and vanished into the Communications Center, taking with them a few bewildered secretaries and office workers that they had bumped into on the way.

But no Borftein was present to save the situation at the side entrance. "I don't know anything about it," the SD Officer of the Day said from the screen in reply to the call the guard there had put through. "Those orders are incorrect. Detain those men." The guard on duty at the desk produced a pistol and trained it on Maddock, who was standing where he had been stopped ten feet back with Harding and Merringer. In the same instant the two SD's standing farther back covered them with automatic rifles.

"*Down!*" Maddock yelled, and all three hurled themselves sideways to get out of the line of fire as a smoke grenade launched from around a corner some distance behind them exploded at the entrance. Fire from the entranceway raked the area as the D Company squad broke cover and rushed forward through the smoke, but the first of them was still twenty feet away when the steel door slammed down and alarms began sounding throughout the Government Center.

Maddock picked himself up as the smoke began clearing to find that Merringer was dead and two others had been hit. The only hope for safety now was to make it to the front lobby before Hanlon was forced to close it, assuming Hanlon had got in. "Go first with four men," he shouted at Harding. "Fire at any SD's who get in the way. They know we're here now." He turned to the others. "Grab those two and stick with me. You two, stay with Crosby and cover the rear. Okay, let's get the hell out."

But SD's were already pouring out of the guardroom behind the main doors of the Government Center and racing along the corridor toward the communications facility while civilians flattened themselves against the walls to get out of the way, and others who had been working late peered from their offices to see what was happening. The engineer in coveralls who had been working inconspicuously at an opened switchbox through an access panel in the floor closed a circuit, and a reinforced fire-door half-way along the corridor closed itself in the path of the oncoming SD's. The SD major leading the detachment stared numbly at it for a few seconds while his men came to a confused halt around him. "Back to the front stairs," he shouted. "Go up to Level Three, and come down on the other side."

On the other side of the fire-door, Bernard dropped his tools and ran back to the front lobby of the Communications Center, praying that the alarm hadn't been raised from there. Hanlon and Stanislau were waiting outside the entrance with a handful of the others. Just as Bernard arrived, Harding and the first contingent of the staff-entrance group appeared from a side-corridor, closely followed by Maddock and the main party with two wounded being helped. Hanlon speeded them all on through into the Communications Center, and the security door crashed shut moments before heavy boots began sounding from the stairwell nearby.

Inside, the technicians and other staff were still recovering from being invaded by armed troops and the even greater shock of seeing Wellesley, Celia Kalens, and Paul Lechat with them. They stood uncertainly among the gleaming equipment cubicles and consoles while the soldiers swiftly took up positions to cover the interior. Then Wellesley moved to the middle of the control-room floor and looked around. "Who is in charge here?" he demanded. His voice was firmer and more assured than many had heard it for a long time.

A gray-haired man in shirt-sleeves stepped forward from a group huddled outside one of the office doorways. "I am," he said, "McPherson—Communications and Datacenter Manager." After a short pause he added, "At your disposal."

Wellesley acknowledged with a nod and gestured toward Lechat. "Speed is essential," Lechat said without preamble. "We require access to all channels on the civil, public service, military, and emergency networks immediately . . ."

* * *

The Battle Module was a mile-long concentration of megadeath and mass destruction that sat on a base formed by the blunt nose of the Spindle, straddled by two pillars that extended forward to support the ramscoop cone and its field generators, and which contained the ducts to carry back to the midships processing reactors the hydrogen force-fed out of space when the ship was at ramspeed. Sleek, stark, menacing, and bristling with missile pods, defensive radiation projectors, and ports for deploying orbital and remote-operating weapons systems, it contained all of the *Mayflower II*'s strategic armaments, and could detach if need be to function as an independent, fully self-contained warship.

The Battle Module was not intended to be part of the *Mayflower II*'s public domain, and restriction of access to it had been one of its primary design criteria. Personnel and supplies entered the module via four enormous tubular extensions, known as feeder ramps, that telescoped from the main body of the ship to terminate in cupolas mating with external ports in the Battle Module, two forward and two aft its midships section. One pair of feeder ramps extended backward and inward from spherical housings at the forward ends of the two ramscoop-support pillars, and the other pair extended forward and inward from the six-sided, forwardmost section of the Spindle, called, appropriately enough, the Hexagon. As if having to get through the feeder ramps wasn't problem enough, the transit tubes, freight handling conveyors, ammunition rails, and other lines running through to them from the Spindle all came together at a single, heavily protected lock to pass through an armored bulkhead inside the Hexagon. Aft of the bulkhead, the lock faced out over a three-hundred-foot-long, wedge-shaped support platform upon which the various lines and tubes converged through a vast antechamber amid a jungle of girder and structural supports, motor housings, hoisting machinery, ducts, pipes, conduits, maintenance ladders, and catwalks. There was no other way through or round the bulkhead. The only route forward from the Hexagon was through the lock.

It's impregnable, Colman thought to himself as he lay

prone behind a girder-mounting high up in the shadows at the back of the antechamber and studied the approaches to the lock. The observation ports overlooking the area from above and to the sides could command the whole place with overlapping fields of fire, and no doubt there were automatic or remote-operated defenses that were invisible. True, there was plenty of cover for the first stages of an assault, but the final rush would be suicidal . . . and probably futile since the lock doors looked strong enough to stop anything short of a tactical missile. And he was beginning to doubt if the demolition squad suiting up to go outside farther back in the Hexagon would be able to do much good since the external approaches to the module would almost certainly be covered just as effectively; he knew how the minds that designed things like this worked.

"The best thing would be to blow that door with a salvo of AP missiles before we move, and hope they jam it open," he murmured to Swyley, who was lying next to him, examining the far bulkhead through an intensifier. "Then maybe drench the lock with incendiary and go in under smoke."

"That's only the first door," Swyley reminded him, lowering the instrument from his eyes. "There are two of them. Whatever we do to that one won't stop them from closing the second one."

"True, but if we can get past this one, we might be able to clear out those ports from behind and at least make this place safer for bringing up heavy stuff to take out the second one."

"And then what?" Swyley said. "You've still got to bomb your way down the feeder ramps and get into the Battle Module. Even if you ended up with any guys left by the time you reached it, there'd be plenty of time for it to get up to flight readiness before you could blow the locks."

"Got any better ideas?" For once Swyley didn't.

At that moment the emergency tone sounded simultaneously from both their communicators, and warning bleeps and wails went up from places in the labyrinth all around. They looked at each other for a second. The noise died away as Colman fished his unit from his breast pocket and held it in front where both of them could watch it, while Swyley deactivated his own. A few seconds later, the faces of Wellesley, Borftein, and Lechat appeared on the tiny screen. Colman closed his eyes for a moment and breathed a long, drawn-out sigh of relief. "They made it," he whispered. "They're all in there."

"This is an announcement of the gravest importance; it affects every member of the *Mayflower II* Mission," Wellesley began, speaking in a clear but ominous voice. "I am addressing you all in my full capacity as Director of this Mission. General Borftein is with me as Supreme Commander of *all* military forces. Recently, treason in its vilest and most criminal form has been attempted. That attempt has failed. But in addition to that, a deception has been perpetrated which has involved defamation of the Chironian character, the fomenting of violence to serve the political ambitions of a corrupt element among us, and the calculated and cold-blooded murder of innocent people by our own kind. I do not have to remind you . . ."

"That has to give us the rest of the ship and the surface," Swyley said. "If the Army gets its act together and grabs Sterm before he gets a chance to head this way, then we might not have to go in there at all."

Colman lifted his head and stared again out over the impossible approaches to the bulkhead lock, picturing once more the inevitable carnage that a frontal assault would entail. Who on either side would stand to gain anything that mattered to them? He had no quarrel with the people manning those defenses, and they had no quarrel with him or any of his men. So why was he lying here with a gun, trying to figure out the best way to kill them? Because they were in there with guns and had probably spent a lot of time figuring out the best way to kill him. None of them knew why they were doing it. It was simply that it had always been done.

On the screen of the communicator, the view closed in on Celia as she began speaking in a slightly quavery but determined voice. But Colman only half heard. He was trying to make himself think the way a Chironian would think.

CHAPTER THIRTY-SEVEN

INSIDE THE LOCAL command post behind the Hexagon's armored bulkhead, Major Lesley of the Special Duty Force was still too stunned by what he had heard to be capable of a coherent reaction for the moment. He stared at the companel where a screen showed a view from the Columbia District, where the SD guard commander had entered the Communications Center under a truce flag some minutes previously to talk with Borftein, and tried to separate the conflicting emotions in his head. Captain Jarvis, Lesley's adjutant officer, and Lieutenant Chaurez watched in silence while around the command post the duty staff averted their eyes and occupied themselves with their own thoughts. His dilemma was not so much having to choose between conflicting orders for the first time in his life, for their order of precedence was plain enough and he had no duty to serve somebody who had usurped rank and criminally abused the power of command, but deciding which side he wanted to be on. Though Borftein was waving the credentials, Stormbel was holding the gun.

Jarvis scanned the screen on the far side of the post. "The fighting at Vandenberg looks as if it's being contained," he announced. "Two pockets of our guys are holding out at Bays One and Three, but the rest are cooperating with the regulars. The regulars have pretty well secured the whole module already. Stormbel won't be getting any help from the surface through there."

"What's the latest from the surface?" Chaurez inquired.

"Confused but quiet at the barracks," Jarvis told him. "A lot of shooting inside the base at Canaveral. Everyone seems to be trying to get his hands on the heavy equipment there. A shuttle's on fire in one of the launch bays."

Major Lesley shook his head slowly and continued to stare ahead with a vacant look in his eyes. "This shouldn't be happening," he murmured. "They're not the enemy. They shouldn't be fighting each other."

Jarvis and Chaurez glanced at each other. Then Jarvis looked away as a new report came up on one of the screens. "Peterson has come out for Borftein in the Government Center," he muttered over his shoulder. "I guess it's all over in the Columbia District. That has to give them the whole Ring."

"So they'll be coming for the Spindle next," Chaurez said. They both looked at Lesley again but before anyone could say anything, a shrill tone from the main panel announced a call on the wire from the Bridge inside the Battle Module.

Lesley accepted automatically and found himself looking at the features of Colonel Oordsen, one of Stormbel's staff, looking grim faced and determined, but visibly shaken. "Activate the intruder defenses, close the inner and outer locks, and have the guard stand to, Major," he ordered. "Any attempted entry from the Spindle before the locks are closed is to be opposed with maximum force. Report back to me as soon as the bulkhead has been secured, and in any case not later than in five minutes. Is that understood?"

At that moment a local alarm sounded inside the command post. Within seconds the sounds of men running to stations came from the passageways and stairs to the rear. One of the duty crew was already flipping switches to collect report summaries, and Chaurez got up to go to the outer observation room just as the Watch Officer appeared in the doorway from the other side. "There are troops approaching the lock," the Watch Officer announced. "Regulars—thirty or more of them."

Leaving Colonel Oordsen peering out of the screen, Lesley rose and walked through the door in the steel wall dividing the command post from the observation room and looked down through one of the ports at the approaches to the lock below. Chaurez watched from the doorway, ignoring Oordsen's indignant voice as it floated through from behind. "Major Lesley, you have not been dismissed. Come back at once. What in hell's going on there? What are those alarms? Lesley, do you hear me?"

But Lesley was not listening as he gazed down at the platform below, which fanned outward from the arc lights above the lock to become indistinct in the darkness of the antechamber. Figures were moving slowly from the shadows by the transit tubes and freight rails, spread thinly at the back, but closing up as they converged with the lines of the platform. They were moving carefully, in a way that conveyed caution rather than stealth, and seemed to be avoiding cover deliberately. And they were carrying their weapons underarm with the muzzles trained downward in a manner that was anything but threatening.

"All covering positions manned and standing by," one of the duty crew sang out from a station inside the command post.

"LCP's standing by and ready to fire," another voice reported.

"Intruder defenses primed and ready to activate."

"Lock at condition orange and ready to close."

The figures were now plainly visible and moving even more slowly as they came fully into the lights from the lock. They were regular infantry, Lesley could see. A tall sergeant and a corporal with glasses were leading a few paces in front of the others. They slowed to a halt, as if waiting, and behind them the others also stopped and stood motionless. Lesley's jaw tightened as he stared down through the observation port. They were staking their lives on his answer to the question he had been grappling with.

Jarvis appeared suddenly in the doorway beside Chaurez. "Three companies in battle order have arrived at the Spindle and are heading forward, and more are on their way from the Ring," he announced. "Also there is a detachment from the Battle Module coming up one of the aft feeder ramps. They must be coming back to close the lock."

Lesley looked at the two of them, but they said nothing. There was nothing more they could tell him. He could close the lock and commit himself to the protection of the Battle

Module's armaments; alternatively, with the added strength of the regulars who had arrived below, he could hold the lock open against the SD's coming from the Battle Module until the rest of the Army arrived. It was time for him to decide his answer.

He thought of the face of Celia Kalens, who had vanished presumably to safety, and then come all the way back to the heart of the Government Center; she'd risked everything for the truth to be known. Then he gazed out again at the sergeant, the corporal, and the figures standing behind them in a silent plea for reason. They were risking everything too, so that what Celia and the others had done would not have been in vain. Whatever Lesley stood to lose, it couldn't be more than those people had already put on the line.

"Tell the men to stand down," he said quietly to Jarvis. "Deprime the intruder systems and revert the lock to condition green. Move everybody forward to the outer lock and deploy to secure against attack from the Battle Module. Chaurez, get those men down there inside. We're going to need all the help we can get." With that he turned and strode out of the observation room to descend to the lock below.

Jarvis and Chaurez caught each other's eye. After a moment, Jarvis breathed a sigh of relief. Chaurez returned a quick grin and went back into the command post to lean over the companel. "Lieutenant," Oordsen demanded angrily from the screen. "Where is Major Lesley? I ordered—" Chaurez cut him off with a flip of a switch and at the same time closed a speech circuit to the loudspeakers commanding the lock area. "Okay, you guys, we're standing down," he said into the microphone stem projecting from the panel. "Get in here as quick as you can. We've got trouble coming up a feeder ramp on the other side."

As Chaurez finished speaking, an indicator announced an incoming call from the Government Center. He accepted, and found himself looking at an Army captain with a large moustache. "Forward Security Command Post," Chaurez acknowledged.

"Sirocco, D Company commander, Second Infantry Brigade. Is your commanding officer there?"

"I'm sorry, sir. He just went down to the lock."

"What about his adjutant?" Sirocco asked.

"Gone forward to the outer lock."

Sirocco looked worried. "Look, there is a force on its way forward to occupy the nose. We want to avoid any senseless bloodshed. Those locks must be kept open. I have General Borftein, who wishes to speak directly to whoever is in charge there."

"I can speak for them," Chaurez said. "You can tell the general that the news is good."

Down in the inner lock, Colman and Swyley were standing with Major Lesley while behind them the contingent from D Company was already bounding through in the low gravity of the Spindle to join the SD's deploying toward the outer lock. "You took a hell of a chance, Sergeant," Lesley said.

"Fifty-fifty," Colman answered. "It would have been zero the other way."

"You think pretty smart."

"We're all having to learn how to do that."

Lesley held his eye for a second, then nodded. "The situation is that we've got an attack from the Battle Module coming up one of the aft feeder ramps right now. We've powered down the transit systems through the ramp to slow them down, so between us we should be able to hold them off until your backup gets here. How long should they take?" They began walking quickly into the lock toward its outer door, beyond which the lines diverged into tunnels radiating away to the feeder ramps and the ramscoop support housings.

"How far have they penetrated?" Colman asked.

"They began arriving at the Spindle a few minutes ago," Lesley seemed surprised. "How come you didn't know?"

"It's been kind of . . . an unorthodox operation."

Ahead of them, Jarvis had positioned soldiers to cover all of the tunnel mouths, with the strongest force concentrated around the outlet from the feeder ramp along which the SD's from the Battle Module were approaching, and he had retired to a sheltered observation platform from which he could direct operations with a clear view into the tunnel. Lesley, Colman, and Swyley moved behind a stanchion where Driscoll and a couple more from D Company were crouched with their weapons. A few seconds later the soldiers all around tensed expectantly.

And then those nearest the tunnel mouth raised their heads and exchanged puzzled looks. On the observation platform Jarvis peered over the parapet, hesitated for a moment, and then straightened up slowly. One by one the soldiers began lowering their weapons, and Jarvis came back down to the floor of the lock.

An SD major with a smoke-blackened face and one of his sleeves covered in blood emerged unsteadily from the tunnel mouth; immediately behind him were four more SD's looking disheveled and one of them also blood-stained around the head. Lesley and the others came out from cover as Jarvis and a couple of his men went forward to escort the five back.

Lesley and the major obviously knew each other. "Brad," Lesley said. "What in hell's happened? We were expecting a fight."

"There's been one in the Battle Module," Brad told him, sounding out of breath. "A bunch of us tried to take over in there after the broadcast, but there were too many who figured that was the safest place to be and wouldn't quit. It was all we could do to get out."

"How many of you are there?" Lesley asked.

"I'm not sure . . . maybe fifty. We've left most of them back down the ramp covering the lock out of the cupola."

"You mean the way's clear right down to the Battle Module?" Colman asked.

Brad nodded. "But Stormbel's people are in the cupola. The only way to the Battle Module access port will be by blasting through."

Lesley turned to Jarvis. "Power the tubes back up and get some more guys down there fast. Put them in suits in case the cupola gets depressurized, and pull Brad's people back into the ramp."

"We've got a section already suited up," Colman said. "Are those cars running?" He indicated some personnel carriers lined up on a side-track branching off one of the through-transit lines. Jarvis nodded. Colman turned to Swyley. "Get the section loaded up and move them on down the ramp." Swyley and Jarvis hurried away.

"The Army's on its way through the Spindle," Lesley said to Brad. "They should start arriving here any time now."

"Let's hope they don't waste any time," Brad replied. "Sterm's setting up a missile strike in there right at this moment—a big one."

Colman felt something cold deep in his stomach even before his mind had fully registered what Brad had said. "Sterm?" he repeated numbly. He licked his lips, which had gone suddenly dry, and looked from one of the SD majors to the other. "You mean he's already in there?"

Lesley nodded. "He's been there all evening. Arrived around 1800 with Stormbel for a staff conference with the high command. They're all in there . . ." He frowned at the expression on Colman's face. "Nobody knew?"

Colman shook his head slowly. There had been too much to think about in too little time. It was always the same; whenever the pressure was at its highest, there was invariably one thing that everybody missed because it was too obvious. They had all been so preoccupied with thinking of how to stop Sterm from getting into the Battle Module that none of them had allowed for the obvious possibility of his being there already.

"What's the target for the missile strike?" Colman asked hoarsely.

"I don't know," Brad replied. "I haven't been in on it at the top level. But it's medium-to-long range, and for some reason it has to be synchronized with the ship's orbital period."

Colman groaned. The target could only be the *Kuan-yin*. If the strike succeeded it would leave Sterm in sole command of the only strategic weapons left on the planet, and in a position to dictate any terms he chose; if it failed, then Sterm and his last few would take the whole of the *May-*

flower II with them when the *Kuan-yin* rose above Chiron's rim to retaliate. Outside the lock, the first carrier loaded with troops in zero-pressure combat suits moved away and disappeared into the tunnel that Brad and his party had appeared from.

"You look as if you might know something about it," Lesley said to Colman. "Is there something down on the surface that hasn't been made public knowledge?"

"No . . ." Colman shook his head distantly. "It's too much to go into right now. Look—"

An SD sergeant interrupted from behind Lesley. "They're here sir. Carriers coming through the lock." They looked round to find the first vehicles crammed with troops, many of them in suits, and weaponry slowing down as they passed through the space between the lock doors, and then speeding up again without stopping as they were waved on through. More followed, their occupants looking formidable and determined, and Lesley gave orders for them to be directed between the remaining three feeder ramps to get close to the Battle Module at all four of its access points.

Then Colman's communicator started bleeping. Bernard Fallows was calling from the Communications Center. "I guess you did it," he said. "But it's not over yet. We've found out where Sterm is."

"So have I," Colman said. "And it's worse than that. He's setting up a missile strike right now. The target has to be the *Kuan-yin*."

Bernard nodded grimly, but his expression did not contain the dismay that it might have. Evidently he had been half-prepared for the news. "Borftein's been checking on that possibility," he said. "It'll be forty minutes before the *Kuan-yin* goes behind the rim. Sterm won't launch before then."

"Will the Chironians let him wait that long?" Colman asked. "Do they know he's in there and what it means?"

Bernard shook his head. "No. We're in touch with them, but Wellesley vetoed any mention of it." Colman nodded. He wouldn't have risked their deciding to fire first either. Bernard went on, "Wellesley's tried contacting

the Battle Module too, but Sterm won't talk. We figure
he'll keep the module attached until after the attack goes
in—in other words if he doesn't pull it off and gets blasted,
we all get blasted. The same thing applies if the Chironians
decide to press the button. We have to assume he's on a
forty-minute countdown. Hanlon and Armley are on their
way there, and Sirocco left a few minutes ago. Borftein
is sending through everybody he can scrape together. What
are the chances?"

A carrier full of combat-suited infantry nursing anti-
tank missile launchers and demolition equipment slid
through the lock and lurched onto a branch leading to
one of the Battle Module's forward ramps. "Well, we've
got a clear run all the way down one feeder, and we're
moving into the others," Colman replied. "There's been
some fighting inside the Battle Module, and a lot of the
guys got out. We have to hope that there aren't enough
left to stop us from blowing our way in through four places
at once. Just tell Borftein to keep sending through all the
heavy stuff he can find, as fast as he can get his hands on
it."

CHAPTER THIRTY-EIGHT

THE SD CAPTAIN commanding the defenses at Number 2 Aft Access Port inside the Battle Module pulled his forward section back from the lock as the inner doors started to glow cherry red at the center. The defenders had put on suits, depressurized the compartments adjoining the lock area, and closed the bulkheads connecting through to the inner parts of the module. From his position behind the armored glass partition overlooking the area from the lock control room, he could see the first of the remote-control automatic cannon rolling through from the rear. "Hurry up with those RCC's," he shouted into his helmet microphone. "Yellow section take up covering positions. Green and Red prepare to fall back to the longitudinal bulkhead locks."

"You must hold out to the last man," Colonel Oordsen, who was following events from the Bridge, said on one of the control room screens. "We're almost ready to detach the module."

"We will if we have to, sir," the captain assured him.

Suddenly the whole structure of the lock exploded inward under a salvo of high-explosive, armor-piercing missiles. Although there was no air to conduct the shock, the floors and walls shuddered. Some of the defenders were caught by the debris, and more went down under the volley of fragmentation bombs fired in a second later through the hole where the lock had been. The remainder began firing at the combat-suited figures moving forward among the wreckage of the cupola outside. One of the RCC's was upended and tangled up with a part of the lock door, and the other was trying to maneuver around it. "Red section, move to fallback positions," the captain yelled. "Covering—"

Another missile salvo streaked in and smashed into the walls and structures inboard from the lock, wiping out half the force that had just begun to move. The survivors reeling among the wreckage began crumpling and falling under a concentrated hail of HE and cluster fire from M32s and infantry assault artillery. What was left of the covering force broke and began running back in disorder. "Get everybody out! Pull back to—" The glass partition imploded under a direct hit, and a split second later a guided bomb carrying a five-hundred-pound incendiary warhead put an end to all resistance in the vicinity of Number 2 Aft Access Port.

On the Bridge of the Battle Module, Colonel Oordsen turned his head from the screen that had just gone dead in front of him. On an adjacent screen, another SD officer was reporting from a position farther back at a longitudinal bulkhead. "Negative at Number Two Aft," Oordsen said to Sterm, who was watching grim faced. "They'll be through there in a matter of minutes."

"How long before the *Kuan-yin* is eclipsed?" Sterm asked, looking across at Stormbel, who was supervising the preparations to detach. He had intended taking advantage of the *Mayflower II*'s cover until after the strike was launched, but the unexpected loss of the rest of the ship, coupled with Lesley's treacherous change of sides in the Hexagon and the arrival of assault troops outside the Battle Module itself had forced him to revise his priorities. There would be little point in destroying the *Kuan-yin* if he lost the Battle Module in the process.

"Eight minutes," Stormbel replied. "But its reaction dish is still aimed away from us. We are now ready to detach."

"You are certain that we could make the cover of Chiron safely?"

"The *Kuan-yin* will not be able to maneuver instantly," Stormbel answered. "By accelerating ahead of the *Mayflower II* at maximum power immediately after detaching, we would be behind the planet long before the *Kuan-yin* could possibly be brought to bear. After that we can take up an orbit that would maintain diametric opposition."

"Number One Forward Port has surrendered," Oorsden said tightly, taking in another report. "The firing has stopped there. Nickolson is leading his men out, including his reserve. We have no choice."

Sterm's eyes smoldered. "I want a full record kept of every officer who deserts," he reminded Stormbel. "The ones in the Government Center, the one in Vandenberg, Lesley in the Hexagon, that one there—all of them." His voice was calm but all the more menacing for its iciness. "They will answer for this when the time comes. General, detach the Battle Module immediately and proceed as planned."

Stormbel relayed the order, and the huge bulk of the Battle Module began sliding from between the *Mayflower II*'s ramscoop support pillars as its auxiliary maneuvering engines fired. The sound of twisted steel scraping across the outside of its hull reverberated throughout the module's stern section as one of the feeder ramps, none of which was retracted, first bent, and then crumpled. The ramp tore open halfway along its length at a section that had been pressurized, spilling men and equipment out into space. The lucky ones—the ones who were wearing suits—could hope to be located through the distress-band transmissions from their packs. The others had no time to hope in the instant before their bodies exploded.

"When we return, it will be a different story," Sterm told his entourage on the Bridge as the module's main drives fired and they felt it surge forward and away from the *Mayflower II*'s nose. "But first, we have to deal with our Chironian . . . friends. What is the report on the *Kuanyin?*"

"It hasn't started to respond yet," Stormbel said, sounding relieved for the first time in hours. "Perhaps we took them by surprise after all." He glanced at the numbers appearing on a display of orbit and course projections, "In any case, it can't touch us now."

Sterm nodded slowly in satisfaction. "Excellent. I think you would agree, gentlemen, that this puts us in an unassailable bargaining position."

* * *

In the *Mayflower II's* Communications Center, Borftein, Wellesley, and the others who had been coordinating activities all over the ship and down on the surface watched and listened tensely as pandemonium poured from the screens around them. Spacesuited figures were cartwheeling away from the mangled remains of one feeder ramp, and the exposed interiors of the cupolas at the ends of the others; all showed battle damage and one of them was partly blown away. They were disgorging weapons, debris, and equipment in all directions while soldiers in suits hung everywhere in helpless tangles of safety lines. "Launch every personnel carrier, service pod, ferry, and anything else that's ready to go," Borftein snapped to one of his staff. "Get them from Vandenberg or anywhere else you have to. I want every one of those men picked up. Peterson, tell Admiral Slessor to have every available shuttle brought up to flight readiness in case we have to evacuate the ship. And find out how many more we can get up here from Canaveral."

"Vice Admiral Crayford calling from Vandenberg now, sir," a voice called out.

"The Chironians on channel eight are requesting a report, sir."

"Major Lesley calling from the nose, sir."

"Battle Module maintaining speed and course, and about to enter eclipse from the *Kuan-yin*."

Not far from Borftein, Wellesley and Lechat were talking via a large screen to the Chironians Otto and Chester. Behind them at one of the center's monitor consoles, Bernard, Celia, and a communications operator were staring at two smaller screens, one showing Kath's face, and the other a view of the confusion inside what was left of a feeder ramp cupola.

On the second screen Hanlon, in a spacesuit blackened by scorch marks, was clinging in the foreground to the remains of a buckled metal structure sticking out into empty space, and hauling on a pair of intertwined lines with his free arm, while behind him other soldiers were pulling figures back into the shattered cupola and helping them climb to the entrance into the feeder ramp. "I think this might be the man himself now," Hanlon's voice said from the grille by the screen. "Ah, yes . . . a little the worse for wear, but he'll be as good as new." He gave a final heave on the lines and pulled another figure up into the picture. Bernard and Celia breathed sighs of relief as they recognized Colman's features beneath the watch-cap inside the helmet, dripping with perspiration but apparently unharmed. Colman anchored himself to another part of the structure that Hanlon was on, unhitched his safety line and untangled it from the other one, and then helped Hanlon pull it in to produce another spacesuited figure, this time upside down and with a pudgy, woebegone face that was somehow managing to keep a thick pair of glasses wedged crookedly across its nose.

"Hanlon's got him," Bernard said to the screen that was showing Kath. "He looks as if he's all right. They've got Swyley too. He seems okay."

Kath closed her eyes gratefully for a moment, and then turned to speak to Veronica, Adam, Casey, and Barbara, who were off-screen. "They've found Steve. He's all right."

Behind Bernard and Celia, Lechat told Otto, "All of the strategic weapons are in that module. The remainder of this ship represents no threat whatsoever."

"We are aware of that," Otto said.

"We had to try," Wellesley insisted from beside Lechat. "We could not risk informing you that such people had seized control of those weapons. The decision was mine and nobody else's."

"I think I'd have done the same thing," Otto told him.

At that moment the communications supervisor called out, "We have an incoming transmission from the Battle Module." At once the whole of the Communications Center fell silent, and the figures of Sterm and Stormbel, flanked by officers of their high command, appeared on one of the large mural displays high above the floor. Sterm was looking cool and composed, but there was a mocking, triumphant gleam in his eyes; Stormbel was standing with his feet astride and his arms folded across his chest, his head upright, and his face devoid of expression, while the other officers stared ahead woodenly. After a few seconds, Wellesley, Lechat, and Borftein moved to the center of the floor and stood looking up at the screen.

Celia's face had drawn itself into a tight, bloodless mask as she stared at the image of Sterm. "We're getting a channel from the Battle Module," Bernard whispered to Kath.

"I know," Kath told him. "He's through to Otto and Chester as well via one of our relay satellites. It's a three-way hookup."

"A good try, Wellesley," Sterm said from the large screen. "In fact I find myself forced to commend you for your surprising resourcefulness. Unfortunately from your point of view, however, we now see it was in vain." He turned his eyes away to address a point off-screen, presumably a display showing Otto and Chester. "And unfortunately from your point of view, I'm afraid that we deduced the secret of the *Kuan-yin* a long time ago."

"Bernard," Kath said quietly from the console screen.

He turned his head back to look at her. "Yes?"

"Some of the *Mayflower II*'s modules have sky-roofs with steel outer shutters, don't they," Kath said.

Bernard frowned uncomprehendingly. "Yes . . . Why . . . What—"

Kath's voice remained low but took on a note of urgency. "Make sure all of them are closed. Do it now." Bernard shook his head, mystified, and started asking questions again. "Just do it," Kath said, cutting him off. "There might not be much time."

Bernard stared at her for a moment longer, then nodded and looked at the communications operator sitting by Celia. "Can you get Admiral Slessor on line here?" The operator nodded and sat forward to begin entering a code.

From the center of the floor Wellesley asked, "What do you want?"

"Good." Sterm nodded approvingly. "I detect a cooperative disposition." He turned his face toward the Chironians. "I take it that we are all beginning to understand one another."

"We're listening," Otto replied tonelessly.

"Perhaps it would be of benefit if I were to summarize the situation that now exists," Sterm suggested. "We command a complete strategic arsenal, the potency of which I do not have to spell out to you, and the only weapon capable of opposing us is now neutralized. Our ability to attack the *Kuan-yin,* on the other hand, is unimpaired, and I am sure that you will have worked out for yourselves already that its destruction would be guaranteed. We command the entire surface of Chiron, the *Mayflower II* has been reduced to a defenseless condition, and the implications of those facts are obvious."

Sterm allowed a few seconds for his words to sink in, and then made a slight tossing motion with his hands as if to convey to those watching him the hopelessness of their position. "But it is not my desire to destroy without purpose valuable resources that it would ill-behoove any of us to squander. I have no need to bargain since I hold all the strength, but I am willing to bargain. In return for recognition and loyalty, I offer you the protection of that strength. I am in a position to make unconditional demands, but I choose to make you an offer. So, you see, my terms are not ungenerous."

"Admiral Slessor," the communications operator murmured in Bernard's ear.

Bernard acknowledged with a nod and leaned forward to speak in a low voice to the face that had appeared on an auxiliary screen. "This is urgent, Admiral. Make sure that all the sky-roof outer shutters are closed immediately."

Slessor recognized Bernard as one of Merrick's former officers. "Why?" he asked, looking puzzled. "What are you doing there . . . Fallows, isn't it?"

"I'm not sure why, but it's important . . . from the Chironians."

Slessor's brow furrowed more deeply. He hesitated, thought for a moment, and then nodded. "Very well, I'll see it's done." He moved away from view.

"That's a strange offer," Otto said to Sterm. "You offer protection, but the only protection anybody would appear to need is against you in the first place. After all, you've just told us that you hold all the weapons. You seem to entertain a curious notion of logic."

For the first time a hint of anger flashed across Sterm's

face. "I would advise you not to use this as an opportunity for demonstrating your cleverness," he warned. He allowed himself a moment to calm down. Then he resumed speaking more slowly. "Earth is tearing itself apart because it has failed to produce the strong leader who would crush"— Sterm raised a hand and closed his fist in front of his face —"the petty rivalries and jealousies which throughout history have frustrated any chance of expression of the full potential grandeur of collective unity and power. Earth has always been in turmoil because it has inherited a legacy of chaos of global proportions against which the efforts of even its most capable organizers have been of no avail. Is that the future that you would wish upon Chiron?

"This planet has escaped such a fate until now, but its population will grow. It has a chance to profit from what Earth has learned, and to plant the seeds of a strong, unified, and unshakable order now, before the diseases of disunity have had a chance to germinate and become virulent. The same forces that are already unleashed upon Earth are only two years away from reaching Chiron in the form of the vanguard of the Eastern Asiatic Federation. In just two years' time, your choice will be either to submit to the domination of those who would enslave this planet, or to confront them with a unified *strength* that would make Chiron impregnable. Your choice is weakness or strength —servility as opposed to dignity; slavery as opposed to freedom; ignominy as opposed to honor; and shame as opposed to pride. Weakness or strength. I offer the latter alternatives."

Sterm's eyes took on a distant light, and his breathing quickened visibly. "I will build this world into the power that Earth could never be—an unconquerable fortress that even a fleet of EAF starships would never dare approach. I will build for you the first-ever stellar empire here at Centauri, one people united under one leader . . . united in will, united in action, and united in purpose. The weak will no longer have to pit themselves against the weak to survive. The weak will be protected by the strength that will come from that unity, and by that same unity the strong who protect them will be invincible. That . . . is what I offer to share."

"Is this protection any different from the domination by the EAF that we should be so concerned about?" Chester asked.

Sterm looked displeased at the response. "Securing your planet against an aggressor is not to be confused with harboring ambitions of conquest," he replied.

Otto shook his head. "If Earth is tearing itself apart, it is because its people allowed themselves to believe the same self-fulfilling prophecies that you are asking us to accept, Mr. Sterm. But we reject them. We need no more protection from you against the people in the EAF starship than they need from their Sterms to protect them against us. We have no need of that kind of strength. Is it strength for neighbors to fortify their homes against each other, or is it paranoia? You must feel very insecure to wish to fortify an entire star system."

Sterm's mouth clamped into a grim, downturned line. "The EAF is committed to a dogma of conquest," he said. "They understand no language apart from force. You cannot hope to deal with them by any other means."

"On the contrary, Mr. Sterm, they understand the same language that people everywhere speak," Chester said. "We will deal with them in the same way that we have already dealt with you."

"And exactly what is that supposed to mean?" Sterm demanded.

Otto smiled humorlessly. "Take a look at the other lunatics around you," he suggested. "What happened to all the people? Where did your army go? They're all Chironians now. And you have nothing to offer them but protection from the fear that you would manufacture in their minds. But they have Chironian minds. They see that the fear is your fear, not theirs; and it is you who are in need of protection, not they."

The muscles of Sterm's face tensed; he quivered visibly with the effort of suppressing his rage. "I was willing to bargain," he grated. "Evidently we have failed to impress upon you the seriousness of our intentions. Very well, you leave me no further choice. Perhaps a demonstration will serve to convince you." He turned to Stormbel. "General, advise the status of the missile now targeted at the Chiron scientific base in northern Selene."

"Primed and ready for immediate launch," Stormbel replied in a monotone. "Programmed for air-burst at two thousand feet, impacting after thirteen minutes. Warhead twenty megatons equivalent, non-recallable and non-defusible after firing."

"Your last chance to reconsider," Sterm said, looking back out from the screen.

"We have nothing to reconsider," Otto replied calmly.

Sterm's face darkened, and his mouth twisted into an ugly grimace. His suave veneer seemed to peel away as his eyes widened, and for an instant, even from where he was sitting, Bernard found himself looking directly into the depths of a mind that was completely insane. He shivered involuntarily. Beside him Celia gripped his arm. "General," Sterm ordered. "Launch the missile in sixty seconds."

Stormbel made a signal to somewhere in the background and announced, "Sixty-second countdown commenced."

"The countdown can be halted at any time," Sterm informed them.

Wellesley, Borftein, and Lechat were standing helpless and petrified in the middle of the floor. "He'll do it," Celia whispered, horrified, to Bernard.

Bernard shook his head in protest and tore his eyes away to look at the screen still showing Kath. "You can't let this happen," he implored. "Those are your own people up there in Selene. This will just be the first example. Then it'll get worse."

"We don't intend to let it happen," Kath said.

"But you are. What can you do to stop it?"

"You've already worked most of that out."

Bernard shook his head again. "I don't know what you mean. The *Kuan-yin* can't fire effectively. It's eclipsed from the Battle Module."

"It couldn't fire anyway," Kath replied. "It's modifications aren't completed yet. We've already told you that."

Bernard frowned at her in bemusement. Nothing was making any sense. "But—its antimatter drive . . . that's your weapon, isn't it?"

"We never said it was," Kath replied. "You assumed it. So did Sterm." Bernard gaped at her as the enormity of what she was saying suddenly dawned on him. Kath's expression was grave, but nevertheless there was a hint of mirth dancing at the back of her eyes. "We could hardly disguise our scientific work," she said. "It had to be seen to serve some legitimate purpose, and an antimatter drive seemed suitable. But the *Kuan-yin* project has been low down on our list of priorities."

Bernard's eyes widened incredulously. "But if the *Kuan-yin* isn't finished, then what made the crater in Remus?"

"Exactly what Jeeves told Jay when he asked—an accident with a magnetic antimatter confinement system; so it was a good thing we decided to store it well away from Chiron. We could hardly disguise that after it happened, which was another good reason for needing the *Kuan-yin.*"

"We—we never believed that story," Bernard said weakly.

"Well, that was up to you. We told you."

Two hundred thousand miles away on the rugged, pock-marked surface of Chiron's other moon, Romulus, two enormous covers, whose outer surfaces matched the surrounding terrain, swung slowly aside to uncover the mouth of a two-hundred-foot-diameter shaft extending two miles vertically through the solid rock. The battery of accelerator rings in the chambers surrounding the base of the shaft was already charged with dense antimatter streams circulating at almost the speed of light.

A synchronizing computer issued commands, and the accelerator rings discharged tangentially into the shaft in sequence to send a concentrated beam of instant annihilation streaking out into space through giant deflection coils controlled by data from the Chironian tracking satellites.

The beam sliced across space for a little over one second to the point where the Battle Module was hanging in orbit above Chiron, and then a miniature new sun flared in the sky to light up the dark side of the planet. The flash of gamma rays ionized the upper atmosphere, and the sky above Chiron glowed in streaks that extended for thousands of miles. Sensitive radiation-monitoring instruments were burned out all over the outside of the *Mayflower II*, and because of the electrical upheaval, it was twelve hours before communications with the surface could be resumed.

CHAPTER THIRTY-NINE

WELLESLEY STOOD TO deliver his final address from in front of the Mission Director's seat at the center of the raised dais facing out over the Congressional Hall of the *Mayflower II*'s Government Center. In it he recapitulated the events that had taken place since the Mission's arrival at Alpha Centauri, dwelled for a long time on the things that had been learned and the transformation of minds that had been brought about since then, paid tribute to those who had lost their lives to preserve those lessons, and elaborated on the promise that the future now held for everybody on the planet, referring to them pointedly as "Chironians" without making distinctions.

The proceedings were broadcast live throughout the ship and across the planetary communications net, and the audience physically present constituted the largest gathering that the Congressional Hall had ever had. All of the members who had been absent had returned for the occasion, and the only seats left vacant were those of the Deputy Mission Director, the Director of Liaison, the Commanding General Special Duty Force, and two others who had chosen to throw in their lot with Sterm. Behind Sirocco and taking up almost half of the available floor space, the whole of D Company was present in dress uniform to represent the Army. Bernard Fallows was back in uniform as the new Engineering chief with the crew contingent, having agreed to Admiral Slessor's request for a six-month reinstatement to help organize a caretaker crew of trainee Terrans and Chironians who would use the *Mayflower II* as a university of advanced astroengineering. Jean Fallows, Jay, and Marie were present with Celia, Veronica, Jerry

371

Pernak, and Eve Verritty in the front row of the guests included by special invitation, and with them were Kath and her family alongside Otto, Chester, Leon, and others from the base in Selene and elsewhere. As if to underline and reecho Wellesley's acknowledgment of how the future would be, there was no segregation of Terrans and Chironians into groups; and there were many children from both worlds.

Wellesley concluded his formal speech and stood looking around the hall for a moment to allow a lighter mood to settle. In the last few days some of the color had returned to his face, his posture had become more upright and at ease, and his frame seemed to have shed a burden of years. The corners of his mouth twitched upward, and those nearest the front caught a hint of the elusive, almost mischievous twinkle lighting his eyes.

"And now I have one final task to perform," he said. He paused again, and the hall grew curious and attentive, sensing that something unexpected was about to take place. "May I remind the assembly that the declaration of a state of emergency has never been revoked, and that therefore, by the processes that we are still formally pledged to uphold, that emergency condition continues to remain in force, along with its attendant suspension of Congress and the vesting of all congressional authority in me." Puzzled expressions greeted his words, and a ripple of surprised murmurings ran around the hall. "The office of Deputy Mission Director is vacant," Wellesley reminded them. "Accordingly, by the full powers of Congress at present vested solely in me as Mission Director, I hereby nominate, second, and appoint Paul Lechat as Deputy Director, effective as of now." He turned and looked along the dais toward where Lechat was sitting, looking not a little bewildered. "Congratulations, Paul. And now would you kindly take your rightful place." He gestured at the empty chair next to him. Lechat rose up, moved along behind the intervening places, and sat down in the Deputy Director's seat, all the time shaking his head at the other members to convey that he was as confused about what Wellesley was doing as they were. Wellesley looked slowly around the hall one last time. "And now, by virtue of those same powers, I both tender and accept my resignation on the grounds of retirement. It has been an honor and a privilege to serve you all. Thank you." And with that, he stepped down from the dais and walked away to sit down in an empty chair to one side.

Lechat stared at the Director's seat next to him, and while he was still turning his head perplexedly from one side to the other, the first approving murmurs and ripples of applause began coming from among the members as one by one they realized what it meant. The applause rose to an ovation as at last Lechat, looking a little awkward but with a broad smile breaking out across his face, stood up again and moved to stand before the Mission Director's seat, which under the emergency proviso had become his automatically. Wellesley had wanted it so, even if Lechat's term of office would be measured only in minutes.

Lechat waited for the noise to die away and managed to bring his feelings under control sufficiently to muster a semblance of dignity appropriate to the moment. But simplicity and brevity were appropriate too. "I am honored and privileged by this appointment, and I will dedicate myself for the duration of my term to serving the best interests of our people to the best of my ability," he announced. "In accordance with that promise, my first official act is to restore the full powers of Congress as previously suspended, and my second is to declare the state of emergency ended as of this moment." Another round of applause, this time briefer than before, greeted the statement. "Next, I have two proposals to put to the vote of the assembly," Lechat said. "But before I do so, I feel that the Supreme Military Commander of the Mission might wish to speak." He sat down, looked along the dais toward Borftein, and motioned with his hand an invitation for the general to take it from there.

Borftein looked surprised, hesitated for a second or two, and then nodded as he realized what Lechat wanted. He rose slowly to his feet and paused to collect his words. "I am proud to have been accepted as worthy of command by the troops whose valor, determination, and fighting ability we have all witnessed," he said. "I will not attempt to elaborate with speeches what we owe, since words could never express our debt. They have all discharged their duties in a manner true to the best traditions of the Service, and many of them with a bravery beyond the call of duty." He paused, and his face became more solemn. "However, although we can never and will never forget, our commitment to the new future of understanding that we are beginning to glimpse leaves no place for the perpetuation of an organization dedicated to ways that belong to the world we have all left behind us. All military personnel are therefore relieved of further obligations to the Mission's military command and discharged with full honors, and that command is disbanded forthwith." The hall remained quiet while Borftein sat down. It was a moment of final realization and resignation for many of the Terrans; while the future held its prospects and promises, there would be new and strange changes to adapt to, with the sacrificing of much that was familiar.

Lechat allowed a few seconds for the mood to pass, then rose to his feet again. "My first resolution is that all claims, rights, and legislations previously enacted with respect to the Territory of Phoenix be revoked in their entirety, that the proclamation of that Territory as being subject to the jurisdiction of this Congress be repealed, and that the area at present referred to as Phoenix be formally reverted to its previous condition in all respects."

"I second the motion," a voice called out promptly.

"Those for?" Lechat invited. All of the members' hands went up. "Against?" There were no hands. "The resolution is passed," Lechat announced. Phoenix had officially become a part of Chiron once again.

Lechat slowly scanned the expectant faces. They all knew what was coming next. "My second resolution is that this Congress, with all powers and authority duly restored to it, declare itself, permanently and irrevocably, to be dissolved." The motion was passed unanimously.

The colonization of Chiron was over.

EPILOGUE

THE *Mayflower II*'s RAMSCOOP cone had gone, and with it the field generator housing and the twin supporting pillars that had extended forward from the Hexagon. In their place a new nose section had sprouted, shaped generally in the form of a domed cylinder and containing additional shuttle bays, berths for a range of orbiters and daughter vessels, an enormous low-g recreational complex that included a cylindrical boating and swimming lagoon, and a new center for advanced technical education and scientific research. The stern of the ship had undergone even vaster changes, its original fusion drive having been replaced by a scaled-up antimatter system developed from the prototype successfully tested on the *Kuan-yin*.

Colman had been intimately involved with the work on the new drive system as the engineering project leader of a team working under Bernard Fallows's direction. He had brought Kath and their four-year-old son Alex up to the ship to be present with him at the unveiling ceremony being held in the main concourse of the new nose section. Many of the faces from five years back were there too. Few of them had lost contact during that time, but it was rare for so many of them to be in the same place at the same time, except for their annual reunions. Most of D Company had assembled for the event—Sirocco, with Shirley and their twin daughters; Hanlon, who now instructed at the martial arts academy in Franklin, with Janet and their two children; Driscoll, who had taken a rest from his touring magic show, one of Chiron's major entertainment attractions; Stanislau, now a computer software expert; Swyley, who directed and produced movies, usually

375

about the American underworld, along with a couple of the pretty girls who seemed to surround him wherever he went; . . . and there were others. Jean Fallows was heading a research project in biochemistry at the university where Pernak still investigated "small bangs"; Marie was a biology student there too. Jay, now twenty and with a young son, had built an old-fashioned railroad into Franklin—now a sizable and thriving city—which used full-scale steam locomotives and provided a sight-seeing attraction and historical curiosity that every visitor to the area had to ride on at least once. Veronica, a practicing architect, was there with Casey, Adam, and Barbara. Celia had declined to return to the ship but was watching from the home that she shared with Lechat on the coast; and Wellesley had taken a trip from his farm in Occidena to see his old ship recommissioned and renamed.

Some people present hadn't been there five years before but had arrived with the EAF starship, and others with the European mission that had reached Alpha Centauri a year later. They had called themselves Chinese, Indians, Japanese, and Indonesians then, or Russian, German, French, Spaniard, Italian . . . but now they were all simply Chironians. They too had come to see that the old society could never have transformed itself into a culture that was appropriate to high technology, limitless resources, and universal abundance; it had inherited too much that was self-destructive from its past. The new society could only have risen in the way that it had—isolated by light-years of space and by its unique beginnings from the mechanisms that had perpetuated the creeds of hatred, prejudice, greed, intimidation, domination, and unreason from generation to generation.

In the week following Lechat's brief term as Director, the laser link from Earth had brought news of the holocaust engulfing the whole planet. Then the signals had ceased, and for five years there had been nothing. No doubt many pockets of humanity had managed to survive, but mankind's first attempt to establish an advanced civilization had ended in failure . . . or almost in failure, for it had served its purpose; it had lifted humankind from its primitive, animal beginnings to a level where human, not animal, values could evolve, and it had hurled a seed of itself outward to take root, grow, and blossom at a distant star. And then it had died, as it had to.

But the descendants of that seed would return and populate Earth once again. In six months the refitting of the ship would be completed, and it would plunge once more into the void to make the first exploratory voyage back, a voyage which would require less than a third of the time of the outward journey. Lechat would be the Mission Director, Fallows the Chief of Engineering, and Adam would head one of the scientific teams. Colman would be returning too, as an Engineering officer; Kath would fulfill her dream of seeing Earth; and Alex would be about Jay's age by the time they returned to Chiron. Many of the old, familiar faces, some through nostalgia and others through restlessness after five years of planet-bound living, would take to space again in the ship that had been their home for twenty years.

Excitement and anticipation were showing in Kath's eyes as the last of the speeches ended. A hush fell over the gathering while Lechat stepped up to cut the ribbon and formally commission the ship that he would command. Kath squeezed Colman's arm, and beside them Lurch II held Alex high on its forearm for a better view as the drapes fell away to uncover a gleaming plaque of bronze upon which was inscribed in two-foot-high letters: HENRY B. CONGREVE—the new name of the ship that would bring Earth's children home.

ABOUT THE AUTHOR

JAMES HOGAN WAS born in London in 1941 and educated at the Cardinal Vaughan Grammar School, Kensington. He studied general engineering at the Royal Aircraft Establishment, Farnborough, subsequently specializing in electronics and digital systems.

After spending a few years as a systems design engineer, he transferred into selling and later joined the computer industry as a salesman, working with ITT, Honeywell, and Digital Equipment Corporation. He also worked as a life insurance salesman for two years ". . . to have a break from the world of machines and to learn something more about people."

In mid-1977 he moved from England to the United States to become a Senior Sales Training Consultant, concentrating on the applications of minicomputers in science and research for DEC.

At the end of 1979, Hogan opted to write full-time. He is now living in northern California.